Their sizzling pa[...]
deny...but can [...]
to happi[...]

Mistress

TAMING THE PLAYBOY

Three fantastic novels from favourite authors
Sharon Kendrick, Melanie Milburne and
Sabrina Philips

Mistress

TAMING THE PLAYBOY

SHARON KENDRICK

MELANIE MILBURNE

SABRINA PHILIPS

MILLS & BOON

Mills & Boon, an imprint of Harlequin (UK) Limited, Eton House,
18-24 Paradise Road, Richmond, Surrey TW9 1SR

MISTRESS: TAMING OF THE PLAYBOY
© Harlequin Enterprises II B.V./S.à.r.l. 2011

Constantine's Defiant Mistress © Sharon Kendrick 2009
Androletti's Mistress © Melanie Milburne 2007
Valenti's One-Month Mistress © Sabrina Philips 2008

ISBN: 978 0 263 89666 4

025-0112

Harlequin (UK) policy is to use papers that are natural, renewable
and recyclable products and made from wood grown in sustainable
forests. The logging and manufacturing processes conform to the
legal environmental regulations of the country of origin.

Printed and bound in Spain
by Blackprint CPI, Barcelona

Constantine's Defiant Mistress

SHARON KENDRICK

Sharon Kendrick started story-telling at the age of eleven and has never really stopped. She likes to write fast-paced, feel-good romances, with heroes who are so sexy they'll make your toes curl! Born in west London, she now lives in the beautiful city of Winchester—where she can see the cathedral from her window (but only if she stands on tiptoe). She has two children, Celia and Patrick, and her passions include music, books, cooking and eating—and drifting off into wonderful daydreams while she works out new plots!

CHAPTER ONE

IT WAS hearing his name on the radio which made her senses scream. Laura never had time for newspapers—even if her dyslexia hadn't made reading so difficult—she relied on the morning news programme to keep her up to date. Usually she only listened with half an ear, and usually she wasn't remotely interested in anything to do with international *finance*.

But Karantinos was an unusual name. And it was Greek. And didn't anything to do with that beautiful and ancient land put her senses on painful alert for very obvious reasons?

She had been busy making bread—sprinkling a handful of seeds into the dough before she popped the last batch into the oven. But with shaking hands she stopped dead-still and listened—like a small animal who had found itself caught alone and frightened in the middle of a hostile terrain.

'Greek billionaire Constantine Karantinos has announced record profits for his family shipping line,' intoned the dry voice of the news-reader. 'Playboy Karantinos is currently in London to host a party at the Granchester Hotel, where it is rumoured he will announce his engagement to Swedish supermodel Ingrid Johansson.'

Laura swayed, gripping the work surface to support herself, her ears scarcely able to bear what she had just heard, her heart pounding with a surprisingly forceful pain. Because she had preserved Constantine in her heart, remembering him just as he'd been when she'd known him—as if time had stood still. A bittersweet memory of a man who still made her ache when she thought of him. But time never stood still—she knew that more than anyone.

And what had she expected? That a man like Constantine would stay single for ever? As if that lazy charm and piercing intellect—that powerhouse body and face of a fallen angel—would remain unattached. She was just surprised that it hadn't happened sooner.

She could hear the sounds of movement from above as she took off her apron. But her heart was racing as she mechanically went through her morning routine of tidying up the kitchen before going upstairs to wake her son. She often told herself how lucky she was to live 'over the shop', and although helping run a small baker's store hadn't been her life's ambition, at least it gave her a modest income which she supplemented with occasional waitressing work. But most of all it provided a roof over their heads—which was security for Alex—and that was worth more than anything in Laura's eyes.

Her sister Sarah was already up, yawning as she emerged from one of the three poky bedrooms, running her fingers through the thick dark curtain of her hair, which so contrasted with her sister's finer, fairer mane.

'Mornin', Laura,' Sarah mumbled, and then blinked as she saw her older sister's face 'What the hell's happened? Don't tell me the oven's gone on the blink again?'

Mutely, Laura shook her head, then jerked it in the direction of her son's bedroom. 'Is he up yet?' she mouthed.

Sarah shook her head. 'Not yet.'

Laura glanced at the clock on the wall, which dominated her busy life, and saw that she had ten minutes before she had to get Alex up for school. Pulling Sarah into the small sitting room which overlooked the high street, she shut the door behind them and turned to her sister, her whole body trembling.

'Constantine Karantinos is in London,' she began, the whispered words falling out of her mouth like jagged little fragments of glass.

Her sister scowled. 'And?'

Laura willed her hands to stop shaking. 'He's throwing a party.' She swallowed. 'And they say he's getting engaged. To a Swedish supermodel.'

Sarah shrugged. 'What do you want me to say? That it's a surprise?'

'No... But I...'

'But what, Laura?' demanded Sarah impatiently. 'You can't seem to accept that the no-good bastard you slept with hasn't an ounce of conscience. That he *never gave you another thought.*'

'He—'

'He what? Refused to see you? Why, you couldn't even get a single meeting with the great man, could you, Laura? No matter how many times you tried. He's never even taken your phone calls! You were good enough to share his bed—but not good enough to be recognised as the mother of his child!'

Laura shot an agonised look at the closed door, straining her ears as she wondered if Alex had done the unheard-of and managed to get himself out of bed without his mother or his auntie gently shaking him awake. But then, seven-year-old boys were notoriously bad at getting up in the morning, weren't they? And they became increasingly curious as they got older…kept asking questions she wasn't sure how to answer…

'Shh. I don't want Alex to hear!'

'Why not? Why shouldn't he know that his father happens to be one of the richest men on the planet—while his mother is working her fingers to the bone in a bread shop, trying to support him?'

'I don't want to…' But her words tailed off. Didn't want to *what* exactly? Laura wondered. Didn't want to hurt her beloved son because it was the duty of every mother to protect her child? Yet she had been finding it increasingly difficult to do that. Just last month Alex had come home with a nasty-looking bruise on his cheek, and when she had asked him what had happened he had mumbled and become very defensive. It had only been later that she'd discovered he'd been involved in some kind of minor skirmish in the playground. And later still that she had discovered the cause, when she'd gone tearing into the school, white-faced and trembling, to seek a meeting with the headmistress.

It transpired that Alex was being bullied because he looked 'different'. Because his olive skin, black eyes and towering height made him look older and tougher than the other boys in his class. And because the little girls in the class—even at the tender ages of six and seven—had been following the dark-eyed Alex around like eager little puppies. Like father, like son, she had thought with a pang.

Laura had felt a mixture of troubled emotions as she'd gone home that day. She'd wanted to ask her son why he hadn't hit back—but that would have gone against everything she had taught him. She had brought him up to be gentle. To reason rather than to lash out. For two pins she would have withdrawn her son from the school and sent him somewhere else—but she didn't have the luxury of choice. The next nearest state school was in the neighbouring town, and not only did Laura not have a car but the bus service was extremely unreliable.

Lately her son had been asking her more and more frequently about *why* he looked different. He was an intelligent little boy, and sooner or later he wouldn't allowed her to fob him off with vague and woolly pieces of information about a father he had never seen. If only Constantine would just *talk* to her. Acknowledge his son. Spend a little time with him—that was all she wanted. For her beloved boy to know a little of his heritage.

She was distracted while she gave Alex his breakfast, and even more distracted during the short walk to his school. Although it was almost the summer holidays, the weather had been awful lately—nothing but rain, rain, rain—and this morning the persistent drizzle seemed to penetrate every inch of her body. She shivered a little, and tried to chatter brightly, but she felt as if she had a heavy lead weight sitting in the pit of her stomach.

Alex looked up at her with his dark olive eyes and frowned. 'Is something wrong, Mum?' he questioned.

Your father is about to marry another woman and will probably have a family with her. Telling herself that the blistering shaft of jealous pain was unreasonable under the circumstances, she hugged her son to her fiercely as she said goodbye.

'Wrong? No, nothing's wrong, darling.' She smiled brightly, and watched as he ran into the playground, praying that the head teacher's recent lecture on bullying might have had some effect on the little savages who had picked on him.

She was lost in thought as she walked back to the shop. Hanging up her damp coat in the little cloakroom at the back, she grimaced at the pale face which stared back at her from the tiny mirror hung on the back of the door. Her grey eyes looked troubled, and her baby-fine hair clung to her head like a particularly unattractive-looking skull-cap. Carefully, she brushed it and shook it, then crumpled it into a damp pleat on top of her head.

Pulling on her overall, she was still preoccupied as she walked into the shop, where her sister was just putting on the lights. Five minutes until they opened and the first rush of the day would begin—with villagers keen to buy their freshly baked bread and buns. Laura knew how lucky she was to have the life she had—lucky that her sister loved Alex as much as she did.

The two girls had been orphaned when Sarah was still at school, after their widowed mother had died suddenly and quietly in the middle of the night. A stricken Laura had put her own plans of travelling the world on hold, unsure what path to take to ensure that Sarah could continue with her studies. But fate had stepped in with cruel and ironic timing, because Laura had discovered soon after that she was carrying Alex.

Money had been tight, but they had been left with the

scruffy little baker's shop and the flat upstairs, where they had spent most of their childhood years. They had always helped their mother in the shop, so Laura had suggested modernising it and carrying on with the modest little family business, and Sarah had insisted on studying part-time so that she could help with Alex.

Up until now the scheme had worked perfectly well. And if the shop wasn't exactly making a huge profit, at least they were keeping their heads above water and enjoying village life.

But recently Sarah had started talking longingly of going to art school in London, and Laura was horribly aware that she was holding her back. She couldn't keep using her little sister as a part-time child-minder, no matter how much Sarah loved her nephew—she needed to get out there and live her own life. But then how on earth would Laura cope with running a business and being as much of a hands-on mum as she could to Alex? To Alex who was becoming increasingly curious about his background.

Sarah was giving the counter a final wipe, and looked up as Laura walked into the shop. 'You still look fed up,' she observed.

Laura stared down at the ragged pile of rock-cakes and boxes of home-made fudge under the glass counter. 'Not fed up,' she said slowly. 'Just realising that I can't go on hiding my head in the sand any longer.'

Sarah blinked. 'What are you talking about?'

Laura swallowed. Say it, she thought. Go on—*say* it. Speak the words out loud—that way it will become real and you'll *have* to do it. Stop being fobbed off by the gatekeepers who surround the father of your son. Get out there and *fight* for Alex. 'Just that I've got to get to Constantine and tell him he has a son.'

Sarah's eyes narrowed. 'Why the new fervour, Laura?' she asked drily. 'Is it because Constantine is finally settling down? You think that he's going to take one look at you and decide to dump the Swedish supermodel and run off into the sunset with you?'

Laura flushed, knowing that Sarah spoke with the kind of harsh candour which only a sister could get away with—but her words were true. She had to rid herself of any romantic notions where the Greek billionaire was concerned. As if Constantine would even *look* at her now! He certainly wouldn't fancy her any more—for hadn't hard work and a lack of time to devote to herself meant that her youthful bloom had faded faster than most? At twenty-six she sometimes felt—and looked—a whole decade older than her years. And even if the fire in her heart still burned fiercely for the father of her son she had to douse the flames completely.

'Of course I don't,' she said bitterly. 'But I owe it to Alex. Constantine has *got* to know that he has a son.'

'I agree. But aren't you forgetting something?' questioned Sarah patiently. 'Last time you tried to contact him you got precisely nowhere—so what's changed now?'

What *had* changed? Laura walked slowly towards the door of the shop. She wasn't sure—only that perhaps she'd realised time was running out, that maybe this was her last chance. And that she was no longer prepared to humbly accept being knocked back by the tight circle which surrounded the formidable Greek. She was fired up by something so powerful that it felt as if it had invaded her soul. She was a mother, and she owed it to her son.

'What's changed?' Slowly, Laura repeated Sarah's words back to her. 'I guess *I* have. And this time I'm going to get to him. I'm going to look him in the eye and tell him about his son.'

'Oh, Laura, exactly the same thing will happen!' exclaimed Sarah. 'You'll be knocked back and won't get within a mile of him!'

There was a pause. Laura could hear the ticking of her wristwatch echoing the beating of her heart. 'Only if I go the conventional route,' she said slowly.

Sarah's eyes narrowed. 'What are you talking about?'

Laura hadn't really known herself up until then, but it was one of those defining moments where the answer seemed so blindingly simple that she couldn't believe she hadn't thought of it before. Like when she'd decided that they ought to start making their own loaves on the premises rather than having them delivered from the large bakery in the nearby town—thereby enticing their customers in with the delicious smell of baking bread.

'The radio said he's giving some big party in London,' she said, piecing her whirling thoughts into some kind of order. 'In a hotel.'

'And?'

Laura swallowed. 'And what industry has the fastest turn-over of staff in the world? The catering industry! Think about it, Sarah. They'll…they'll need loads of extra staff for the night, won't they? Casual staff.'

'Just a minute…' Sarah's eyes widened. 'Don't tell me you're planning—'

Laura nodded, her heart beating faster now. 'I've done waitressing jobs at the local hotel for years. I can easily get a reference.'

'Okay, so what if you do manage to get on the payroll?' Sarah demanded. 'Then what? You're going to march over to Constantine in your uniform, in the middle of his fancy party, and announce to him in front of the world, not to mention his soon-to-be wife that he has a seven-year-old son?'

Laura shook her head, trying not to feel daunted by the audacity of her own idea but her fervour refused to be dampened. 'I'll try to be a bit more subtle about it than that,' she said. 'But I'm not going to leave until he's in full possession of the facts.'

She reached up and turned over the sign on the shop door from 'Closed' to 'Open'. Already there was a small cluster of shoppers waiting, shaking off the raindrops from their umbrellas as they filed into the shop.

Laura pinned a bright smile to her lips as she stood behind the counter and took her first order, but the irony of her plan didn't escape her. After all, she had been waitressing when she'd first met Constantine Karantinos, and had tumbled into his arms with embarrassing ease.

Afterwards she had looked back and wondered how she could have behaved in a way which had been so completely out of character. And yet it had been such a golden summer in those carefree months before her mother had died, and she'd felt as if she had the world at her feet as she saved up to go travelling.

She had been an innocent in every sense of the word—but a few months of waitressing in a busy little harbour town had trained her well in how to deal with the well-heeled customers who regularly sailed in on their yachts.

Constantine had been one of them, and yet unlike any of them—for he'd seemed to break all the rules. He'd towered over all the other men like a colossus—making everyone else fade into insignificance. The day she had first set eyes on him would be imprinted on her mind for ever; he had looked like a Greek god—his powerful body silhouetted against the dying sun, his dark and golden beauty suggesting both vigour and danger.

She remembered how broad his shoulders had been, and how silky the olive skin which had sheathed the powerful muscle beneath. And she remembered his eyes, too—as black as ebony yet glittering like the early-morning sunlight on the sea. How could she have resisted a man who had seemed like all her youthful fantasies come to life—a man who had made her feel like a woman for the first and only time in her life?

She remembered waking up in his arms the next morning to find him watching her, and she had gazed up at him, searching his face eagerly for some little clue about how he might feel. About her. About them. About the future.

But in the depths of those eyes there had been…nothing.

Laura swallowed.

Nothing at all.

CHAPTER TWO

'YES, Vlassis,' Constantine bit out impatiently, as he glanced up at one of his aides, who was hovering around the door in the manner he usually adopted when he was about to impart news which his boss would not like. 'What is it?'

'It's about the party, *kyrios*,' said Vlassis.

Constantine's mouth flattened. Why had he ever agreed to have this wretched party in the first place? he found himself wondering. Though in his heart he knew damned well. Because there had been too many mutterings for much too long about people in London wanting to enjoy some of the legendary Karantinos wealth. People always wanted to get close to him, and they thought that this might give them the opportunity. And it was always interesting to see your friends and your enemies in the same room—united by those twin emotions of love and hate, whose boundaries were so often blurred.

'What about it?' he snapped. 'And please don't bother me with trivia, Vlassis—that's what I pay other people to deal with.'

Vlassis looked pained, as if the very suggestion that he should burden his illustrious employer with trivia was highly offensive to him. 'I realise that, *kyrios*. But I've just received a message from Miss Johansson.'

At the mention of Ingrid, Constantine leaned back in his chair and clasped his fingers together in reflective pose. He knew what the press were saying. What they always said if he was pictured with a woman more than once. That he was on the verge of marrying, as most of his contemporaries had now done. His mouth flattened again.

Perhaps one of the greatest arguments in favour of marriage would be having a wife who could deal with the tiresome social side of his life. Who could fend off the ambitious hostesses and screen his invitations, leaving him to get on with running the family business.

'And?' he questioned. 'What did Miss Johansson say?'

'She asked me to tell you that she won't be arriving until late.'

'Did she say why?'

'Something about her photo-shoot overrunning.'

'Oh, did she?' said Constantine softly, his black eyes narrowing in an expression instinctively which made Vlassis look wary.

Unlocking his fingers, Constantine raised his powerful arms above his head and stretched, the rolled-up sleeves of his silk shirt sliding a little further up over the bunched muscle. Slowly he brought his hands down again, lying them flat on the surface of the large desk. The faint drumming of two fingers on the smooth surface was the only outward sign that he was irritated.

Ingrid's coolness was one of the very qualities which had first attracted him to her—that and her white-blonde Swedish beauty, of course. She had a degree in politics, spoke five languages with effortless fluency—and, standing at just over six feet in her stockinged feet, she was one of the few women he had ever met who was able to look him in the eye. Constantine's mouth curved into an odd kind of smile. As well as being one of the few *natural* blondes he'd known...

When they'd met, her unwillingness to be pinned down, her elusiveness when it came to arranging dates, had contrived to intrigue him—probably because it had never happened before. Most women pursued him with the ardour of a hunter with prized quarry in their sights.

But over the months Constantine had realised that Ingrid's evasiveness was part of a game—a master-plan. Beautiful enough to be pursued by legions of men herself, she had recognised the long-term benefits of playing hard-to-get with a man like him. She must have realised that Constantine never had to try very hard, so she had made him try very hard indeed. And for a while it had worked. She had sparked his interest—rare in a man whose natural attributes and huge wealth meant that his appetite had become jaded at an early age.

She had been playing the long game, and Constantine had allowed himself to join in; Ingrid knew what she wanted—to marry an exceptionally wealthy man—and deep down he knew it was high time he took himself a wife. And surely the best kind of wife for a man like him was one who made few emotional demands?

He didn't want some clingy, needy female who thought that the world revolved around him. No, Ingrid came close to fitting almost all his exacting criteria. Every hoop he had presented her with she had jumped through with flying colours. Why, even his father approved of her. And, although the two men had never been close, Constantine had found himself listening for once.

'Why the hell don't you marry her?' he had croaked at his son, where once—before age and ill-health—he would have roared. 'And provide me with a grandson?'

Good question—if you discounted his father's own foolish views on love. Didn't there come a time when every man needed to settle down and produce a family of his own? A boy to inherit the Karantinos fortune? Constantine frowned. Circumstances seemed to have been urging him on like a rudderless boat—and yet something about the sensible option of marrying Ingrid had made him hold back, and he couldn't quite work out what it was.

How long since they had seen one another? Constantine allowed his mind to flick back over the fraught and hectic recent weeks, largely filled with his most recent business acquisition. It had been ages since Ingrid had been in his bed, he realised. Their paths had been criss-crossing over the Atlantic while their careers continued their upward trajectory. Constantine gave a hard smile.

'What time is she arriving?' he questioned.

'She hopes before midnight,' said Vlassis.

'Let's hope so,' commented Constantine, as a faint feeling of irritation stirred within him once more. But he turned to a pile of papers—to the delicate complexity of an offshore deal he was handling. And, as usual, work provided a refuge from the far more messy matter of relationships. For Constantine had learned his lesson earlier than most—that they brought with them nothing but pain and complications.

He left the office around six and headed for the Granchester, whose largest penthouse suite he always rented whenever he was in town. He loved its glorious setting, overlooking lush green parkland, its quiet luxury and the discretion of its staff. And he liked London—just as he liked New York—even if they were too far from the sea for him to ever let complete relaxation steal over him....

To the sound of opera playing loudly on the sound system, he took a long, cold shower before dressing in the rather formal attire which the black-tie dinner warranted. His eyes glittered back at him as he cast a cursory glance at himself in the mirror.

Slipping on a pair of heavy gold cufflinks, he made his way downstairs, his eyes automatically flicking over to his people, who were discreetly peppering the foyer. He knew that his head of security would be unable to prevent the paparazzi from milling around by the entrance outside, but there was no way any of them would be getting into the building to gawp at the rich and the powerful.

Ignoring the gazes of the women who followed his progress with hungry eyes, he walked into the ballroom and looked around. The Granchester had always been a byword for luxury—but tonight the hotel had really surpassed itself. The ballroom was filled with scented blooms, and chandeliers dripped their diamond lights...

A soft voice cut into his thoughts.

'Could...could I get you a drink, sir?'

For a brief moment the voice stirred a distant memory—as faint as a breath on a still summer's day. But then it was gone, and slowly Constantine turned to find a waitress standing staring up at him—chewing at her lip as if she hadn't had eaten a meal in quite a while. His eyes flicked over her. With her small, pinched face and tiny frame she looked as if she probably *hadn't* eaten a meal in ages. Something in her body language made him pause. Something untoward. He frowned.

'Yes. Get me a glass of water, would you?'

'Certainly, sir.' Miraculously, Laura kept her voice steady, even though inside she felt the deep, shafting pain of rejection at the way those black eyes had flicked over her so dismissively. She had tried to hold his look for as long as was decently possible under the circumstances—willing him to look at her with a slowly dawning look of incredulity. But instead, what logic told her would happen *had* happened. *The father of her son hadn't even recognised her!*

Yet had she really bought into the fantasy that he might? That he would stare into her eyes and tell her that they looked like the storm clouds which gathered over his Greek island? He had said that when he had been charming her into his bed, and doubtless he would have something suitable in his repertoire for any woman. Something to make every single woman feel special, unique and amazing. Something which would make a woman willingly want to give him her virginity as if it were of no consequence at all.

It had been her moment to tell him that he had a beautiful little son—while there was no sign of the supermodel girlfriend all the papers had been going on about—and she had blown it. The shock of seeing him again, coupled with the pain of realising that she didn't even qualify as a memory, had made her fail to seize the opportunity. But surely you couldn't just walk up to a man who was essentially a total stranger and come out with a bombshell like that?

Laura hid her trembling fingers in her white apron as she quickly turned away—but the emotional impact of seeing Constantine again made her stomach churn and her heart thump so hard that for a moment she really thought she might be sick.

But she couldn't afford to be sick. She had to stay alert—to choose a moment to tell him what for him would be momentous news. And it wasn't going to be easy. Getting an agency placement to waitress at the Karantinos party had been the easy bit—the hard stuff was yet to come.

'What the hell do you think you're doing?' demanded a severely dressed middle-aged woman as Laura walked up to the bar to place her order.

Laura smiled nervously at the catering manager, who had summoned all the agency staff into a cramped and stuffy little room half an hour earlier to tell them about the high expectations of service which every Granchester customer had a right to expect. 'I just offered the gentleman a drink—'

'Gentleman? *Gentleman*? Do you know who that *is*?' the woman hissed. 'He's the man who's *giving* this party which is paying your wages! He's a bloody world-famous Greek shipping tycoon—and if anyone is going to be offering him drinks then it's going to be me. Do you understand? I'll take over from now on. What did he ask for?'

'Just…just water.'

'Still or sparkling?'

'He…he didn't say.'

The manager's eyes bored into her. 'You mean you didn't ask?'

'I…I… No, I'm sorry, I'm afraid I didn't.' Inwardly,

Laura squirmed beneath the look of rage on her supervisor's face, and as the woman opened her mouth to speak she suspected that she was about to be fired on the spot. But at that moment there was some sort of hubbub from the other end of the ballroom, as the harpist arrived and began making noisy demands, and the manager gave Laura one last glare.

'Just do what you're supposed to do. Offer him both still and sparkling, and then fade into the background—you shouldn't find *that* too difficult!' she snapped, before hurrying away towards the musician.

Laura tried to ignore the woman's waspish words as she carried her tray towards Constantine. But inside she was trembling—mainly with disbelief that she had managed to get so close to him. And thrown into the complex mix of her emotions at seeing him again was also her body's unmistakable reaction to seeing the biological father of her son. It was something she stupidly hadn't taken into account—the powerful sense of recognition at seeing him. The sense of familiarity, even though this man was little more than a stranger to her.

Because here was Alex in adulthood, she realised shakily—or rather, here was a version of what Alex *could* become. Strong, powerful, prosperous. And wasn't that what every mother wanted for her son? A lion of a man, as opposed to a sheep.

Whereas the Alex she had left back at home being looked after by a frankly cynical Sarah—well, that Alex was headed in a completely different direction. Bullied at school and living a life where every penny mattered and was counted—how could he possibly achieve his true potential like that? What kind of a future was she offering him?

And any last, lingering doubt that she must be crazy to even contemplate a scheme like this withered away in that instant. Because she owed Alex this.

It didn't matter if her pride was hurt or the last of her stupid, romantic memories of her time with Constantine was crushed into smithereens—she owed her son this.

But as Laura approached him again, it was difficult not to react to him on so many different levels. His had always been an imposing presence, but the passing of the years seemed to have magnified his potent charisma. There had been no softening of the hard, muscular body—nor dimming of the golden luminance of his skin. And, while there might be a lick of silver at his temples, his wavy dark hair was as thick as ever. But with age had come a certain cool distance which had not been there before. He carried about him the unmistakable aura of the magnate—a man with power radiating from every atom of his expensively clad frame.

Laura felt the erratic fluttering of her heart. Yet none of that mattered. His eyes were still the blackest she had ever seen, and his lips remained a study in sensuality. She still sensed that here was a man in the truest sense of the word—all elemental passion and hunger beneath the sophisticated exterior.

'Your water, sir,' she said, trying to curve her mouth into a friendly smile and silently praying that he would return it.

Hadn't he once told her that her smile was like the sun coming out? Wouldn't that stir some distant memory in his mind? And didn't they say something about the voice always striking a note of recognition—that people changed but their voices never did?

She spoke the longest sentence possible under the circumstances. 'I…I wasn't sure if you wanted still or sparkling, sir—so I've brought both. They both come from…from the Cotswolds!' she added wildly, noticing the label. A fact from a recent early-morning farming programme on the radio came flooding back to her. 'It's…um…filtered through the oolitic limestone of the Cotswold Hills, and you won't find a purer water anywhere!'

'How fascinating,' murmured Constantine sardonically, taking one of the glasses from the tray and wondering why she sounded as if she was advertising the brand. She didn't *look* like the kind of out-of-work actress who would moonlight as a waitress, but you could never be sure. 'Thanks.'

He gave a curt nod and, turning his back on her, walked away without another word and Laura was left staring at him, her heart pounding with fear and frustration. But what had she expected? That he would engage her in some small-talk which would provide the perfect opportunity for her to tell him he had a son? Start remarking that the slice of lemon which was bobbing around in his glass of fizzy water was vastly inferior to the lemons he grew on his very own Greek island?

No. The smile hadn't worked and neither had the voice. Those black eyes had not widened in growing comprehension, and he had not shaken his coal-dark head to say, in a tone of disbelief and admiration, *Why, you're the young English virgin I had the most amazing sex with all those years ago! Do you know that not a day goes by when I don't think about you?*

Laura chewed on her lip. Fantasies never worked out the way you planned them, did they? And fantasies were dangerous. She mustn't allow herself to indulge in them just because she had never really got over their one night together. She was just going to have to choose her moment carefully—because she wasn't leaving this building without Constantine Karantinos being in full possession of all the facts.

The evening passed in a blur of activity—but at least being busy stopped her from getting too anxious about the prospect which lay ahead.

There had been a lavish sit-down dinner for three hundred people, though the space beside Constantine had remained glaringly empty. It must be for his girlfriend, thought Laura painfully. So where was she? Why wasn't she sticking like glue to the side of the handsome Greek who was talking so carelessly to the women in a tiara on the other side of him. *It was a royal princess!* Laura realised. Hadn't she recently come out of a high-profile divorce and walked away with a record-breaking settlement?

Laura had managed to pass right by him with a dish of chocolates, just in time to hear the Princess inviting him to stay on her yacht later that summer—but Constantine had merely shrugged his broad shoulders and murmured something about his diary being full.

The candlelight caught the jewels which were strung around the neck of every woman present—so that the whole room seemed to be glittering. In the background, the harpist had calmed down, and was now working his way through a serene medley of tunes.

It was not just a different world, Laura realised as she carried out yet another tray of barely touched food back to the kitchens, it was like a completely alien *universe*. She thought of the savings she had to make so that Alex would have a nice Christmas, and shuddered to think how much this whole affair must be costing—why, the wine budget alone would have been more than the amount she lived on in a single year. And Constantine was paying for it all. For him it would be no more than a drop in the ocean.

The guests had now all moved into the ballroom, where the harpist had been replaced by a band, and people had started dancing. But the minutes were melting by without Laura getting anywhere near Constantine, let alone close enough to be able to talk to him. People were clustering around him like flies, and it was getting on for midnight. Soon the party would end and she'd be sent home—and then what?

There was a momentary lull before a conversational buzz began to hum around the ballroom, and then the dancing crowd stilled and parted as a woman began to slowly sashay through them, with all the panache of someone whose job it was to be gazed at by other people. Her flaxen fall of hair guaranteed instant attention, as did the ice-blue eyes and willowy limbs which seemed to sum up her cool and unattainable beauty.

She wore a dazzling white fur stole draped over a silver dress, and at over six feet tall she dominated the room like the tallest of bright poppies. And there was really only one person in the room who was man enough not to be dwarfed by her impressive height—the man she was headed for as unerringly as a comet crashing towards earth.

'It's Ingrid Johansson,' Laura heard someone say, and then, 'Isn't she *gorgeous*?'

Convulsively, she felt her fingers clutching at her apron as she watched the blonde goddess slink up to Constantine and place a proprietorial hand on his forearm before leaning forward to kiss him on each cheek.

Constantine was aware of everyone watching them as Ingrid leaned forward to kiss him. 'That was quite an entrance,' he murmured, but inside he felt the first faint flicker of disdain.

'Was it?' Ingrid looked into his eyes with an expression of mock-innocence. 'Must we stay here, *alskling*? I'm so tired.'

'No,' Constantine said evenly. 'We don't have to stay here at all—we can go upstairs to my suite.'

To Laura's horror she saw the couple begin to move towards the door, and she felt her forehead break out into a cold sweat.

Now what?

She saw some of the bulkier security men begin to follow them, and the slightly disappointed murmur from the rest of the guests as they began to realise that the star attractions were leaving. Soon Constantine would be swallowed up by the same kind of protection which had shielded him so effectively from her all those years ago...

And then a terrible thought occurred to her—a dark thought which came from nowhere and which had never even blipped on her radar before. Or maybe she had simply never allowed it to. What if it *hadn't* been his security people who had kept her away from him all those years ago? What if he'd *known* that she was trying to make contact? And what if he'd actually *read* the letter she'd sent, telling him about Alex, and had decided to ignore it?

What if he had simply *chosen not to have anything to do with his own son*?

A cold, sick feeling of dread made her skin suddenly clammy, but Laura knew it was a chance she had to take. If that had been the case, then maybe she would find out about it now. And if he chose to reject his son again…well, then she wanted to see his face while he did it.

She went over to the bar and ordered a bottle of the most expensive champagne and two glasses.

'Put it on Mr Karantinos's account,' she said recklessly, and took the tray away before the barman could query why the order hadn't gone through room service.

Her flat, sensible shoes made no sound as they squished across the marble foyer, but within the mirror-lined walls of the lift she was confronted with the reality of her appearance and she shuddered. Hair scraped back into a tight bun, on top of which was perched a ridiculous little frilly cap. A plain black dress hung unflatteringly over her knees and was topped with a white-frilled apron.

She looked like a throwback to another age, when people in the service industry really *were* servants. Laura was used to wearing a uniform in the bread shop—what she was not used to was looking like some kind of haunted and out-of-place ghost of a woman. A woman who must now go and face one of the world's most noted beauties, who happened to be sharing a bed with a man whose child Laura had borne.

The lift glided upwards and stopped with smooth silence at the penthouse suite, its doors sliding open to reveal

Laura's worst fears. Two dark and burly-looking men were standing guard outside the door. So now what? Fixing on a confident smile, which contradicted the awful nerves which were twisting her stomach like writhing snakes, Laura walked towards the door.

One of the guards raised his eyebrows. 'Where do you think you're going?'

His accent was thickly Greek, and somehow it only added tension to her already jangled nerves. Laura's smile widened, though a bead of sweat was trickling its way slowly down her back. 'Champagne for Mr Karantinos.'

'He told us he didn't want to be disturbed.'

Because of what was at stake, Laura found herself digging deep inside herself, finding courage where she had expected to find fear. Her smile became conspiratorial; she even managed a wink. 'I think he's about to announce his engagement,' she whispered.

The other guard shrugged and jerked his head in the direction of the door. 'Go on, then.'

Rapping loudly on the door, Laura heard a muffled exclamation—but she knew she couldn't turn back now. She had to get this over with—because if she left it much longer she might find them…find them…

Blocking out the unbearable thought of Constantine and the supermodel beginning to make love, Laura pushed open the door, and the scene before her stamped itself on her gaze like a bizarre tableau.

There was Constantine, staring hard at the supermodel. And there was Ingrid staring back at him, her expression disbelieving. She had removed her fur wrap, and her dress was nothing but a sliver of silver which clung to her body and revealed the points of her nipples.

They both looked round as she walked in.

'What the hell do you think you are doing?' demanded Constantine, and then frowned as he saw the tray she was carrying. 'You don't just walk into my suite like this—and I didn't order champagne.'

Not even he was cold-hearted enough to celebrate the fact that he'd just finished with his girlfriend—even though Ingrid was still standing there staring at him as if she didn't quite believe it.

Putting the tray down on a table before she dropped it, Laura looked up at him, her voice low and trembling. 'I need to talk to you.' She glanced over at the model, who was glaring at her. 'Alone, if that's all right.'

'Who the hell is this?' snapped Ingrid.

He had absolutely no idea, and for one moment Constantine wondered if the insipid little waitress was some kind of set-up. Were her male accomplices about to burst in with cameras? Or did her uniform conceal some kind of weapon? Hadn't kidnap attempts been suspected enough times in the past?

But he remembered her from the ballroom—her pinched, pale face and her inappropriate babbling on about some type of water. She didn't look like the kind of woman capable of any kind of elaborate subterfuge. And her expression was peculiar; he had never seen a woman look quite like that before—and it made him study her more closely.

Her cheeks were pale but her grey eyes were huge, and she looked as if she was fighting to control her breathing. Her breasts—surprisingly pert breasts for such a tiny frame, he thought inconsequentially—were heaving like someone who had just dragged themselves out of the water after nearly drowning.

'Who are you?' he demanded hotly. 'And what do you want?'

'I told you,' answered Laura quietly. 'I need to talk to you. Alone, if I may.'

Constantine's eyes narrowed as some primeval instinct urged him to listen to what this woman was saying. And something in her strange urgency told him to ensure that they had no audience. He turned to the supermodel, praying that she wouldn't make the kind of scene which some women revelled in when a man had just ended a relationship.

'I think you'd better leave now, don't you, Ingrid?' he questioned quietly. 'I have a car which will take you wherever you want to go.'

For a moment Laura felt eaten up with guilt and shame as she saw the supermodel's stricken face, and her heart went out to her. Because what woman wouldn't be able to identify with the terrible battle taking place within the gorgeous blonde? Anyone could see she wanted to stay—but it was also easy to see from the obdurate and cold expression on Constantine's face that he wanted the supermodel out of there.

Oh, this was just terrible—and it was all her fault. Awkwardly, she shifted from one foot to the other. 'Look, perhaps I can…come back.'

'*You* are not going anywhere,' snapped Constantine as he flicked her a hard glance. 'Ingrid was just leaving.'

At this, Ingrid's mouth thinned into a scarlet line. 'You

bastard,' she hissed, and marched out of the suite without another word.

For a moment there was silence, and Laura's heart was pounding with fear and disbelief as she lifted up her hands in a gesture of apology. 'I'm sorry—'

'Shut up,' he snapped, two fists clenching by the shafts of his powerful thighs as a quiet fury continued to spiral up inside him. 'And don't give me any misplaced sentiments. Do you think you can hysterically burst in here making veiled threats and then act like a concerned and responsible citizen who cares about the havoc she's wreaked along the way? Do you?'

Nervously, Laura sank her teeth into her bottom lip. She supposed she deserved that—just as she supposed she had no choice other than to stand there and take it. Maybe if she let him vent his anger then he would calm down, and they could sit down afterwards and talk calmly.

His black eyes bored into her like fierce black lasers. 'So who *are* you?' he continued furiously. 'And why are you really here?'

Brushing aside her hurt that he *still* didn't recognise her, Laura tried again. 'I…' It sounded so bizarre to say it now that the moment had arrived. To say these words of such import to a man who was staring at her so forbiddingly. But then Alex's face swam into the forefront of her mind, and suddenly it was easy.

She drew a deep breath. 'I'm sorry it has to be this way, but I've come to tell you that seven years ago I had a baby. Your baby.' Her voice shaking with emotion, she got the final words out in a rush. 'You have a son, Constantine, and I am the mother of that son.'

CHAPTER THREE

CONSTANTINE stared at the trembling waitress who stood before him, and who had just made such a preposterous claim. That *she* was the mother of *his* son. Why, it would almost be laughable were it not so outrageous.

'That is a bizarre and untrue statement to make,' he snapped. 'Especially since I don't even know you.'

Laura felt as if he had plunged a stiletto into her heart, but she prayed it didn't show on her face. 'Then why didn't you have the guards take me away?'

'Because I'm curious.'

'Or because you know that deep down I could be telling the truth?'

'Not in this case.' His lips curved into a cruel smile. 'You see, I don't screw around with waitresses.'

It hurt. Oh, how it hurt—but presumably that had been his intention. Laura forced herself not to hit back at the slur, nor to let herself wither under his blistering gaze. 'Maybe you don't now—but I can assure you that wasn't always the case.'

Something in her calm certainty—in the way she stood there, facing up to him, despite her cheap clothes and lowly demeanour—all those things combined to make Constantine consider the bizarre possibility of her words. That they might be *true*. He looked deep into her eyes, as if searching for some hint of what this was all about, but all he saw was the stormy distress lurking in their pewter depths, and suddenly he felt his heart lurch. Eyes like storm clouds.

Storm clouds.

Another memory stirred deep in the recesses of his mind. 'Take down your hair,' he ordered softly.

'But—'

'I said, take down your hair.'

Compelled by the silken urgency of his voice, and weakened by the derision in his eyes, Laura reached up her hand. First, off came the frilly little cap, which she let fall to the floor—she certainly wouldn't be needing *that* again. Then, with trembling fingers, she began to remove the pins and finally the elastic band.

It was a relief to be free of the tight restraints and she shook her hair completely loose, only vaguely aware of Constantine's sudden inrush of breath.

He watched as lock after lock fell free—one silken fall of moon-pale hair after another. Fine hair, but masses of it. Hair which had looked like a dull, mediocre cap now took on the gleaming lustre of honey and sand as it tumbled over her slight shoulders. Her face was still pale—and the dark grey eyes looked huge.

Storm clouds, he thought again, as more memories began to filter through, like a picture slowly coming into focus.

A small English harbour. A summer spent unencumbered by the pressures of the family business. And a need to escape from Greece around the time of the anniversary of his mother's death—a time when his father became unbearably maudlin, even though it had been many years since she had died.

His father had promised him far more responsibility in the Karantinos shipping business, and that summer Constantine had recognised that soon he would no longer be able to go off on the annual month-long sailing holiday he loved so much. That this might be the last chance he would get for a true taste of freedom. And he'd been right. Later that summer he'd gone back to Greece and been given access to the company's accounts for the first time— only to discover with rising disbelief just how dire the state of the family finances was. And just how much his father had neglected the business in his obsessive grief for his late wife.

It had been the last trip where he was truly young. Shrugging off routine, and shrugging on his oldest jeans, Constantine had sailed around the Mediterranean as the mood took him, lapping up the sun and feeling all the tension gradually leave his body. He hadn't wanted women—there were always women if he wanted them—he had wanted peace. So he'd read books. Slept. Swum. Fished.

As the days had gone by his olive skin had become darker. His black hair had grown longer, the waves curling around the nape of his neck so that he had looked like some kind of ancient buccaneer. He'd sailed around England to explore the place properly—something he'd always meant to do ever since an English teacher had read him stories about her country. He'd wanted to see the improbable world of castles and green fields come alive.

And eventually he'd anchored at the little harbour of Milmouth and found a cute hotel which looked as if it had been lifted straight out of the set of a period drama. Little old ladies had been sitting eating cream cakes on a wonderful emerald lawn as he strolled across it, wearing a faded pair of jeans and a T-shirt. Several of the old ladies had gawped as he'd pulled out a chair at one of the empty tables and then spread his long legs out in front of him. Cream cakes which had been heading for mouths had never quite reached their destination and had been discarded—but then he often had that effect on women, no matter what their age.

And then a waitress had come walking across the grass towards him and Constantine's eyes had narrowed. There hadn't been anything particularly *special* about her—and yet there had been something about her clear, pale skin and the youthful vigour of her step which had caught his attention and his desire. Something familiar and yet unknown had stirred deep within him. The crumpled petals of her lips had demanded to be kissed. And she'd had beautiful eyes, so deep and grey—a pewter colour he'd only ever seen before in angry seas or storm clouds. It had been—what? Weeks since he had had a woman? And suddenly he'd wanted her. Badly.

'I'm afraid you can't sit there,' she said softly, as her shadow fell over him.

'Can't?' Even her mild officiousness was turning him on—as was the pure, clean tone of her accent. He looked up, narrowing his eyes against the sun. 'Why not?'

'Because…because I'm afraid the management have a rule about no jeans being allowed.'

'But I'm hungry,' he murmured. 'Very hungry.' He gave her a slow smile as he looked her up and down. 'So what do you suggest?'

As a recipient of that careless smile, the girl was like putty in his hands. She suggested serving him tea at an unseen side of the hotel, by a beautiful little copse of trees. Giggling, she smuggled out sandwiches, and scones with jam and something he'd never eaten before nor since, called clotted cream. And when she finished work she agreed to have dinner with him. Her name was Laura and it made him think of laurels and the fresh green garlands which ancient Greeks wore on their heads to protect them. She was sweet—very sweet—and it was a long time since he'd held a woman in his arms.

The outcome of the night was predictable—but her reaction wasn't. Unlike the wealthy sophisticates he usually associated with, she played no games with him. She had a vulnerability about her which she wasn't afraid of showing. But Constantine always ran a million miles from vulnerability—even though her pink and white body and her grey eyes lured him into her arms like a siren.

In the morning she didn't want to let him go—but of course he had to leave. He was Constantine Karantinos— heir to one of the mightiest shipping dynasties in the whole of Greece—and his destiny was not to stay in the arms of a small-town waitress.

How strange the memory could be, thought Constantine—as the images faded and he found himself emerging into real-time, standing in a luxury London penthouse with that same waitress standing trembling-lipped in front of him and telling him she had conceived a child that night. And how random fate could be, he thought bitterly, to bring such a woman back into his life—and with such earth-shattering news.

He walked over to the drinks cabinet and poured himself a tumbler of water—more as a delaying tactic than anything else. 'Do you want anything?' he questioned, still with his back to her.

Laura thought that a drink might choke her. 'No.'

He drank the water and then turned round. Her face looked chalk-white, and something nagged at him to tell her to sit down—but his anger and his indignation were stronger than his desire to care for a woman who had just burst into his life making such claims as these.

A son....

'I wore protection that night,' he stated coldly.

Laura flinched. How clinical he sounded. But there was no use in her having pointless yearnings about how different his reaction might have been. She knew that fantasies didn't come true. Try to imagine yourself in his shoes, she urged herself. A woman he barely knew, coming back into his life with the most momentous and presumably unwelcome news of all.

'Obviously it failed to do what it was supposed to do,' she said, her voice as matter-of-fact as she could make it.

'And this child is you say…how old?'

'He's seven.'

He felt the slam of his heart and an unwelcome twist of his gut. Constantine turned and stared out of the vast windows which overlooked the darkened park before the unwanted emotions could show on his face. A son! Above the shadowed shapes of the trees he could see the faint glimmer of stars and for a moment he thought about the stars, back home, which burned as brightly as lanterns. Then just as suddenly he turned back again, his now composed gaze raking over her white face, searching for truth in the smoky splendour of her eyes.

'So why didn't you tell me this before?' he demanded. 'Why wait seven long years? Why now?'

Laura opened her mouth to explain that she'd tried, but before she had a chance to answer him she saw his black eyes narrow with cynical understanding.

'Ah, yes, but of course,' he said softly. 'Of course. It was the perfect moment, wasn't it?'

Laura frowned. 'I don't know what you're—'

But her thoughts on the matter were obviously super-fluous, for ruthlessly he cut through her words as if he were wielding a guillotine. 'You wait long enough to ensure that I can have no influence—even if the child *is* mine. How is it that the old saying goes? *Give me a child until he is seven and I shall give you the man.*' He took a step towards her, his posture as menacing as the silken threat in his voice. 'So what happened? Did you read the papers and hear that that Karantinos stock has soared, and then decide that this was the optimum time to strike? Did you think that coming out with this piece of information now would put you in a strong bargaining position?'

'*B-bargaining* position?' echoed Laura in disbelief. He might have been talking about a plot of land…when this was their *son* they were discussing.

His voice was as steely cold as his eyes. 'I don't know why you're affecting outrage,' he clipped out. 'I presume you want money?'

Automatically, Laura reached her hand out and steadied herself on a giant sofa—afraid that her trembling knees might give way but determined not to sit down. Because that would surely put her in an even weaker position—if she had to sit looking up at him like a child who had been put on the naughty chair. But even her protest sounded deflated. 'How dare you say that?' she whispered.

'Well, why else are you here if you haven't come looking for a hand-out?'

'I don't have to stay here and listen to your insults.'

'Oh, but I am afraid that you do. You aren't going anywhere,' he said with silky menace as he glittered her a brittle look. 'Until we get this thing sorted out.'

This thing happened to be their son, thought Laura—until she realised with a pang that maybe the Greek's angry words had the ring of truth to them. Because Alex was *her* son, not his. Constantine had never been a part of his life. *And maybe he never would be.* For a moment she felt a wave of guilt as Constantine's black gaze pierced through her like a sabre.

'Just by telling me you have involved me—like it or not,' he continued remorselessly as his gaze burned into her. 'Didn't you realise that every action has consequences?'

'You think I don't know that better than anyone?' she retorted, stung.

Something in her response renewed the slam of his heart against his ribcage, and Constantine narrowed his eyes, searching for every possible flaw in her argument the way he had learnt to do at work—an ability that had made him a formidable legend within the world of international shipping. 'So why didn't you tell me about this before—like seven years ago?'

She still wanted to turn and run, but she doubted that her feet would obey her brain's command to walk, let alone run. 'I tried…' She saw the scorn on his face. 'Yes, I tried! I tried tracking you down—but you weren't especially easy to trace.'

'Because I hadn't meant it to be anything more than a one-night stand!' he roared, steeling himself against the distressed crumpling of her lips.

'Then don't you talk to *me* about consequences,' she whispered.

There was a pause as he watched her struggling to control her breathing, her grey eyes almost black with distress. 'So what happened?' he persisted.

Laura sucked in a low, shuddering breath. 'I managed to find out the address and phone number of your head-quarters in Athens.' She had been completely gobsmacked to discover that her scruffy jeans-wearing, slightly maverick Greek lover turned out to be someone very important in some huge shipping company. 'I tried ringing, but no one would put me through—and I sent you a letter, but it obviously never reached you. And I've tried several times since then.'

Usually around the time of her son's birthday, when Alex would start asking questions, making her long to be able to introduce the little boy to his father.

'The result has always been the same,' she finished bitterly. 'It doesn't matter how I've broached it or what approach I've made—every time I've failed to even get a phone call with you.'

Constantine was silent for a moment as he considered her words, for now he could imagine exactly what must have happened. An unknown English girl ringing and asking to be put through to Kyrios Constantine—why, she would have been swatted away as if she were a trouble-some fly buzzing over a plate of food. Likewise any letters. They would have been opened and scrutinised. Who would have made the decision not to show him? he wondered, and then sighed, for this was something he *could* believe.

The ancient Greek troop formation of a tightly-knit and protective group known as the phalanx still existed in modern Greece, Constantine thought wryly. It was not the right of his workers to shield him, but he could see exactly why they had done it. Women had always shamelessly pursued him—how were his staff to have known that this woman might actually have had a case. *Might*, he reminded himself. Only *might*.

There was a pause. 'Do you have a photo?' he demanded. 'Of the child?'

Laura nodded, swallowing down her relief. At last! And surely asking to see a picture of Alex was a good sign? Wouldn't he set eyes on his gorgeous black-eyed son and know in an instant that there could only be one possible father? 'It's…it's in my handbag—downstairs in the staff cloakroom. Shall I go and get it?'

He was strangely reluctant to let her out of his sight. As if she might disappear off into the night and he would never see her again. *But wouldn't that be the ideal scenario?* The question came out of nowhere, but Constantine pushed it away. He stared down into those deep grey eyes and inex-plicably his mouth dried. 'I'll come with you.'

'But I'll…'

Black brows were raised. 'You'll what?'

She had been about to say that she would be sacked if she were seen strolling through the hotel with one of the guests—but, come to think of it, it wasn't as if she was planning to work here again. 'People will talk,' she said. 'If you're seen accompanying one of the waitresses to the staff cloakroom.'

'So let them talk,' he snapped. 'I think it is a little late in the day for you to act concerned after your dramatic entrance into my suite!' And he pulled open the door and stalked out, leaving Laura to follow while he spoke in rapid Greek to the two guards.

They rode down in the penthouse lift, which seemed to have shrunk in dimension since the last time she had been in it. Laura was acutely aware of his proximity and the way his powerful frame seemed to dominate the small space. She was close enough to see the silken gleam of his skin and to breathe in that heady masculine tang which was all his. Close enough to touch…

And Constantine knew that she was aware of him; he could sense it in the sudden shallowness of her breathing— the way a pulse began fluttering wildly beneath the fine skin at her temple. Did she desire him now, as women always did, and was anger responsible for the answering call in his own body? The sudden thick heat at his groin? The furious desire to open her legs and bring her right up against him, so that he could thrust deep into her body and spill out some of his rage? What was it about this plain little thing which should suddenly have him in such a torrent of longing?

He swallowed down the sudden unbearable dryness in his throat as the lift came to a halt and the door slid open on some subterranean level of the hotel he hadn't known existed. Laura began to lead the way through a maze of corridors until she reached the women's cloakroom.

'Wait here,' she said breathlessly.

But he reached out and levered her chin upwards with the tips of his fingers, feeling her tremble as he captured her troubled gaze with the implacable spotlight of his own.

'Don't run away, will you?' he murmured, with silky menace.

Laura stilled. In the light of all the vicious accusations he had hurled at her, his touch should have repelled her—but it did no such thing. To her horror, it reminded her of what it was like to be touched by a man, and the hard, seeking certainty of this man's particular touch.

With an effort she jerked her head away. 'I wasn't pl-planning to.'

'Hurry up,' he ordered, as the heat at his groin intensified—for he had seen the sudden darkening of her eyes and sensed her body's instinctive desire for him. That in itself was nothing new—women always desired him—what perplexed him was the answering hunger which stirred in his blood.

Laura nodded. 'I…I can't stay in this uniform. I'd better change while I'm in there—so I may be a couple of minutes.'

'I'll wait,' he ground out, but her words triggered an unwanted series of explicit and strangely powerful memories as the door closed behind her. Of the young woman who had shed her clothes with such unashamed pleasure—taking him into her pink and white body and gasping out her pleasure. Had that same woman conceived his child that night? he found himself asking, the question spinning round and round in his brain as he stared at the dingy wall of the staff corridor.

Laura took off her uniform and, leaving it neatly folded

beside one of the laundry baskets, she pulled on her jeans, T-shirt and thin jumper—she'd experienced too many cold winters not to have learnt the benefits of layering. Then she picked up her handbag and waterproof jacket and walked outside, to where Constantine stood in exactly the same spot, like a daunting dark statue.

Beneath the harsh glare of the overhead light, she began delving around in her handbag until she pulled out the picture of Alex taken at school, just a few months ago—she handed it to him.

Constantine stared down at it in silence for a long moment. The child had black eyes and a faint olive tint to his skin, and the dark curls of his hair looked as if an attempt had been made to tame them especially for the photo—but already they were beginning to escape. He remembered his own hair being just as stubborn at such an age.

Narrowing his eyes, he studied the image more carefully. The child was smiling, yes—but there was an unmistakable wariness about that smile, and Constantine felt a sudden wild leap of protectiveness, mixed in with an innate sense of denial. As if the logical side of his mind refused to accept that he could start the evening by hosting a glittering party and then the evening would end with a paternity claim foisted on him out of the blue. That he should suddenly be a father. He shook his head.

'He looks just like you!' Laura blurted out, wanting him to say something—anything—to break this tense and awful silence.

An icy feeling chilled his skin. He had never felt quite so out of control as he now found himself—not since his mother had died and he had watched his father fall to pieces before his eyes, and had decided there and then that love did dangerous things to a man. 'Does he?'

'Oh, yes.'

'That proves nothing,' he snarled as he thrust the photograph back into her hand. 'For all I know this might just be a very clever scam.'

Laura swayed, unable to believe that he would think her so cold and calculating. So *manipulative*. So sexually free and easy. But why shouldn't he think that? He didn't know her—just as she didn't know him. Though the more of himself he revealed, the more she was beginning to dislike him. Had he forgotten that she had gone into his arms an innocent, unable to resist the powerful sexual pull he had exerted?

'B-but you knew that I was a virgin that night,' she reminded him painfully.

He shrugged, as if her words meant nothing—but the concept of a woman's purity was both potent and important to a man as traditional as Constantine. He forced himself to remember his incredulity that a young woman should so casually give her virginity to a man she knew she would never see again. Or had *he* been naïve? With her he had played the man he had never allowed himself to be— the itinerant traveller without a care in the world. What if her sweet and supposed ignorance of his wealth and his status had all been an act? Suppose she'd seen his yacht and started asking questions in between serving him tea and having dinner with him? Wouldn't that make her eagerness to lose her innocence to a man who was little more than a stranger more understandable?

Constantine had spent his whole life being surrounded

by people who wanted something from him—maybe this woman was no different.

'You *told* me you were a virgin, but those could have simply been words. And, yes, I know that you gasped as I entered you,' he said brutally, before pausing to add a final, painful boast. 'But women always do—maybe it is something to do with my size, or my technique.' He shrugged as her fingertips flew to her lips, hardening his heart against her obvious distress. 'Maybe you thought that affecting purity would guarantee you some sort of future with the kind of man you were unlikely to meet again. That if I thought you were a virgin I would think more highly of you—rather than just as a woman who had casual sex with a man she'd just met.'

Laura felt ill. It was as if he had taken her memories of the past and ground them to dust beneath his heel. 'Well, if you think that,' she said, putting the photo back in her wallet with trembling fingers, 'then there's nothing more to be said, is there?'

But Constantine moved closer, so close that she could feel his body heat, and she hated the thought that flashed through her mind without warning. This was the man who had planted a seed in her body...whose child had grown within her. The image was so overwhelming that it made her instinctively shudder. And wasn't nature famously canny, if cruel—conditioning women to desire the biological father of their child, even if that man was utterly heartless? Laura swallowed, because now he was lowering his head towards her so that she was caught in the intense ebony blaze of his eyes. Surely he wasn't going to...?

But he was.

He caught her against him, crushing her tiny frame against his and enfolding her within his powerful arms. She could feel the fierce hard heat of his body where it touched hers, and knew that she should cry out her protest—but she could no sooner stop this than she could have stopped the earth spinning around the sun.

His mouth came down to capture hers, and even though Laura was desperately inexperienced when it came to men she could sense the simmering anger which lay behind his kiss. This was a kiss which had more to do with anger than desire. But that didn't stop her responding to it—didn't stop her body flaring up with desire as if he had just ignited it with some hidden fuse. *He despises me,* was her last sane thought as the expert touch of his mouth made her lips part willingly beneath his.

His hands were tight around her waist and her own were splayed over the hard chest, where she could feel the rapid thundering of his heart. And through the kiss Laura made a little sound of disbelief—wondering how she could respond with such melting pleasure to a man who clearly viewed her with utter contempt.

The sound seemed to startle him, for just as suddenly as he had taken her in his arms he let her go, so that she had to steady herself against the wall as she stared up at him.

'Wh-what was that all about?' she breathed.

What, indeed? With an effort, Constantine controlled his ragged breathing and stared at her, shaking his head as if to deny the intensity of that kiss. It had been all about desire, he told himself fiercely—a powerful desire which was no respecter of circumstance or status. And how extraordinary that he should feel such overwhelming lust for this washed-out little waitress. Inappropriate, too—when to do so would surely weaken his case against her preposterous claim.

He looked down at her, his heart pounding so powerfully in his chest and his groin so hard with need that for a moment he couldn't think straight. 'You will need to get a DNA test done as quickly as possible,' he grated.

Laura's eyes widened in distress. 'But… But…'

'But what?' he cut in scornfully, and gave a short laugh as the aftermath of the kiss faded and reality flashed in like a sharp knife. 'Did you really think that I was going to acknowledge the boy as a Karantinos heir—giving him access to one of the world's greatest fortunes—simply because you say so and because the boy bears a passing resemblance to me?'

'But you—'

'Yes, he looks Greek,' he finished witheringly. 'But for all I know you might be one of those women who turn on for Greek men.' He gave a blistering smile as his gaze raked over her kiss-swollen lips. 'I think you've just demonstrated that to both our satisfaction.'

Laura slumped back against the wall and stared up at him. Was that why he had kissed her—to make her look morally loose? And then to follow it up with a cold-blooded demand that she prove Alex was his child? 'Why, you…you *bastard*!' she gasped.

Constantine reflected that women were remarkably unimaginative when it came to insults. And didn't they realise that *they* were the ones who put themselves into situations which gave men ammunition to criticise them?

But inside he was hurting for reasons he wasn't even

close to understanding—a state of being so rare for him that it made him want to hurt back, and badly.

'I should be careful about my choice of words, if I were you, Laura,' he informed her coldly. 'It isn't *my* parentage which is in doubt. If tests prove that the boy is mine, then I will take responsibility—but first you're going to have to prove it.'

CHAPTER FOUR

'WHAT do you mean, he wants a DNA test?'

Laura stared at her sister, trying to snap out of the terrible sense of weariness which seemed to have settled over her like a dank cloud. After leaving the Granchester last night she had spent a few restless hours in a cheap London hotel before catching the first train back to Milmouth—her mind still spinning with all the hurtful things Constantine had said to her. On the plus side, she had arrived back in time to take Alex to school, but now she was back in the shop, Sarah having coped with the morning rush of customers. This quiet spell meant that Laura was now forced to face Sarah's furious interrogation.

She shrugged her shoulders listlessly—she had gone through every emotion from anger and indignation through to sheer humiliation and had worn herself out with them. 'It's fairly self-explanatory, isn't it? He wants a DNA test done. He wants proof that Alex is his son.'

'Did you show him the photo?'

'Of course I did.'

'And?'

There was a pause while Laura thought about how best

to put it, strangely reluctant to repeat Constantine's wounding words. Was it her own hurt pride which stopped her from telling her sister how much he clearly despised her and all she stood for? 'He said that although Alex looked Greek he couldn't possibly risk acknowledging an heir to such a vast fortune as his without proof.'

'The bastard!'

And even though she'd hurled exactly the same word at him last night, Laura now found herself in the bizarre position of putting forward a contrary point of view. One that she had been thinking about during her early morning train journey. 'I can see his point,' she said carefully. 'I mean, he doesn't know that he's the only possible contender who could be Alex's father, does he?'

'Didn't you tell him?'

'No.' His anger had been too palpable; the mood between them too volatile. Why, he'd even accused her of using her virginity as a bargaining tool. 'And even if I had he might not have believed me. Why should he?'

Sarah frowned. 'Laura—I don't believe this! You're not *defending* him, are you?'

'Of course I'm not,' replied Laura stiffly.

But the truth was far more complex. She *could* see Constantine's point—even though it hurt her to the core that he should think her capable of having lots of partners and just wanting to foist paternity on the richest candidate. The way she had acted the day she'd met him had been uncharacteristic behaviour she'd never repeated—but Constantine wasn't to know that, was he?

'For all he knows, there might have been a long line of Greek lovers in my life,' she told her sister fiercely, blinking furiously to stop the rogue tears from pricking at her eyes.

'What? All of them sailing their yachts into Milmouth?' questioned Sarah sarcastically. 'I didn't realise our town was twinned with Athens!'

'Very funny,' said Laura as she pulled on her apron.

But at least Sarah's acerbic comments had helped focus her mind, and she went on the internet at lunchtime—cursing the dyslexia which made her progress slow as she laboriously pored over websites which offered information about DNA-testing. Sitting in the cramped little corner of the sitting room where they kept the computer, she studied it until she was certain she knew all the facts—and she was startled by the sudden sound of her cellphone ringing. She used it mainly for emergencies—only a few people had the number—and this was one she didn't recognise.

But the voice she did. Instantly.

'Laura?'

Briefly, she closed her eyes. Away from the cruel spotlight of his eyes, it was all too easy to let the honeyed gravel of Constantine's faintly accented voice wash over her. It tugged at her senses, whispering over her suddenly goosebumpy skin, reminding her of just how good a man's kiss could make a woman's starved senses feel.

Appalled at the inappropriate path of her thoughts—especially when he was forcing Alex to go through the indignity of a DNA test—Laura sat up straight and glared at the computer screen. Get real, she told herself furiously.

'Hello, Constantine.'

'Ah, you recognised my voice,' he observed softly.

'Funny that, isn't it? Yet, strange as it may seem, there

aren't scores of Greek men growling down the telephone at me.'

Detecting a distinctively spiky note in her voice, Constantine frowned. Was she daring to be sarcastic—to *him*? And under such circumstances, too? 'You know why I'm calling?'

'Yes.'

'You will agree to the DNA test?'

Laura gripped the phone tightly. What choice did she have? 'I suppose so.'

'Good.' Leaning back in the sumptuous leather of his chair, Constantine surveyed the broad spectrum of the glittering London skyline. 'I've been making some enquiries and I can either arrange for you to have it done at my lawyer's office here in London—or he tells me that he can arrange for you to use somewhere closer to you, if that's more convenient.'

She heard an unexpected note of silky persuasion in his voice, and suddenly Laura was glad that she had done her research, glad that she wasn't just going to accept what the powerful and autocratic Greek was telling her. *What it was in his best interests to tell her*.

'I'm not using a lawyer's office,' she said quietly.

There was a disbelieving pause. 'Why not?'

'Because I believe that doing so carries all kinds of legal implications,' she said. 'This test is being done to establish paternity to your satisfaction; it is not a custody claim. So I'm doing the test at home on a purely need-to-know basis.'

Another pause, longer this time. Constantine had not been expecting her to query his wishes—to be honest, he had expected her simply to accept his agenda. Because people always did; they bowed to the dominance of his will. So just who did this mousy little waitress think she was to dare to oppose his wishes? He lowered his voice. 'And if I object?'

'You aren't in any position to object!' she declared, refusing to let that silky tone intimidate her. 'You're the one who wants this damned test—who is going to force me to take a swab from my seven-year-old son's mouth. Have you thought what I'm going to tell him? How I'm going to explain *that* to a seven-year-old boy?'

'And didn't you think through any of this before you came to me?' he flared back.

The terrible truth was that she *hadn't* thought through all the repercussions—instead she had been swept along by feelings which had been too primitive to allow any room for reason. She had felt an overpowering sense of injustice—because Constantine might be about to marry another woman and have a family with *her* without realising that he had another son who might know nothing but penury and spend his life living in the shadows. And she had thought he would recognise her—remember the night they had spent together with surely a *bit* of fondness. And then, in true fairy-tale fashion, she had imagined him acknowledging his son with a certain amount of Greek pride.

And it was about you, too, wasn't it? prompted the uncomfortable voice of her conscience. *Aren't you forgetting to put that into the equation? You were unreasonably jealous of the woman you thought was going to share his life—even though you had no right to be. And your actions*

*helped contribute to the fact that the supermodel stormed
out of the hotel suite, didn't they?*

'Or did you think I was just going to roll over like a
pussycat and sign you a big, fat cheque?' he persisted.

She had been about to admit her hastiness and lack of
forethought, but his hateful remark made her bite it back.
What an unremittingly cruel man he could be. Perhaps she
had opened a whole can of worms, and Alex might be
about to discover what kind of man his father really was.
'I—I'll organise the test,' she said shakily.

Constantine heard the faint tremble in her voice, and unwillingly he frowned. He remembered the photo of the
little boy with the stubborn curls and the wariness which
had peeped out from his black eyes. Could he really put
the child through the worry of a test? Had she not proved
herself by now? Because surely if she had been bluffing
then she would not have dared sustain such a fiction for so
long. And the fact that he had been trying to block from
his mind now came slamming into focus—that little boy
was *his* little boy.

'Forget the test,' he said suddenly.

Staring out at Milmouth high street, where the hazy
sunshine spilling onto the cobbled streets seemed to mock
at her dark mood, Laura froze. 'F-forget it?' she questioned incredulously. 'Why?'

'I've changed my mind,' he said slowly.

Laura's lips parted—she was scarcely able to believe
what she'd just heard. Constantine magnanimously telling
her that the test was unnecessary when he was the one who
had insisted on it in the first place—like a teacher at school
deciding to let her off a hastily handed-out detention. He

has all the power, she realised bitterly. And she still wasn't clear what the motives were for his sudden about-face.

'But you said you wanted proof.'

'I no longer need it. I believe you,' he said unexpectedly.

'You believe that he's your son?'

'Yes.' There was a long silence as Constantine acknowledged the power of the single word of admission which would now change his whole life—whether he liked it or not. 'Yes, I believe he's my son,' he said heavily, as if the full statement would reinforce that fact to both of them. He had known it the moment he had stared at the photo and seen those disobedient curls—and on some subliminal level he had accepted it even before that. Because some instinct had told him to—an instinct he had not understood at the time and probably never would.

'But...why?' Her confused words cut into the turmoil of his thoughts. 'Why now, after all you said? All you accused me of?'

Constantine curled his hand into a tight fist and stared at it. All he had said had been rooted in denial; he hadn't *wanted* to believe her. He had been reluctant to accept the enormity of the possible consequences if what she said *had* been true. But suddenly he allowed himself to see that this news could have all kinds of benefits—and perhaps it had dropped into his life at just the right time. A solution had begun to form in his mind—as perfect a solution as such circumstances would allow. All he needed was to convince her to go along with it.

The determination which had driven him to rebuild one of the most powerful companies in his native Greece now emerged in a different form. A form which could be used to tackle a private life which had suddenly become complicated. Constantine's mouth hardened, and so did his groin as he remembered the way she had let him kiss her in that scruffy little hotel corridor last night. Of *course* she would go along with his wishes! She wasn't exactly the kind of woman who was going to turn down a golden opportunity if it fell into her lap, now, was she?

For a moment he was tempted to put his proposition to her there and then—until he was reminded that she had shown signs of stubbornness. Better to have her as a captive audience and to tell her face to face. Better to allow his lips and his body to persuade her if his words couldn't.

'Your co-operation has convinced me that you are telling the truth,' he said silkily. 'A woman like you would be unlikely to pit herself against an adversary like me if she was lying.'

The unexpected reprieve made Laura blink her eyes rapidly. 'Th-thank you,' she said, after taking a moment to compose herself—though when she thought about it afterwards she realised that she had completely missed the sting behind his words.

Constantine was aware that this was the moment to choose—when she was both vulnerable and grateful. 'We'll need to discuss some kind of way forward,' he said smoothly. 'Obviously, if I am the child's father, then there are a great many possibilities available to us all in the future.'

Laura felt a conflicting mixture of fear and hope. She didn't like to ask what he meant in case she came over as greedy, or grasping—but her senses had been put on alert. His sudden mood-switch from anger and accusation to honeyed reasonableness was unsettling—she felt like a starving dog, about to leap on a tasty-looking piece of meat, only to discover that it was a mangy old stick. What did he want?

'Such as?' she questioned cautiously.

'I don't really think it's the kind of discussion we should be conducting on the phone do you, *mikros minera*?' His voice deepened. 'So why don't we meet somewhere and talk it over like two sensible adults?'

It didn't seem to matter how many times she swallowed—Laura just couldn't lose the parchment-dryness which seemed to be constricting her throat. Why did she feel as if she was being lured into some trap—as if Constantine Karantinos was taking her down some path to an unknown and not particularly welcome destination? She snatched a glance at her watch. She was already ten minutes over her lunch break, and Sarah would go mad if she was much longer.

'Okay,' she said cautiously. 'I'll meet you. Where and when?'

'As soon as possible,' he clipped out. 'Let's say tomorrow night. I can come there—'

'No!' The word came out in a burst before she steadied her voice. 'Not here. Not yet. People will talk.'

'Why will they talk?' he bit back, more used to his presence at a woman's side being flaunted.

Laura stared out of the window to where she could see the distant glimmer of the sea. Did he have no idea about a small town like this and the ongoing mystery of Alex's paternity? Her night with the handsome Greek had been clandestine enough, and no one had known about it. Previously innocent and still relatively naïve, her pregnancy had come as a complete shock. If Laura's mother had still been alive, it might all have been different—she would have been there to support her and help her face the rest of the world.

As it was, Laura had felt completely on her own—not wanting to burden her young sister with any of her fears about the future. She had been proud and defiant from the moment she'd started to show right up to the moment she'd brought her baby home from the hospital.

Alex had been so very cute, and Laura so tight-lipped about his parentage, that people had given up asking who his father was—even if they still sometimes wondered.

But imagine if a man as commanding and as striking as Constantine should suddenly show up in Milmouth! His black hair and golden-olive skin were exactly the same physical characteristics which marked her son out at school. Why, she might as well take out a front-page advertisement in the *Milmouth Gazette*! People would talk and word might reach Alex—and whatever Alex was going to be told it needed to be carefully thought out beforehand. Oh, *what* was she going to tell her beloved son?

'Because people always talk,' she said flatly. 'And I don't want my son hearing speculative gossip.'

Constantine frowned. 'Where, then? London?'

'London's not easy for me to get to.'

'I can send a car for you.'

How easily practical problems could be solved when you had money, thought Laura. But a Greek billionaire's limousine was just as striking as its owner. 'No, honestly— there's no need for that. I'll meet you in Colinwood—it's our nearest big town.'

Constantine waved away the secretary who had appeared at the door of his vast office, carrying a bundle of papers. 'And is there a good restaurant there?'

She thought about what Colinwood had to offer. 'There's a hotel called the Grapevine, which is supposed to have a good restaurant, but I won't be eating because I like to have tea with my...my son,' she said. And besides, if the evening turned out to be really uncomfortable then she'd be trapped, wouldn't she? Forced to sit enduring food she didn't really want to eat and growing silent every time the waiter appeared. 'I'll meet you in the bar at nine.'

'Very well,' he said softly, and put the phone down—feeling slightly perplexed that she had not instantly fallen in with his wishes as he had expected her to do. *As women always did.*

Laura sat in silence for a moment after the connection was broken, and then ran back down to the empty shop, blurting out her news before her sister had a chance to berate her for being late.

'I'm meeting him for a drink tomorrow night. He's changed his mind about the DNA test.'

Sarah paused in the middle of brushing some icing sugar off the counter. '*Why?*'

Laura shook her head, and a terrible combination of fear and excitement shivered over her skin. 'I *don't know*,' she whispered. 'I just don't know.'

CHAPTER FIVE

DURING the build-up to her meeting with Constantine, Laura tried to carry on as usual—but inside she was still a seething cauldron of nerves, fear, and a terrible sense of *excitement,* too. And how she hated that heart-pounding awareness that she was going to see him again…that she *wanted* to see him again.

Even her choice of clothes for the outing proved a headache—she wasn't used to going out on dates and so had no idea what to wear. And this *wasn't* a date, she reminded herself—in fact, it was anything but. She knew it was wrong to go looking all dressed-up—it might look as if she was *expecting* something, mightn't it? But he had only ever seen her dressed as a waitress—or naked—and she had her pride. She didn't want him to look at her and wonder what the hell he had ever seen in her.

So, the following evening, she tucked Alex into bed and went to shower and change. It was a hot, sticky evening, and a light, flowery dress was about the only thing she had which was suitable—but it worked with bare legs and strappy wedge sandals. She added some seed pearls which had belonged to her mother, and went into the sitting room to face her sister's assessment.

'No make-up?' questioned Sarah critically as she looked her up and down.

'I am wearing a *bit*.'

'Hardly going to knock his socks off looking like that, are you?'

'That was never my intention,' said Laura as she picked up her handbag. 'Anyway, I'll see you later.' She wobbled her sister a smile as nerves came back to assail her. 'And thanks for babysitting.'

'Any time. Ring me if you want rescuing.'

'And how are you going to rescue me?' asked Laura, her mouth curving into a wry smile. 'By sending in the cavalry?'

She caught the bus to Colinwood—a pretty journey, which took in part of the dramatic coastline before tunnelling into lanes lush and thick with summer greenery. Normally she might have enjoyed just sitting back and taking in the scenery, but her heart was full of fear and the sky was heavy with the yellow-grey clouds which preceded a storm. As Laura alighted in the market square in the still and heavy air, she could already feel the oppressive beads of sweat which were prickling at her forehead.

The Grapevine was already quite full—mainly with young professionals, as well as couples out together for the evening. Laura found herself watching them the most—their close body contact proclaiming to the world that they were in love.

She knew that envy was an unappealing trait, but sometimes she just couldn't help herself. She wondered what it must be like to do things the 'right' way round. To fall in love and get engaged and then married. To have a man sit and hold your hand and look as if he had found heaven on earth. She tried to imagine the shared joy of a first baby—the breathless wonder of news being broken to friends and relatives. Not like her—with her unplanned pregnancy and her young son who had never laid eyes on his father...

She saw Constantine immediately—somehow he had bagged the best table in a quiet corner which commanded an enviable view of the stunning gardens outside. A waitress was buzzing around him, smiling for an extra beat as she placed a small dish of olives in front of him, smoothing her manicured hand down over a slender hip as if she wanted to draw his attention to it.

Please give me the strength to stand up to him, Laura said to herself silently as she picked her way through the room towards him, trying to fix her face into a neutral expression. But what kind of expression did she wear in circumstances like these?

Constantine watched her, observing her with a clinical detachment made easier by the fact that she was not wearing a uniform tonight. Tonight her long, fine hair was fizzing down over her shoulders—he could see its brightness as she approached. And she wore a thin little summer dress which made the most of her firm, young body and slender frame. The shoes she wore were high and drew attention to her legs. Amazing legs, he thought suddenly, as if remembering why she had captivated him all those years ago—and then instantly regretted it as she walked up to his table.

'H-hello, Constantine.'

He should have risen to greet her, but his trousers were stretched so tightly across his groin that he did not dare move. It wasn't textbook behaviour—but then he reminded himself that this wasn't exactly a textbook situation. They weren't out on some kind of cute, getting-to-know-you evening; they were here to discuss a small child. And once again the shimmering of some unknown emotion whispered at his heart.

'Sit down,' he drawled.

'Thanks.' She perched on the edge of the plush leather banquette, her skin clammy and her heart thumping loudly with nerves. It was so hot in here! When he handed her a glass of wine, she automatically took it with boneless fingers, even though she'd decided on the way over that alcohol was a bad idea. She took a sip. 'Have…have you been waiting long?'

There was silence for a moment, and Constantine leaned back, taking his time as he studied her, noting the way her knees were pushed tightly together and the stiff set of her slender shoulders. Her body language screamed out her tension—and he knew then that this was not going to be a walk-over. 'No, I've only just arrived,' he said, and in the fading light his eyes glittered. 'So…that's the niceties out of the way. Have you told the boy anything yet?'

Laura shook her head. She wished he would stop looking at her like that. As if he was stripping her completely bare with his black eyes. 'No.'

Fractionally, he leaned towards her. 'Do you realize,' he said softly, 'that I don't even know his name?'

It sounded like an accusation, and maybe it was—though it was actually the first time he'd asked. She sucked in a breath, disorientated by his proximity. *What if he hates the name I've chosen?* she thought—*in that inexplicable*

way that people often did take against names because they
reminded them of someone or something from their past.

'It's Alex,' she said quietly. 'Short for Alexander.'

There was a moment of silence before Constantine let
out a long, low breath. It was a name which meant warrior.
A proud name which carried with it all the weight and
honour of his heritage. 'A Greek name,' he observed.

'Yes. It seemed somehow *appropriate*.'

He felt a wave of something approaching helplessness
wash over him. 'In a situation which was entirely *inappropriate*?' he countered—because didn't giving the child a
name make him seem real in a way that a photo never
could? A person was beginning to emerge from the scraps
of information he was being fed. A person about whom he
knew absolutely *nothing*. 'What else did you decide was
appropriate?' he snapped.

Laura recoiled from the anger which was emanating in
heated waves from his powerful frame, and she put her
wine glass down on the table before it slid from her fingers.
'We can't keep apportioning blame!' she said in a low
voice. 'What happened *happened*. We can't change it—we
just have to deal with the situation as it is.'

'And the situation is what?' he retorted. 'A woman who
is clearly living from hand to mouth having sole charge of
my son and heir? Don't you think it's time I had a little
input into his life as well, Laura?'

'Of…of course I do. That's why I'm here.' She stared
at him, twisting her fingers nervously in her lap. 'We could
arrange a first meeting, if you like.'

He gave a short laugh. 'Slot me into the diary like an
appointment at the dentist, you mean? You want me turning

up on a Saturday afternoon to take a reluctant child for a hamburger while he counts away the minutes he has to spend with this stranger?'

Laura bit her lip. 'I didn't mean like that.'

'No? Then just what *did* you mean?' His black eyes blazed into her. 'What kind of future had you anticipated when you made contact with me again?'

His dominance was formidable, and Laura felt herself swamped by its dark power. *'I don't know,'* she admitted desperately.

Constantine's mouth hardened. 'Well, I *do*. I have given it a lot of thought and weighed up all the possibilities.' He had spoken to his lawyers, too—but maybe now was not the best time to tell her *that*. He lowered his voice, the way he did in the world of business when he was about to close a deal. 'And there is a future which makes perfect sense for all parties. Which is why I want you to accompany me to my island home in Greece, Laura, occupying the only position which is appropriate.' He paused, and his eyes gleamed like cold, black stones as he looked at her. 'As my wife.'

CHAPTER SIX

LAURA stared at Constantine, her heart beating wildly, scarcely able to believe her ears. 'Your *wife*?' she repeated incredulously. 'Why on earth would I want to marry *you*?'

'*Want* has nothing to do with it,' he iced back, outraged at her shocked and unflattering response. '*Need* is a far more fitting word. For a start, you need money.'

'I never said—'

'You're a *waitress* who also works in a damned shop!' he shot out.

The beating of her heart increased. 'How did you know that?'

His lips twisted. How naïve she was! 'It wasn't difficult. I got someone to find out for me.'

Laura swallowed. 'You mean you've been *spying* on me?'

Dismissively, he batted the question away, with an arrogant flick of his hand. If only it were as easy to bat away the memory of the photos his private detective had dropped in front of him: Laura taking the boy to school in clothes which were clearly too small for him. Not to mention the pictorial evidence of his son growing up in some scruffy apartment over a seedy little shop.

But it was more than that. There had been the dawning realisation that perhaps this trembling little waitress might actually make ideal marriage material. Poor and desperate—wouldn't she be so swept away by his power and his riches that she would be completely malleable, so that he could mould her to the image of his perfect wife? And of course added to all this was the inexplicable fact that he hadn't been able to stop thinking about that stolen kiss in the dark basement of the hotel... Why, even now the memory of it made him want to do it all over again. It was crazy. It was inexplicable. And it was as potent as hell...

He scowled, forcing his mind back to her ridiculous claim that she'd been spying on him. 'Don't be hysterical, Laura,' he snapped. 'When a woman comes to a man in my position, making claims of enormous significance, it is inevitable her background will be investigated. For all I knew you might have had some male partner at home, his eyes fixed greedily on the main chance—seeing your ex-lover as a meal ticket.'

'You...you...*cynic*...' she breathed.

'Or simply a realist?' he countered. 'Oh, come on—you can lose the outrage, *agape mou*. You see, I *know* the corrupting power of money. And I've seen what people will do in its pursuit.'

Laura stared at him. His *wife*? Had he really just asked her to be his wife? 'But I thought you were marrying that other woman—'

'What other woman?'

She saw his eyes narrow dangerously and wished she hadn't started this. 'The Swedish supermodel,' she said reluctantly.

'Who told you that?'

'I heard it on the radio,' she admitted, and from the look of slowly dawning comprehension which crossed his face she wished she'd kept quiet. Because now she sounded like some kind of stalker.

'You shouldn't believe a word the media tells you,' he snapped. 'But at least that explains why you suddenly appeared out of nowhere the other night.' His eyes fixed her with icy challenge. 'Actually, the press have been trying to marry me off for years—but *I* will chose whom and when to marry, not the media!'

She stared up at him, full of bewilderment. 'I still don't understand…after everything you've said—why you want to marry *me*.'

'Don't you? Think about it. Marriage has always been on a list as something that perhaps I ought to do when I get around to it—but there's been no real sense of urgency. Until now.' His black eyes glittered. 'You see, I possess a vast fortune, Laura,' he elaborated softly, 'and my father is old and frail. His greatest wish is to see me provide him with an heir. This could be a surprisingly easy way of accomplishing both objectives.'

Laura shook her head. 'But that's so…*cold-blooded*!'

'Is it?' He gave a cynical laugh. 'Unlike you, I have not grown up on a diet of believing in romance and happy-ever-after.' In fact, he knew better than anyone that reality never matched up to dreams, and that emotion robbed men of sense and of reason. He lowered his voice. 'Why not look at it practically rather than emotionally? Marriage will serve a purpose—it will legitimise my son and it will give you all the financial security you could ever need.'

But deep down Laura's suspicions were alerted. It would also give Constantine power, she recognised. And once he had that power wouldn't he be tempted to use it against her? Pushing her to the sidelines until he dominated Alex's life as she suspected that he could all too easily? Everything that she'd fought and worked for could be threatened by this man's undeniable wealth and charisma.

'No! No and no and no!' she flared back, as the emotion and the humid atmosphere of the bar began to tighten her throat. Suddenly she needed to get away from Constantine's heady proximity and the danger he represented.

Grabbing her handbag, she stood up—and without another word walked straight out of the bar, uncaring of the sudden lull in conversation from the couples around them, or the curious eyes watching her as she tried not to stumble in her high wedges.

Outside in the fast-fading light the atmosphere was just as sticky, and the heady scent of roses was almost overpowering. Laura dimly wondered if she should take off her shoes and run to the bus stop in an effort to escape from him, when she felt a hand gripping her arm. Constantine spun her round to face him, his black eyes blazing.

He stared at her, a nerve working furiously in his cheek. Because no woman had ever said no to him before. And no woman ever turned her back on him, either.

'Don't you ever walk out on me like that again!' he bit out.

'I'm a free agent and I can do exactly as I please!'

'You think so?' His mouth hardened with lust. 'Well, in that case, so can I!'

Without warning he pulled her right up against him—so close that she could feel every hard sinew. And she wanted to resist him—just as she was resisting his demand that she marry him. But it seemed that her body had other ideas. To her horror she found herself wanting to sink against him. Into him.

Did he sense that? Was that why he gathered her closer still—with a small moan of what sounded like his own surrender?

In the pale light, he tilted her face up. 'Now, this *is* a time when the word *want* is appropriate. And you want me, Laura—just as I want you. Don't ask me why, but I do,' he ground out, and he drove his mouth down onto hers.

She had meant to gasp out her protest, but instead her lips opened beneath his like a sea-anemone, and suddenly her feelings ran away with her. Was it anger or frustration which fuelled her desire, causing her fingers to clutch at his shoulders—finding the butter-soft silk of his shirt and the hard sheath of the muscular flesh beneath? Or was it something infinitely more dangerous—the fierce clamour of her heart for a man who would never grant her access to his?

'*Oh,*' she breathed, as she felt his free hand move down to splay with intimate freedom over the globe of one buttock, and a shudder rocked through her as her body melted into his.

'*Theos mou!*' he ground back in response. Through waves of hunger, which came with a strength he had not been anticipating, Constantine pulled her into a darkened recess at the side of the building and continued to plunder her mouth with kiss upon kiss. The fingers which had been on her bottom now slipped underneath the little sundress, and he slid his hand round until it lay over the cotton-covered warmth of her mound. He felt her gasp out a little cry. Her passion had not abated over the years, he thought grimly. Nor had her eagerness dulled or softened around the edges. He felt himself grow so hard that he thought he would explode.

Should he do it to her here? Unzip his trousers and thrust himself in her sweet, wild wetness? He moved his hand over what felt like a pair of functional cotton panties.

'If only you weren't wearing any…then how easy it would be,' he commented unevenly.

His graphic words broke into the darkly erotic spell which had captivated her, and Laura opened her eyes to see the face of Constantine—taut and tight with sexual hunger. Reality washed over her like a cold shower. *What the hell was she doing? Standing there while he put his hand between her legs and incited her to…to…*

'Stop…stop it,' she whispered.

'Stop what?'

'T-touching me.'

'But you like it. You know you do.' He moved a finger against her and heard her breathing quicken. 'Don't you?'

'*Oh.*'

His fingertips continued to tease her moist heat—and even in the dim light he could see the sudden dilation of her eyes before the lids came down to obscure them. She relaxed against him once more and he felt her imminent surrender. Should he carry on? Bring her to an orgasm she would be unable and unwilling to prevent? Kiss away the gasping little sounds as those sweet spasms pulsed through her? It would be a turn-on to watch her, and perhaps she would be more amenable to his plans if he had her glowing and basking in his arms afterwards.

But at that moment he heard the sound of a car approaching, and saw the powerful beam of its headlights snaking up the drive. He realised just what he was doing. He, Constantine Karantinos, was standing by the side of a hotel, making out with a woman, in an aroused state such as he had not been in since his teenage youth!

'Let's go upstairs,' he murmured, his lips soft as they whispered over the long pale line of her neck.

Through the mists of sweet, sensual hunger warning bells sounded like fire alarms in her head, and Laura opened her eyes in confusion. 'Up-upstairs?' she echoed blankly.

'Mmm. Much more comfortable there. Enormous bed. Enormous pleasure.' He kissed her neck and guided her fingers to where he was hard and aching for her. 'Enormous everywhere,' he whispered, on an arrogant boast.

But Laura shrank back, snatching her hand away from his tantalising heat as she looked up at him, aghast. 'You have a *room* here?'

'A suite, actually. Not the best I've seen—but not bad.'

'Let me get this straight.' Her heart was pounding. 'You thought…you thought that I'd just meekly go to bed with you?'

He smiled. 'Meekly is not the word I was hoping for, *agape mou*—since your response so far tells me that you are a very passionate woman. But then as I recall you always were,' he added softly.

And it was those last words of his which were almost her undoing—because they gave the situation a *faux* intimacy, almost as if they had some kind of tender, shared past between them. But they didn't, she reminded herself painfully. What they had shared had been nothing but a powerful sexual chemistry which had flared out of control. And just because that sexual chemistry was as explosive as ever, it didn't mean she had to give in to it. To behave in a way which would afterwards have him insulting her as if she were no better than a cheap little tramp.

'I'm not going upstairs with you,' she said sharply, pulling herself out of his arms and tugging her dress down defiantly as she moved away from the alcove.

To Constantine's astonishment, he could see that she meant it. Had he thought that she would capitulate as easily as she had done all those years ago? The way women always did? For a moment frustrated longing pulsed around his veins as he searched her face for a sign that she might be on the verge of changing her mind, but there was none.

With the steely self-control for which he was renowned he forced his own desire to evaporate, like droplets of water sizzling onto a hot Greek street. There would be plenty of time for sex once she had agreed to his other demands—and, banishing the tantalising memory of her heated response to him, Constantine switched to the real reason he was here.

'Hasn't that little interlude convinced you that we could make a creditable stab at matrimony?' he questioned softly as he followed her, his feet crunching over the soft gravel.

'How delightfully you put it—but the answer is still no.' Her knees still weak, Laura sank down onto a wooden bench in full view of the main entrance into the hotel, where cars were coming and going. Let him *dare* try to start touching her here!

Constantine sat down next to her. Was this like a board-room battle? he wondered. With her supposedly stubborn resistance being used as a lever to increase her demands? He gave a small smile. She would soon learn that *he* called all the shots. 'I'd like to know what your main objection to my proposal is?' he questioned silkily.

'Why—Alex, of course,' she shot back. 'Do you really think I can just announce to him that I'm marrying his father—whom he's never even met—and that we're all going off to Greece to live happily ever after?'

'Why not?'

'Why *not*? Don't you know *anything* about children?'

'Actually, no, I don't,' he snapped. 'Since I've been denied that opportunity up until now!'

Laura swallowed as she stared into the shadowed flint of his features. Be reasonable, she told herself as she worked out what to say. Because if she expected him to come round to her way of thinking then she was going to have to be convincing. And convincing a man like this about anything wasn't going to be easy. She had to show him how it would look from a little boy's point of view.

Her voice softened. 'Alex's life is here in England— it's all he's ever known. Don't you think that suddenly landing all this in his lap would be overloading him with too much, too soon? Tearing him away from his home and his school? A new father who turns up out of the blue and a new life he has no say in? What if Greece doesn't work out?'

'We will make it work out,' he vowed grimly.

And in a way that stubborn insistence only reinforced her determination. Laura suddenly got an ominous vision of the finality of being trapped in a loveless marriage with a man like Constantine, and a shiver ran down her spine. 'You can't *make* things happen like that,' she said. 'Human beings aren't puppets that you can play with and control. I don't think you realise the impact of taking a child who's never even been abroad and plonking him in a foreign land.'

His body tensed as if she had hit him, and he clenched his fists. 'Don't ever…*ever*…refer to Greece as a "foreign land" in front of me or in front of my son,' he hissed. 'It is the land of his forebears with a rich and glorious heritage. And one which I intend that he will learn about.'

The fingers which had tightened into two fists now slowly unfurled, and Laura found herself watching them with a horrible kind of fascination.

'I want contact with Alex,' he continued inexorably. 'And I want him to meet his grandfather. Those two things are non-negotiable—so how do you intend to let me go about doing it, Laura?'

And Laura knew then that she didn't have to be stuck on an island to be trapped. Entrapment could be emotional as well as geographical, she realised—and in a way her fate had been sealed from the moment she had made contact with him again. She could see the determination etched on his face, and she realised that there was no way she was going to be able to escape his demands. Which meant that she had to fashion them to best suit her and Alex's purpose. And no one could deny that it was in a child's best interests to learn about his father—no matter what *she* thought about him.

She laced her fingers together. 'I think it's best for Alex to get to know you…gradually.'

'And how do you suggest I do that?' he demanded. 'Start coming into that bread shop you run and buying some damned bun every morning?'

If the circumstances hadn't been so fraught then Laura might almost have laughed, because the image of this powerful Greek going into her little village shop was both bizarre and amusing. But there was no place for humour here; this was deadly serious. Yet neither was there was any need for him to be so scathing about her method of earning a living. Working in a shop wasn't up there with being a supermodel, but it was honest and it was decent—even if it didn't reap the huge kind of rewards which *he* obviously considered essential.

'Of course I don't,' she said stiffly.

'*My* life and *my* work are in Greece,' he clipped out.

'I realise that.' Just as hers and Alex's was here—a cultural and geographical world away. Laura's mind starting spinning as she searched desperately for some sort of solution to their dilemma, when suddenly a thought occurred to her. Unseen in the folds of her cheap summer dress, her fingers tightened as an idea of breathtaking simplicity came to her. 'But the long summer holidays are coming up,' she said slowly.

Constantine stilled. 'And what has that got to do with anything?'

'I could come to Greece,' she said carefully. 'But not as your wife. A complete lifestyle change would unsettle Alex— but he could cope with the kind of situation he's used to.'

'You aren't making any sense,' he snapped.

'Well, I…I presume that your father employs staff at his home in Greece?'

'Of course he does.'

'How many?'

'I am not in the habit of keeping an inventory,' he drawled. But her eyes continued to regard him steadily and he gave an impatient kind of sigh. 'There is a permanent house-keeper who lives within the complex, and several people who come in from the village to help out.'

'And do…do any of them have children?'

'Not young children, no—but there are plenty of those in the village.' He frowned. 'What the hell does that have to do with anything?'

Laura let out a long breath. 'I know exactly what we can do,' she breathed. 'You take me on for the summer as a temporary member of staff. I can work in your father's house—'

'*Work in my father's house?*' he roared in disbelief, staring at her as if she had taken complete leave of her senses. 'Doing *what?*'

Laura lifted her chin up, determined not to be intimidated by the fierce blaze from his eyes. 'The skills of which you've already been so very critical—I can clean and make beds. I can serve food. I can even cook—though not to any cordon bleu standard.'

Constantine stared into her face. 'Such lowly and subservient pursuits!' he bit out. 'What kind of a woman would want this?'

A woman with pride, thought Laura ardently. And a woman with dignity—or rather one who was trying to claw back some of the poise which always seemed to fly out of the window whenever Constantine was around.

'Meanwhile, Alex gets a few weeks in the sun,' she carried on, her enthusiasm growing now. 'If he plays with other children he can learn a little Greek, and they can learn English. It'll do him good to have a holiday—and in that relaxed environment he can get to know you.'

There was an ominous kind of silence while Constantine mulled over her words—there was no doubt that he was surprised by the humbleness of her request. She wanted to come to his house as a *servant*! And yet maybe it would work out better this way—for wouldn't it place strain on his father's heart to suddenly produce a seven-year-old grandson out of nowhere? And wouldn't she be more expendable as a servant than as a wife? Easier to dispose of afterwards, if her presence began to grate on him, without having to go through all the publicity and disruption of a divorce?

He stared at her, aware that her impudent idea was distracting him from the most important question of all. 'And when do you propose telling Alex that I'm his father?' he asked softly.

The eyes she turned to him were huge. 'Can we…can we wait until the moment is right?'

He hardened his heart against the tremulous appeal in her voice. 'I will not wait for ever, Laura,' he warned.

'No. No, I can understand that. We will tell him as soon as it's appropriate. I promise. Oh, thank you. Thank you, Constantine.' She flashed him a grateful smile, but the look he gave in response was like ice.

'This is not a situation I am happy with,' he bit out.

How hard the years had made him, she thought fleetingly. He was a completely different person from the ruffle-haired man who had sailed in and out of her life all those summers ago.

And what about her? Had *she* changed that much? Laura bit her lip. Quite honestly, that brief period of freedom and sexual awakening had been so unlike anything she had known since that she had almost completely forgotten it.

Or maybe she had just blocked it from her mind. Maybe it was too painful to remember being carefree and unencumbered by worry.

She forced her mind back to practicalities. 'The only problem I can think of is that I'm going to need a replacement to help my sister in the shop while I'm away—but I assume you'd be able to help me sort that out?'

The *only* problem? he thought. Was she crazy? He could see a few more than that.

'I can fix that,' said Constantine heavily—because for the first time in his life he had not got what he wanted. Despite her reduced circumstances and tiny stature, he could see that here was a woman who had her mind set on something, and nothing he could do or say was going to change her mind. Was this a unique version of mother-love? he wondered bitterly. A mother fighting tooth and nail for what was best for her child?

Briefly, Constantine found himself wondering what it must be like to have a mother who felt like that about you. A mother who cared about your welfare more than she cared about her own—but he vetoed the thought instantly. He never wasted time thinking about things which were beyond his own comprehension.

It was one of the reasons behind his success.

CHAPTER SEVEN

LAURA was aware of a surprisingly green oval rising up to meet them as the helicopter landed with the agility of a large moth. Ringed with silver-white sand, from the sky the island had looked like a jewel in the middle of a sea so intensely blue that she'd felt quite shaken with the beauty of it all.

And shaken by her first ever trip in a helicopter, of course.

She stole a glance at Alex, who also seemed completely rapt by the splendour unfolding before him, and wondered what kind of effect this trip was going to have on him. Because although she'd insisted on travelling out to Greece on a regular airline, since 'servants don't arrive in private jets,' as she had told Constantine firmly, there had been a helicopter waiting at Athens airport to whisk them off to the island of Livinos.

It had all proved a little distracting—and Laura found herself wondering if experiencing these enormous riches from such an early age had been instrumental in fashioning Constantine's character? She stared out at the gradually slowing helicopter blades. Of course it had! Your early experiences always shaped your development like nothing else. If he'd been used to snapping his fingers from an early age and getting whatever it was he wanted then no wonder he was so autocratic and demanding.

She held Alex's hand tightly as she helped him down from the helicopter, with his beloved blue bear clutched tightly to his chest. He'd been worried that the scruffy old toy was too babyish to bring with him—but Laura had insisted the bear come too. Heaven only knew he wouldn't go to sleep without him.

Thinking she heard someone call her name, she looked up, her eyes narrowed against the blinding heat of the hot sun, and there, standing beside a four-wheel drive, was the man who had been dominating her thoughts all week.

Constantine! Here! Her mouth dried and her heart began to race erratically as he fixed his piercing gaze on them. So much hung on what happened next, and for Alex's sake she prayed that this first meeting would be a success as they made their way across the scorching tarmac towards the Greek billionaire.

Constantine felt a sudden lurching of his heart as he watched them approach, unprepared for the powerful feelings which came surging over him as he stared at the boy. The photos he had seen had made him take seriously her claim that the child was his—even though he had done his best to deny it at the time. But seeing him now, in the living and breathing flesh—well, that was something entirely different. Put a hundred—no, a thousand seven-year-old boys in front of him and Constantine would have instantly picked out this particular boy as having sprung from Karantinos loins.

He sucked in a ragged breath as they grew closer, his heart now pounding with a terrible combination of recognition and regret—that they were strangers to one another, and yet he knew that they were linked in the most primeval way of all.

With an effort he tore his gaze away from Alex and let it travel instead to Laura, whose eyes were fixed on him with a certain amount of trepidation. As well they might be. Constantine's lips curved with contempt. Another cheap little dress and a pair of sandals which had seen better days—and her fine hair all mussed up in a cloud around her head. Had she deliberately come here today emphasising her lowly status, after stubbornly insisting that she be employed in the house as a member of staff? Was she perhaps hoping that he might make some kind of generous settlement on her if she insisted on highlighting the differences between them?

Yet despite the anger he felt towards her there was a fair amount of it directed at himself, for the inexplicable lust he still felt for her. That his groin should instantly ache with an unquenchable desire to make love to her—this pale and insipid little shop-worker who had turned down his offer of marriage!

But he composed his face into a smile of welcome as they grew closer—because he was clever enough to know that he could never win the boy if he was seen to be openly critical of his mother.

'C-Constantine,' stumbled Laura. 'I…well, I certainly wasn't expecting to find you here to meet us.'

'What an unexpected pleasure it must be,' he murmured sardonically, but his eyes were fixed on the child and he was aware of a strange beating of his heart. 'Hello, Alex.'

Alex turned a confused face up towards Laura 'Who's this, Mum?'

Constantine crouched down so that he was on a level with the boy, wondering if there would be some kind of instant recognition on the part of his son—but of course there was none. Had he perhaps been secretly hoping that Laura might already have told him—that there would be some kind of touching scene outside the airport? But things like that only happened in movies, he told himself grimly. This was real life.

Usually he did not care what kind of impression he made—people could either take him or leave him. His careless attitude stemmed from the fact that other men were always anxious to be his friend, while women were eager to be his lover. But now he realised that unexpectedly his heart was beating fast with something approaching concern. I want him to like me, he thought fiercely. I *need* him to like me.

'My name is Constantine Karantinos,' he said softly. 'And you are going to be staying in my father's house.'

Alex nodded, as if this were nothing untoward, and Laura supposed that after the excitement of the day itself he would have calmly accepted being told he was taking a trip to the moon. 'Is it a nice house?'

'Oh, it's a very nice house,' answered Constantine, with a smile of rare indulgence. 'With a big swimming pool.'

Alex blinked. 'You mean, just for us?'

'Just for us,' replied Constantine gravely.

Alex bit his lip in the way he always did when he was worried, and Laura's heart turned over as she watched him. 'But I'm not very good at swimming,' he said.

Constantine wondered why. 'Then we shall have to teach you—would you like that?'

Alex nodded, his dark eyes wide. 'Yes, please!'

'Let's get in the car, then.' And Constantine helped the child into the back seat and strapped him in, before stepping back to allow Laura to pass.

His eyes narrowed as she moved close enough for him to be able to get the drift of some light scent, and despite its cheapness he swallowed with another unexpected wave of lust.

'You look…' He allowed his gaze to drift over her pale skin and pinched expression and saw her bite her lip in response to his critical scrutiny. 'Pretty tired,' he conceded.

'Yes,' said Laura, thinking that tired didn't even come close—she felt physically and mentally exhausted. Truth to tell, she hadn't had a full night's sleep since she'd met Constantine at the Grapevine that night—plus she'd been working some of Sarah's shifts, to make up for the time she was going to take off. 'It's been a long week,' she said wearily.

For a moment—just for a moment—he felt the faintest tug of sympathy. For the first time he noticed that the grey eyes were shadowed, and that her pale skin was almost translucent with fatigue.

'Then for heaven's sake get in the car and relax,' he said roughly, climbing into the driver's seat himself and starting up the engine, while the helicopter pilot put their small and rather battered suitcases in the boot.

'Wow! Get in, Mum!' Alex enthused. 'It's huge.'

Uncomfortably conscious of trying to keep as much of her pale, bare legs hidden as possible, Laura got in next to her son. She caught sight of a pair of black eyes mocking her as they glanced at her from the rearview mirror, and her reaction to that unmistakably sensual look was instinctive, though completely unwelcome. She felt the weak, thready patter of her heart and the icing of her skin, but she stared straight ahead at his broad shoulders and prayed that he would just let her get on with her work while he got down to the important business of getting to know Alex. Did he realise that she was determined to fight her desire for him—since no good could come out of their renewing a sexual relationship?

'Do you live near the sea?' piped up Alex.

'No place on the island is far from it,' answered Constantine. 'And if you're very lucky you might see one of the Karantinos ships sailing by.'

Alex failed to keep the sense of wonder from his voice. 'You mean *real* ships?'

Constantine laughed. 'Yes. Very real. And very big.'

'I'd love that,' said Alex wistfully, and then bit his lip in the way he'd unconsciously picked up from his mother. 'But Mum will be working, won't she? And she says I'm not to get in anyone's way.'

There was an awful silence, and if there had been a dark corner nearby then Laura would have gone away and crawled into it. She had never felt sorry for herself—ever. She had always embraced hard work and considered it a part and parcel of bringing up a child out of wedlock. But Alex's words prompted a deep dislike of her predicament—and of what it was doing to her son.

His words had set them apart. Making him sound like some servant's child from a different century—almost as if he was going to be sent up the chimney and asked to sweep it! And Constantine clearly felt it, too—because once more he caught her gaze in the driving mirror, but this time the look was not remotely sensual, it was spitting with a slow, burning anger. As if it was an insult to *his* honour to hear his son speaking in such a way.

'You must not worry about your mother's working hours,' he said abruptly. 'Since I know that she will be happy for you to enjoy yourself.'

'I just don't want her to feel left out,' said Alex loyally, and Laura could have wept. It was supposed to be *her* protecting him, and not the other way round.

'Of course you must let Constantine show you all his ships,' said Laura, as if she discussed the ownership of ships every day of her life.

'I used to live here when I was about your age,' said Constantine conversationally.

'Oh, *wow*!' Alex sighed. 'Lucky you.'

Something in the boy's wistfulness made a rush of unwilling memories come flooding back—and for once Constantine could not block them out. In many ways it had been a textbook and idyllic upbringing—with none of the stresses surrounding life spent in the city. The beauty of Livinos, and the ability to swim and to fish and to climb trees without fear—those were gifts which every other child on the island had experienced. He hadn't needed to be the son of a wealthy man to enjoy the carefree freedoms of childhood in this part of Greece.

But, essentially, it had been a lonely time for Constantine. Materially rich but emotionally neglected by a mother who had never been there—even when she had been physically present. His beautiful, fragile mother, who had captivated his father like a moth to a flame—who had consumed all those around her but given little back. Who had not known—nor been able to learn—how to love the strong-minded baby she had given birth to.

'Look out of the window, Alex,' said Constantine gently. 'As well as some of the most wonderful beaches you will ever see, we have mountains, and forests of cedar, oak and pine. And mines of silver and gold.'

'*Gold*?' spluttered Alex. 'Not really?'

'Yes, really. It was first discovered by the Parians, who came from the island of Paros.'

This time Laura sent Constantine a silent message. *Stop it,* her eyes appealed. *Stop painting for him the kind of pictures he has only ever seen in films or books before. Please don't make his life in England fade into pale and boring insignificance.*

And Constantine read the appeal perfectly, deliberately choosing to ignore it. Did she really expect him to play his heritage down, when it was his son's heritage, too? His expression didn't alter.

'We have white marble, too,' he continued. 'Which is exported all over the world. And there are all the other components which are an essential part of Greek life—fruit and honey and olives. Now, look closely as we drive up this road, Alex, and you will see my father's house.'

House, he had said, noted Laura suddenly, her quibble forgotten as she gazed curiously out of the window. Not home. Did that have any significance? But then she peered out through the window and her breath caught in her throat as the most beautiful place she had ever seen suddenly came into view.

Surrounded by orange and lemon trees, the villa was large and imposing, dominating the landscape while somehow managing to blend into it. It stood almost at the top of the mountain, and the views around it were panoramic. Dark sapphire brush-strokes of a sea threw off a brilliant light, and as Laura opened the car door she could smell the scent of pine and citrus and hear the unfamiliar sound of beautiful birdsong.

'We're here,' said Constantine, as he held his hand out to help Alex down. The boy took it as naturally as breathing.

How easily Alex is learning to trust him, thought Laura—knowing that she should be glad for her son's sake, and yet unable to prevent the strange spike of envy which tugged at her stomach.

The huge front door opened and a middle-aged woman wearing a floral pinafore dress came out immediately to meet them—as if she had been standing waiting for their arrival.

'I'll introduce you to Demetra,' Constantine said, an odd glint in his eyes. 'She's in charge of the staff here— so you'll be directly answerable to her. Oh, and don't worry—she speaks excellent English, so you won't have any problems understanding her instructions, Laura.'

Instructions. Answerable. His words brought Laura tumbling back down to earth with a crash. And with a shock she realised that all the privileges she had been enjoying up until that moment were now about to evaporate. She was to become one of the domestic staff. *But that's what you wanted*, she reminded herself painfully. *That's what you insisted on.*

At least she had spent the last few evenings poring over a phrasebook—but her usual slowness with reading coupled with the difficulty of the complex Greek language meant that she had retained only a few words. Still, now was the time to start using them.

'*Kalimera*,' she said, with a nervous smile at the older woman.

Demetra's eyes swept over Laura in rapid assessment, and she said something in Greek to Constantine, to which he made a drawled reply. It seemed to satisfy her, for she nodded and returned the smile.

'*Kalimera*, Laura. You are very welcome at Villa Thavmassios.' Her eyes crinkled fondly as she stared at Alex's dark curls. 'And this your boy?'

'Yes, this is Alex.' Laura gave a Alex a little push, and to her relief he stepped forward and shook the Greek woman's hand, just the way she'd taught him to. Demetra gave a delighted exclamation before enfolding him in a bear-hug, and Laura bit back a smile as she saw Alex send her a horrified look of appeal.

'We bring children from the village to play with you, Alex,' said Demetra. 'And my own son is home from university—he is a very fine sports student. He teach you to swim and to fish. You would like that?'

'Yes, please,' said Alex shyly, as Demetra finally let him go. She said something else to Constantine, but he shook his head.

'*Ochi*,' he said in negation, and then smiled. 'Shall I show you to your room now, Alex?' Then he turned to Laura, almost as if it was an afterthought. 'And I might as well show you yours,' he added softly.

Laura tried to tell herself not to react to the unmistakable provocation in those dark eyes—telling herself that nothing was going to happen because she didn't want anything to happen. But even as she made the silent vow she had to fight to suppress the glimmer of longing which had begun to whisper its way over her skin.

Liar. You know that you want him. That you would give a king's ransom for his lips to rove all over your naked body.

Laura's cheeks flushed, and she could feel their colour intensify simply because Constantine was looking at her with that hateful half-smile playing around his lips—as if he knew exactly what she was thinking. As if he knew that her breasts were prickling and her heart racing like a piston. Her fist clenched around the strap of her handbag and she dug her nails into it—as if she were digging them into his rich, silken flesh.

What on earth was going on? Why was she suddenly reacting to him as if she was the kind of woman who was prey to carnal desires, when nothing could be further from the truth?

Nothing.

Why, there hadn't been a single man in her life since Constantine had sailed away all those years ago—because the truth was that she had never wanted another man in the way she'd wanted him, even if single motherhood didn't exactly encourage romantic entanglements. But suddenly Laura's lack of another lover seemed more like a failure rather than anything to be proud of. As if she was one of those pathetic women who had been carrying a flame for a man who'd never even given her a second thought. Who hadn't even remembered that they'd been lovers!

His voice cut across her thoughts. 'Ready?' he questioned.

Forcing a smile, she took Alex's hand. 'Let's go and see your room, darling.'

The villa was cool and huge—it made her Milmouth apartment look like a shoebox—and Laura found herself wondering how long it would take to get her bearings.

Alex's suitcase had already been brought into a bright room which had been transformed into a small boy's dream. There was a bookcase filled with any number of books, and a table on which sat a drawing block and a rainbow collection of colouring pens. A giant castle reposed in one corner—with small figures of knights and horses—and a beautiful wooden train-set sat curved and just itching to be put in motion.

Seeing the castle, Alex turned to Constantine with a look of breathless excitement on his face.

'Did Mum tell you I liked horses?' he demanded excitedly.

'I thought that all little boys liked horses,' answered Constantine solemnly.

'Can I play with it? Now?'

'That is what it is there for. You play with it while I show your mama her room—which is just along the corridor—then we will go downstairs and eat something, and later on you can swim. Would you like that?'

Alex's eyes were like dark, delighted saucers. 'Oh, *yes*!' And he ran over to the castle.

Laura looked up at Constantine, fighting to keep her emotions in check—but, whichever way you looked at it, the Greek tycoon had gone out of his way to make the small boy feel welcome, and she found that she was having to blink back sudden tears. She wanted to say thank you, but the look which had darkened his features into a steely mask was not one which readily invited gratitude.

'Let's go,' said Constantine softly, and Laura's heart was pounding heavily as they walked along the cool, marbled corridor. She felt like a prisoner whose fate had been sealed, yet she was filled with a terrible kind of excitement when Constantine halted before a door. As he threw it open, all she could see was a bed.

'What did Demetra say to you outside?' she questioned quickly, wanting something—anything—to distract her attention from that bed.

'That you looked too small and too slight for any kind of physical work.'

'And what did you tell her?'

Constantine paused as he stared down into the stormy beauty of her grey eyes, registering the dormant strength which lay within her petite frame. 'I told her that you were no stranger to hard work,' he said unexpectedly.

'Oh.' The words caught her off-guard, and Laura found herself feeling ridiculously warmed by the nearest thing to a compliment he'd paid her. She looked up at him, heart racing. 'Why, thank you—' But she got no further, because Constantine's gaze was raking over her face. He took her hand, pulling her inside the bedroom, shutting the door on the rest of the world.

'Be very clear about this, Laura. I don't want your thanks,' he said softly. 'I want you. *This...*' And suddenly he was kissing her with a fervour which sapped the last of her resistance. Her knees sagged and she fell against him as with a low moan he tightened his arms around her, his lips prising hers open with effortless mastery.

It was a frantic, seeking kiss, and for a few seconds Laura gave herself up to it completely. She felt the lick of his tongue exploring hers, the sweet pressure of his mouth as it seemed to plunder deeper and deeper within her mouth—until she felt as if he had stripped her bare with his kiss. Suddenly she was vulnerable. Too vulnerable.

She could feel her breasts begin to prickle as they pushed against the hard wall of his chest, and an unbearable aching clamoured at the fork of her thighs. She wanted him to lift her skirt up. She wanted him to touch her. She wanted…

Had she silently transmitted those wishes to Constantine? Because suddenly he was making them all come true. His hand was impatiently rucking up the cotton of her sundress and splaying with indolent possession over the cool silk of her inner thigh.

'Constantine,' she moaned into his mouth, and the sound seemed to incite him.

'Ah, *ne, ne*,' he breathed, as he deepened the kiss, moving his fingertips upwards so that they scorched their way over the moist fabric of her panties and he felt her buck beneath him. Would there be time? he wondered distractedly as his hand moved down to his belt.

Through the hot heat of a fierce sexual hunger which seemed ready to consume her Laura felt the sudden tension in his body, and became graphically aware of his growing hardness. And with a certainty born of instinct rather than experience she saw just where all this was leading. Was that the rasping of a zip she could hear? With a stifled cry of horror and recrimination she tore her lips away and pushed helplessly at the solid wall of his chest, but her head dipped against it for support.

'We...we mustn't,' she breathed against his racing heart. 'You know we mustn't.'

Constantine caught his breath before disengaging himself, propelling her away from him as if she had suddenly become poison in his arms. He turned away to adjust his trousers even as hot, sexual hunger coursed round his veins, and it was a moment or two until he had composed himself enough to face her.

And in a way he knew she was right to stop things before they went too far, but—damn her—he didn't *want* her to be right! Especially when she was so turned on and struggling to control her breath. *He* was the one who always controlled the situation, and women the ones who clung to him like limpets as they waited for his command. The whole encounter had lasted only a couple of minutes but fierce frustration made him turn on her.

'Do you always conduct yourself in such a way?' he accused hotly. 'Using your eyes to beg silently for a man to *take you* when your son is just along the corridor? How many times has he witnessed his mother in an intimate embrace with a man, Laura—tell me that? How many?'

Laura's mouth opened in an 'oh' of protest. 'Never,' she breathed fiercely, shaking her head so that her hair flew round it like a cloud. 'Never, ever.'

'A woman who turns on as quickly as you do? I don't believe you,' he said with soft scorn.

'Don't you? Well, that's your problem, not mine, Constantine—you can believe what you damned well like!' Injustice bubbled up in her blood to replace the aching fires of frustration. Why should he apportion blame solely to *her*? Smoothing her hands down over her heated cheeks, she stared at him. 'You had nothing to do with what just happened, of course—you were just standing there like an innocent while I threw myself at you.'

'I wouldn't advise that you go down the accusation path,' he drawled arrogantly. 'Because when a woman has sent out the unmistakable message that she wants a man to make love to her then I'm afraid that nature has programmed that man to follow through.'

Laura stilled as she stared at him in horror. *Had* she? Her heart began to pound anxiously. Maybe she had—though certainly not consciously—and yet wasn't his reaction to it about as insulting as it was possible to get? As if kissing her had been nothing more than a conditioned response for him, while for her it had been…

What? Her betraying body shivered with sweet memory. What had it been? Like being transported straight to paradise without stopping? Or—even worse—a reactivation of that passionate longing he had awoken in her the very first time she'd looked into his eyes all those years ago? When she'd believed in love at first sight and had cried for months after he'd gone.

But such emotion was completely wasted. *He doesn't like you*, she reminded herself bitterly—*and he certainly doesn't respect you*. For him you're just another willing body in a long line of willing bodies who have been welcoming him into their arms all his life.

Once she had been blinded by youth and inexperience and his sheer charisma, and she had willingly fallen into bed with him. But now things were different. She had too much to lose to risk throwing it all away on some feel-good sex which would leave her physically satisfied but emotionally bereft. Sex which he might use against her to paint a black picture of her morals. Or which might prejudice her attempts to have a reasonable relationship with him for the sake of his son.

'Shall we just put it down to experience and make sure it doesn't happen again?' she questioned unsteadily.

Black eyes mocked her. 'You think it's that easy? That desire is like a tap you can just turn on and off at will?'

'I think you can try.'

'But I don't want to try,' he said softly. 'And what is more I don't intend to.'

Their eyes met in a silent battle of wills, and Laura felt her mouth dry, hating the fact that his thinly veiled threat thrilled her instead of shocking her. 'I think that…that you'd better leave now while I freshen up and then help get Alex properly unpacked,' she said. But she couldn't help noticing the pulse which beat so frantically at his throat as his gaze continued to rake over her in a look of unashamed sexual hunger.

Laura swallowed as she turned away and walked over to the window, blind to the beauty of the sapphire sea and cerulean sky outside, suddenly realising how difficult this whole situation was going to be. But you're here as his *employee*, she reminded herself. So why not remind him of that? Put some space and some barriers between the two of you. Remind yourself that you are most certainly not equals.

She turned round and fixed the kind of smile to her lips which she gave to the Milmouth office workers when they came into the shop for their lunchtime sandwich. 'So…what happens next in terms of me starting work?'

Constantine gave a slow smile. He knew exactly what she

was doing—but he recognised that it was a kind of game she was playing. So let her be confronted by the reality of waiting on him and see how she liked *that!* 'Tonight you and Alex will eat with Demetra, and she will familiarise you with our customs. She will tell you what she expects from you and answer any questions you might have,'

'You mean…you…won't be there?' questioned Laura tentatively.

'No, *agape mou*,' he said softly. 'I'm going out.'

'Out?' she echoed, aware that she sounded crestfallen. And *possessive*?

'Indeed I am.' His black eyes glittered. 'As your new husband I should not, of course, have dreamt of abandoning you on your first evening. But this was the choice you made, Laura—and you must live with the consequences even if they are not to your liking.'

'At least I can live with my conscience,' she said tightly.

'Well, bravo for you!' he mocked, as he finished tucking in his silk shirt. 'And tomorrow Alex will join me and my father for lunch. The child will meet his grandfather for the first time.'

'That's good.' Laura stared at him, suddenly aware of just how little she really knew about him. 'And…your mother?'

There was an infinitesimal pause before he spoke. 'My mother died many years ago,' he said.

'Oh, I'm sorry,' said Laura, interpreting his flat tone as grief, knowing from her own experience that the dead must always be acknowledged, even if the subject sometimes made you feel miserable. 'What happened?' she questioned gently.

'She died of pneumonia a long time ago,' he said, his face stony. 'But my family history need not concern you, Laura.'

'It's Alex's family history, too,' she reminded him, taken aback by the sudden venom in his tone.

'Then I will discuss such matters with Alex,' he said. 'And it's pointless looking at me with those wounded grey eyes—because as my wife you could have legitimately shared such discussions. As it is there are plenty of other things to occupy you. So why don't you run along and speak to Demetra.'

He paused deliberately, enjoying seeing the flush of colour to her cheeks, wanting to rub in the subservience she had insisted on. Wanting to wound her as she had somehow wounded him, though he couldn't for the life of him work out how. 'And then prepare to wait on my table,' he finished cuttingly.

CHAPTER EIGHT

LAURA awoke to that confusing sensation of being in a strange room and not realising quite where she was—until she saw the stripes of bright sunlight shafting in through the bottom of the shutters and felt unaccustomed warm air wafting her body. She was in Greece—on the Karantinos island—and all night long she'd dreamt of Constantine, remembering the coldness in his voice when she'd tried to ask him about his mother, his dismissing her and her questions with a crisp arrogance clearly intended to drive home her reduced status in his household.

Some time during the night she must have kicked off the crisp cotton sheet, and now she was lying sprawled and exposed in a little nightdress which had ridden up over her hips during her very restless sleep. Which was surprising, given how tired she'd been following a delicious supper eaten with Demetra and her son in the cosy informality of the large kitchen.

Afterwards she and Alex had gone for a walk around the vast estate, with Demetra's son, Stavros, acting as their guide. The young Greek student had pointed out all the bright constellations in the night sky and Alex had had the time of his life as a brand-new world of astronomy had opened up for him.

And then Laura sat bolt upright in bed. Alex! She hadn't heard a peep out of him all night—when she'd tucked him and Blue Bear up in bed he'd barely been able to murmur goodnight before he was out for the count. What if he'd had nightmares? Got up and gone looking for her? Or wanted a drink and found himself lost in this vast and unknown house?

Grabbing her matching wrap, she hurried from her room and burst into Alex's room—to find it completely empty. 'Alex!' she gasped.

'He's outside,' came a voice from behind her, and she whirled around to find Constantine standing in the doorway of the room—an unfathomable look on his face as he studied her.

Aware that her hair was unbrushed and her eyes still full of sleep, Laura blinked. 'Outside where?'

'By the pool—with Demetra's son.'

'You mean you left my son—'

'*Our* son,' he corrected.

'With someone who's virtually a stranger—by a swimming pool when he *can't even swim that well*!'

'Oh, for heaven's sake—do you really think I would have placed him in any danger? I've known Stavros all his life, and he swims like an eel!' he snapped. 'I've been with them all morning, and apparently you all had dinner together last night. They've been getting along famously. If you hadn't overslept you could have seen that for yourself.' His expression darkened. 'What I want to know is why he can't damned well swim in the first place?'

'Because…'

'Because *what*, Laura?' he queried archly.

'Because—' Oh, what was the point in hiding anything from him? 'Well, the lessons were expensive...' Her voice tailed away as she realised he was looking at her in disbelief.

'Expensive?' he repeated incredulously.

She thought he sounded as if he were trying out a new and unknown word. But how *could* he understand what it was like to have to make every penny count when he had spent a life with an abundance of wealth?

'He has football coaching at the weekends instead,' she justified. 'And I couldn't afford everything.'

'So here we have my son, the pauper,' he said bitterly. 'A Karantinos heir living on the breadline!'

Laura swallowed, suddenly realising how exhausted he looked—as if he hadn't had a wink of sleep all night. His black eyes were hooded and tired, and the dark shadow at his jaw suggested that he might not yet have shaved. The expensively dressed Greek billionaire was a world away from this barefoot and elemental-looking man in faded jeans and T-shirt who stood in front of her.

It seemed all too disturbingly intimate and familiar—a glimpse of the old Constantine—and Laura shrank back, suddenly and dangerously aware of his proximity and the fact that while he was fully dressed she was wearing very little. Nothing but a very short wrap over an equally short night-dress that barely came to the middle of her bare thigh. And from the sudden tightening of his features the realisation had begun to dawn on him at precisely the same moment.

Without another word, Laura turned and walked out of the room and back along the corridor to her own—but to her horror and shameful excitement, she realised that Constantine was right behind her.

'No,' she whispered ineffectively, as he shut the door behind him and she felt his warm breath on her neck.

'Oh, yes,' he said grimly, turning her round as if she were a mannequin in a store window. 'You should not walk around the house half-naked if you don't want this particular outcome—nor make big eyes at me and allow your body to tremble with such obvious hunger whenever you come near me.'

Afterwards, she'd try to tell herself that she had done everything to resist him—but that would be a complete lie. She did nothing. Nothing but stare up at him, her parched lips parting with unashamed yearning, a tiny little whimper of desire escaping from them as he moved closer still. And then it was too late. His kiss was like dynamite, his touch the fire which made it combust—and Laura went up in flames.

'*Oh,*' she moaned, clawing at his shoulders as he caught her by the waist and brought her up hard against the aroused cradle of his desire, so that she could feel the shockingly unfamiliar hard ridge of him pressing up against her through his jeans.

With an uncharacteristic disregard for foreplay, he slid up her nightdress and this time found her bare and ready for him, giving a little groan of delight as he tangled his fingers in her hair and then greedily delved inside her honeyed moistness as she gasped out her fevered response. He closed his eyes helplessly as she swayed against him, her hips moving with sudden instinct against his fingers.

Laura clung to him, her love-starved body hungry for his kiss and for everything else she knew he could give her.

His fingers were moving purposefully between her legs now, and he was driving his mouth down on hers in a kiss which quite literally took her breath away—a kiss she never wanted to end.

And then she felt a change taking place in her body; the rhythm of his fingers was changing pace—quickening against her blossoming heat. She felt the wild beat of her heart—the momentary lull before she tumbled over—her body spasming helplessly against his hand, his kiss silencing her little gasps of fulfilment as she slumped weakly against him until the last of her orgasm died away.

'Constantine,' she breathed eventually, her cheeks flushed and her heart beating fast. 'Oh, Constantine.'

'I want you,' he whispered fiercely into her ear. He guided her hand to lie over the achingly hard ridge in his jeans. 'Feel how much I want you.'

And she wanted him, too. But it was broad daylight in the middle of the morning, and she had responsibilities which were far more urgent that the siren call of her body. 'N-Not now…' The words stumbled out of her mouth. 'A-And not here. We can't. You know we can't.'

Through the dark, erotic mists of his desire came her unsteady voice of reason. At first he tried to ignore it—but something at its very heart made Constantine still and pull his lips away from hers, to stare down into the flushed confusion of her face, the tumbled gold of her unbrushed hair.

His heart was thundering so powerfully he could barely think, let alone speak. 'You think that it is right to deny me pleasure now that you have taken your own? Is that right?'

Dumbly, she shook her head.

Fuelled by a savage wave of frustration, he felt the slow

flare of anger begin to burn. 'You think you can keep tantalising me and that I will be like a tame puppy who will just keep trotting behind you and taking whatever it is that you dish out to me? Letting you turn me down, time and time again—so that I can't sleep at night for thinking about your pale, curved body? Taking me so far with your sweet, soft promise and then acting outraged? Is that what men usually let you do, Laura?'

She was too busy catching her breath to rise to the taunt.

'Have you become a *tease*, Laura?' he persisted.

Her lips were trembling, 'No. *No.*'

'Just a woman who promises so much, who lets a man touch her so intimately and then freezes up? If that isn't your definition of a tease, then I'd like to know what is.'

Frustratedly, she shook her head—knowing that he spoke nothing but the truth. She was acting like a naïve little virgin around him, when they both knew she was anything but. The kind of woman who would let a man only go so far... Was that because she thought that her continued resistance to full-on sex might make him respect her? When just one look at the contemptuous mask of his features proved that respect was the very last thing he was feeling?

And what of her *own* desires? Hadn't she been living like a nun for the past eight years? Though it had not felt like denial because no one had moved her to passion. But Constantine had. Constantine still did. It was all there for the taking if only she could accept that it would just be no-strings sex.

'I'm not saying I don't want you—how could I when I've just proved the very opposite?' she whispered. 'Just not now and not here—when Alex might come back from the pool and start looking for me.'

His unyielding expression did not alter. 'So, when?'

Laura could have wept. How matter-of-fact he sounded. It had taken a lot for her to say that, and yet it was as if the significance of her declaration was irrelevant and all he wanted was to pin her down to a time and a place. Her breath came out in a shuddering sigh, but she knew that she couldn't back out of it now, even if she wanted to.

'Come to me tonight,' she whispered. 'Late. When the house is quiet and when I know for sure that Alex is asleep.'

He felt the urgent leap of anticipation at his groin and he stared deep into the storm clouds of her eyes. Taking her slender waist between his hands, he bent his head to graze his lips over hers, feeling her tremble as he did so. Had she learnt somewhere along the way that a woman's most effective weapon was resistance? Was that why she had applied it so effectively, making him desire her with a power which set his blood on fire for her?

And yet with Laura it did not feel like a game she was playing with him in an attempt to ensnare him. This felt real—as if she was fighting herself as well as fighting him.

'I shall spend the whole day thinking about it, *agape mou*,' he murmured. 'Imagining you naked in my arms. Pinned beneath my body as I drive into you over and over again. Yes, I will come to you tonight.' He smiled as he brushed an indolent finger over her trembling lips. 'Now, hurry up and get dressed before I change my mind about waiting.'

With a mounting feeling of disbelief, Laura watched as he left the room, hugging her flimsy little wrap closer to her still flushed and trembling body.

She felt calmer after she'd showered and dressed and pulled on the floral pinafore Demetra had given her to wear. Not the most flattering garment in the world—but that wasn't supposed to be its function, was it?

She stared at her rather drab image in the mirror. It was stupid to feel ashamed of waitressing when it was a job she had done with pride and efficiency during many periods of her adult life. But this felt different, and maybe that was because it *was*. She was going to have to wait on the father of her child and pretend that he meant nothing to her.

Shutting the door quietly behind her, Laura went outside to find Alex splashing around with Stavros in the shallow end of an enormous swimming pool.

'Mum!' he yelled. 'Look! Stavros is teaching me breaststroke!'

Laura smiled as the seal-dark wet head of the student emerged from the water. 'Thank you, Stavros.'

The student grinned as he gestured for Alex to come forward. 'I like to teach, and he shows promise. Young children learn quickly. Come, Alex, show your mama what you can do.'

Alex doggy-paddled over to the edge of the pool and stared up at her, and Laura's heart turned over as she saw the look of pure joy on his little face. 'Don't get tired, will you, darling?' she said.

'*Mum!*'

'Did you have breakfast?'

'Yes, I had it with Constantine.' Alex grinned. 'We had yoghurt—with *honey*! And Constantine and me went and picked oranges from the tree and then we squeezed them!'

She gazed down at him, thinking how easily her son

had slotted into life here—already. *And* how easily he seemed to be slotting into a relationship with Constantine, too. Why, he must have felt as if he had landed in heaven with all the space and beauty which surrounded him

The dark flicker of fear invaded her heart once more. Fear that Alex might just fall in love with Greece and the powerful man who had fathered him—and might not want to return with her to their grey and penny-pinching life back in England…

'Lovely, darling,' she managed to say. 'Well, I'm supposed to be working, so I'd better go and see what Demetra wants me to do.'

Laura made her way to the kitchen to find Demetra, who seemed to have assumed the role of mother hen. First she insisted that Laura sit outside and eat some bread and honey, and drink some of the thick, strong coffee.

'You are too thin,' Demetra commented as she pushed a bowl of bread towards her. 'A woman needs her strength.'

Tell me about it, thought Laura wryly, as she sliced a peach into gleaming rose-tinged slices. But mental strength was surely just as important as the physical kind—and you couldn't build *that* up with bread and honey! But she felt oddly moved by the older woman's kindness—because it had been so long since someone had fussed over her like this.

And at least working was therapeutic—it was hard to stay troubled when your fingers were busy chopping salads and stuffing vine leaves. Demetra showed her how to make a sweet pastry dish which was soaked in lemon syrup after baking—as well as a pudding studded with nuts and raisins and flavoured with cinnamon and cloves.

Laura leaned back against the range. 'Where did you learn how to cook like this, Demetra?'

'Oh, I have cooked all my life,' answered Demetra simply. 'First for my husband and then for my living. You see, I was widowed when Stavros was just a baby, and so I came here to work for the Karantinos family. They have been good to me. And Kyrios Constantine is a good man,' she added fiercely. 'He used to fish with my husband—and when he died he put Stavros through school and university and made sure the boy wanted for nothing.'

The housekeeper's words of praise for Constantine pre-occupied Laura as she began to lay the table on the terrace, beneath a canopy of leaves. But the last thing she needed was to hear praise lavished on him. She wanted to put him out of her mind—at least until tonight.

'Do you know, I could stay here all day watching you do that?' murmured a deep voice from the shadows, and Laura whirled round to find Constantine at the other end of the terrace, his black eyes fixed on her. Clearly fresh from the shower, with tiny droplets of water bejewelling the black hair, he had changed from jeans and T-shirt into dark trousers and a thin silk shirt, and he had shaved, too.

'How long have you been standing there?' she accused, her heart beginning to race with a ridiculous excitement.

He began walking towards her, his progress made slow by an exquisitely painful arousal. 'Long enough to see that delightfully old-fashioned pinafore dress stretched tight over the delectable curve of your bottom,' he murmured. 'Making me want to touch it again, quite urgently.'

Laura sent an agonised glance in the direction of the kitchen, even though the rattle of china told her that

Demetra was not within earshot. 'Constantine, don't. Please. Somebody might hear.'

His black eyes mocked her. 'Ah, Laura! You see how already we are colluding like lovers—even though we are not yet lovers? For that pleasure I must wait—and I am not a man who is used to waiting.'

'No, I can believe that,' she said quietly, holding the tray in front of her as if it were a shield.

He lowered his voice until it was nothing but a silken caress which whispered over her skin. 'Do you know that I feel as a man in prison must feel, ticking off the seconds and the minutes and the hours?'

Laura swallowed. 'Constantine—'

'So that the whole day seems stretched out in front of me like a piece of elastic,' he continued inexorably. 'Which is tightening unbearably—tighter and tighter—until the time when it snaps and I can once more feel your lips on mine and your honeyed heat as it welcomes me into your body.'

'Stop it,' she whispered as the siren song of desire began a slow pulsing through her veins 'Please, stop it. Or how will I compose myself in front of the others?'

'You didn't think through the potential problems of making such an erotic date with destiny, did you?' he taunted.

She hadn't counted on being on such an erotic knife-edge, no. 'Do you think your father's going to ask me anything?'

'If he does, then just answer his questions truthfully,' he said, his whole mood suddenly sobering. 'If you think you can manage that.'

'You're…making it sound as if you think I'm a liar,' said Laura unsteadily, trying to read his expression—but it would have been easier to have sought some sort of meaning from a statue.

Constantine shook his head. 'I haven't quite decided what you are,' he said softly. 'Or just what your agenda is.'

Her heart slammed against her ribcage. 'Who says I have an agenda?'

'Women always do—it's in their genetic make-up.'

'You're a cynic, Constantine.'

'No, *agape mou*,' he contradicted softly. 'I am simply a very rich man who has seen female ambition in its every form. And you—of all women—have the opportunity to try to take me for everything you can get your hands on.'

'You think that I'd do that?' she demanded breathlessly.

'I told you—I haven't made up my mind yet,' he returned.

And yet Laura had confounded every one of his expectations of her. Her refusal to marry him and her stubborn insistence on coming here to work instead had left him feeling unsettled. After a lifetime spent dodging matrimonial commitment to some of the world's most eligible women, he had assumed that this humble waitress would leap at the chance of being a rich man's wife—yet she had done the very opposite. So was she simply being devious, or principled?

'Now—if you'll excuse me—I have some business calls I need to make before lunch.' His eyes glittered with erotic intent. 'And roll on midnight, my stormy-eyed little temptress, so that we can at last finish off what we've started.'

For a moment after he'd gone Laura stood rooted to the spot—unable to believe how a man could switch so quickly from desire to distrust and then back to desire again. She finished laying the table for lunch, and then went to help Alex get ready.

'Is Constantine's daddy very old?' he wanted to know, as he wriggled into a brand-new T-shirt.

'I believe so, darling—and he hasn't been too well recently, so you must be well-behaved.' Surprisingly, Alex let her attempt to tame his dark waves into shape and, stepping back, her eyes shone with maternal pride as she looked at him. 'But I know you will.'

The lunch table looked beautiful—with little pots of purple and white flowers dotted everywhere—and Stavros and Alex sat at their places, waiting until Constantine appeared with his father. Laura watched as they made slow progress across the terrace, the old man leaning heavily on a stick.

He's so *old*, realised Laura suddenly. Why, he must be in his mid-eighties. Which meant that he... She frowned as she worked out what age he'd have been when Constantine was born. Fifty, at least. Had his wife also been elderly? she wondered. Was that why she'd succumbed to a bout of pneumonia?

Kyrios Karantinos was, as Constantine had said, very frail—but it was easy to see how handsome he must once have been. He had the most amazing bone structure, and Laura found herself wondering with a pang whether Alex would look a little like this when he was an old man. Whether Constantine would.

And whether she would still be around to see it.

The faded eyes looked her up and down as he waved Constantine away and looked at Laura. Was it wrong to play the part of being some kind of waitress in this elderly man's house? she wondered, as a sudden pang of guilt washed over her. But it *wasn't* a part, was it? She *was* a waitress. This was far more honest than turning up here as

Constantine's new bride, married to a man who seemed to alternate between despising and desiring her—now, that really *would* have been a living lie. And one that any father would surely veto.

Nervously, Laura smoothed down the front of her pinafore dress. 'I'm very pleased to meet you, Kyrios Karantinos,' she said.

'My son tells me that you met in England?'

'Yes, sir.'

'And that you persuaded him to let you come and work here for the summer?'

'That's right. It seemed a great opportunity to give my son a holiday.'

There was a momentary pause before he gestured towards the curly-haired little boy in his new shorts and T-shirt. 'And this is your little boy?'

'Yes, this is Alex.'

The faded eyes were now turned in the direction of the child, and for a moment Laura thought that she saw them narrow. But the moment passed, and slowly he sat down and began asking Alex about his morning. To Laura's delight and pride her son began to chatter away. He began to tell the old man about his swimming lesson, and she longed to stay and listen, but Constantine was raising his hand to get her attention.

Her cheeks burned as she met the mocking look in his black eyes and registered the arrogant tone in his voice as he clipped out an order for wine. He's enjoying this, she thought to herself suddenly as she hurried out towards the kitchen. He's enjoying rubbing in my subservient status.

She tried to tell herself not to be affected by Constantine's sardonic scorn, but that was easier said than done. When he gestured arrogantly for the bread basket she found herself wanting to hurl its contents at his hateful head. Or to tip the cool yoghurt and cucumber dish of *tzatziki* all over his lap.

In fact, she was so busy keeping everyone's glasses filled and bringing out dish after dish that Laura had no real opportunity to take in what was going on—much as she longed to listen to what Alex was saying to his grandfather, or to see whether the old man showed any sign of guessing who the little boy really was. And it felt peculiar to be serving her own son his lunch in the guise of a waitress.

Never had she felt more of an outsider than she did during that seemingly endless meal—it was as if she was an observer, watching a play unfold before her. As if she had no real place anywhere.

And wasn't there a rather frozen lack of communication between Constantine and his own father? As if the two men tolerated each other rather than loving one another? Is that the kind of role model Constantine is planning to provide for Alex? she wondered, feeling suddenly fearful. That of emotional containment?

But at least Alex himself seemed to have come into his own, blossoming in a way she had never seen him doing before. He was lapping up all the attention, she realised. From Constantine, from his father, and from young Stavros, too. *Because he wasn't used to the company of men.* For the first time she could see how limiting his life must be, living with two women in a cramped apartment above a village shop.

And all the time she was aware of Constantine watching the scene too, his shuttered black eyes hidden behind the dark lashes, his gaze drifting to the animated features of the little boy. Had he sat at that very table and chattered away like that when he was Alex's age? she wondered.

She watched as he began to peel an orange for his son, her gaze drawn inexorably to the strong fingers as they pulled away petal-shaped segments of the peel. Shadows fell from the high-angled slash of his cheekbones and the sensual curve of his lips had relaxed into a half-smile. And then he suddenly looked up, and the ebony spotlight of his gaze swept over her, and she found herself flushing as he raised his glass in her direction.

'Can you fetch me some more ice for my water?' he questioned carelessly, and Laura's colour heightened as she nodded and went off to the kitchen in search of some.

He watched her go. Watched the high, tempting curves of her buttocks thrusting against the dowdy clothes, and once again he felt his heart-rate soar. What was it this plain little creature had which made his body ache like this? he asked himself bitterly. Was it because she was the mother of his child? Or because she was the only virgin he had ever bedded? Perhaps his desire for her was stronger than anything he had ever known simply because she had refused him time and time again. More importantly, would this terrible hunger cease once he had possessed her? His lips curved. Of course it would. As if someone like her could hold his attention for more than one night!

Laura returned, carrying the ice, and bent to put some in his glass, temptingly aware of the tantalising warmth of his body and the faint trace of his musky scent. Was he silently laughing at the image she presented as she served him—and when those black eyes swept over her in insolent assessment what did they see? A too-slight woman serving drinks in an unflattering floral pinafore dress? A mother who had willingly put herself in the role of outcast by waiting at her lover's table?

Laura wondered if that was all they saw. Perhaps his gaze was perceptive enough to delve beneath the surface and guess at her feelings of apprehension and vulnerability. Was he feeling quietly triumphant as he anticipated the assignation she had so willingly agreed to tonight—and might he use it against her? *To do what?*

She thought of all the empty promises she had made to herself—that she would not succumb to the overwhelming chemistry which still sizzled between them. That she would protect her heart from pain by not getting close to him in any way.

And then she thought of their midnight assignation, closing her eyes as her body registered an automatic thrill of anticipation—despite the damning quality of the words he had whispered. What had they been? *Ah, yes. To finish off what they'd started.*

Laura bit her lip as she carried out a dish of almonds to the table. Was there any scenario more potentially heartbreaking than the one which lay ahead of her?

CHAPTER NINE

A CRACK of light slanted across the floor as the door opened, and Laura held her breath as she saw the dark and formidable shape of Constantine standing silhouetted there. If he thought she was sleeping, would he creep away again? she wondered. Would he remember that she had been working and perhaps might need her rest? Spare her this sensual ordeal which she suspected might open the door to a terrible kind of heartache? And yet her heart was pounding so hard that she was certain he must be able to hear its frantic beat.

A low laugh beside the bed put paid to her half-hearted hopes. 'Surely you don't expect me to believe you are asleep do you, *ghlikos mou*?' he questioned softly.

She heard the rasp of a zip, and then the soft thump of something slithering to the ground—presumably his jeans—before a rush of air to her skin as he peeled the sheet away from her body and climbed into bed. Laura trembled as she felt that first contact with his warm, muscular flesh.

'You're…*naked*,' she breathed.

'What did you expect?' With comfortable assurance he hooked his arms around her and drew her close, the glitter of his eyes discernible in the moonlight, his breath warm on her face. 'Ah…perhaps you wanted to watch me strip?'

'I….' His easy provocation left her feeling cheated and out of her depth. *He does this kind of thing all the time,* she reminded herself—*and he has no idea that it's been eight long years since you slept with a man. This man.* Had she mistakenly hoped that there might be some kind of wooing, and that he might be gentle with her? Perhaps taking her tenderly in his arms and tossing her a few compliments, before beginning a slow lovemaking? Was she *crazy*?

'Meanwhile, you…are most definitely *not* naked,' he murmured, as he skated his hand down over one cotton-covered hip, and she heard the faint deprecation in his voice. 'Shame on you, Laura—I cannot believe you always wear something this unflattering in bed when you make an assignation with your lover.'

She guessed that now was not the time to tell him that this was her first such assignation. But she realised that Constantine hadn't been expecting a reply—his question had merely been the precursor to skimming the nightie up and over her head, and tossing it over the side of the bed like a flag of surrender. She shivered as her nakedness was revealed.

'Cold?' he murmured, as his lips found the line of her jaw and began to whisper along its curve.

'N-no.'

'Surely not scared?'

Scared? She was *terrified*—because didn't sex play havoc with a woman's emotions? And weren't hers already see-sawing their way towards chaos and a terrible feeling of vulnerability? But she shook her head, unwilling to admit to fear or doubt or anything else which might put her at even more of a disadvantage in his arms.

'Good.' He lifted his hand to smooth some of the fine mass of pale hair away from her face. 'You see, you have made me wait too long for this, Laura. Much too long…longer than any other woman would have dared or been able to. You have driven me half mad with temptation—do you realise that?' His voice was unsteady as he drove his mouth down on hers with a hunger so fierce that it made his body shudder, and her hands reached up to cling to him so that even his taunting words about other women were forgotten beneath the power of his kiss.

Constantine groaned as her lips opened eagerly to welcome him and he felt the softness of her breasts. His fingers skimmed her body, reacquainting themselves with all its curves and secret places, luxuriating in the soft, silken feel of her skin—and he groaned again.

He had found the delay before getting into her bed almost unendurable—their snatched and teasing foreplay something he had not experienced since he was a teenager—and it had been compounded by the fact that she was the mother of his child. For once his feelings were less than straightforward—she had captured his imagination as well as his desire. But in the sweetness of the moment all that was forgotten, and now she was so compliant beneath his embrace that Constantine knew this was all going to happen very quickly. Too quickly.

And perhaps Laura sensed it too, because she suddenly pulled away from him, her eyes huge in her face.

'Contraception?' she whispered.

'You?'

'I don't…have anything.'

Swearing softly in Greek, he reached blindly for the jeans he'd left on the floor until he found a condom. Gingerly he slid it on, and then pulled her soft body back into his arms. 'Let's hope it's a little more reliable than last time,' he drawled.

Laura stiffened as the impact of his words hit home, and half tried to pull away from him. 'That's a hateful thing to say.'

'You want to hide from the truth? Is that it?'

'I think there's a time and a place for everything—and that remark was wrong on just about every level.'

He gave a brief half-smile. 'You dare to scold me, *ghlikos mou*?' Before she could answer, he tipped her chin upwards and stared down at her with erotic intent. 'But then you dare to do many things which surprise me, Laura. Now, where was I? Was it here?' He lowered his head until his mouth found the lobe of her ear and whispered over its plump little oval. 'Or here?' His lips moved to hers, felt them tremble, and that involuntary little shudder moved him more than it should have done.

He kissed silent her little cries, his greedy fingers exploring her body with a thoroughness which left her gasping—finding her most vulnerable places and tantalising her until he felt her squirm with impatient longing. And her fervour filled him with a strange kind of disquiet, even while it set his senses on fire. 'Are you always this eager?' he murmured.

'Are you?' she parried.

No, he thought suddenly. No, he was not—but then this was the only woman who had had his child grow within her body. 'That doesn't answer my question,' he said unevenly.

No, it didn't—and while Laura knew that there was no earthly reason why she should respond, instinct told her that her answer would please him. And why not please him when he was in her arms and in her bed and soon to be in her body?

'I am only this eager with you,' she said, her voice dipping a little with sexual shyness. 'For you are the only lover I have ever known.'

There was a moment of disbelief while he sucked in a ragged breath, and suddenly the power of that thought made him feel momentarily weak—or as weak as Constantine was ever capable of being. 'The *only* one?' he demanded.

'Yes. And now will you please shut up about it? Or you'll give me a complex.'

He groaned as she kissed him back, boldly tracing her soft and seeking lips over every inch of his body, and then he gave a low laugh as he took her soft breast in his hand and stroked it.

He held back until he could hold back no longer, and then he touched her once again between the sweet haven of her thighs and felt her quiver with pleasure. Tearing his lips away from hers, he stared down into her face for an infinitesimal moment before—with one long, delicious stroke—he filled her and let out a long moan of pleasure.

The feel of him inside her again after so long was a sweet shock—but Laura barely had time to accommodate him, or to savour the sensation of Constantine moving within her, thrusting deep into her body and deep into her heart. Because all too quickly she was spiralling once more towards that dizzy destination he'd led her to that very afternoon, when he had brought her to orgasm with his fingers. But this was something else. This was the real thing. *He* was the real thing. Her heart gave a sudden lurch in time with her limbs.

'Oh, *Constantine*,' she cried, and she felt tears spilling from beneath her eyelids. '*Constantine*!'

Smothering her little gasps with his lips, he felt her bucking uncontrollably beneath him, and the spasming of her body sent his own pleasure hurtling right off the radar. He waited until he could wait no longer—until his orgasm took him under completely, instead of his more usual controlled riding it out, like a wave. And the unexpectedness of that surrender momentarily took his breath away.

Afterwards, he felt as though she had taken something from him, but he wasn't quite sure what. Abruptly he rolled away from her, and lay beside her on the rumpled sheets, staring at the moon-dappled ceiling, waiting for her words—the words that women always said at moments like these, when they were at their weakest. Praise, adoration and undying love—Constantine had heard them all in his time. Words which were his due and yet words he often scorned because of their transparent predictability. Yet Laura said nothing.

He turned his head to look at her—she was lying perfectly still, with her eyes closed and her pale hair spread out like a fine cloud across the pillow. She was so still she might almost have been sleeping—the fading gleam of tears drying on her heated cheeks the only clue as to what had just taken place. She must have sensed that his gaze was on her, yet still she did not open her eyes and look at him.

Which made the next step easy, didn't it? An early exit

from her bed—which was what he had planned on making all along. Besides, he preferred sleeping on his own once his passion had been spent, and the cloying emotions of waking up with a woman always left him cold. So why the hell was he lying here in a state of indolent bliss, heavy-limbed and unwilling to stir?

For a moment Laura didn't move, couldn't think—her equilibrium thrown off kilter by what had just happened between them. She found herself biting back inappropriate words—telling him that sex with him was one of the most glorious things which had ever happened to her, and so was he. Telling him that she had been a rash and stupid fool to have turned down his offer of marriage and please could she reconsider? But as her shattered senses returned to something approaching normality she knew she had to put some distance between them in order to protect herself.

Because sex could make you feel too close to a man—it could make you start concocting all kinds of emotional fantasies about that man. And hadn't she just been doing exactly that? Imagining herself half way in love with him? She should never forget that the man in question had a heart of stone—why, he'd moved as far away from her as possible as soon as their bodies had stilled. And hadn't he made this 'assignation' of theirs sound completely unemotional—mechanical, even? Well, then, pride should make her do the same.

'I think...I think that perhaps you'd better go now,' she suggested huskily.

Constantine, who had been mentally preparing himself to do exactly that, stilled. '*Go*?' he echoed in soft disbelief.

She risked opening her eyes then, and wished she

hadn't—for in the bright moonlight Constantine lay on the bed like a beautiful dark statue, with the rumpled sheet which lay carelessly over one narrow hip only just covering his manhood.

Laura swallowed. 'Well, yes. I mean…Alex might come in early and I don't… Well, I don't want him to find us in bed together.'

'How very admirable of you, Laura,' he murmured, but inside his feelings were at war. He felt anger that she—*she*—should be the one to eject Constantine Karantinos from her bed—and yet this went hand in hand with an undeniable and fierce approval that she should demonstrate such sound morality around his impressionable young son.

He pushed the sheet back from his inconveniently hardening body and watched the way that her nipples were peaking in response. He saw the movement of her throat as she swallowed down her desire, and the way her eyes were now drawn irresistibly to his groin. 'Though if you continue to lie there looking at me like that, then I might just change my mind,' he said thickly.

The statement—or was it a question?—hung on the air as she saw the sudden tension return to his body, and Laura's tongue snaked around her lips, her thighs parting by a fraction as she shifted uncomfortably on the bed.

Constantine rolled over. Kissed her nipple. Heard her gasp as he stroked between her legs and then slicked on a condom. Suddenly she was urging him inside her, and it seemed like only seconds before she felt her spasming helplessly around him and he followed her almost immediately, his mouth pressed against her shoulder as he bit out his fulfilment. But he withdrew from her as soon as the last sweet wave shuddered away, moving from the bed with an elegant grace as he began to pull on his clothes.

'Constantine—'

Zipping up his jeans, he looked down at the flushed and startled expression on her face. 'Mmm?'

'Maybe…' Her voice was tentative. 'Maybe I might change my mind this time. About you staying. As long as you leave early.'

Although he was now on the much more familiar ground of a woman trying to inveigle him back into her bed, Constantine narrowed his eyes with a slowly smouldering anger. Did she really think he was the kind of man who would pander to her whims—the kind of man to be played with as a kitten played with a mouse? Wasn't she in danger of over-estimating her appeal to him?

His mouth twisted. 'I don't think so, *agape mou*. Alex is asleep down the hall—and until he knows that I am his father, then I don't think it's a good idea if he finds me in your bed, do you? Sweet dreams,' he said softly, and turned and left the room without another word.

For a moment Laura just lay there, watching the door close behind him, her body still glowing with the aftermath of pleasure but her heart aching with a terrible kind of pain. Had she mistakenly thought that sex might bring about some sort of closure? Maybe give her some guidance about how she was going to extricate herself and Alex from this situation while causing the least amount of hurt all round?

If so, then she had been hugely mistaken. Because behind all the passion she had felt Constantine's bitterness, and the knowledge that it could take her to a dark, dark place.

She must have drifted off to sleep, because when she opened her eyes she was surprised to find it was six o'clock. The house was still silent and for a moment she lay there, reliving the night before and its horribly unsatisfactory ending. She showered and dressed, and spent ten minutes tugging the rumpled bed back into some sort of order before going to the other end of the corridor and poking her head around Alex's door.

He was fast asleep, his dark lashes feathering down into two sooty arcs, the faint colour to his skin an indication that he had been playing in the sunshine. He looked really contented, she thought with a sudden glow—and her heart felt a little lighter as she went down to the empty kitchen and made herself a coffee.

Taking the cup outside, she went to stand at the top of the stone steps at the end of the garden and stood looking out to sea, where the giant crimson globe of the sun was rising up over the milky horizon. It was such a beautiful place, she thought wistfully—and yet it seemed to have its own shadows and secrets. Though maybe every place on earth did.

Later, she was busy constructing a giant plate of fruit for breakfast, while Demetra pounded away at some dough and bemoaned the fact that the village no longer had a bakery, when Laura heard a rapid clicking sound and looked up.

'What's that?' she questioned.

Demetra paused. 'Oh, the helicopter.' She shrugged. 'It will be Kyrios Constantine, going to Athens.'

'To...to *Athens*?' questioned Laura shakily, her heart crashing uncomfortably against her ribcage. She told herself that it was unreasonable of her to expect him to inform her of his movements. But didn't last night's love-making entitle her to the common courtesy of him at least coming to say goodbye? She could see Demetra looking at her curiously, and found herself struggling to say something suitably conventional. What would a casual servant say at such a time? 'Er…the pilot lives on the island, does he?'

'Oh, he needs no pilot,' answered Demetra. 'Kyrios Constantine flies the helicopter himself!'

'And is he…working in Athens?' questioned Laura

'Work, yes—and probably women, too.' Demetra's eyes crinkled conspiratorially. 'Always the women—they flock to Kyrios Constantine like ants around the honeypot.'

The housekeeper's words made her hand jerk, and the fruit knife she was holding inadvertently nicked her thumb. Laura quickly put it down as a small spot of crimson blood welled up and began to drip onto the wooden table.

CHAPTER TEN

'YOU'VE cut your thumb,' observed Constantine softly.

'Oh, it's nothing.'

'Nothing?' he murmured. 'Come here—let me see.'

Laura squirmed as he took the injured digit in his hand and even that innocent contact sent her senses spiralling. Earlier that day he had flown back, after spending three nights in Athens, and while she was ridiculously pleased to see him she couldn't dispel her terrible aching insecurity and jealousy at the thought of what he might have been doing there.

They were sitting by the edge of the sea, on a beach more beautiful than any beach she could ever have imagined—just her, Alex and Constantine, who had insisted that she and her son both needed to see more of the island, especially as today was officially her day off.

Alex had spent the morning playing with a magnificent sandcastle which his father had constructed while demonstrating a sweet kind of patience which had made Laura's heart turn over with an aching wistfulness. Because it was like glimpsing the sun appearing from behind a thick, dark cloud. This was the Constantine who usually lay hidden behind that formidable exterior—the one he rarely allowed people to see. The side he had shown her all those years ago…the side which had made him all to easy to love—and still did.

They had just eaten salads and cheese for lunch, and now their son was lying in the cool shade of a rock, fast asleep—a cute cotton hat shielding his little face from the occasional sand-fly. It felt strange to be out like a normal family—without her floral pinafore dress and the subtle sense of subservience which she adopted whenever she put it on. And strange too to be in the company of the man she had not seen since he had left her room after that passionate night of lovemaking.

When he had left without a word about why or where he was going, she reminded herself.

'How did you do it?' questioned Constantine as he continued with his mock-examination of her thumb, which was raising her heart-rate significantly.

'I…I cut it on a fruit knife.'

'Clumsy of you, Laura.'

'Yes.' She wanted to tell him not to touch her like that—yet she knew that such words would sound like hysterical nonsense, because to the outside world it would look like nothing more than an innocent assessment of her thumb. But to Laura it felt as if he were trailing sizzling fire where he made contact. As if her nerve-endings became instantly raw and clamouring wherever his fingertips brushed against them.

And yet conversely she wanted him to touch her in a far more inappropriate way altogether. To have him pull her into his arms—to at least give *some* indication that they'd actually been lovers. But of course he did not touch her, and Laura tried to tell herself it was because Alex was nearby.

'So…what were you doing in Athens?' she questioned suddenly, even though she had vowed she would not.

For a moment Constantine didn't answer as he let her hand go, an odd, mocking kind of smile curving the corners of his lips. 'I don't think that's any of your business, do you?'

It was the response of her worst nightmares, and it made all her uncertainties bubble to the surface. Heart pounding with fear, she glanced quickly over at Alex, but he was fast asleep, worn out by the morning and oblivious to the low, urgent tones of his parents. 'Did you go straight from my bed to another's?'

His black eyes sent her a mocking challenge. 'Why? Is that the kind of behaviour you normally indulge in yourself?'

She clenched her hands into tiny fists. 'You know very well that you're the only person I've ever slept with!'

On hearing this for a second time, Constantine felt his heart accelerate into a thundering kind of triumphant beat. He was Greek, and he was pure alpha-male, and he would have been lying if her declaration hadn't thrilled him to every fibre of his being—but he was damned if he would let it show.

'Ah, if only I could say the same, *agape mou*,' he sighed regretfully.

Tears stung her eyes. 'Why do you delight in hurting me?' she demanded, realising too late how vulnerable that made her sound. But Constantine didn't seem to have noticed.

'Don't you think that hurt is an inevitable part of a relationship?' he returned with a shrug. 'Of *all* relationships?'

She disregarded his careless use of the word 'relationship,' because the clue was in the emphasised word and Laura seized on it. 'Is that what happened with you, Constantine? You got hurt?'

'I've seen how women can hurt and manipulate, yes.'

'Girlfriends, you mean?'

'No, not *girlfriends*,' he answered scornfully.

'You mean…your mother?' she guessed, as she remembered the odd, strained look on his face when he'd mentioned her.

He shrugged in affirmation but didn't bother to reply. Hopefully she might take the hint and quit interrogating him.

'What happened?'

Did she never learn when to leave well enough alone—that her probing questions were unwelcome? 'What happened happened a long time ago,' he snapped. 'So forget it.'

Laura leaned a little closer. 'But I don't want to forget it. This is Alex's grandmother we're talking about, and one day he may want to know. Won't you tell me, Constantine? Please?'

What was it about her softly spoken question that sparked a need to reply—*to confide about things he had never told another?* he wondered, raking his dark hair back from his brow in frustration. He was a man who never confided, who was strong for everyone. The buck stopped with Constantine and it had done for many years, but now words came spilling from his lips like a stream of dark poison.

'She was years younger than my father—decades, in fact. A beautiful, fragile beauty who bewitched him—and because he was almost fifty when they married her youth and her beauty hit him like a hurricane. When a man has never known passion until late in life it can take him over like a fever.' He shrugged. 'He neglected everything in pursuit of a love she was ill-equipped to return—but then she was incapable of loving anyone but herself.'

'Even you?' said Laura slowly.

Her question broke into the tumult of his thoughts, but Constantine was in too far to stop now. 'Even me,' he answered, and the admission was like a hammer blow—for was there not something almost shameful about admitting that the most fundamental bond of all, between mother and child, had simply not existed in their case? But the precise side of Constantine's nature meant that he needed to attempt to define it.

'She was one of those people who did not seem to be of this earth—she was too fey and too delicate, and she did not look after herself,' he continued. 'She partied and drank wine instead of eating—smoked cigarettes instead of breathing in the pure Greek air. And when she died her enchantment still did not end—for my father went to pieces. He became one of those men who are obsessed by a ghost and who live in a past which only really exists in their own imagination. It was only when I took over the business properly that I was able to see just how badly he had let things go.'

Laura stared at his hard and beautiful features, transformed now into a mask hardened by pain and memory. So even his father had not been there for him—which explained the lack of closeness between the two men. 'I'm so sorry,' she said simply.

He turned, angry with her, but far angrier with himself for having unleashed some of the dark secrets of his soul. 'I do not want your sympathy,' he snapped.

'But I think that—'

'And neither do I want your advice—no matter how well intentioned! You are a woman from humble circumstances who knows nothing of this life of privilege which you have entered solely because you are the mother of my son! And you would do well to remember your place here!'

Laura reached for her sunglasses and rammed them down over her eyes before he could see the tears which were brimming up behind her lids. *Remember your place here.* How cheap did that make her feel? His words were barely any different from her own thoughts about them occupying different worlds—but, oh, how it hurt to hear them flung at her with such venom. He didn't like women, she realised—and, while it was easy to see why, it wasn't going to change, was it? Nothing *she* said would ever change it.

She saw Alex begin to stir—had their low but angry words wakened him? she wondered guiltily. But her primary feeling was of relief that she would no longer have to endure any more hurt provoked by Constantine's cruel comments. And she would protect herself from further heartache by staying as far away from him as possible.

'I think in view of what's just been said that we should try to avoid each other as much as possible while I'm still here,' she whispered.

Constantine's eyes narrowed. 'Are you *crazy*?' he questioned silkily, and without warning he splayed his hand over the sun-warmed expanse of her thigh, watching with triumph as her lips parted involuntarily in a soundless little gasp of pleasure. He lowered his voice. 'We may as well enjoy the one good, satisfactory thing which men and women *do* give each other. And—just for the record—I've done nothing but work in Athens; there have been no other women.' His black eyes gleamed with predatory anticipation. 'To be perfectly frank, your passion has left me unable to think of any other woman but you, *agape mou*.'

'And should I be flattered by that?' she questioned bitterly.

'I think perhaps you should,' he murmured.

But Laura was already scrambling to her feet and packing up the picnic basket.

'Oh, and Laura?' he said softly.

She looked up, some new steely quality in his voice warning her that what he was about to say would be more than another remark about their sexual chemistry. 'What?'

'I think it's about time we told Alex who I really am, don't you?'

Laura bit her lip. She had known this would happen, and it was happening sooner than she had hoped. But what was the point in delaying any more? Wouldn't that look as if they were hiding something shameful rather than giving them the opportunity to bond? Just because change was disrupting—and just because Laura was afraid of how telling Alex might affect their lives—it didn't mean that she could keep putting it off because it suited *her*.

'And your father?' she said softly. 'He'll need to know, too. Alex shouldn't be expected to keep the news to himself.'

In the end, the moment for telling Alex came quite naturally later that afternoon, when the three of them were sitting in the main town square of Livinos. Alex was eating ice-cream—an elaborate concoction of lemon and chocolate curls—and it seemed that every island resident stopped to ruffle his dark curls as they passed by.

'Why does everyone keep patting my head?' he questioned, not unhappily. 'And what do they keep saying to you?'

'By and large, the Greek people love having children around,' said Constantine, and Laura felt her heart lurch as she thought about his own mother. *But he's told you quite emphatically that he doesn't want your sympathy*, she reminded herself.

'Some of the older ones say that you look very much as I did at the same age,' added Constantine carefully.

'Do I?'

There was a pause. 'Very much so,' said Constantine gruffly, and then he looked across the table at Laura. She nodded. 'Do you have any idea why that might be?'

To Laura's surprise, Alex didn't answer straight away—just glanced from Constantine, to her, and then back to Constantine again. His dark eyes fixed on his father's face, a look of hope and longing tightening his boyish little features.

'Are you my daddy?' he asked.

Had it been the spoonful of ice-cream Alex had insisted on giving him which had caused this damned lump in his throat, making him momentarily incapable of words? Constantine swallowed. 'Yes, I am,' he said eventually.

There was no Hollywood movie scene of the son flinging himself onto his father's lap—that would have been too much in the circumstances. As they began to walk back towards the villa, Laura noticed Alex's fingers creep up towards the hand of the man by his side. And that Constantine took his son's little hand and was clasping it firmly, while looking fixedly ahead and blinking furiously, as if some piece of grit had just flown into his eye.

That evening, Constantine—with Laura standing nervously by his side—told his father that the Karantinos family did indeed have an heir, and that he had a grandson.

The old man stared at his son for a long moment and then gave a short laugh. 'You think I haven't already guessed that?' he questioned quietly. 'That you could bring a young child into this house out of the blue, with some flimsy excuse about him and his mother needing a holiday, a child who is the mirror-image of you at the same age, and that I would not realise that he was yours?'

Laura tried not to stare as she felt emotion build up like a gathering storm. She saw the old man take one tentative step forward, and silently willed the two men to embrace—to try to wipe out some of the heartache and bitterness which had built up between them. But Constantine took a corresponding step backwards—a step so subtle that many people would not have noticed. But Laura noticed. *Damn you, Constantine*, she thought furiously. *Damn you and your hard and unforgiving soul*. And his father noticed, too—for the lined face momentarily crumpled before he turned to look at her and nodded.

'You have a fine child in Alex, my dear. A happy and contented son for you to be proud of.'

'Th-thank you,' said Laura tremulously. 'It may seem odd to you that we kept it secret, but—'

Kyrios Karantinos shook his head. 'I can understand that circumstances may have been difficult,' he said gently. 'For I am not a complete ogre.' This was accompanied by a mocking glance at the silent figure of Constantine. 'Far better to approach things cautiously than to dive in. And Alex—he is happy to learn of the news?'

'He's ecstatic,' said Laura truthfully. As far as Alex was concerned it was *Constantine this* and *Constantine that*. Constantine had quickly become the centre of the impressionable young boy's universe. She'd watched the relationship developing between them and seen how badly her boy wanted a father—a man as a role-model. And Constantine never showed his fierce side with Alex, realised Laura.

'We must have a party to celebrate!' announced Kyrios Karantinos suddenly. 'We could invite some people over from the mainland. It's a long time since we've thrown a big party.'

And, to Laura's surprise, Constantine nodded.

'Why not?' he questioned, with a shrug of his broad shoulders.

Laura turned away before either of them noticed the conflict of emotions she suspected were criss-crossing over her face, knowing that it was wrong to feel scared—but she did.

Despite their differences, the two proud men were gearing themselves up to announce to the world that the Karantinos family now had an heir—and the importance of such an heir to such a family could not be over-estimated. But aside from the bloodline issue there was something else which was just as important...and deep-down Laura hoped that Constantine and his father might be making the first steps towards a true reconciliation.

But where did that leave her? And Alex? She wanted him to forge a close relationship with both his father and his grandfather—of course she did. It was just the future which worried her now. Because how on earth were they going to handle it when she took Alex back to England at the end of the holidays? When he left sunshine and luxury behind him and returned to an old life which was looking greyer by the minute?

CHAPTER ELEVEN

'WHAT the hell are you doing?' demanded Constantine as he walked into the kitchen.

'What does it look like?' questioned Laura steadily, finding herself in the awkward situation of having to pretend to be normal and pleasant to Constantine in a situation which defied definition—made doubly difficult by the fact that she had been writhing passionately underneath the man in question in the early hours of that very morning. Pushing the erotic memory from her mind, she positioned another olive on one of the little feta tartlets, wanting to look at something—anything—other than the mocking distraction of his black eyes.

'Laura, put the damned dish down and look at me!'

Laura complied—knowing that if she didn't want to create discord then she didn't really have a lot of choice. 'What is it?'

'Why…?' He drew a deep breath. 'Why are you helping out in the kitchen?'

'Because we both agreed that would be my role here.'

'No, Laura,' he said heavily. '*You* insisted on it and *I* was railroaded into agreeing.'

'That must have been a first,' she said gravely.

Unwillingly, his mouth twitched. 'Very probably,' he agreed, before the sight of her beautiful body in that hideous-looking floral pinafore made the smile die instantly. 'I don't want you doing any more of this kind of work in the house and neither does my father. It is no longer appropriate. You are Alex's mother—and at the party tonight you will be introduced to the people of Livinos as such, not serving damned pastries to the guests!'

'But won't…?' She could feel her heart racing with nerves. How would the Karantinos family's friends and neighbours accept her—a pale little English waitress—as the mother of the Karantinos heir?

'Won't what?'

'Won't people think it strange? I mean, it's a small island. Everyone's going to want to know why I've been working here and now suddenly I've been revealed as the mystery mother. Why, even Demetra's been dying to ask, but she's so loyal to you and your father that she wouldn't dare.'

'I do not *care* what other people think,' he iced back. 'It is what *I* think that matters.'

'If you knew just how arrogant that sounded—'

His black eyes glittered. 'You didn't seem to be complaining about my arrogance when I ordered you to strip for me last night, *agape mou*. In fact, you told me that you had never been so turned on in your life.'

Laura flushed. Well, no—but characteristics which worked well within the bedroom did not always work in everyday life. 'Oh, very well,' she said quickly, in an effort to change the subject. 'I'll come to the party—if you insist.'

Fleetingly, it struck him as ironic that she—of all

people—should sound as if she were conferring upon him a favour, when just about every other female of his acquaintance would have bitten his hand off for an invitation to what would be an undeniably glittering event.

'You will, of course, need something to wear.'

Laura felt her body stiffen with tension. 'What's the matter with the clothes I brought with me?' she questioned defensively. 'Too small-town and humble for the Karantinos family? Is that it?'

'Frankly, yes,' he drawled, his eyes mocking her as she took an angry step towards him. '*Ne*, just try it,' he murmured. 'Go on, Laura. Jab an angry finger at my chest and we both know what will happen. Except that it won't, because we can't—since Alex is having a chess lesson with my father just along the hall and Demetra is getting half the women in the village to bake bread for her. That is why I'm not able to ravish you here in the kitchen, or by the pool—or anywhere else for that matter.' He paused and he gave the flicker of a smile. 'So maybe you'll lose that indignation when I tell you about the dresses I've bought for you.'

Laura stared at him. 'You've...bought me *dresses*?'

He nodded as he met her uncomprehending look with one of his own. *Didn't* all *women like to be bought beautiful dresses?* he wondered. In his experience, the more money you lavished on a female, the more she adored you for it. 'When I was in Athens I took the opportunity to pick some up. You see, I knew that this kind of situation was bound to arise at some time, and that you'd need to look the part of a Karantinos woman.'

Her heart raced with anger and shame and hurt. Look

the *part*? Because she was playing a role instead of being the real thing? Of course she was—or that would be how Constantine saw it.

The arrogant swine! He had bought her finery with his millions so that she would blend in, had he? Well, for once in her life—she would make sure she did the exact opposite and stand out at his wretched party!

'How very kind of you,' she said, mock-demurely, and saw him frown. 'I'll go and look at them.'

'No. Not now,' he said softly, and caught her wrist, bringing it up to his lips and whispering them against the fine tracery of veins which clothed the thready hammering of her pulse.

Just that brief touch weakened her, and Laura swayed and closed her eyes. 'Don't,' she whispered. 'You've just said yourself that the house is full of people.'

'Which is why we're going for a drive.'

Laura swallowed. 'Alex—'

'Is fine with my father. I've checked. Now, take off that damned pinafore and let's get going.'

Minutes later they were zipping their way along an isolated coastal road in a little silver sports car she hadn't seen before. 'Where exactly,' she questioned, 'are we going?'

'You'll see.'

The wind whipped through her hair and Laura felt ridiculously light-hearted. 'Suddenly you're an international man of mystery?'

'If that's what you'd like me to be,' he declared evenly, but her bright mood had affected him too, and he smiled.

Their destination turned out to be a beautiful stone house set back from the beach—but its simple beauty went unnoticed because they were barely inside the door before Constantine started kissing her and tugging at the zip of her dress.

'Aren't you going to...show me around?' she gasped.

'Aren't you?' he countered, and then closed his eyes as his fingers found her soft breasts. 'Come on, Laura. Show me around your body, *oreos mou*, show me deep inside your body—for that is the only place I want to go right now.'

His erotic words only spurred on Laura's own frantic desire. Half-clothed, they sank onto the marble floor—its cool surface contrasting perfectly with his hot flesh as it covered hers, their gasps morphing into ecstatic shuddered cries which split the silence.

Afterwards, they lay there—both with a fine dew of sweat drying on their skin—and Constantine stroked the mass of blonde hair which clouded her shoulders.

'Hot?'

'Boiling.'

'Fancy a swim?' he questioned idly.

Lazily, she stirred against his body, and yawned. 'I didn't bring a costume.'

Regarding her discarded panties, he splayed his hand possessively over one bare, warm globe of her bottom. 'Who says you'll need one? You can swim naked, my beauty.'

'Providing fodder for any passing voyeurs?' she said primly, even though she shivered beneath his touch and at the blatantly untrue compliment which had sprung from his lips.

Constantine laughed. 'It's utterly private and we won't be observed by a soul,' he said softly. 'That's why I brought us here. To see your body by daylight—for I am tired of having to be furtive. Of having to sneak into your room at night as if we are committing some sort of crime. I want the freedom to cry out when I come, and to watch while you do, too. To watch you walk around unfettered. I want to have sex with you in the sea, Laura,' he said thickly. '*Oreos mou*, I want to have sex with you all day long—until our bodies are exhausted and our appetites sated.'

It wasn't the most romantic declaration she had ever heard, but it echoed Laura's own haunting desire for him. With her body she could show him her passion, even if her heart and her lips were prevented from giving voice to it. You could love a man with your lips in a different way than using them to tell him, she thought. And Constantine was right—the freedom to behave without constraint was completely intoxicating…

The afternoon sun was still bright when they drove back. Laura tried to tell herself that they were too exhausted for much conversation, but it was more than that. Her head was full of spinning thoughts.

Constantine had remained true to his vow that he was going to make love to her until they were both exhausted—she had never known that it was possible for desire to be ignited over and over again. He had made love to her on the beach, and then carried her down to the sea to wash the grains of sand from her skin. But the act of washing had awoken their sensual hunger once more—he had made her gasp and giggle until at last he had pulled her wet body against his and let the sea foam surge deliciously over their nakedness. Slippery and salty, she had let him part her legs beneath the water and felt their warm flesh join once more beneath the waves. And Constantine had been right—the freedom to make love without worrying about being overheard or seen was utterly intoxicating.

She thought about the party which lay ahead, and which until fairly recently would have terrified the life out of her. But that had been before this journey here to Livinos—a journey which had taught her as much about herself as about Greek life.

It had taught her that she loved the man who sat beside her, despite his cold heart which had been so damaged in his own childhood that it seemed to have no hope of healing. She loved him because he was Alex's father—but she suspected that she had loved him all those years ago, when she had given him her virginity so joyfully on that warm summer night. For wasn't love at first sight both the great dream and yet the admittedly rare reality of human relationships? Even if it hadn't been reciprocated it didn't mean it had necessarily gone away—and since she had become his lover that feeling had been growing as inexorably as a new shoot towards the spring sunshine. Hadn't the afternoon they'd just spent added to the magic?

She glanced at his hard and rugged profile as he stared at the coastal road ahead. The wind whipped through the black, tousled curls and the dark glasses shaded his eyes against the light—preventing her from reading anything of his own thoughts.

But who was she kidding? Those ebony eyes never gave anything away. And neither did he. He could buy her new dresses so that she wouldn't disgrace him at his fancy party— but he couldn't give her any of his heart or his soul even if he wanted to. He had locked those away a long time ago.

Back at the villa, they parted without a kiss or embrace— only the briefest of glittering looks from Constantine reminding her of how they'd spent the afternoon.

'I'll see you later,' he said softly, and resolutely turned his back on her before he was tempted to kiss her again.

Laura watched him go. Maybe for him it had just been an afternoon of amazing sex, she thought. He probably wasn't—like her—stupidly reliving every glorious second of it and pretending that it had anything to do with emotion.

It was with heightened colour that she went off to find Alex, who was now playing tennis with Stavros.

He waved his arm at her in greeting, and then adopted a fierce expression on his little face, wanting desperately to show his mother how good he'd become at the game.

How he'd grown to love sport, she thought tenderly. She stood by the side of the tennis court and watched as her son batted the ball over the net with what looked like incredible natural skill to her proud, motherly eye. Alex had been on a journey too, she recognised—he had realised some of his own dormant talents as well as getting to know his Greek family. And deep down she knew that nobody would ever dare bully him again. Laura watched as they changed ends, wondering once again how on earth he would ever be able to bear to leave this paradise of a place to go back to the very different life he knew in England.

She went to her room and showered off the sand, slipping into jeans and a T-shirt before surveying the garments Constantine had bought her, which someone had hung up in her wardrobe while she'd been out at the beach house. And although she'd told herself that she wasn't going to swoon over a few expensive articles of clothing she found herself doing just that.

Finest silk, cashmere and organza were here—represented in gowns which unbelievably fitted her like a glove.

She twirled in front of the mirror in a vivid emerald silk. Though maybe it wasn't unbelievable at all—for wasn't Constantine one of those men who seemed to instinctively know more about a woman's body than she did?

But Laura didn't have a clue about dressing up. She'd never had the time, the money or the opportunity before— and suddenly she found herself longing for advice. Surely she could phone Sarah? She hadn't spoken to her sister for ages, and she missed her. With her artistic streak, Sarah had a brilliant eye and knowledge of clothes—she'd know which of these dresses would be most suitable.

She walked through the house, looking for Constantine, but he was nowhere to be found—only Kyrios Karantinos was in his study, sitting hunched over a book. He looked up as she tapped on the door.

'Looking forward to the party?' he questioned with a smile.

Laura wondered what he'd say if he had any idea of the confused emotions which were swirling around inside her. 'I'm not quite sure what to wear,' she admitted. 'And I wondered if it would be okay to use the telephone to ring my sister in England?' She hesitated, but then thought of the Karantinos billions and her own modest income. 'I've…I've got a cellphone, but it's…'

The old man gave a small smile as he gestured towards the telephone on the desk and began to get up. 'Please— say no more and come in. You must feel free to use the phone whenever you like, my dear.' His smile became a little wider. 'It is quite clear to me that Constantine has not ended up with a materialistic woman!'

She wanted to tell him that Constantine had not 'ended

up' with this woman at all. 'Thank you—but I can go somewhere else to make the call. I don't want to push you out of your own study.'

'I was leaving shortly anyway.' He looked at her. 'I've been wondering what your future plans are?' he questioned, his faded eyes narrowing. 'Or maybe I shouldn't ask?'

Laura hesitated, knowing that she should not confide in Constantine's father—for mightn't Constantine see that as some kind of betrayal? 'No arrangements have been made yet,' she said uncertainly.

'You're good for him,' the old man said suddenly.

'No—'

'*Yes*. Better than anyone else has ever been for him.' A ragged sigh left his lips, as if it had been waiting for a long time to escape, and the old man looked at her with pain in his faded eyes. 'Better than I or his mother ever were, that's for sure.'

'I don't think—'

'I was a *bad* father—a very bad father,' interrupted Kyrios Karantinos fervently. 'I know that. I worshipped his mother—I was one of those foolish men who become obsessed by a woman. She dazzled me with her beauty and her youth so that I couldn't see anything but her.' There was a pause. 'And that kind of love is dangerous. It is blind. It meant that I could not tell the difference between fantasy and reality—and somewhere along the way was a very small and confused boy, cut adrift by the very two people who should have been looking out for him.' He gave a shuddering sigh. 'We both neglected him.'

How her heart ached for that little boy. 'Have you…have you tried to explain all this to Constantine?' she ventured cautiously. 'Tried to tell him how it was? I mean, how...how *sorry* you are now?'

'Oh, maybe a million times,' he admitted. 'But my proud and successful son will only hear what he wants to hear, and he finds the past too painful to revisit. Forgive me, Laura—for I do not mean to speak ill of him. You see...I love him.' His voice trembled. 'And I am an old man.'

She stared at him, suddenly understanding the subtext which lay behind his words. Soon he might die. And then the painful past might never be resolved—instead spreading its poisonous tentacles far into the future.

Briefly, he squeezed her arm and then left the study, and Laura stared out of the window at the beautiful Greek day, her heart almost breaking as she thought about the terrible distance between the two men which might never be bridged.

But she was here with a purpose. And—even if her worries about what to wear seemed rather flippant in comparison to what Kyrios Karantinos had just told her—she gathered together her troubled thoughts before dialling England.

It was strange speaking to her sister—it felt as if a lifetime had passed since they had last spoken—and Sarah was sounding very bubbly. 'The girl Constantine hired to work in the shop is *lovely*!' she enthused, and her voice dipped mischievously. 'And she has this *cousin*...he's called Matthius and he's just *gorgeous*!'

Aware of the rapidly spiralling cost of the call, Laura butted in. 'Sarah, I need your advice about clothes...'

Once Sarah had been given a brief run-down on all the dresses in the picture, she was emphatic. Laura must wear her hair up—'because sometimes when you wash it it goes into a cloud, and you end up looking like Alice in

Wonderland.' And she should opt for the most fitted dress—'because what's the point of having a great figure if you can't show it off?'

That evening, Laura's hands were trembling as she swept an extra layer of mascara onto her lashes. She couldn't ever remember feeling this nervous before a party before—but maybe that wasn't so surprising. She'd overseen Alex getting dressed—Constantine had ensured that his son would be suitably kitted-out, too—and her heart had swelled with pride when she saw her little boy in a pair of long, dark trousers and a white shirt and little bow-tie. He looked so *Greek*, she thought.

But he is Greek. Or at least half-Greek.

Suddenly filled with fear, she stood in front of the mirror, but her head was so buzzing with disquiet that for a moment she did not see the image which reflected back at her. *Alex isn't going to want to leave this place*, she realised with a sinking heart. And could she really blame him?

Her eyes focussed on the mirror at last, and Laura blinked because for a moment it felt as if she was looking at a complete stranger. A sleek and sophisticated stranger with a costly dress and big, dark eyes?

There was a tap at the door and she turned round to see it opening. Constantine was standing there—his dark expression completely unreadable as he looked her up and down.

Nervously, Laura swallowed. 'Do you…do you like it?'

'I'm not sure,' he drawled.

'But you bought it! You're the one who wanted me to wear something grand.'

'*Ne.* I know I did,' he said slowly. He just had not been expecting such a complete…*transformation*. On the model in the showroom—who had flirted with him quite outrageously until his stony indifference had caused her to stop—the dress had looked completely different. But the blue satin moulded Laura's curves so closely that it looked as though she had been dipped in a summer sky. Above the low-cut bodice her skin glowed softly golden, and the curve of her breasts was a perfect swell. Her fine blonde hair was piled high on her head, with just a couple of recalcitrant locks tumbling down by the side of her face like liquid gold.

And her face! She rarely wore much make-up—sometimes nothing and she always looked as sexy as hell—but tonight the unaccustomed darkening of her eyes and the slick of gloss to her lips made her look like a siren. Every man would look at her and want her, thought Constantine—and a nerve flickered furiously at his temple.

'Do you like it?' repeated Laura, half tempted to tear the damned thing off and put on the little floral dress she'd brought with her from England.

'You look very *beautiful*,' said Constantine carefully. Putting his hand in his pocket, he withdrew a slim leather case. 'You'd better have these.'

'What are they?'

He flipped the lid open to reveal a bright scattering of ice-white jewels, and it took Laura's disbelieving eyes a couple of seconds to realise that she was in fact looking at a diamond necklace and a pair of long, glittering earrings.

'I can't wear these,' she breathed.

'Why not?'

'What if I lose one?'

'Don't worry—they're insured,' he said carelessly as he

clipped the exquisite necklace around her neck. 'Put on the earrings, Laura.'

With trembling fingers she complied, and the piled up hairstyle complemented the waterfall earrings brilliantly as she stood before him for his assessment.

'Perfect,' he said softly. 'Now you look like a Karantinos woman.'

But as they walked out together towards the strings of lights which were already twinkling against the darkening sky Laura felt like a prize pony in a show, decked out with unfamiliar ribbons and with its mane plaited.

She was an impostor, she thought. A fraud. Externally she carried all the displays of wealth which would be expected of the mother of Constantine's son. But inside? Inside she felt like a cork from a bottle which was lost on a vast and tossing ocean.

The party had all the elements for a successful evening, and the guests were determined to enjoy the fabled Karantinos hospitality. The weather was perfect, the finest wines flowed, and the village women had outdone themselves with the food. But part of Laura wished that she could hide behind the anonymity of her waitress's uniform instead of being subjected to the curious looks of the women of Livinos and—even more intimidating—of the society beauties who had flown in from Athens. They seemed to have no qualms about failing to hide their surprise when they were introduced to Laura. And neither did they abstain from flirting with Constantine.

Maybe she couldn't blame them, for he drew the eye irresistibly; no other man came even close to him. His hair looked ebony-black when contrasted against the snowy whiteness of his dinner jacket, which emphasised his powerful physique. And Alex stayed close by his side as Laura heard him being introduced over and over again as 'my son'.

My son, too she thought bitterly, ashamed of the great flood of primitive jealousy and fear which washed over her.

Because one look around at all the good and the great gathered here tonight was enough to ram home the extent of Constantine's power and influence. And not just here in his native Greece. Why, a world-famous architect had flown in from New York especially for this party!

But Laura knew how to behave. She knew that people couldn't tell how you were feeling if you disguised your nerves and concerns behind a bright party smile. It must be working too, because several of the men went out of their way to be charming to her.

The toast—to health and happiness and the continuation of the Karantinos bloodline—was taken early, so that Kyrios Karantinos could retire. He looked exhausted, thought Laura—and she accompanied him back to the house, keen to see he got there safely as well as enjoying a break from the sensation of being watched by the other guests.

She managed to get an excited Alex into bed before midnight, and by the time she had pulled the sheet over Blue Bear he was fast asleep. It was late, she reasoned. Too late to go back—and she was exhausted, too. All that endless smiling and trying not to sound like some gauche little woman who had shoe-horned her way into the life of the Greek billionaire by getting pregnant had completely wiped her out.

She showered and slipped into bed—half hoping that Constantine would not come to her tonight and half praying

that he would. Couldn't she lose this terrible sense of insecurity in the warm haven of his arms? Forget life and all its
problems in the dreamy pleasure of his lovemaking? Even
if those feelings came crowding back in the moment he left.

The door opened and Constantine stood there
unmoving—still in his dinner suit—just staring at the bed
in silence before walking into the room and quietly shutting
the door behind him.

'H-hello,' she said, sitting up and feeling rather stupid—
why hadn't he come over to pull her hungrily into his arms?

'Can you get up and put some kind of robe on?' he
asked, in a strained and distant kind of voice.

'Sure.' She looked up at him for some kind of hint as to
what this was all about—but then she wished she hadn't.
Because it was like a cruel flashback to all those years ago
when she had looked into his eyes and seen nothing.

Nothing at all.

CHAPTER TWELVE

'Is…is something wrong?' asked Laura tentatively.

Constantine turned round. The silky gown came to mid-thigh, and covered her in all the right places—but it did nothing to disguise the luscious curves and he did not want to be distracted by her body. Not yet.

'Nothing is wrong,' he said coolly. 'Why don't you sit down?'

He indicated the long window seat, which was scattered with squashy embroidered cushions, and Laura sank down onto it, wondering why he was talking to her in that strange tone. And why he hadn't kissed her. 'Why are you acting like this?' she asked, bewildered.

'I'm not *acting* like anything,' he ground out. 'I'm just wondering why you ran back to your room without saying goodnight to any of our guests?'

'Because they weren't *my* guests, they were *yours*!' she returned. 'They weren't here to see me, but you—and your father—and your son. I only had curiosity value as the woman who had given birth to him. Once they had seen me, I was superfluous to requirements.'

'Not to some of the male guests, you weren't!' he snarled. 'They could hardly stop undressing you with their eyes!'

'Well, you have only yourself to blame for that, Constantine,' she hissed back. 'Since you're the one who bought me the dress!'

'And I don't know why I did!'

'Oh, yes, you do,' she contradicted hotly. 'Because I just wasn't good enough, looking the way I normally look. You were afraid that I'd show you up!'

'I didn't want you to feel awkward.'

'You don't think I felt *awkward* with half a million pounds worth of diamonds strung around my neck?' She glanced over at the leather box. 'And can you please take them away with you? Just having them in the room makes me nervous.'

'Laura, why are you being like this?' he exploded.

Why, indeed? Because he made her feel cheap? As if the real Laura could only be tolerated if she was dressed up to look like someone else? *Because he would never love her as she wanted to be loved?* She raked her loose hair away from her face and looked at him in the bright moonlight which flooded in from the unshuttered windows.

'Being like *what*? *You're* the one who's burst in here with a face like ice!' she returned. 'So have you come here for something specific? Because I'm tired and I'd like to get to sleep.'

His eyes narrowed—it was the first time she had not melted automatically into his arms, eager for the closeness of his body.

'Yes, I came here for something specific,' he said, and his mouth hardened as he bit the words out. 'To ask you once again to marry me.'

It was ironic, thought Laura fleetingly, how something which you had only ever pictured in your wildest dreams should dissolve when it happened in real life. This was different from the last time he'd asked her—when they'd barely known each other. Because now they did. Now they were lovers who had shared time with one another—so that him asking her to marry him could be given proper consideration.

A proposal of marriage from the man she loved—supposedly the one thing her aching heart longed for. And yet it had been delivered with all the warmth of a giant chunk of ice floating in an Arctic sea.

She drew in a deep breath. 'Presumably to legitimise your son?'

He looked at her. Hadn't they been through too much for him to dress up the truth with niceties? He shrugged. 'Of course.'

Laura could have wept—or hurled the nearest object at his hard-hearted head. But since that happened to be the diamond set she didn't dare risk it.

He sensed her displeasure. 'Of course there would be more to our marriage than that.'

'There would?' she questioned hopefully.

He nodded. 'We have shown that we can live compatibly, *ne*?' His voice softened into a tone of pure silk. 'And in bed—or out of it—we are pure dynamite together, *agape mou*. You know that.'

Yes, she knew that—but wasn't that the most frightening thing of all? To have physical chemistry up there as one of the main reasons for being together. Because didn't everyone say that it faded in time? And then what would they be left with? A cold shell of a marriage. Already she could imagine the reality of such a marriage, and an icy chill made her begin to shiver, despite the heavy warmth of the night.

'No,' she said.

'No?' His voice was incredulous, and he took a step forward. 'How can you say no when you know that it is what Alex would want,' he said, his voice dangerously soft. 'What Alex *wants*.'

Her fingers flew to her throat and she stared at him in fear. 'Have you asked him? Gone behind my back to get him to side with you?' she demanded hoarsely.

His mouth twisted. 'You think me capable of such an act, Laura? No, I have not—but you know that what I say is true. The boy loves it here—you have only to look at him to see how much he has blossomed since he arrived.'

Guilt shafted through her heart. Hadn't she thought the very same herself—and had he guessed that? 'But that's…*blackmail*,' she whispered.

No. It was fighting for what was truly his—something which he had discovered meant more to him than all his properties and ships and the international acclaim he enjoyed. His son meant far more to him than the continuation of a bloodline…young Alex had crept into his heart and found a permanent home there. Was Laura prepared to ride rough-shod over their son's wishes purely for her own ends?

'Ask him,' he taunted. 'Go on—ask him!'

But Constantine's cruel words focussed Laura's mind on what really mattered, and now she got up and faced him, staring mulishly up at him. It was true that he towered over her, and made her feel ridiculously small, but she didn't care. She might be small but she certainly wasn't insignificant. And he *would* hear her out!

'No, I *won't* ask him—because I wouldn't marry you if you were the last man on earth!' she hissed. 'A man so cruel and so cold that he can't bear to forgive his own father. Even though that father has asked him time and time again to forgive him for all the wrongs he admits he did!'

'Have you been speaking with my father?' he demanded furiously.

'And what if I have? Is that such a heinous crime?' she retorted. 'Am I supposed to ask your permission if I want to speak to somebody?'

'You dare to accuse me of going behind *your* back, and now I discover that you have done exactly the same!' he thundered.

'Oh, please don't try and get out of it by using logic!' she flared, showing a complete lack of it herself. 'Your father made mistakes, yes—and so did your mother. Though it sounds to me as if she couldn't help her own behaviour, and some people are like that. Weak. Unable to give love—even to their own children. And *they can't help it*, Constantine—they were born that way!'

He clenched his fists in fury. How dared she? How *dared* she? 'Have you quite finished?'

That intimidating tone would have silenced many people, but Laura was too passionate to stop. This meant far too much for her to be able to stop. 'No, I have *not* finished! I can't believe you even made the suggestion that I marry you. You're still angry about the coldness of your own childhood and yet you want to subject Alex to more of the same!'

'What the hell are you talking about, Laura?'

This was painful; maybe too painful—and Laura was not prepared to go as far as admitting that if they married then the balance of love would be as one-sided as in his parents' own marriage. Because he didn't realise she loved him, did he? And wouldn't it give him power over her if he did?

'I'm talking about bringing a child up within a loveless marriage—it's just not fair. Things would only get worse between us—never better—and as Alex grew he would have to tiptoe around our feelings and our animosities. What kind of example is that to set him?' she said, her voice beginning to tremble as she thought of her darling son. 'What hope is there for him to be happy in his own life if he looks around and sees discord all around him? How can he believe in love and happiness for himself if he never sees an example of it at home, Constantine?'

Her breath had deserted her and her words died away. She had nothing left to say—but she did not think she needed to. For Constantine's face had suddenly become shuttered. And his eyes—always enigmatic—now looked like strange, cold stones. As if a light had gone out behind them.

'This is what you think?' he demanded.

'Yes,' she whispered, although it broke her heart to admit it. 'Because it's the truth.'

For a moment there was silence—a heavy and uncomfortable kind of silence—and then Constantine's mouth hardened.

'Very well, Laura,' he said, in a voice of pure steel. 'I can see the sense behind your words, since they are—as you say—the truth. And at least if you go then I will no longer have to endure your intolerable interference in things which do not concern you.'

She prayed her lips would not crumple, nor her eyes give her pain away. 'Constantine—'

But he silenced her with his next statement. 'We will need to make plans. And we must do it so that everyone benefits as far as possible. You will require financial assistance. *No!*' He held his hand up peremptorily, anticipating her objections. A harsh note of bitterness entered his voice. 'This is not the time for pretty displays of unnecessary pride,' he spat out. 'You are the mother of my son and I insist that you have an adequate income to support him in a manner which I hope we can both agree on. I want him to go to a school where he isn't bullied—'

'Who told you that?'

'He did, of course,' he said impatiently. 'Not in so many words—but it was clear to me that he is not as happy as he could be. He needs a school where there is plenty of sport, and you need enough money to take that haunted look out of your eyes, never to have to supplement your income with damned waitressing jobs again. And I...' He drew a deep breath as pain like he had never known rushed in to invade the heart he had tried to protect for so long. 'I want to see as much of Alex as possible—we'll need to come to some agreement on that.'

She wanted to reach out to him. To tell him that he could see as much of Alex as he wanted—to reassure him and to comfort him that they would do the best they possibly could. But there was something so icy and forbidding about his words and demeanour that she did not dare. Suddenly he had become a stranger to her. 'Of course,' she said stiffly.

'I will arrange for you to return to England as soon as possible. I think that best, in the circumstances. My lawyers will be in touch on your return. But I want some time alone with Alex tomorrow morning.' He drew a deep breath as reality hit him, seeming to turn his whole body into stone. He forced the next words out. 'To say goodbye to my son.'

CHAPTER THIRTEEN

'BUT Mum, *why* do we have to go home?'

Laura's smile didn't slip, even though her face felt as if it had been carved out of marble—but during the sleepless night which had followed her furious row with Constantine she had decided the best way to handle questions like this. And the best way was to present her and Alex leaving Livinos as something perfectly normal. *Which it was.*

'Well, we only ever planned to come out for a few weeks,' she reminded him. 'Remember?'

'It's been less than that,' said Alex sulkily. 'And I like it here.'

She knew that—and it broke her heart to have to drag him away—but what choice did she have? He'd been happy in England before and he would be happy again—especially if there was no more bullying and if he changed schools, as Constantine himself had suggested. And didn't all the books on child-rearing say that the worst thing you could do was to subject your children to a hostile atmosphere and infighting between parents? She could do worse than remind herself of the bitter words she and Constantine had exchanged last night if she needed any more convincing that the two of them were basically incompatible.

'Anyway,' said Laura, with a brightly cheerful smile, even though the thought of the future terrified her, 'you'll be coming back to Livinos lots…to see your daddy. And he'll be coming to England to take you out. You'll…well, you'll have the best of both worlds, really, Alex!'

Alex bit his lip, as if he couldn't bring himself to agree with this. 'Can I go swimming with Stavros, please?'

Laura felt her heart threaten to break as she saw his pinched little face. 'Of course you can,' she whispered. 'But you've only got a couple of hours. The helicopter will be leaving straight after lunch, and we mustn't be late.'

He didn't say another word as she took him outside to find the affable Greek student, and Laura stood there, watching the two of them heading towards the pool area, her eyes full of rogue tears which she fiercely blinked back.

Returning to her room, she finished packing—folding her cheap clothes into neat piles and then stuffing them into the equally cheap suitcase. For a brief moment her fingers strayed towards the costly gowns Constantine had bought her, and then strayed back again. Because what was the point of taking them back to England? They had been purchased with the sole purpose of making her look like a Karantinos woman—and she wasn't one and never would be. She had no right to wear the exquisite garments and they had no place in her life—where on earth could she possibly wear them in Milmouth?

Packing up Alex's stuff was harder—because here she really was tempted to take some of the wonderful toys and books Constantine had provided for him. But even if they took a whole load back—where on earth would they find room to accommodate them in their tiny apartment? And besides, they would always be here for him when he visited.

Laura swallowed the sudden acrid taste of fear. Because wasn't that an additional cause of her fretting heart? The fact that Alex would have his wonderful little world kept intact here—a world of toys and swimming pools, boats and planes, and the growing knowledge that he was heir to the fabulous Karantinos fortune…not simply the son of a struggling single mother. Would the day come when he chose to live out the Greek side of his heritage—rejecting her and the country of his birth?

Alex wouldn't *do* that, she told herself desperately—but still the fear ate away at her.

Their packing completed, Laura stole a glance at her watch. She had already said a brief and upsetting farewell to Constantine's father, and to Demetra, too. Goodbyes were awful at the best of times, but these felt a million times worse—loaded down with the terrible and aching significance of all that she was leaving behind. And most upsetting of all was the thought of leaving Constantine.

Was she being crazy? Wouldn't it make more sense if she gritted her teeth and accepted the fact that, while he didn't love her, Constantine would provide a secure childhood for Alex?

But not a *loving* childhood, she reminded herself. And she knew that this was about far more than her ego being bruised because Constantine didn't love *her*. Why, he couldn't even forgive his father. How could she let Alex exist in an emotionally cold world like that?

Laura glanced at her watch. The time was ticking away,

and her stomach was churning with the kind of slow dread she got before an exam. What the hell was she going to do between now and the arrival of the helicopter, which would whisk them to Athens to catch the private jet which this time she had been unable to refuse? Maybe she would take one last lingering tour of the beautiful grounds which surrounded the Karantinos property.

Slipping out of the villa into the dappled sunlight, Laura thought how strange the atmosphere around the place seemed today. Was it because Constantine was nowhere to be seen? Or maybe it was just her.

She could hear the distant splash of Alex and Stavros larking around in the pool, and she could see a sleek white yacht down on the sapphire waters of the sea—but none of it seemed real. She felt as if she was insubstantial; a ghost of a woman who walked through the fruit orchards and tried to focus on the scent of the pine trees rather than the tearing ache in her heart.

Walking further across the property than she had ever ventured before, she came across a small bougainvillaea-tumbled grove. It was a scented, secret sort of place, reached through a dusty tract of olive trees and shaded from the glaring heat of the sun by tumbling blooms, and she sank down on a stone bench, wishing that she'd drunk some water before leaving the house.

For a while she sat there, trying to decide about what she would do when she got back to Milmouth. Maybe she'd think about selling more local produce in the shop—asking villagers if they wanted to shift any leftover crops from large gluts of home-grown vegetables. That would benefit everyone in the community, wouldn't it? But the question seemed to have no real relevance in her life. *Please help me to feel part of that community again,* she prayed. *And not like some sad woman who's left her heart and her soul behind in this paradise.*

'Hiding away, are you, Laura?'

A deep and familiar voice shattered the silence, and Laura's heart leapt as Constantine stepped into the grove— his hard face shuttered, the dappled light casting shadows over the high slash of his cheekbones. She looked up into his eyes, but met nothing but cool curiosity in their ebony depths.

'Why would I be hiding?' she questioned, her voice sounding light in contrast to the hard thundering of her heart.

He shrugged as he sat down beside her. 'This isn't a place you usually frequent.'

'Then how did you know I was here?'

There was a pause. 'I followed you.'

Another pause. Longer this time. And now her heart was beating so hard and so fast that Laura could barely stumble the words out. 'Wh-why would you do that?'

His eyes rested on the lightly tanned length of her slender thighs, their shape clearly outlined by the thin cotton dress she wore. Why, indeed? Because she continued to mesmerise him—even though he had vowed not to let her? Constantine's mouth twisted as he felt the slow throb of blood to his pulse points. How many times had he told himself that she exerted an allure simply because she had refused him—because she had done the inexplicable and turned down his offer of marriage for a second time?

He met the wide grey eyes which were observing him so guardedly, and noted the fall of fine blonde hair which was hanging around her narrow shoulders like a pale cloud.

Had she read one of those books which advised holding out in order to increase her worth as a woman? He felt the stab of desire jerking insistently at his groin. Well, she would learn soon enough that he would not be played with—not any more. She had had her chance and that chance would not return. But in the meantime he would have her one last time!

'Why, Constantine?' she persisted. 'Why did you follow me?'

He picked up her unresisting hand and studied it. 'Oh, I don't know.' Running the pad of this thumb questingly over the centre of her palm, he felt her shiver. 'Any ideas?'

Laura felt her already dry throat grow completely parched. His touch. His proximity. The sudden glint from his eyes. All those things were making her feel weak and helpless.

She told herself to pull her hand away. To move. To distract him.

So why did she stay exactly where she was? Letting Constantine stroke enchanting little circles over her skin and feeling herself tremble in response?

'Mmm, Laura?' he questioned, as he shifted his body a little closer on the bench. 'Any ideas?'

'N-no.'

'Really? How remarkably unimaginative of you, *agape mou*. Why, I'm quite disappointed that someone whom I have coached so tirelessly in the art of love shouldn't immediately take advantage of a sweet and final opportunity presenting itself like this.'

His words were in a muddle in her head. Dangerous words—of which *final* seemed to be the most dangerous of all. *You both know it's over*, she told herself desperately—

so why are you letting him pull you onto his lap? And why aren't you stopping him from sliding your panties right down, from putting his fingers between your legs and...

'Constantine!' she gasped.

He kissed her to shut her up—but also because he wanted to kiss her. *Needed* to kiss her. To punish her and to make her hurt as he was hurting. But the kiss didn't stay that way—infuriatingly, it transformed itself into a terrible aching hunger which could be eased in only one way. He tore his mouth away and shuddered out a harsh entreaty.

'Undo my jeans.'

Laura didn't even hesitate before she tremblingly obeyed—indeed, she thought that she might have been scrabbling at his belt even before that terse instruction had been whispered in her ear.

She gasped again as she freed him—marvelling at the sheer power of him. He looked and felt so big and so erect in her tiny hand as she stroked on the condom he gave her. And then he began impatiently to tug at the jeans, until they had slithered down to his ankles. He didn't even bother to kick them off. Instead, he just lifted her up, as if she were made of cotton wool, bringing her down deep onto his aching shaft and kissing her again with a fierce hunger—sensing that her shuddering little cries of fulfilment were only minutes away. As were his. A few ecstatic movements of her hips and he was groaning into her mouth as he felt himself spasming against her own honeyed contractions.

Afterwards, she collapsed against him, burying her head on his shoulder, willing the tears not to come, and wondering why everything felt so confused. Why had he done this—and why had she let him? Registering that sex had a dark power which managed to distort what had seemed such a straightforward decision, she found herself wondering if she had been wrong to tell him she was leaving.

If he asks me again to stay, then I might just say yes, she thought weakly—but the next thing she knew was Constantine firmly lifting her off him.

'Straighten your clothes,' he said abruptly as he began to pull up the zip of his jeans. He hated his weakness around her—the way he couldn't seem to resist her when every logical pore in his formidable body told him that it should be easy. Would she see this as another little triumph? he wondered bitterly. Another perfect demonstration of how she had the powerful Constantine Karantinos eating out of her hand?

'I'll leave you to find your own way back,' he finished, raking angry fingers back through the tousled waves of his black hair.

And then he was gone, and Laura could hardly believe what had just taken place. How she could have let him arrive and just…*do* that to her? But she *had* let him. More than let him—had squirmed with pleasure and enjoyed every erotic second of it—so if Constantine had now lost all respect for her as a woman then she had only herself to blame.

But in a way her orgasm had emptied her of all feeling and all emotion—and at least that made the last preparations for her departure bearable. So that she was able to chat excitedly to Alex about the conkers which would be on the autumn trees in England—ignoring the morose set of his little face in response. Only once did her composure threaten to buckle, and that was when Constantine clasped his son in a hug which went on and on.

Then he ruffled the little boy's dark curls and smiled. 'I'll come and see you soon in England,' he said.

Alex's crumpled face was turned upwards, as if he had just seen the first light in a dark sky. 'When?'

'How does next month sound?'

'Oh, it sounds wonderful, Papa.'

The helicopter blades whirred round and round, and Laura glanced out of the window to see Constantine staring up intently at his son. She felt a real pang of remorse. Was she doing a wrong and selfish thing by taking Alex back to England? Yet how many women would willingly trap themselves on an island this size with a man who didn't love them?

The island retreated as the craft took off, but Constantine stood there long after the black speck had grown smaller and smaller and then finally disappeared, his shoulders bowed with the weight of something too painful to analyse.

Something which made all the Karantinos billions fade into pale insignificance.

CHAPTER FOURTEEN

As THE last of Alex's footsteps died away, Laura closed the front door and let out a long sigh of something which felt like relief. *Please let him have a nice day with my sister,* she prayed silently. *Please remove some of the inevitable disappointment which has clouded my son's face since returning home from Greece last week.* A week which had felt more like a year.

It was strange to be back in England, and even stranger to be back in their small flat which no longer seemed to feel like home. *And why was that?* she wondered guiltily. Because it was small and poky after the vast Karantinos villa? Or because the powerful presence of Constantine was absent—making the place seem soulless?

'I miss my papa,' Alex had told her on more than one occasion—in a way which tore at Laura's conscience.

And, so do I, she thought. *So do I.* A decision she had made for all the best reasons was now proving to be unbearable—and it seemed that she had no one in the world to turn to or confide in.

Because even Sarah seemed to have moved on. Her sister

had been hurtling up to London at every opportunity to see Matthius—the cousin of the Greek student Constantine had roped in to help while Laura had been away. It seemed that like Demetra, Mattius was also a member of the Constantine Karantinos fan-club, having convinced Sarah that the billionaire was only arrogant and cold to the many people who wanted something from him—but that to friends and family he was loyalty personified.

For Laura, who was trying desperately hard to put the Greek tycoon from her mind, this was the last thing she wanted or needed to hear. Was it her stricken face which had made Sarah offer to take Alex out for the day? Or the fact that she couldn't seem to settle to anything and was driving everyone mad?

Whatever the reason, it was very kind of her sister, and Laura knew it was good for Alex to have something to occupy his thoughts other than the life he had left behind on Livinos. But the free day yawned emptily ahead of her, and Laura found herself wondering how she was going to fill the aching hours ahead when she heard a loud banging on the door. She ran back into the hall to throw it open with more than a little relief.

'Now what have you forgotten—?' she began to say, but the words died on her lips when she saw who was standing there. Not Alex. Nor Sarah. But…

Constantine?

Laura swallowed, shaking her head a little, blinking back the stupid sting of disbelieving tears as she stared up at him. She'd been thinking about him non-stop. Dreaming about him constantly. Her thoughts about him had driven her half mad and her heart had been unable to stop aching—so that for a moment it just felt like an extension of all her desires that he would somehow magically appear. As if the man who stood in front of her wasn't real. As if he couldn't be real.

But he was. Laura stared at the formidable physique of Constantine Karantinos—standing on her doorstep, with his dark hair all windswept and a look on his face she had never seen before. Had she forgotten just how gorgeous he was? How strong and how vital? How he could dominate a space simply by existing in it?

'Constantine,' she breathed, and her heart began to pound with frantic yearning. She wanted to touch him. To throw her arms around him. To whisper her fingertips wonderingly along the hard, proud line of his jaw—as if only touch alone would convince her that he was really here. 'Wh-what are you doing here?' she questioned.

It was then that she realised. Of course! He had come to see his son. Their heartbreaking farewell on the airstrip must have made him vow to come and see Alex earlier than he had intended. And even though she would have liked some warning that he was about to appear, so that she wouldn't have answered the door in a scruffy old pair of jeans and a T-shirt which had seen better days, she managed a brisk kind of smile.

Think of Alex, she told herself—he's the one who matters.

So she was able to look up at him with genuine regret. 'Oh, what a pity. Alex has just gone out.'

'I know he has.'

She looked at him blankly. 'You do?'

'Yes. I rang Sarah this morning and asked her if she would take him out for the day.'

'You rang Sarah?' she repeated. 'And she...*agreed*?'

'Yes, she did.'

Laura blinked at him in confusion. It was true that her sister no longer seemed to think that he was the devil incarnate—but agreeing to Constantine's request behind her back sounded awfully like *collusion*, and...and... Well, it threw up all kinds of questions. 'But *why*?' she whispered.

He raised his dark brows in sardonic query. 'Do you want me to tell you when I'm standing on the doorstep?'

Registering the faintly reprimanding tone of his question, she pulled the door open wider. 'No. No, of course not. Come in.' But as he passed her she had to clutch the door handle to balance herself—his very proximity was producing a terrible wave of weakness and longing which threatened to destabilise her.

He was standing in their cramped little hallway—making it look even smaller, if that were possible—and Laura shook her head uncomprehendingly. Because if he wasn't here to see Alex, then...then...

'Please tell me why you're here,' she said, her voice a whisper as thready as her erratic heartbeat.

His black gaze was calculating. 'No ideas at all, Laura?'

Numbly, she shook her head, and it was then that Constantine realised that there was no easy way to do this—or she wasn't going to make it easy for him—and maybe that was the way it should be. Maybe he too needed to experience doubt and uncertainty, as well as the fear that she might reject him again.

But words describing feelings didn't come easy when you'd spent a lifetime avoiding them—and for a moment he felt like a man who had found himself on a raft in the middle of the ocean, unsure of which direction to take. He sucked air into lungs which suddenly felt empty.

'I have thought about everything you said that last night. About love and about the past.' He saw the way she was staring at him, her pale face fierce, chewing on her bottom lip the way she always did when she was concentrating hard. 'And the impact of both those things on the present and the future.' There was a pause. 'They were things I didn't want to hear,' he whispered. 'Things I tried to block my ears to. But somehow—I couldn't do it. And when my anger had died away, I realised that you were right. That I needed to forgive my father—and in a way I needed to forgive my mother, too.'

'Constantine—'

'So that's what I've come to tell you. That I have. I have had a long talk with my father and told him…'

Momentarily his voice tailed away, and Laura lifted up her hand. 'You don't…have to tell me if you don't want to,' she whispered, seeing the pain of memory etched on his hard features and finding that it was hurting her, too.

'Oh, but that's where you're wrong. You see, I do, Laura. I need to tell you plenty of things—just as I did my father.' He sucked in another breath—because although Constantine was a brave man, opening up his heart to her like this took courage of a different kind. 'I told him that it was now time for us to be a true father and son to each other—and for him to be a grandfather to Alex.'

Laura nodded as his sudden appearance at last began to make sense. She guessed what was coming. He was going to ask her to take Alex back to Greece, to help facilitate his relationship with his father—a man too old and infirm to travel great distances. And, although it wasn't ideal, Laura knew she was going to say yes. It didn't matter if he wasn't offering her the dream ticket of love *with* marriage—she'd settle for whatever she could get. For everyone's sake. Because she'd had a chance to live the alternative—a life without Constantine—and that life was bleak. Like a vase which was permanently empty of flowers. And didn't she have more than enough love to go round—for all of them? Couldn't she perhaps show him *how* to love—with the hope that one day he might be able to give a little love back to her? Was it pathetic of her to be prepared to settle for that?

'That sounds perfect,' she agreed.

Constantine's eyes narrowed. 'Does it?' he questioned, and suddenly his voice sounded harsh. 'Not to me, it doesn't.'

And now a very real fear lanced through her. Perhaps he *wasn't* asking her to marry him at all—hadn't he already asked her twice and she'd turned him down? Would a proud man like this really ask her a third time? Why, she was probably being completely arrogant in not accepting that deep down he'd been delighted to see the back of her. 'Why not?' she breathed painfully.

He stared at her. The bare feet. The shapeless jeans—and a T-shirt which Demetra would probably have used to polish the tiles with. It was inconceivable that such a woman as Laura had captured his heart, but captured it she had—and so tightly that at this moment it was threatening to burst right out of his chest. Her physical ensnarement of him had never been in any doubt—but her purity and loyalty to him as a lover thrilled him to the very core of his being. As did her fierce determination to protect her son, and her admirable refusal to accept his offer of marriage, showing him that she was not a woman who could be bought by his colossal wealth.

'Because I have been a fool,' he declared hotly. 'I have failed to see what was right beneath my very nose—that you, Laura, are the woman who makes me laugh, who challenges me. The woman who is not afraid to tell me the truth. Who kisses more sweetly than I ever thought it possible to kiss. Who makes diamonds look dull and starlight seem mediocre.'

He drew a ragged breath, knowing that he had still not gone far enough—but admitting love for the first time in his life was hard for a man who had only ever seen warped examples of that emotion.

He stared at her, his heart pounding in his chest, aware as he looked at her that if he said it he had to mean it. *Really* mean it. And suddenly it was easy.

'You are the woman I love,' he said softly. 'I love you, Laura. I love you so much.'

'Oh, Constantine...' she breathed, scarcely able to believe what he was saying to her. But just one look at the incredible tension on his beautiful face told her that every word was true.

'But the question is do you love *me*?' he demanded.

Was he *crazy*? 'Yes—*yes*!'

'As fiercely as I do you?'

'Oh, yes!'

'Then for the third time of asking—and because I am finally running out of patience—will you please marry me, Laura?'

Her smile broke out, so wide it felt as if it would split her face in two. 'Yes! Oh, God, yes. I love you. I *love* you,

Constantine! I've loved you for so long that I don't know any other way—but, oh, I can't tell you how wonderful it is to actually be able to say it out loud!'

'Promise me you'll never stop saying it,' he declared, amazed at his own need to hear it.

'Oh, I won't—my sweet, darling Constantine.'

He pulled her into his arms, and this time he really *did* destabilise her, for her knees gave way—but Constantine was holding onto her as tightly as could be as he began to kiss her. And this kiss was different from any other they had ever shared. It was tender and healing as well as passionate, and it sealed their love properly—ending all twists and turns along the way which had brought them here to this point.

And if it was a kiss which was mingled with their tears—then didn't that somehow make it sweeter and more precious still?

EPILOGUE

THE wedding took place in Greece—with Sarah as brides-maid and Alex carrying two platinum rings on a little cushion. Knowing the sensibilities of young boys, Laura had told him that he didn't *have* to be involved in the ceremony, but Alex had insisted. He was so happy, Laura realised—blissfully contented that his mother and his father were going to be married at last.

It was a small ceremony, with a big party afterwards, and because it was held on the island it meant that the press could be kept largely in check. Unexpectedly, the message of congratulations which brought most satisfac-tion to bride and groom was sent by the supermodel formerly known as Ingrid Johansson, who was now Mrs Ingrid Rockefeller, and living in luxury in the centre of Manhattan. It read:

You did me a favour, *alskling*—I have now a man who adores me, and we were married last month.

Laura had long ago realised that Constantine had already finished with the supermodel when she had burst into his life again, but it gladdened her heart to know that the Swedish beauty was happy.

Sarah had landed herself a place at art school in London, and was planning a new life for herself there. So they'd sold their bakery shop and the flat for a very respectable sum which had gone towards buying her an apartment near her college. And Sarah—after a little persuasion—had allowed Laura and Constantine to pay off the balance of her new home.

'You've helped me for years,' Laura had told her fiercely. 'So please let me pay back something for all your time and kindness.'

It was decided that Alex would go to the school on Livinos until he was old enough to continue his studies on the mainland—just as his father had done. And, as well as taking an intensive course in Greek, Laura was planning to open a bakery on the island. Demetra had moaned about the lack of a bread shop often enough, and Laura recognised that she had a real gift for making a small business work. Two local women had been employed to help her, and if other babies came along—well, then Laura knew there were heaps of people she could call on.

But for now the shop gave her a role and a purpose on Livinos—it meant that she was more than just Constantine's new wife, and that was important to her. And, she suspected, to him. One of the reasons he had fallen in love with her—so he told her on their wedding night—was because she was so proud and independent. She was the only woman he'd ever known who hadn't coveted diamonds.

In fact, this lack of enthusiasm for fine jewels had

proved to be the only problem in the blissfully problem-free time leading up to their wedding.

'It is traditional for the groom to give his beautiful bride a gift,' he murmured, pulling her into his arms and drifting his lips against hers. 'But—since diamonds don't impress you—what on earth can I give you as a wedding present that is equally precious, *agape mou*?'

And Laura smiled, because the question was superfluous. She already had the thing she most wanted—the most precious thing on this earth. The love of a man she adored.

Constantine's love.

Androletti's Mistress

MELANIE MILBURNE

Melanie Milburne says: "I am married to a surgeon, Steve, and have two gorgeous sons, Paul and Phil. I live in Hobart, Tasmania, where I enjoy an active life as a long-distance runner and a nationally ranked top ten Master's swimmer. I also have a Master's Degree in Education, but my children totally turned me off the idea of teaching! When not running or swimming I write, and when I'm not doing all of the above I'm reading. And if someone could invent a way for me to read during a four-kilometre swim I'd be even happier!"

To my mother-in-law, Joyce, and my late
father-in-law, Alf Wilkinson. I dedicate this book
to you for the very special gift you gave me in
producing the most adorable man in the world—
your son. Thank you from the bottom
of my heart. Love you.

CHAPTER ONE

IT WAS the sort of funeral where no one shed a tear.

Nikki accepted everyone's condolences with a composed expression on her face, even though in spite of everything she still felt a sense of deep sadness as the coffin was lowered into the cold, dark soil.

'So sorry about Joseph,' one of the sales managers said as he shook her hand a few minutes later. 'But he wouldn't want to have lingered on any longer.'

'Thank you, Henry,' she said, even managing to crack a small, grateful smile. 'No, indeed he wouldn't.'

'Mrs Ferliani?' A journalist pushed through the small knot of mourners. 'Have you any comment on the successful takeover bid of Ferliani Fashions conducted by your late husband's stepson Massimo Androletti?'

Nikki felt a shockwave go through her body at the mention of that name. She'd already scanned the small congregation repeatedly, in case he'd had the audacity to appear, but so far she hadn't caught sight of him. 'No, I haven't,' she said coolly. 'Now, please leave; this is a private ceremony.'

'Is it true there is nothing left of your late husband's

estate?' the journalist persisted. 'That Massimo Androletti now owns the business and even the house you live in?'

Nikki set her mouth. 'I have no comment.'

Another reporter joined the first. 'Our sources say Joseph Ferliani lost a fortune on the stock exchange, and in an effort to recoup the losses gambled away everything he and you owned.'

'Mrs Ferliani has already told you she has no comment to make,' a deep male voice said from just behind Nikki.

She swung around to look a long way upwards into the black, diamond gaze of Massimo Androletti. She fought hard not to reveal how seeing him after all this time affected her, but Nikki was almost certain he had noticed the tiny up-and-down movement of her throat. His expression was mask-like, but there was a glint of steely purpose in his eyes that secretly terrified her. Her stomach hollowed out, her legs began to tremble and her chest felt as if something hard and thick had lodged itself halfway down, making it almost impossible to draw in the air necessary to breathe.

'Come this way,' he said, putting a hand beneath her elbow, the touch of his fingers sending a current of tingling awareness right through the thick sleeve of her winter coat.

Nikki considered resisting his attempt to lead her away, but thought better of it when she felt the subtle tightening of his hold, as if he'd already sensed her intention. As she felt his latent strength, her heart began to thump behind the wall of her chest as she thought of being alone with him.

He led her to his waiting limousine parked outside the cemetery. 'Get in,' he commanded curtly. 'We have things to discuss.'

Nikki sat on the plush leather seat, her legs pressed tightly together as he joined her, the huge car now seeming far too small with his long legs and six-foot-three frame taking up most of the available space. Even the air inside the car seemed to have been reduced; it physically hurt to take in each breath as she tried to steady her growing panic with deep, calm breaths.

'To the house, thank you, Ricardo,' Massimo said as he leaned forward to speak through the panel.

Nikki shifted even further away as he sat back in the seat, her nostrils flaring slightly as the spicy fragrance of his after-shave drifted towards her. Her stomach gave a little flutter as her eyes went to the long, hard length of his thighs within touching distance of hers. She had once felt those strong legs entwined with hers, had felt his hard male body drive into her silky moistness, his hot, commanding mouth wreak havoc on all of her senses.

'So,' he said as he swung his cold, hard gaze towards her. 'Your plans to land yourself a fortune failed in the end, did they not?'

Nikki tightened her mouth without responding to his embittered jibe. He had a right to be bitter, she had to admit. She would have felt the same, if not worse, if he had done the same to her. But explaining her actions five years down the track would be pointless. Given the choice, she would have done the same thing again in spite of all it had cost her.

'It is true what the journalist said. I now own everything,' he said into the silence, which was taut as a violin bow. 'But then I expect the lawyer has already explained that to you.'

'No,' she said, stripping the one word of any trace of emotion. 'I haven't yet met with him, but I plan to do so tomorrow.'

His dark brows rose slightly. 'I would have thought that would have been your very first priority,' he said with a cynical glint in his eyes. 'A sluttish little gold-digger like you would surely check to see what has been left to her on her husband's death?'

Nikki refused to show the despair she was feeling at his comment. Instead she elevated her chin and sent him an arctic look. 'Joseph was far more important to me than his money,' she said. 'I don't care if he's left me nothing.'

His mouth tilted into a calculating smile. 'Such wifely devotion,' he drawled. 'But then you are very good at acting when it suits you, are you not?'

She turned her head away to stare sightlessly out of the window.

'He has left you nothing,' Massimo said into the strained silence. 'Nothing except debt, that is. Even the house is now mine.'

This time it was harder not to reveal how his statement affected her. She fought to control her expression, but she could feel the tensing of her jaw regardless as she turned back to glare at him. 'I don't believe you. Joseph promised he would provide for me.'

'The way I see it, you are in a rather precarious position,' he went on evenly, although his coal-black eyes still shone with hatred. 'You have no income unless I choose to give it to you, no car, no house, and as of a week ago, no sugar daddy.'

Nikki really loathed that term. It demeaned everything she had come to admire and respect in Massimo's stepfather.

Joseph Ferliani had had his faults; he had been a hard-nosed businessman for most of his life. But for all that, she had come to know him in a way she suspected few people ever had. The long, agonising months of his terminal illness had shown a side to him that he had kept well hidden, and most particularly from his stepson and arch-enemy Massimo Androletti.

'Your stepfather was not my sugar daddy,' she said in a clipped tone as she faced his obsidian gaze head-on.

His top lip lifted in disdain. 'What was he, then?'

'He was my husband and my friend,' she answered with quiet dignity.

Something flickered in his eyes at the word 'husband', for which again Nikki couldn't really blame him. It would gall most men to think they had been replaced by someone much older and richer than they were, and Massimo was clearly no different. She could feel his blistering rage in the air that separated them; her skin felt tight and prickly, and the hairs on the back of her neck lifted one by one as his eyes clashed with hers.

'You forgot to mention he was your lover,' he pointed out with another curl of his lip. 'Or did he not come up to scratch in the bedroom?'

Nikki turned away again so he wouldn't see the way her face flamed with colour. 'I don't wish to discuss my private details with you,' she said. 'It's disrespectful, considering Joseph is not even cold in his grave, and to be quite frank it's none of your business.'

'It was my business five years ago, wasn't it, Nikki?' he reminded her. 'But little did I know then that one drink would lead to a one-night stand with my stepfather's future child bride.'

She ground her teeth together and bit out, 'I was nineteen years old, surely old enough to know my own mind?'

'You went from my bed straight to his,' he said, his dark eyes flashing with livid sparks of fury.

Nikki felt her insides twisting with anguish. 'I didn't know who you were,' she said. 'Joseph never mentioned your name to me prior to our…marriage.'

'So what are you saying?' he asked with a cynical twist to his features. 'That if you had known who I was you would not have fallen into my arms at all?'

How could she defend herself? Nikki wondered. Was there any way she could package what she had done to make it more palatable? At nineteen, she had been so very young and so heavily traumatised. She had wanted something different for herself, something so far removed from the dark, spreading stain of her childhood that she had accepted Joseph Ferliani's offer of a lucrative marriage contract without really looking into the details as closely as she should have. As the enormity of what she'd been committing herself to had begun to dawn, she had insisted on a few days to call her own before she signed away her future into his hands.

One last week of freedom.

And on the very first day of it Massimo Androletti had been the right man at the wrong time….

CHAPTER TWO

'CAN I buy you a drink?' Massimo said as she walked up to the bar the first night of her stay at the city hotel Joseph had paid for as part of their agreement.

Nikki turned her head and looked at the tall, dark, handsome man sitting with a glass of spirits half finished in front of him. He was dressed in a suit, but not just any old off-the-rack suit, one that fitted him superbly. She could tell he was taller than average by the way she had to raise her head to meet his brown, almost-black eyes as he got to his feet. She was five-foot-nine without heels, so it was a bit of a novelty to have to crane her neck for a change.

He had a thick head of curly dark hair but it was cut close to his scalp, as if he was a person who liked control. His jaw and chin were determined, if not a little forceful, and yet his smile was easy and involved his dark eyes in a totally compelling way.

'Why not?' she suddenly found herself replying. What had she got to lose? After the harrowing afternoon she'd just been through visiting her younger brother, a drink with a perfect stranger who knew nothing of her past was just what she needed. Besides, what was that quote: 'Eat, drink and be merry for tomorrow we die'?

'What would you like to drink?' he asked, leading her to one of the plush chairs in a quiet corner.

Nikki vaguely registered the hint of an Italian accent in his slightly formal use of English. How incredibly ironic, she thought. 'Champagne,' she said, and because she was feeling uncharacteristically reckless added, 'But not the cheap stuff, it gives me a headache. I want the best there is.'

'Then the best you will have,' he said, and signalled for the bar tender.

A couple of glasses later, Nikki ended up agreeing to have dinner with him, enjoying his company in a way she hadn't expected. She had been on very few dates; she hadn't been all that comfortable in the company of men other than her brother. But Massimo was charming and polite, amusing and attentive, and she couldn't help lapping it up while it lasted. But whenever the subject drifted into the territory of her background she papered over the cracks of her conscience with the parcel of lies she had constructed ever since the day her mother had died and her brother's life had been changed for ever.

'I'm a personal assistant,' she said, which at least was true. 'I'm having a week off. I thought I'd do some shopping, have some beauty treatments—you know, pamper myself a bit, that sort of thing.'

'You do not need beauty treatments,' he said, running his dark gaze over her. 'You are the most naturally beautiful woman I have ever met.'

A flicker of uncertainty momentarily flashed across her features. 'Do you really think so?' she asked in a soft, breathless whisper.

He leaned forward to take one of her hands in his, the curl of his fingers around hers sending shooting sparks of heat to her most secret place. 'Of course I think so,' he said. 'I have never met a more beautiful or desirable woman in my life.'

Nikki pulled her hand out of his to reach for her champagne glass, her stomach still flip-flopping all over the place. 'I'm sure you've met plenty of women much more attractive than me,' she said, her mouth going down at the corners.

'On the contrary, I have met very few that compare with your translucent beauty,' he said. 'Your blonde hair is like a skein of silk. Your eyes are the most amazing grey-blue and you are tall, slender and graceful. You are any man's dream.'

She looked at him searchingly. 'You don't think I'm too tall?'

He gave her a reproving look. 'You are surely not going to apologise for being tall, are you? You are doing my neck a huge favour. I do not have to bend down to hear what you are saying.'

Nikki giggled, which in itself was a novelty. She couldn't remember the last time she had found anything or anyone amusing. 'You're the first man in ages that I've looked up to,' she said, still smiling. 'It's quite a change, I can tell you.'

'Is there a current man in your life?' he asked.

Nikki hesitated for a fraction of a second. How could she tell him she was engaged to be married to a man twenty-five years older than her? A man who was offering her a passport out of the shame that had haunted and hunted her for so long.

'No,' she said, rationalising that for a week at least there was no one. She was a free agent until the following Saturday, and after that she was off the market for who knew how long.

'I find that hard to believe,' he said. 'What is wrong with all the young men in Melbourne?'

She smiled at him again, and took another sip of her champagne. 'What about you?' she asked. 'Are you currently unattached?'

'Yes,' he said on a little jagged sigh. 'I was involved with a woman in Sicily a few months back, but it did not work out.'

'Have you recently arrived from Italy?' she asked.

'I have dual citizenship,' he said. 'I travel back and forth a lot on business.'

'What sort of business?'

'I am building up an international investment portfolio. My plan is to seek ailing companies to buy and then resell them for a profit,' he said. 'With proper management teams in place, a flagging business can be turned around within a year or two, or even a few months.'

'It sounds very interesting, but rather expensive and extremely risky,' she commented.

'It is,' he agreed. 'I have a meeting later this week to hopefully organise financial backing for a company takeover I have planned for years.'

'You sound very determined,' she said, reaching for her glass and taking a little sip.

'I am.' A frown brought his dark brows together as he reached for his glass. 'The company I want to take over was launched using money defrauded from my father. He was swindled by someone he trusted as a friend. I am on a mission to get every cent of it back.'

Nikki felt a faint shiver run up her spine at the determination in his tone. His expression had darkened, his eyes losing their playfulness, and instead they had begun to glitter with hatred. 'So you're after revenge?' she asked.

He nodded grimly. 'It is all I think about. I want to take

my father's enemy down, and I will do so, even if it takes me a lifetime to achieve it.'

'How will you take him down?' she asked, her heart beginning to thud with alarm. 'You're not going to do anything…er…underhand, are you?'

He smiled at her worried expression. 'Of course I am not going to do anything illegal. I am simply going to outwit him in business. It should not be too hard. The best tactic in any sort of successful campaign is to know your enemy. I know all his weak spots, and so it will be relatively simple to disarm him when the time is right.'

'He sounds like a truly horrible person,' Nikki said, suppressing a tiny shudder. 'Is that why you're here?'

'Yes and no,' he said, his expression clouding slightly. 'I have some meetings to attend…' He appeared to give himself a mental shake and exchanged his serious expression for a smile. 'But enough about my troubles,' he went on in a lighter tone. 'Tell me about your family.'

Nikki felt her stomach drop with all-too-familiar panic. 'M-my family?'

'Yes; have you any brothers or sisters?' he asked.

She concentrated on the bubbles in her glass rather than meet his gaze. 'I have a brother two years younger than me.'

'What about your parents? Are they still married?'

'Yes,' she said, reflecting wryly that it was more or less true. Her mother had still been married to her father on the day he had taken her life and ruined Jayden's for ever.

'You are lucky to have come from such a loving and stable background,' Massimo said as he refilled the glasses. 'My parents divorced when I was sixteen.'

Lucky? Nikki almost laughed out loud. The last word she

would ever use to describe her background was 'lucky'. Each day had been a fight for survival, each night an agonising wait for disaster to unfold as soon as her father had walked through the door.

'Losing the business was bad enough, but losing my mother tipped him over.' He paused, as if searching for the words to continue, the flash of pain in his dark eyes all the more evident.

'What happened?' Nikki prompted gently.

His gaze meshed with hers. 'He took his life a few months later,' he said. 'I came out to the garage and found him unconscious. He had killed himself—the fumes had poisoned him, and he was unable to be revived.'

Nikki felt tears burn in her eyes for what he must have suffered. 'I am so sorry,' she said, reaching for his hand, her fingers curling around his. 'No wonder you are after revenge. This ghastly man took everything away from you.'

Massimo gave her another grim look. 'But I am going to get it all back, every single cent of it. I do not have the money to do it yet, but I will do it eventually. I know I will.'

'Do you know something, Massimo?' she said with an encouraging smile. 'I believe you will, too.'

He squeezed her hand. 'I have never met anyone like you before,' he said, his dark eyes melting as they held hers. 'I feel this amazing connection with you. Our backgrounds are very different, but I feel as if I have known you for a very long time—and yet we have only just met.'

Nikki felt her belly start to quiver as his long fingers stroked the underside of her wrist, the slow, sensual movement stirring her body into a whirlpool of feeling. Her breasts tightened, her nipples pressing against the lace of her bra as she held his dark-as-night gaze. 'I feel it too,' she said, her voice coming out low and husky.

A shadow of regret passed over his features. 'I am only here for a week,' he said. 'I have to go back to Italy first thing on Sunday. But, when I return, can I see you again?'

Nikki hoped he couldn't see the panic in her eyes as they came back to his. 'I'm sure you will have forgotten all about me by the time you return,' she said with a weak smile.

'No, Nikki,' he said, his fingers strong and determined around hers. 'I will *not* forget you.'

She moistened her lips with her tongue. 'I—I should have told you earlier,' she said, dropping her gaze as she hastily composed her lie. 'I don't come from Melbourne. I'm just here on a little holiday. I won't be here when you get back.'

'Where will you be?'

'Umm…Cairns.' She said the first place that came to mind.

'Then I will come and see you in Cairns,' he said. 'We can go to the Great Barrier Reef together, eh?'

'Massimo…' She forced her eyes to meet his. 'I'm not sure I'm the person you—'

'Do you believe in love at first sight?' he asked before she could finish her sentence.

A few hours ago Nikki would have answered a resounding 'no', but after spending the evening in Massimo's company she was now not so sure. She was attracted to him in a way she had never been attracted to anyone before, but it wasn't just a physical thing—although that in itself was as overwhelming as it could ever be. It was more a sense of being in the company of a man who stood up for what he believed in. His loyalty to his father's memory was truly admirable. It was so far removed from what she had experienced in her childhood she couldn't help but be impressed, and indeed incredibly moved.

She thought then what a wonderful husband and father he would make. His sense of family was so strong that no one would be hurt, while under his protection. He was quite simply the most amazing man she had ever met.

'You are taking a long time to answer.' Massimo sent her a rueful look. 'I have made a fool of myself, yes?'

'No,' she said, shivering all over again as he brought her hand up to his mouth. 'I'm not sure about love at first sight, but I definitely feel something I've never felt before.'

He pulled her to her feet, bringing her to stand in front of him. 'We have the next six days to explore and get to know each other,' he said. 'I do not want to rush you, but I cannot bear the thought of finding someone so special and wasting time in case we do not get this chance again.'

Nikki drew in a wobbly breath and did her best to smile. 'If it's meant to be, then we will get our chance,' she said as his mouth came down to hers.

CHAPTER THREE

NIKKI spent the happiest six days of her life in Massimo's company. She stalwartly refused to think about her wedding on Saturday. It was as if by not thinking about it she could really be the person Massimo believed her to be. She was a young carefree woman in love for the first time, relishing every moment of being truly adored and treated like a princess.

She knew it would have to end when the week was up, but she tried not to dwell on it too much. She comforted herself that Massimo was a man of the world. He would forget about her as soon as he boarded the plane back to Italy; his brief fling with the tall, blonde Australian girl would no doubt be a distant memory as soon as the first drink was served on the flight back home.

They explored the sights of Melbourne together, walking through the Bourke Street Mall to window shop, dining at some of the restaurants along the Southbank complex, and even spending some time at the world-famous Crown Casino where Nikki watched in awe as Massimo won a small fortune at one of the black-jack tables.

Later in the week they hired a car and visited the beautiful

Yarra Valley, notorious for its picturesque vineyards, where the rolling green hills and valleys they passed prompted Massimo to say how much it reminded him of Sicily.

'I would love to show you my homeland,' he said as they drove back after spending a wonderful afternoon at Healesville Wildlife Sanctuary. 'We do not have koalas and kangaroos and wombats, of course, but there are many wonderful historic buildings and artifacts.'

'I would love to travel the world one day,' Nikki said dreamily, looking out of the window as the verdant fields went by. 'I've only ever been to…' She stopped, her heart thumping at how close she had been to revealing how she had lied about where she had originally come from.

'You were saying?'

'Er…I've only ever lived in Australia,' she said. 'I know it's a big and diverse continent, but I haven't seen much of it really…'

He sent her a smile. 'You have no need to be ashamed, *cara*,' he said. 'You are young. You have plenty of time to see the world.'

On the last day Massimo arranged to meet her after he had his meeting in the city. As soon as she saw him walking towards her outside the art gallery, where she had spent the morning filling in time, she knew things had not gone well for him. His handsome face looked pinched and his mouth tight.

'Are you OK?' she asked, touching him on the arm.

He placed his hand over hers and gave it a tiny squeeze. 'I do not want to spoil our last afternoon and evening together talking about my business. Suffice to say things did not go according to plan.'

'I'm so sorry.'

He gave her a strained smile. 'I will just have to wait a little longer to achieve what I want, but then the best things in life are worth waiting for, no?'

'I guess…' she answered, looking down at their linked hands.

They walked past the Shrine of Remembrance through to the Botanic Gardens, stopping to have afternoon tea at the café overlooking the lake, where ducks waddled in search of crumbs and cheeky sparrows darted in amongst the chairs and tables in spite of the shooing actions of the staff.

Massimo smiled indulgently as she surreptitiously bent down to scatter some crumbs from the coconut cake he'd bought her. 'You are not supposed to encourage them,' he said, indicating the DO NOT FEED THE BIRDS sign nearby.

'I know, but I can't help feeling sorry for them,' she said, a fleeting shadow of sadness moving across her face. 'They've probably got little babies to feed.'

He reached across the table for her hand and brought it up to his mouth, kissing each fingertip in turn, his intense gaze holding hers. 'You have such a kind and tender heart,' he said in a deep, gravelly tone. 'I have waited a long time to meet someone as sensitive to the needs of others as you are.'

Nikki gently pulled her hand out of his, her whole body tingling with awareness. As each day had passed, she'd found it harder and harder to resist him. He had not pressured her to sleep with him, which surprised her. She had assumed, like many men with his jet-setting lifestyle, that he would have leaped at the chance of a one-week fling with a woman he had singled out for his attention. His kisses had been passionate and tender, enthralling and tantalising, and yet each time their mouths had touched he seemed to be keeping himself in check.

'You are feeling nervous and uncertain, *cara*?' he asked into the little silence.

'W-what do you mean?'

He reached for her hand again and began stroking the sensitive skin on the underside of her wrist in slow, sensual movements that sent a riot of sensation to her toes and back. 'I want you,' he stated bluntly. 'I have wanted you from the first moment I saw you but something about you made me realise you are not a one-night stand sort of girl. I deeply respect that about you.'

Somehow she found her voice in time to croak out, 'T-thank you.'

'I have a bit of a reputation for working hard and playing harder,' he confessed. 'I can assure you, it is highly unusual for me to have spent more than three dates with a woman before bedding her.'

Nikki swallowed.

He smiled at the twin flags of colour on her cheeks. 'You are a virgin, yes?'

Her eyes fell away from his. 'No,' she said in a small voice. 'I wish I still was. My first and only time was horrible…'

He frowned, and his hand encircling her wrist tightened protectively. 'You were…' he paused over the word '…raped?'

Her eyes came back to his, her colour still high. 'No, I just didn't realise it would be so…so one-sided, if you know what I mean.'

His fingers began their sensual magic against the satin surface of her skin. 'You did not experience pleasure, Nikki?'

'Not really.' She gave a little wry grimace and added, 'Not at all, actually.'

His eyes darkened with tenderness as he pulled her to her feet. 'We have one night left, *cara*,' he said, linking her arm through his. 'I want to make it as memorable as possible.'

Nikki had not dreamt how truly memorable it would be. They went back to the hotel hand in hand, the silence that hung between them heavy and pulsing with promise.

She felt it all through their last dinner together in the hotel restaurant. Each time his eyes caught and held hers, she sensed the sexual tension building in him. She could feel it thrumming in her own body, a deep and low pulse that begged to be assuaged.

She felt it in the lift as they silently climbed the floors to his room, each number showing above their heads like a countdown to paradise.

And she felt it in the thudding pulse in his fingers as they tilted her face to receive his kiss, the self-control he had been reining in all week finally slipping as the door of his room closed behind them.

'I should not be doing this,' he said, pressing hot kisses to the side of her neck as he lifted her hair out of the way. 'I told myself I would wait until I return from Sicily, but I want you so much I am burning inside and out with it.'

Nikki raised her face for more of his drugging kisses. 'I want you too,' she whispered against his lips. 'I want you to make love to me. I want to feel pleasure… Your pleasure as well as mine.'

He held her from him, looking deeply into her eyes. 'Are you absolutely sure, *cara*? I can wait for you. I will *make* myself wait for you if you do not feel ready to take this step.'

She pulled his mouth back down to hers. 'Don't make

me wait,' she pleaded desperately. 'I don't want to wait another minute.'

He undressed her, the slow movements of his hands belying the true state of his arousal. She felt it against her, the hard surge of his body and how he fought to control it in order to prepare her properly for his passionate possession. His mouth was on hers, and then on each of her breasts, sucking gently at first, and then harder until her back arched with intense longing.

He laid her carefully on the king-sized bed, trailing a hot blaze of kisses all over her body, her mouth, her neck, her breasts and the tiny cave of her belly button before moving lower. She totally melted under the sweep and stroke of his tongue as it separated her feminine folds, the sensation of such an intimate caress sending her pulse skyrocketing. Her body began to convulse, the earth-shattering release beyond anything she had ever imagined.

He waited until she was calm once more before reaching for a condom. She watched with wide eyes as he came back to her, taking his time again in kissing and caressing her, until she was begging him to fill her. 'Oh, please…oh please…'

'You are getting impatient, Nikki,' he said playfully, kissing her lingeringly, the sexy saltiness of her own body on his lips inciting her to grab at him greedily, her pelvis rising to meet the downward thrust of his.

Nikki heard his deep groan of pleasure as the small, tight sheath of her body grasped at him, the honeyed warmth enveloping him totally. He tried to control his thrusts to keep them slow and not too deep, but she was having none of it. She clung to him, her fingers digging into the tautness of his buttocks to keep him where she wanted him.

She felt herself begin to climb the mountain again, the pinnacle getting closer and closer with each surging movement of his body within hers.

The overwhelming power of his release surprised her, as did her own. It was like an earthquake rumbling between them, rocking them back and forth, shaking them, shattering them into a thousand tiny pieces.

She held him against her as his breathing gradually came back to normal, the skin of his back raised in tiny goose-bumps, under the soft pads of her fingertips.

He lifted himself up on his elbows to look at her, his dark eyes full of wonder. 'Do you realise what you have just done, Nikki?' he asked.

'W-what?' she asked, a shadow of uncertainty flitting across her face.

'You have made me fall in love with you,' he said. 'For ever.'

Nikki felt her throat tighten. Oh God! What had she done? This should not have happened. She should *not* have let it happen. She had no right to sleep with a man to whom she could offer nothing but a one-night stand, for that was all it could ever be.

He reached past her to take something out of the bedside drawer. 'I have something for you,' he said.

Nikki tensed as he retrieved the small package. Throughout the week he had bought her gifts—not expensive ones, which had made it easy for her to accept them, with perhaps not an entirely clear conscience, but she'd reasoned she wanted something to keep as a reminder of what she could have had if life had dealt her a different hand of cards.

She took the tiny package from him, her fingers beginning to tremble slightly as she felt the cushioning of velvet beneath the tissue wrapping. 'What is it?' she asked, her voice sounding rusty.

'Open it and see,' he said, smiling at her.

She began to undo the tiny silk ribbon, each movement of her fingers meticulously slow. The tissue fell away, and the red velvet box lay in her hand like a square of blood. She knew what was in it before she opened it, knew too that she should have handed it straight back and told him the truth, but instead she slowly lifted the lid.

A diamond solitaire ring gleamed up at her, its sheer brilliance taking her breath away.

'Put it on,' he said into the silence.

Nikki had never hated herself more than at that moment. The shame of her past was nothing to what she was experiencing now. But as if her fingers had a mind of their own they lifted the ring from its velvet home, and slid it on her ring finger where Joseph Ferliani's ring was supposed to be. But, unlike the heavy, cumbersome cluster Joseph had insisted she wear, Massimo's ring was exquisitely delicate, suiting her slim hand perfectly.

'Will you marry me, Nikki?' Massimo asked as he took her hand in his. 'I know this is terribly rushed, but I love you and want to spend the rest of my life with you.'

Nikki bit her lip in anguish, tears springing in a crystal stream from her eyes as she met his. 'I don't know what to say…' she began. 'It's been so sudden…so totally unexpected.'

He brought her closer to the warmth of his body and, holding her hand to his heart, smiled down at her. 'It looks like I will have to be patient and wait for your answer on my return,' he said. 'That will give you time to talk it over with your family. I am forgetting how very young you are. I am nine years older than you, so it is reasonable to expect you to be feeling a bit overwhelmed—especially now, after we have made love for the very first time.'

She *was* overwhelmed, but with guilt. It prodded and poked at her from every angle like a thousand pointed daggers. How could she have let things get to this stage? What had she been thinking? She should have known from the beginning that a man like Massimo Androletti would want more than a quick fling. She should have had one drink with him that first night and left, then he would not have had to suffer the pain of rejection, and she would not have known what it felt like to be truly in love, only to have to walk away because of circumstances beyond her control.

'Massimo, there's something I need to tell you…'

He bent his head to press a soft kiss to her mouth. 'No, *cara*,' he said. 'Do not give me your answer until we meet again. I am flying to Palermo on Sunday. I am sorry I cannot spend the day with you tomorrow, but I have an engagement to attend which I cannot get out of.'

'It's all right,' she said, inwardly blowing out a breath of relief. 'I have something on as well.'

He held her close, his arms strong and protective around her. 'I will miss you, Nikki. Every day we are apart I will miss you.'

'Me too,' she whispered, her heart breaking into a million pieces.

He put her from him. 'I will not say goodbye, but *vederla presto*.'

She looked up at him in puzzlement. 'What does that mean?'

'It means "see you soon",' he said, and sealed his promise with a burning kiss.

CHAPTER FOUR

NIKKI arrived at the church in her stiff-as-meringue dress, the lace itching her all over as she walked up the aisle, her bouquet feeling as heavy as her heart in her hands. She didn't recognise any of the faces, but then it wasn't as if she had a large circle of friends to invite. Ever since she'd moved from Perth with Jayden, there hadn't been time to socialise even if she had felt inclined to do so. Holding down a job in order to pay for her brother's care had taken up every bit of available time.

She just wanted this bit to be over so she could help her younger brother get the extra support he needed. Joseph had offered her a large sum of money in exchange for her hand in marriage. He had told her he needed a trophy wife, and was prepared to pay her a wage on top of the amount he'd promised for as long as she lived with him. He had assured her he was not interested in consummating the union due to his health problems, which he'd insisted no one was to know about. To all intents and purposes, their marriage was to appear normal, and Nikki had only agreed because she knew it would be worth it to see Jayden settled into Rosedale House where he would receive the twenty-four-hour care he so desperately needed.

Finally the vows were over, the register signed and the organ playing as they came out of the church to a cloud of confetti.

It was only then that Nikki saw him.

She stumbled in her tracks, her hand digging into Joseph's arm to steady herself as Massimo Androletti stepped from the crowd to stand in front of them, his black gaze glittering with a rage so intense she felt as if her skin was going to peel away layer by sensitive layer under its scorching heat.

'I would like to be introduced to your new wife,' he said, addressing Joseph in a seemingly polite tone, although the way he said the word 'wife' made it sound more like an insult.

'Nikki,' Joseph said, 'this is my stepson, Massimo Androletti, who has graced us with his presence this afternoon, after telling me for weeks he wouldn't be seen dead at any wedding of mine. Massimo, this is Nikki, my new wife.'

'Il piacere è tutto mio,' Massimo said, and with a sardonic curl of his lip translated, 'The pleasure is all mine.'

Nikki felt the heat of his fingers as he took her hand, the hint of steel in them as they brought it up to his mouth sending a tremor of terror through her body. She knew her face was every shade of red, but there was nothing she could do about it. She had never dreamed that such a fateful coincidence could occur, but, thinking back over the last week, she realised there had been a hundred clues if she had taken the time to reflect on them. But then she hadn't wanted to think about anything, but that precious time with Massimo, for she'd known it had to end.

'So you decided to come after all,' Joseph said to Massimo. 'What changed your mind?'

'I had heard you were marrying your new secretary,' Massimo said, swinging his hardened gaze to Nikki, running it up and down her body insultingly. 'But I had no idea she was so very young and beautiful.'

Joseph's arm came around Nikki's waist in a territorial manner. 'She is to be the new face of the Ferliani Fashions advertising campaign. She is delightful, is she not?'

'Exquisite,' Massimo drawled insolently. 'But then you always want the best, and do whatever you can to get it.'

Joseph gave him an imperious smile. 'Get over it, Massimo. This is one time you are not going to win. I have it all—a beautiful wife, a business that is thriving, and money to play with.'

'What a pity none of it is really yours,' Massimo ground out, his eyes flashing. 'Even your angelic-looking wife is a slut. Why don't you ask her what she was doing all last week?'

Nikki felt the colour of her shame brand her from head to foot. She wanted to sink to the ground at their feet, but a last vestige of pride made her hold her head high.

'Nikki was having a well-earned rest before the wedding,' Joseph said, but even she could see the doubt in his hazel eyes as they came to rest on her. 'Weren't you, Nikki?'

'T-that's right,' she answered, lowering her gaze slightly.

'Yes, well, she certainly spent a lot of time relaxing,' Massimo said with another venomous glance in her direction. 'But perhaps you had better ask her whose bed she was in last night.'

'I think it might be time for you to leave,' Joseph said, indicating for one of his burly staff members to come forward. 'Gino, please show Signore Androletti the way out.'

'You lying little whore,' Massimo said to Nikki as he brushed off the man's hands as if they were pieces of lint. 'I will make you pay for this. I will not rest until I have you begging for my mercy, I swear to God.'

Nikki swallowed convulsively as he stalked out of the church grounds, the tolling of the bells ringing in her ears like an omen for the future...

The car coming to a halt jolted Nikki out of the past. She felt Massimo's burning gaze still pressing against her in accusation. 'You knew who I was that first night, didn't you, Nikki? It was all a game to you, to make me appear a lovesick fool, while you were busily planning your marriage to another man—the one man I hated more than any other.'

'You are entitled to your opinion, but I can assure you it is wrong. Anyway, it was a long time ago,' she said with carefully measured calm. 'It can hardly have any relevance to here and now.'

'It has *everything* to do with here and now,' he returned with chilling determination. 'You see, Nikki, the time has come for my revenge.'

Nikki refused to allow him the satisfaction of seeing how much his words frightened her. She sat casually in her seat, one finely arched brow lifting in scorn. 'This is the twenty-first century, in case you hadn't noticed. The days of an eye for an eye, and what have you, have long gone.'

'We will see,' he said, and unfolded himself from the car. He turned to offer her a hand, but she ignored it as she too exited the vehicle on legs that were not as steady as she would have liked.

She looked up at the imposing mansion before throwing him a questioning glance. 'I take it this is your house?' she said.

'It is.' He turned to the driver. 'Ricardo, you can take the next couple of hours off. Mrs Ferliani and I have business to discuss. I will call you when I need you.'

'Right, boss.'

Nikki pulled her mouth tight as the limousine drove away. 'I have no desire to discuss anything with you,' she said. 'I have things to see to at home, in any case.'

His dark brows lifted expressively. 'Home?' he asked. 'Now, which home are you referring to, I wonder?'

She ground her teeth. 'Even if what you say is true, that the house is now yours, by law I don't have to move out without notice.'

'On the contrary, as the new owner I can evict you at a moment's notice,' he said. 'You have already been living there for several months rent-free—or did your husband not inform you of that?'

Nikki swallowed against the solid lump of dread in her throat. 'What are you talking about?' she asked, her heart stumbling in her chest.

He gave her a cool smile. 'Your husband approached me for financial help in the months before he died. He begged me to dig him out of trouble—but of course I refused.'

'You unfeeling bastard,' she bit out. 'How could you twist the knife like that in a dying man?'

'As you know, I had a score to settle,' he said. 'He took it very well, all things considered. He handed me everything— the house, the cars, the business, and…' He paused deliberately, his gaze locking meaningfully with hers.

Don't ask, Nikki told herself firmly. *You already know the answer, so what would be the point?*

'You do not want to know what else your husband put up for purchase?' he asked.

She met his sardonic gaze with a flare of resentment in hers.

'If by any chance you are presuming to lump *me* in with the goods and chattels, then forget it—I am *not* for sale.'

His smile didn't quite reach his eyes as he came to stand right in front of her. 'He paid you to marry him,' he said. 'He even told me how much. You put quite a high price on yourself, did you not?'

Nikki ran her tongue over her dry lips as his eyes burned into hers. She refused to answer out of a mixture of pride and anger. Let him think what he liked. What did it matter now? Joseph was dead, and if what Massimo had said was true she was going to have to find a way to scrape what she could together to keep Jayden in care. She'd been down on her luck before and pulled herself out of it. It would be hard, but she'd damn well do it for her brother's sake.

'Of course, I will be very generous in my payment for your services,' he said. 'Very generous, indeed.'

She clenched her fists at her sides, her chest heaving against the tide of anger raging within her. 'I am *not* going to sleep with you,' she said. 'Not for any price.'

The look he gave her was full of icy disdain. 'You are very convincing, but I know what you are up to, Nikki. You are used to a high standard of living. You want to make sure it continues, do you not?'

Nikki felt as if her heart was being crushed between two solid bookends. 'Joseph would not have left me with nothing,' she said again, dearly hoping it was true. 'He told me I would be left well-provided for on his death.'

'I already told you, Nikki. Were you not listening? He left you with nothing. Nothing but debts that will take you years to clear, but fortunately for you I have come up with a plan to help you offload them more or less immediately.'

Nikki moistened her lips again, panic beating like a primitive tribal drum inside her chest. 'What p-plan would that be?' she asked, wishing her voice didn't sound so thin and scared.

He gave her one of his inscrutable looks. 'I want you to be my mistress of convenience.'

She frowned as she tried to make sense of his statement. 'I'm afraid you'll have to explain what you mean,' she said after a heart-chugging pause. 'I'm unfamiliar with the term.'

'I have recently ended a relationship,' he informed her in a dispassionate tone. 'The woman I was involved with is not finding it easy to let go. I have always found the best way to deal with such stubbornness is to have physical evidence that I have now moved on with my life.'

'I'm still not sure what it is you want me to do,' she said guardedly.

'You are being deliberately obtuse, are you not?' he asked. 'I want you to do everything for me that you did for my step-father.'

Nikki couldn't imagine Joseph revealing the unconsummated nature of their relationship, and wondered if he had told Massimo a mountain of lies instead in an effort to maintain his sense of male pride.

Massimo waved a hand towards the mansion behind him. 'You see this house?' he asked.

She looked past his shoulder at the huge, two-storey mock-Georgian building before bringing her gaze back to his. 'Yes…'

'I want you to move in with me.'

Her eyes widened. 'I'm afraid that's out of the question,' she said. 'I can't possibly live with you.'

He gave her an ironic glance. 'You find the position I am offering beneath you?'

She narrowed her eyes at him. 'What's this about, Massimo? Some petty payback scheme to make me regret our stupid little fling five years ago?'

'I need a trophy mistress,' he said. 'You need a job—it is as simple as that.'

Nikki felt her stomach lurch sideways in alarm. 'I already have a job, if you remember,' she said, moistening her bone-dry lips again. 'I am still the face of Ferliani Fashions. I only took off the last six months to nurse Joseph.'

His eyes were unreadable as they held hers. 'As the new owner and CEO of Ferliani Fashions, I have decided not to renew your contract,' he said. 'I have other plans for you.'

She gave him a fiery glare. 'What do you want me to do, scrub your floors and fold your socks?'

'That, and a whole lot more.'

Her eyes narrowed into wary slits. 'How much more?'

'I have a busy life,' he said. 'I do not have time to cook proper meals or maintain an immaculate house. Joseph told me what a wonderful wife you were in that respect. He told me how you refused to have a housekeeper—that you preferred to do it yourself. I need someone running things here twenty-four-seven. I am willing to pay you generously for each month the arrangement continues.' He named a sum that sent her brows winging upwards, and added, 'It is twice what you were earning from the Ferliani contract.'

'There are hundreds of women who would give anything to have this job,' she said. 'But I'm not interested.'

'Ah, but you have no choice, Nikki,' he said. 'For if you do not agree you will have to pay back every cent of the money your husband borrowed from me in your name a month before he died. Your signature is on the documents.'

Nikki stared at him, cold fear trickling into every one of her veins like a flow of ice. She vaguely remembered Joseph pushing some papers under her nose, mumbling something about advertising expenses. It had been an astonishing amount of money, she recalled with another quake of apprehension. But she had signed her name and felt grateful that he was taking care of the business side of things while he still could, never realising it would lead to this.

'You've been planning this for months, haven't you?' she bit out caustically. 'You've been watching and waiting like a vulture circling overhead for your stepfather to die.'

'I told you five years ago when we met that I would have my revenge on what he did. He stole my father's money and launched the Ferliani label using it,' he said. 'But I must say my motivation increased even more after our brief assignation. There's a certain irony in it, don't you think? We have come full circle. You are the face of Ferliani Fashions only because my stepfather gave you the leg up you needed, but I now own the company. You do not have a future without me. You need me, Nikki, whether you like it or not. You need me.'

Her grey-blue eyes glittered with sparks of fury. 'You're asking for my degradation, that's what you're doing.'

He gave her a cool, composed smile in return. 'I am not *asking* anything of you, Nikki. I am *telling* you what is going to happen.'

'And I am telling you to go to hell!' she said and, spinning on her heels, began to stalk down the long crushed-limestone driveway.

'If you take even one step outside that gate, I will activate legal proceedings immediately to recoup the money you owe me—every last cent of it,' Massimo said in an indomitable tone.

Nikki's right foot hovered over the boundary line as she thought about her choices. There was so much she didn't know. Joseph's business affairs had always seemed to her to be a little on the complicated side. He'd had money coming in from various local and international investors to float the label, and, while she had been quite content to leave him to it, so she could do her part in fulfilling the modelling contract, she'd known it was quite possible debts had mounted up over the months before he'd finally succumbed to the cancer that he'd been valiantly fighting ever since she'd met him.

The modelling meant nothing to her; it had always been a means to an end. She had hidden behind it, enjoying the benefits of financial security in order to rise above her impoverished background. No one knew that the glamorous Nikki Ferliani was actually Nicola Jenkins, the eldest child of Kaylene and Frank Jenkins, brought up surrounded by poverty, violence and crime. And certainly no one knew her father was serving a life sentence for murder, with 'never to be released' stamped on his file.

Not even Joseph had known about that.

And then there was Jayden.

He was happy at Rosedale House, or at least as happy as someone with permanent and severe physical and mental disabilities could be. The level of care he received there was the best that money could buy. If she had to move him away from the dedicated staff who had grown so fond of him, she would never be able to forgive herself. After all, wasn't it her fault he had been injured in the first place?

She slowly turned around, her expression stripped of all

emotion as she faced her nemesis. 'I need some time to think about this.'

'You have the next ten seconds,' he said, lifting his wrist to look at his watch, and began to count them. 'Nine, eight, seven six, five—'

'All right,' she said, her stomach somersaulting in dread at what was ahead. 'I will be your…er…trophy mistress.'

His eyes came back to hers, his inbuilt cynicism glinting in their smoky depths. 'I knew you would see sense. You are far too mercenary to throw away a fortune such as this.'

She ran her tongue over the desert dryness of her lips. 'When do you want me to…to start?'

He reached into the pocket of his trousers and brought out a set of keys. He walked to where she was standing, took her clenched fist and, unpeeling her stiff fingers, placed the keys in her palm. 'You started five minutes ago,' he said.

Nikki closed her fingers around the cold metal of the keys, wincing as they bit into the soft flesh of her palm.

Now, there's another irony, she thought as she followed him a moment later into the Toorak mansion. Within her very own hand lay the keys to her new prison…

CHAPTER FIVE

IT WAS a stunningly beautiful house. It was decorated throughout in subtle tones of cream and taupe and white, offset
superbly by the black wrought-iron of the balustrade on the
magnificent staircase leading to the upper floor. The marbled
floor of the elegant foyer led into ankle-deep caramel-brown
carpet in the living areas, the large windows offering wonderful views of the lush and very private gardens outside.

It was a house built for entertaining and pleasure, every
room ideally appointed for large numbers with maximum
comfort.

The furniture as well as the artworks on the walls spoke
of unlimited wealth and dignified taste. It was nothing like
the ostentatious layout Joseph had insisted on in his house in
South Yarra, and certainly nothing like the variety of run-
down trailer parks where Nikki had spent most of her childhood.

'I have taken the liberty of organising someone to collect
your belongings from your previous residence.' Massimo's deep
voice broke the silence. 'They will be delivered here tomorrow.
All you will need to do is pack your personal things. They will
do the rest.'

Nikki turned to look at him. 'Aren't you rushing things a bit?' she asked. 'I have been a widow only a week, now I am supposedly your mistress. What will people think?'

He gave an indifferent shrug. 'I do not care for what people think. This is between you and me. The press will no doubt begin to speculate, which brings me to the issue of what we will tell other people.'

'How about the truth?' she said with an arch look. 'That you are blackmailing me for revenge.'

His dark eyes glinted warningly as they held hers. 'It would be in your interests to refrain from revealing the real motivations behind our relationship—both your own and mine.'

'I'm not going to pretend to be in love with you,' she said with a resentful scowl.

He gave her a cynical smile. 'That would indeed be a rather tall order, eh, Nikki? Although you did it quite convincingly in the past, I seem to recall.'

'You're never going to let it go, are you?' she asked with a flash of ire in her grey-blue eyes. 'Your stupid male pride got dented, and now five years later you're still harping on about it.'

He came up close and took her chin between his finger and thumb, his eyes blazing with hatred as he ground out savagely, 'I told you the day you married my stepfather that one day I would have you begging for my mercy. Do not tempt me to make it *this* day, the very day you buried him.'

Nikki swallowed back her fear, her heart chugging like an old engine going uphill. 'L-let me go,' she croaked.

His fingers tightened momentarily, the fire of his gaze raking her face for endless seconds, before he dropped his hand and stepped back from her.

Nikki felt her breath leave her chest in a ragged whoosh, her chin still tingling where his fingers had lain. She wanted to reach up and touch her skin, but knew it would give away her vulnerability, so she clenched her hands into hard little fists by her sides.

'I will send a car for you at 10 a.m. tomorrow,' he said. 'The house you have been living in is going to be redecorated and sold.'

'Removing every last trace of him, are you?' she sniped at him bitterly. 'Isn't that a bit melodramatic even for someone as stuck in the Middle Ages as you?'

Twin spots of white-tipped anger were visible at both sides of his tightened mouth. 'You will have to learn to curb that tongue of yours, Nikki. You might have wound my stepfather around your little finger, but you will not achieve the same success with me. I expect you to be polite and charming at all times, most particularly when we are entertaining guests. I have important clients, corporate investors, who will expect you to be the perfect hostess.'

'So you're expecting me to cook for you, are you?'

'My stepfather informed me of your many talents, both in and out of the kitchen,' he said with another searing look over her heaving form. 'I am sure you will be able to handle the challenge of rustling up a few ingredients from time to time.'

'I'm surprised you haven't made me audition for the part,' she said. 'How do you know Joseph wasn't lying about my capabilities?'

His eyes were steady on hers. 'My stepfather was an inveterate liar and a cheat, but the one thing he had no reason to lie about was his relationship with you. He made no secret of how you gave him pleasure, catering to his every physical need in spite of the difference in your age.'

Nikki felt ill at what he was implying. Surely Joseph hadn't taken things to that extreme in a last-ditch attempt to maintain his male pride?

'I will leave you for a few minutes to wander around the house, to get acquainted with its layout.' Massimo filled the silence. 'You can choose any room you like, but it might be preferable to keep it well away from mine.'

'Why?' she asked with a deliberately taunting look. 'Are you worried you might be tempted to go back on your promise?'

His gaze ran over her indolently. 'No,' he said. 'I am not. For, if you recall, I did not promise anything of that nature.'

Nikki felt her face suffuse with red-hot heat as the significance of his statement began to sink in. 'You're surely not expecting me to sleep with you, are you? You said I was to be a trophy mistress.'

His expression was difficult to read. 'And that is what you will be, unless one or both of us changes our mind.'

She turned away, pretending an avid interest in the view from the window overlooking the garden, her head pounding with uncertainty and fear.

He had control of everything.

How could she have not anticipated this? She had seen the hatred in his look five years ago but had foolishly deluded herself into thinking he would get over it.

He had not done so.

'You…you have a lovely garden,' she said, for the want of something to fill the uncomfortable silence.

'You are at liberty to enjoy it at your leisure,' he said. 'I do not expect you to slave your fingers to the bone.'

She turned back to face him, cynicism sharpening her features. 'So I won't be chained to the house?' she asked.

'Not at all. You can come and go as you please, but there are some ground rules.'

She folded her arms across her chest. 'Which are?'

'No men.'

She twisted her mouth at him. 'Please allow me some measure of decency. In case you have forgotten, I have just buried my husband.'

'Good, for I will not tolerate you entertaining any of your lovers in my house.'

She straightened her spine and glared at him. 'Anything else?' she asked.

'Yes,' he said. 'I expect you to be polite at all times to the young woman who will be replacing you as the face of Ferliani Fashions—Abriana Cavello. She may on occasion come to the house. I will try to keep such visits to a minimum, but if she should be here, I will expect you to treat her just like any other guest.'

Nikki felt her anger towards him skyrocket. She knew how this was going to work; she could feel it in her bones. No doubt this Cavello woman had slept with him to gain his favour and was now going to flounce around the house, acting like a prima donna just to needle her into breaking one of his stupid rules.

'That shouldn't be a problem,' she said, grinding her teeth. 'I am sure we will get along just fine.'

'That will be all for now,' he said, turning away to leaf through some papers he'd picked up from the hall table. 'I will be in my study when you have finished looking over the house.'

'And then?'

He put the papers to one side and met her arched-brow look. 'And then, Nikki, we will have dinner together.'

'Dinner?'

He smiled wryly at her anxious expression. 'Do not worry. I do not expect you to cook tonight. We will go out this evening.'

'Thank you for being so considerate,' she said with heavy sarcasm. 'But if it's all the same to you, I would prefer to go straight home.'

His black-diamond stare clashed with hers. 'You no longer *have* a home, and if I say we will have dinner together then that is what we will do, do you understand?'

Nikki felt like she was standing in front of a stranger. Gone was the gentle and loving Massimo Androletti of five years ago, and in his place was a hard, cold, determined man intent on exacting every gram of revenge he could.

She hated having to bow to his command, but there was nothing else she could do short of telling him about her reasons for marrying his stepfather. But it wasn't just her pride that wouldn't allow her to do it. If she told him who she really was—the daughter of a man who had committed the most heinous of crimes—how could she be sure it wouldn't be all over the papers within hours? Massimo was after revenge, and what better revenge could he have than to bring her past to light?

She drew in a breath, the air feeling like acid as it expanded her lungs. 'It seems I have no say in the matter. You are now the boss.'

'In every sense of the word,' he said. 'You will answer to no one but me until such time that I feel your debt is cleared.'

'How long are you planning this façade of a relationship to last?' she asked.

'It will last as long as I say. Considering what happened between us the last time, I think you owe me that privilege, don't you?'

'In my opinion, I don't owe you a thing,' she said. 'Or I wouldn't if you hadn't exploited Joseph's illness the way you did.'

'Do not speak to me of that man,' he bit out furiously. 'Once we are living together tomorrow you are forbidden to mention his name in my company. Do you understand?'

Nikki held his glittering glare with wavering courage. 'You might be able to stop me saying his name, but you can't stop me from thinking about him,' she said.

Her words angered him more than she had anticipated. She saw the flash of fury come and go in his eyes as they clashed with hers, and her stomach gave a little shudder of trepidation. She had underestimated him all those years ago. She had thought his generous and loving nature would recover quickly from her rejection, but instead it had created something she wasn't sure she could handle.

He came back to stand in front of her, his hand beneath her chin this time like a burning brand. 'Then I will have to find a way to make you stop thinking about him, won't I, Nikki?'

Her eyes went to his mouth, the hard, embittered line of it sending her stomach into another nosedive of panic. If he should kiss her, he would know how terribly vulnerable she was towards him. He would assume she was exchanging one

rich man for another, never once realising she had only ever
loved him.

His thumb traced a sensuous pathway across the cush-
ioned bow of her bottom lip, back and forth, in a careless
movement that stirred her longing for him like a long-handled
spoon in her belly. She held her breath, mentally preparing
herself for the descent of his mouth, when he stepped away
from her without warning.

'I will be in my study if you should need me,' he said. 'I
will have Ricardo pick us up in half an hour.'

She watched him leave the room, disappointment deflating her chest along with the almost inaudible sound of her
rough-edged sigh.

After she'd given the house a quick once-over, Nikki chose
the smallest bedroom five doors down from what she presumed to be Massimo's. She had poked her head in, seen the
huge bed and *en suite* leading off it, and had quickly surmised
it was his domain. She could even smell him in the air, the
clean male scent combined with his signature aftershave, the
citrus and sandalwood aftershave she had still been able to
smell on her skin the day she had married Joseph Ferliani.

She shut the door firmly and moved on, determined to
separate herself from the tempting lure of the past. She didn't
want to think about how it had felt that one precious time to
have her body pinned beneath the hard, surging pressure of
Massimo's. She didn't want to be reminded of how he had
trailed hot kisses down her body, from her peaking breasts to
her quivering thighs, his lips and tongue wreaking havoc on
all of her senses. She didn't want to remember the arch of her
spine as his body had taken her to paradise, the aftershocks

of pleasure triggering his own release as he'd spilled himself into her silky warmth.

She didn't want to remember how she had sobbed in the loneliness of her bed for months after her marriage to Joseph, her heart breaking for what she had lost.

Massimo stared sightlessly at the documents in front of him. They represented everything he had worked so hard for, but somehow he felt as if something was missing. It was an empty victory when the one prize he had longed for had already been snapped up by someone else. He had seen the sadness in Nikki's grey-blue eyes as his stepfather's coffin had been lowered into the ground.

He hadn't been expecting that.

He had her marked as a gold-digger; why else had she married Joseph Ferliani after spending such a phenomenally sensuous night with *him* all those years ago? Quite obviously she had cold-heartedly calculated the bigger returns. He had told her repeatedly over that week that he was still building his business. She had done the sums and come up with Joseph as the one to back with her body and her misleadingly sultry smile.

He clenched his fists where they lay on the desk. She would pay for it. She would pay for it every moment she spent in his house.

Of that he would make sure.

Nikki sat silently beside Massimo as his driver took them to the city, her heart beginning to thud a little unevenly when she realised where they were heading. She stiffened in her seat when the hotel where they had spent that glorious week together came into view. She hadn't been able to bring herself back in all the time she had been married to Joseph. She had come close once or twice, but had never been able to put herself through it, knowing that as soon as she walked in those doors, her longing for what might have been would overwhelm her all over again.

She clutched her bag to her chest as the car came to a halt. 'I'm not getting out,' she said.

'You have the choice of getting out of the car under your own volition, or being subjected to me carrying you into the hotel restaurant,' Massimo informed her in a tone that was undergirded by steel. 'Which is it to be?'

Nikki threw him a blistering glare. 'You're doing this deliberately, aren't you? All of this is part of your stupid revenge-plot.'

'For tonight we are two people having dinner together,' he returned. 'There is no other agenda.'

'With you there is always an agenda,' she said, scowling at him furiously. 'There are thousands of restaurants in Melbourne—why did it have to be this one?'

'It is a nice restaurant, and the view over the city is superb.'

'You brought me here to rub salt in the wound,' she said. 'You knew it would upset me.'

'I do not see why it should upset you, Nikki,' he said. 'After all, it is not as if *I* married someone else the day after we last dined here. That was you—remember?'

Nikki wasn't sure it would be wise to answer. She had already given too much away as it was. She should have feigned indifference, played it cool and composed, instead of emotionally fragile.

The trouble was it wasn't possible for her to be cool and

composed around Massimo, not while she still harboured feelings for him. Her love for him had never gone away; she'd wondered many times over the last five years if it ever would. Even in the face of his hatred she still felt the steady, strong pulse of her love for him beating inside her.

The uniformed man held the door open for her, and, taking a shaky breath, she exited the car, and with Massimo's hand at her elbow she reluctantly allowed herself to be led inside.

The hotel had undergone considerable refurbishment in the time since they'd last been there, but Nikki still felt the press of memories coming towards her from every corner of the foyer and lounge-bar area.

She had sat in that quiet area near the windows, listening intently to Massimo's plans for the future, had smiled at his jokes, held his hand, shared his cocktails and dreamed of a magical life where she could have it all.

'I thought before dinner we would have a drink in the bar for old times' sake.' His voice intruded on her reverie.

Nikki knew it would be pointless refusing, so forced her legs to carry her to the plush sofas a short distance from the white grand-piano. She sat down and looked at the drinks menu, hardly able to read a word for the sudden blur of tears.

Massimo took the sofa opposite and frowned as he saw the play of emotions on her face, wondering if he had rushed things. She had only hours ago buried her husband. Yes, she had married Joseph Ferliani for money and a lucrative modelling contract, but it was still possible she had developed some feelings for him over the last five years.

But then, he quickly reminded himself, no doubt losing everything she had worked so hard to gain was inducement enough to break down emotionally. He had seen the same crocodile-tears in his mother's eyes when her financial supply had finally dried up. He had learned to ignore such emotional displays, and this time would be no different. Nikki Ferliani was after money and position, for why else had she married his stepfather and stayed married to him for five years?

He watched as she put the menu down, her trembling hand reaching for her purse. She took out a scrunched-up tissue and wiped her eyes before stuffing it back inside and snapping the catch closed.

'You are upset.'

Nikki met his eyes with an ironic look. 'You sound surprised,' she said.

'It has been a hard day for you,' he conceded. 'I have perhaps underestimated just how hard.'

Her expression turned sour. 'Don't try and be nice to me, Massimo, it doesn't suit you any more.'

'If I am not nice it is your fault,' he said in a clipped tone. 'What you did to me was unforgiveable, so do not complain if I do not treat you the way I used to. I am not so naïve and stupid these days.'

'We met at the wrong time,' she said, lowering her gaze from the searing scorn of his.

'I disagree,' he said. 'We met at exactly the right time. I found out before it was too late the lengths some women will go to in order to get themselves a meal ticket. You rejected me and married a man two-and-a-half times your age to land yourself a fortune—a fortune I have great pleasure in reminding you that you no longer possess.'

Nikki's hands tightened on the purse in her lap as she brought her eyes back to his. 'You shouldn't have destroyed him,' she said, with bitterness sharpening every word to a dagger point. 'You shouldn't have humiliated him when he had already suffered for so long.'

A tiny nerve flickered at the side of his mouth. 'You are telling *me* what I should have done or not done?' he asked.

She lifted her chin, her eyes glittering at him rebelliously. 'Yes, I am. You could have bought the business from him at a reduced price instead of rubbing his nose in it the way you did.'

His eyes flashed with sparks of anger. 'I did no less than he did to my father.'

'That's not the point,' she argued. 'What good did it do to go after him? What victory is there in destroying a man who was already dying?'

'It was a matter of honour,' he said through clenched teeth.

'What a pity your modus operandi wasn't always honourable,' she tossed back.

His lip curled. 'You sound as if you really cared about him,' he said.

'Yes…' She caught at her bottom lip for a moment. 'Yes, I did.'

'But you still married him for money, did you not?'

The silence left hanging after his question began to drum in Nikki's ears.

'I married him because I had to,' she said after a long pause.

A small frown appeared between his brows. 'Had to?' he asked, leaning forward slightly. 'What do you mean by that?'

Nikki was momentarily caught off guard. 'Um…I…'

'Did he force you?'

It would have been so easy to tell him the truth, she thought.

But in the long months of nursing Joseph through his terminal illness she had learned much of what had made him act so ruthlessly back then. His childhood had its similarities to hers; the loneliness, rejection and guilt he'd spoken about in his last days of life had stirred her very deeply. To talk of such delicate things with his enemy stepson would seem like a betrayal to her of the tentative trust and companionship that had developed between them. Joseph had been a damaged man, but a good one for all that.

'No,' she said after a tense little pause. 'No, he didn't force me.'

'So you married him because you wanted to do so.'

'Yes,' she said, forcing her eyes to hold his. 'I married him because it was what I wanted to do at the time.'

His dark gaze pinned hers determinedly. 'But you did not love him, or at least not then?'

She let a tiny breath escape from between her lips. 'No…'

Another pulsing silence thickened the air between them.

'Why did you not tell me the first night we met that you were engaged to be married the following weekend?' he asked.

She couldn't hold his penetrating look, and stared down at the clasp on her purse. 'I'm not sure…I thought about it several times, but I wanted to forget and be someone else that night.' She dragged her eyes back to his. 'You didn't meet me that night, or indeed for any part of that week, Massimo. Or at least not the real me.'

'Who is the "real you"?'

How could she tell him who she was? How could she confess to such shame? What would he think, to hear of how as a young child she had rummaged through garbage bins in an effort to find something for Jayden and herself to eat when their mother hadn't been able to cope or had lain injured from yet another beating? Or that from the age of eight she'd had to fight off the inappropriate attentions of her father, lying awake in terror most nights, cuddling Jayden close to her in case her father turned his attention to him instead?

And how would he react to find out the terrible truth about why her brother could no longer feed or toilet himself, his body shattered and slumped in a wheelchair, his once-brilliant mind vacant?

Nikki looked away without answering, her eyes stinging with the acid rain of regret and guilt.

'Who is the woman sitting opposite me now?' Massimo asked. 'Is she the social climbing gold-digger or the girl with the golden heart?'

'What if I am both?' she asked, a fleeting shadow of sadness in her eyes as they returned to his. 'What if I am one and the same?'

The drinks waiter appeared at that moment to take their order, giving Massimo time to reflect on her answer. She was a complicated person; he could see that now. She had depths and layers he had not really noticed in that first week of heady passion. But he was determined to uncover each and every one of them now.

He had waited so long for revenge. He had thought of nothing for five long years. Each punishing day working at building his investment empire had been for this chance to turn the tables on her.

He had been ruthless in his pursuit of wealth and power. His anger towards his stepfather had become almost insignificant as he had planned his revenge on her.

Nikki Ferliani had a reputation for being cool and composed; her ice-maiden looks suggested to him she had nothing but a heart of stone beneath that hot, tempting body.

He was not going to be lured in by her innocent act all over again.

This time he would have her where he wanted her, where he had dreamed of having her for the last five years.

In his bed.

CHAPTER SIX

'MR ANDROLETTI, the table you requested is ready now,' the waiter informed Massimo a short time later.

'Thank you,' Massimo said, and, offering a hand to Nikki, helped her to her feet.

Nikki felt her fingers tingle from the contact with his, but when she tried to remove her hand, his hold tightened.

He looked down at the heavy rings on her wedding finger, his brows coming together over his eyes as he turned the cluster of diamonds to catch the light. His eyes came back to hers, his expression like curtains drawn across a stage. 'Did you enjoy being married to him, Nikki?' he asked.

Nikki hesitated over her answer. It seemed she was caught either way. A 'yes' would incite his anger, but a 'no' would probably provoke him to wonder why she had endured an unhappy marriage, no doubt assuming she had done so in order to maintain her glamorous lifestyle.

'Like any marriage it had its good and bad moments,' she said, trying to remove her hand without success.

'Did he treat you well, Nikki?'

She disguised a small swallow. 'Yes…yes, he did,' she said, lowering her eyes to where their hands were linked.

She felt a tremor of desire brush over the base of her belly
as she saw the way his tanned skin contrasted with her creamy
smoothness. He had large, square hands with long, slightly
blunt fingers, the nails neatly maintained, the dusting of masculine hair making her aware of her femininity in a way she
hadn't been in years.

He released her hand and led her by the elbow to their
table, where five years ago he had looked at her with desire
burning in his eyes.

Nikki sat down and hoped he couldn't see how distressed
she was. It was too much. Why had he done this? Surely it
was taking revenge too far? So many young people fell in and
out of love and moved on with their lives. Why couldn't he?
What good was this going to do? It wasn't going to change
anything. She had married another man for reasons he would
probably never understand. How could anyone understand,
unless they had carried the burden of shame as long as she
had carried it?

A vision of her young brother's face came to mind and her
heart tightened painfully. Jayden was always going to be her
top priority. It was the only way she could deal with the
tragedy of the past. If she had to go through hell and high
water, she would do it.

It was the price she had to pay.

Massimo waited until the waiter had left with their order
before he asked, 'Do you still have the ring I gave you?'

Nikki looked at him in confusion. 'I gave it back to you. I
left a message with the concierge on duty that there was a
package for you to collect. Didn't you receive it?'

His eyes hardened with suspicion. 'No, I did not.'

She chewed at her lower lip, her eyes now downcast.

'I'm sorry you didn't get it back. Someone must have stolen it.'

'I think we both know who that someone was.'

Her head came back up at that, her grey-blue eyes wide with appeal. 'I didn't take it, Massimo. Surely you don't think I would do something like that?'

'You stole my heart,' he said with an embittered look. 'Why shouldn't you steal a ring worth a small fortune as well?'

Nikki felt totally crushed by his cynicism, and yet she knew if the ring hadn't been returned to him he had every right to assume she had taken it. 'I wish we had never met that night,' she said on the tail end of a despondent sigh. 'I wish I had never gone into that bar and gone straight upstairs instead.'

'Why did you?'

Nikki compressed her lips as she thought about it. She had spent the afternoon with her brother in the hospice where he had been placed once she'd no longer been able to manage him at home by herself. The nurses had been incredibly caring and attentive but terribly overworked. They'd done the best they could do, but Jayden needed one-on-one care and instant access to a doctor on twenty-four-hour call. That sort of care came at an astronomical cost that few families could afford for their loved ones.

'I'm taking you out of here soon,' she'd promised him as she'd stroked some warmth into his thin, cold hands. 'I'm going to do everything in my power to make sure you get the best help there is.'

One of the nurses had walked past with a bundle of bedding and gave Nikki a tired smile. 'I hear you've organised a place at Rosedale House for him,' she said. 'That will cost you a pretty penny.'

'Yes,' Nikki said, still holding on to her brother's hand.

The nurse had looked at Jayden and shaken her head. 'It's a tragedy what these young folk do to themselves in fast cars,' she'd said. 'We've got a new admission coming in this afternoon. Motorcycle accident. He's in a similar condition to your brother. There's no way of managing him at home. You can't help feeling sorry for the parents—all that potential gone to waste.'

'Yes,' Nikki had said, feeling another arrow of guilt pierce her heart.

'Well, good luck, then,' the nurse said as she'd moved on.

'Thank you,' Nikki said, and with a sigh had turned back to her brother.

Massimo looked at the bowed figure across the table and frowned. 'You didn't answer my question,' he said. 'Why did you go to the bar?'

She lifted her gaze to meet his. 'I didn't want to be alone that night.'

Something shifted in his chest as he saw the way her small white teeth captured her bottom lip, the slight tremble of her chin making her appear as vulnerable as a small child.

He was annoyed with himself for being affected by her after all this time. It wasn't supposed to happen this way. He was the one in control now. He was the one who was calling the tune for her to dance to, not the other way around. For all he knew, this could be another act of hers to gain sympathy. After all, she was now destitute with a mountain of debts banked up behind her. She was no doubt looking for a way to dig herself permanently out of the mess, by getting him to offer to marry her. But he was not going to be played for a lovesick fool again.

'What would you like for the next course?' He diverted the conversation to less treacherous ground. 'The menu has changed from when we last dined here, of course.'

'I'm surprised you didn't talk the chef into recreating it,' she said with an edge of bitterness sharpening her tone.

'Perhaps I should have done. Although I do not think I would be able to remember what we ate that night.'

'I can,' Nikki said, before she'd stopped to think about what she was actually revealing.

'Oh really?' His brows rose in speculation. 'You have that good a memory?'

A frown pulled at her smooth forehead as she looked away from him. 'For some things, I guess…' she said.

Massimo watched as she toyed with the edge of the tablecloth with her fingers, the movements suggesting an inner restlessness he found faintly intriguing. He would have to be careful around her, he decided. That hint of fragility about her was all an act. She was after security and was prepared to do anything to get it. She had pretended to be outraged at his suggestion that they share his bed, but he had seen the looks she had given him when she hadn't thought he was watching. She had hungry eyes, and not just for money. His groin tightened as he thought about her panting beneath him the way she had that one night in the past.

He gripped the stem of his glass as he thought about her doing the same with his stepfather, her slender body bucking beneath the sweating, overweight bulk of a man who had indulged his every appetite to the extreme.

His gut shuddered, and he shook with nausea. How could she have sold herself in such a despicable way?

He pushed his glass aside before he was tempted to smash it against the nearest wall. 'You and Joseph did not have children,' he said in a tone that belied the true state of his feelings.

Her eyes met his briefly. 'No…'

'His choice or yours?'

Nikki wondered what he would say if she told him she had never once slept with Joseph Ferliani. That had been her condition on agreeing to the marriage, and she had been grateful he had accepted it, and had never once gone back on his word.

'The chemotherapy he had a few months before we married made him infertile,' she said, which was also true. 'It was a great sadness to him that he hadn't been able to have a child.'

'And what about you?' he asked after another tiny pause.

Her eyes were fixed on the glass of water in front of her. 'It wasn't an issue for me,' she said.

'Meaning what, exactly?'

'Meaning I don't want to have children.'

'Any particular reason why?' he asked.

Nikki brought her eyes back to his with an effort. 'I don't think I would make a good mother.'

'What makes you believe that? Was your mother a bad mother?'

'No, of course not,' she said, perhaps a little too quickly.

'But?'

'There's no but,' she said. 'I just don't want to go down that path. It's not for me.'

'There are many who would say that a woman who does not want children is being selfish,' he commented.

'That is a very outdated view,' she countered. 'There are

lots of women who don't see children as an option for their lives. There are plenty of childless men out there, and no one would ever dream of calling them selfish.'

'Point taken,' he said agreeably. 'I had not considered that angle.'

'What about you?' she asked, when she could stand the stretching silence no longer. 'Are you hoping to have children one day?'

'It is something I think about occasionally,' he said. 'I am now thirty-three. At the same age my father had been married for seven years. But for now, I am happy as things are. There are many benefits to being a playboy.'

Nikki ground her teeth, and dearly wished the waiter would hurry up and bring their meals so the evening could be over. She had tried so hard over the years not to think about him with other women. She had mostly succeeded, but now seeing him again had brought it all back to her: what she had experienced that one time in his arms—the magic, the joy and the mind-blowing pleasure.

But he didn't want her in that capacity any longer. She was little more than an employee this time around, a trophy mistress with no real status in his life.

She flicked her napkin across her lap as the waiter approached, and in spite of her lack of appetite she worked her way through the delicious meal in an effort to avoid small talk. But she came to realise after a while, that the sound of her cutlery was making conversation for her. Each cut of a knife or jab of a fork seemed to be saying something of an embittered nature.

'You are angry at your food for some reason?' Massimo asked after she had given the delicate meat on her plate a particularly vicious jab with her fork.

Nikki put the fork down with a little clatter. 'I can't do this,' she said and got to her feet, her eyes glistening with moisture. 'I can't sit here and pretend this isn't affecting me.'

His dark gaze collided with hers. 'Sit down, Nikki.'

Her blue-grey eyes tussled with his for a long moment, but then, blowing out a breath of resignation, she sat back down. 'I'm sorry,' she said, looking down at her plate, her shoulders sagging. 'I'm not used to being in public any more. I feel a bit exposed. It's been a while since I've eaten out.'

Massimo reached across the table and took one of her hands in the warmth of his. 'Perhaps, I should not have brought you here. Not today. You are grieving. I did not realise you would be so affected by my stepfather's passing.' *Or by his leaving you destitute*, he said under his breath as he gauged her reaction.

She bit at her lip for a moment, releasing it to say in a subdued tone, 'It was so hard those last few weeks. I know you probably think he deserved it, but I hated seeing him suffer. He was such a big man, and yet he faded away to nothing…' A tear escaped from the corner of her eye and she brushed at it with the back of her hand. 'I'm not usually so emotional. Over the years I've taught myself to keep it inside.'

'That surely cannot be a good thing,' he said, absently stroking her soft palm with his thumb.

'No.' She gave a serrated sigh. 'No…I guess not.'

Massimo gave her hand a little squeeze. 'Come, I will take you home.'

She lifted her reddened eyes to his. 'Are you sure?'

He gave a nod as he helped her to her feet. 'I am not enjoying the meal either.' *Or by being taken for the biggest fool this side of the Nullarbor,* he felt like adding. God, but she was good at this stuff. She had it down to a science—the tears, the despair, even the tiny tremble of her small chin was startlingly realistic. But he hardened his heart as he led her outside. She hadn't yet met with the lawyer, and when she did he could almost predict what would happen. She would learn her financial status and there would be no 'I don't want to sleep with you' statements then, he was sure.

Nikki followed him out to the waiting car and sat silently beside him as they made the short journey to South Yarra, her emotions still seesawing inside her. Being in Massimo's presence disturbed her so deeply. Every time he looked at her she felt his scorn and hatred, when five years ago nothing but melting softness had shone from those eyes.

'I will walk you to the door,' he said as Ricardo pulled into the driveway.

'No, please don't bother,' she said, suddenly desperate to be alone. 'I'll be fine.'

'It is of no bother to me, and besides I would like to see the house I now own.'

Nikki pulled her mouth tight at his imperious tone. 'All right, then. Come this way.'

She walked stiffly to the door and, unlocking it, stepped aside for him to enter. 'Make yourself at home,' she said with a little pointed look.

He moved past her and took his time looking around the lower floor, stopping here and there to inspect a painting on the wall or an object on display.

After what seemed an age, he came back to where she was standing, his gaze taking in her tightly crossed arms and hard expression. 'It is just a house, Nikki,' he said. 'And not a particularly beautiful one.'

'It's not just a house,' she bit out. 'It's my home.' The first she had ever had, in fact. Sure, it wasn't exactly to her taste, but she had loved the privacy and security it offered.

'Not any more, it isn't,' he reminded her.

She gave him an embittered glare. 'No, because you won't be happy until you have total control over me, will you?'

He took her chin between his thumb and index finger, tilting her head so she locked gazes with him. 'Can you blame me for wanting it all?' he asked.

'You're going too far. You know you are. You practically admitted it yourself this evening.'

His eyes dropped to her mouth. 'I do not think I have taken things far enough,' he said, his thumb moving from her chin to press against the soft contours of her bottom lip.

Nikki swallowed against the ground swell of feeling that his simple touch evoked. 'Don't,' she said raggedly. 'Please, don't…'

His mouth came close enough for her to feel the brush of his warm breath on her lips. 'You do not want me to kiss you, Nikki?' he asked softly.

'No,' she breathed as her mouth inched closer to his almost of its own volition. 'No, I don't…'

'Do you not need to be reminded of what it felt like to have my tongue playing with yours?' he asked.

She moistened her lips. 'No…'

'So you have not forgotten, eh, Nikki?' he said, brushing the seam of her mouth with the tip of his tongue.

Her legs swayed beneath her, and she had to clutch at him for stability. 'No, I haven't forgotten a thing,' she said on the back of a shaky sigh.

'Nor have I,' he said and brought his mouth down on hers.

Nikki felt her mouth explode with the burning heat of his, the first entry of his tongue making her toes curl inside her shoes. Her body came to instant life, energy racing like a current of electricity through the intricate network of her veins as his hands slid down her hips to pull her closer.

The hot, hard heat of him against her pelvis sent her pulse soaring; she could even feel her heart slamming against her sternum as he deepened the kiss even further.

Her breasts peaked and swelled against his chest, her belly giving a quick, hard kick of excitement when one of his hands left her hip to move upwards to cup the fullness of her breast. She pressed herself closer, her body acting of its own accord in a desperate need to feel more of his possessive touch.

His mouth ground against hers with increasing fervour, as if the fire he had set alight in her body had now spread to his. She felt it in the bruising pressure of his kiss, felt it too in the hard thrust of his tongue in its quest to subdue hers, and she heard it in the deep groan that came from the back of his throat, as her hands moved to cup his taut buttocks to keep him tightly locked against her.

His tongue flicked against hers, coiling, sweeping and conquering, until she could barely stand upright. She felt the graze of his teeth against her swollen bottom lip, and she began to nip at him in tiny tug-and-release bites that brought another deep, guttural groan from his throat.

Suddenly it was over.

He stepped back from her without warning, leaving her stranded in a swirling sea of unmet needs. She opened her eyes and blinked, feeling disoriented and dishevelled, and, when she encountered his cold, hard gaze, deeply ashamed, as well.

'It seems I was right. You are indeed very keen to find a

replacement for your dead husband after all,' he said with a mocking look.

Pride brought her chin up. 'I think it's time you left,' she said.

'You cannot order me from my own house, *cara*,' he said. 'If I choose to stay then I will stay.'

'I hate you for what you're doing to me,' she said with a fulminating glare.

'Hate is good, Nikki. I prefer that to the lies about love you spoke of five years ago.'

'I never told you I loved you,' she said, doing her best to avoid his eyes. 'You were the one who read more into the relationship than what was there.'

'You cold-hearted little slut,' he ground out viciously. 'You love money and position, not people. You will do anything to get it, won't you? I bet if I had offered to give you this house back you would have let me take you right here where we are standing.'

She turned away so he wouldn't see the tears she was desperately trying to hold back. 'Please leave,' she said in a strangled voice. '*Please*…just go.'

'I will see you tomorrow at my house as arranged,' he said into the brittle silence. 'I will send Ricardo to fetch you. And I think I should advise you against reneging on the deal. You have too much to lose.'

I have already lost it all, Nikki thought once the door had slammed on his exit. She laid her head back against the nearest wall and groaned. *Dear God; I have already lost it all.*

CHAPTER SEVEN

'YOU mean it's true?' Nikki gasped in shock. 'There's really nothing left? Nothing at all?'

Joseph's lawyer, Peter Rozzoli, shook his head. 'I'm sorry, Mrs Ferliani,' he said, his tone anything but apologetic. 'Your late husband left things in an awful mess. I know things got tough towards the end for him, but he really should have organised someone to run things for him when he no longer could manage it.'

Nikki couldn't help feeling the lawyer was laying the blame for that at her door. She'd never really liked the man on the few occasions Joseph had invited him to the house. It had seemed to her he was always looking at her in a predatory manner, but whenever she'd mentioned it to Joseph he had just laughed, and said Peter was jealous of him having such a beautiful young wife.

'Joseph told me everything was going well,' she said, in her defence. 'I asked him numerous times.'

'Joseph as you know was a very proud man,' the lawyer said. 'The way he handled his illness was a case in point. No one would have ever believed he'd been fighting cancer for so long.'

She looked down at the papers on the desk between them and swallowed. 'I can't believe he left things like this,' she said. 'I have bills and…and expenses.'

The prolonged silence brought her head back up to meet a gaze not dissimilar from the one she had spent most of the previous day avoiding.

'You will have to find yourself another rich husband or a very wealthy benefactor, and fast, Mrs Ferliani,' Peter Rozzoli said, his snake-like gaze slithering all over her. 'Otherwise you are going to be held responsible for several-hundred thousand dollars' worth of debt.'

Nikki gathered her bag from the floor and stood up on legs that threatened to give way. 'Thank you for your time,' she said stiffly.

The lawyer gave her a nod without rising to his feet. 'Good luck, Mrs Ferliani,' he said. 'But then, from what I read in this morning's paper, you seem to have already landed on your feet.'

Nikki didn't stay around to ask him what he meant. She closed the door on her exit and, taking a ragged little breath, made her way outside.

There was a news stand on the corner near the lawyer's offices, and she almost stumbled when she saw the billboard advertising the story of the day:

BANKRUPT WIDOW ONE DAY—WEALTHY MISTRESS THE NEXT.

She didn't stop to purchase the paper; she didn't need to read the rest for she knew it wouldn't be pretty. The tall-poppy syndrome, so active in the Australian press, had stung her on previous occasions. It went with the territory of being in the public eye. She had only to turn up at an event with a frown and it was reported she was a surly prima donna, or smile too brightly and be accused of being shallow. She had long given up worrying about it, assuring herself that as soon as she could she would toss it all in. But with Joseph leaving things as he had, her plans for a return to anonymity were going to have to be shelved.

She made her way back to Joseph's house on leaden legs, her stomach rolling in panic. She had so wanted to throw Massimo's offer in his face. She had allowed him to think she was agreeing to it, but she had been desperately hoping he had somehow been misinformed about Joseph's finances.

It didn't seem possible things had gone so badly without her knowing. She had spent long months nursing Joseph, holding his gaunt body as he was sick, bathing him, spooning what little food she could into his mouth, and yet he had said nothing. He had instead assured her things were all in order and she would have no money worries in the future. She wasn't sure what hurt the most—the fact that he had lied to her, or that she had been foolish enough to believe him.

Massimo was waiting for her in the study of his house when she arrived with Ricardo later that morning. He looked up from his desk and asked her to take a seat. 'There are some things I need to ask you about the business,' he said.

'I'm not sure I will be able to help you with any of that,' she said, briefly capturing her bottom lip. 'In the last few months I had less and less to do with things. You'd be better to speak to Kenneth Slade, the business manager.'

'I have already spoken to him. In fact, I have spoken with

everyone in the company,' he said. 'They seemed to think I should talk to you.'

Nikki sat very still, but her hands twitched in her lap no matter how hard she tried to stop them.

'I was not aware until very recently that you took over the designing of the spring-summer collection when my stepfather became too ill to meet the deadlines,' he said. 'The designs are some of the best I have ever seen.'

She met his eyes briefly, unable to disguise her surprise at his compliment. 'Thank you.'

'It seems you have a natural flair,' he went on. 'Which is what I wanted to talk to you about this morning.'

Nikki rolled her lips together, not sure where this was leading. 'I see…'

She heard the creak of leather as he leaned back in his chair, and she chanced a look at him. His dark gaze was watching her steadily, but his expression was as mask-like as ever which made her feel even more uneasy.

'Are you interested in being contracted for the next autumn-winter collection?' he asked.

She blinked at him. 'You're…you're offering me a job?'

'I gave you a job yesterday, if you remember,' he said with another unfathomable look.

She sent the tip of her tongue out to her lips, running it over the dryness in an agitated gesture. 'Yes, I realise that, but I meant another job on top of *that* one…'

'Yes,' he said as his chair creaked again. 'I am offering you another job. Are you interested?'

She pressed her damp palms to her knees and met his eyes. 'Yes, I am interested,' she said. 'But only if you are prepared to pay me well.'

One of his dark brows came up in a perfect arc over one cynical eye. 'I take it you have consulted your husband's lawyer?' he said as he began to toy with his pen.

'I have been informed of the state of affairs, yes,' she answered.

'You are shocked by what you heard?'

'Of course,' she said, looking at him instead of the movement of his pen in his fingers. 'I am very shocked that I seem to have been the last person to find out how bad things had got.'

He tossed the pen to one side and sent a raking gaze over her designer outfit. 'You were probably too busy spending the money to know where it was coming from, or whether or not it was likely to dry up,' he said. 'That was your job after all, wasn't it, Nikki? To act the dumb blonde, the sexy little wife, to see to your older husband's needs in exchange for the wealth and position he could provide.'

Nikki ground her teeth until her jawed ached. 'I was a good wife to your stepfather,' she bit out. 'And money had nothing to do with it.'

He got to his feet so suddenly she felt the rush of air from his movement against her face. He slammed his fist down on the desk between them, his eyes twin pools of black fury.

'You are nothing, but a cheap little slut,' he said. 'You sit here, telling me you were a good wife, when you were flirting with everything in trousers behind my stepfather's back.'

Nikki stared at him in shock. 'That's not true!'

He pushed himself away from the desk, his expression full of disdain. 'Your husband's lawyer told me how you tried to come on to him every time he came to the house.'

Her jaw dropped open, and it took her far too long to find

her voice. 'Peter Rozzoli is a *liar*!' She practically shrieked the words at him as she got to her feet. 'He's a sleazy, double-tongued snake who I've never trusted in all the years he's worked for Joseph. It wouldn't surprise me if he had something to do with the business failing the way it did.'

'What was the problem, Nikki?' he asked with a sardonic tilt of his mouth. 'Didn't he offer you enough to have an affair with him?'

Nikki had to curl her fingers into her palm to stop herself from slapping his arrogant face. 'No amount of money would have tempted me to get involved with him,' she said. 'Besides, he's married.'

'Ah, but you are prepared to do business with me,' he said as he closed the distance between them.

Nikki's startled gaze flicked sideways to instinctively check for an escape route, her heart missing a beat when she couldn't see one. She held her breath as he cupped her cheek with his palm, her eyes unable to avoid the smouldering intensity of his.

'But I am not married, am I, Nikki?' he said, his thumb roving over the curve of her cheek in a slow, imminently sensual motion.

'I-I'm not interested,' she said, pushing his hand away from her face with what little willpower she had left.

He gave her a cool smile. 'We will see,' he said as he returned to his chair behind the desk. 'You have not had long enough to realise how dire your situation is. When you do, I can almost guarantee you will seek refuge in my bed.'

Nikki sat down again only because her legs were refusing to hold her up. 'I thought you wanted to discuss business with me,' she said with a frosty look. 'If that's not the case, then I would like to leave.'

He held her hostile glare for a lengthy moment before announcing, 'I would like you to accompany me to Sicily to look over the garment factory.'

She jerked upright in her seat. 'Sicily?'

His brows lifted again. 'I would have thought you of all people would not be uncomfortable with the notion of travelling abroad,' he said. 'You went everywhere with my stepfather did you not?'

'Not for the last year,' she said, lowering her eyes again.

'Perhaps it is the notion of travelling with me that is the problem, eh, Nikki?' he said, his tone containing a thin, but unmistakable thread of anger.

Her eyes came back to his. 'I am prepared to pretend to be your mistress, but I wouldn't want you to get any ideas about making fiction turn into fact.'

He gave her another cold smile. 'You are very sure of yourself, are you not?'

She refused to answer, and instead sat silently glaring at him.

He leaned back in his chair once more, his pen tapping against the edge of the desk as he observed her. 'You are reeling me in, aren't you, Nikki?' he asked. 'Making me want you all over again. Every look you give me, every flutter of your lashes, and every movement of your tongue across your lips, is all part of your plan to have me make you a permanent fixture in my life.'

'You're imagining it,' she said crisply. 'No doubt because you're so used to women falling over themselves to dive into your bed.'

'Are you going to deny the attraction you still feel for me?' he asked.

Nikki felt the force field of his gaze as it tugged hers back to his, her body tingling all over when his eyes roved over her in male appraisal. She felt the tightening of her breasts, her nipples going to hard little points as if he had brushed them with his lips and tongue as he done so passionately in the past. She clamped her thighs together to stop the rush of liquid longing, but it was a useless exercise; her whole body quivered with the memory of his hard possession, and she was almost certain he knew it.

'Of course I'm going to deny it,' she said. 'I have no interest in any sort of relationship with you.'

He ignored her denial to inform her, 'I have organised our flights for Friday morning. We will spend a week at my villa. I thought after the article in this morning's paper you would be glad of a temporary reprieve.'

Nikki felt her stomach go hollow all over again. 'I haven't read the paper this morning. I took one look at the billboard and decided it wasn't worth it.'

He unfolded the newspaper he had on the desk and handed it to her. 'I should warn you, it is not a very flattering piece of journalism,' he said.

She looked down at the photo taken at Joseph's funeral the day before. The photographer had captured her smiling at the sales manager. It was just a tiny moment in time, and yet the journalist had used it to portray her as a shallow, money-hungry widow who was apparently rejoicing in the demise of her husband.

The article went on to describe her as the latest lover of Italian investment tycoon Massimo Androletti, the new owner of Ferliani Fashions, the journalist even speculating that their affair had been going on behind Joseph Ferliani's back as he'd struggled with terminal cancer.

Nikki tossed the paper down in disgust, her rage directed at Massimo as she got agitatedly to her feet. 'You did this, didn't you?' she blasted him. 'You fed them a pack of lies to make me look like an immoral tart—*didn't you*?'

He gave her a look of implacable calm, which in the presence of her anger made her all the more furious. 'You know what journalists are like, *cara*,' he said. 'They make these things up to ramp up sales.'

She slammed her hand on the desk, her chest heaving as she leaned towards him. '*You* made it up to send a message to your stupid ex-mistress, but you couldn't resist embellishing it to make me appear as tacky and tasteless as possible, could you?'

His gaze travelled lazily to the hint of cleavage she was showing, before returning to her glittering eyes. 'I did no such thing. I am always extremely careful in what I reveal to the press. However, it is perhaps rather unfortunate timing—but as I said, this trip away will allow the dust to settle.'

'*Unfortunate timing?*' she spluttered at him. 'As far as I can see you've timed it to a second, turning up at the funeral like that, issuing your demands like the overbearing tyrant you are.'

'I have already spoken to you about your tendency to speak incautiously when addressing me, Nikki,' he warned her silkily as he got to his feet.

Nikki had to fight with every instinct not to step backwards as he came from behind the desk. She stood stock still, her hands clenched by her sides, her greyish-blue eyes flashing with anger. 'I never thought I'd say this, but I hate you, Massimo Androletti. Do you hear me? I hate you.'

A nerve pulsed like a tiny jackhammer beneath the skin of

his jaw, his gaze black as night as it speared hers. 'You can hate me all you like whilst in the confines of this house, but as soon as we leave it you will have to abide by the rules I lay down— otherwise you will find yourself with legal bills that will take you years to read through, much less pay.'

He took his car keys out of his trouser pocket and added, 'I am going to my office in the city. I will be home for dinner at approximately seven-thirty.'

'If you think I'm going to cook a meal and wait for you to return to eat it you've definitely got rocks in your head,' she said. 'If you're not here on time, I'll toss it in the bin.'

'*La mia piccola padrona arrabbiata,*' he said, with a mocking little smile. '"My angry little mistress".'

She glared at him heatedly. 'Don't call me that.'

'Would you prefer *"la mia padrona, piccola e cara"*?' he asked. 'That is what you are, is it not, Nikki? My *dear* little mistress—for I have paid a lot of money for you.'

She could feel her teeth turning to powder as she clenched her jaw. 'You don't own me.'

He flicked her cheek with the end of one long finger. 'Ah, but I do,' he said, his voice a deep, velvet drawl. 'And when the time is ready, I will take what you have to offer.'

'I'm offering you nothing.'

His dark eyes glinted. 'That was not the impression I got from you last night,' he said.

'Last night was a mistake,' she threw back. 'I wasn't myself. I was upset and overly emotional. And you took advantage of it.'

'I only took advantage of what was going begging,' he returned, neatly. 'And if it is ever on offer again, I will do the very same. You have taught me well, eh, Nikki? I do not wear my heart on my sleeve any more. Once was more than enough.'

'You can't blame me for ever for your own limitations,' she said. 'You have a choice to behave in an honourable way, in spite of what may have happened to you in the past.'

'You speak to me of honour when you have prostituted yourself for five years to a man old enough to be your father?' he snarled. 'Seeing you on his arm the day of the wedding sickened me to my stomach, when only the night before you had been sobbing in my arms in ecstasy.'

She put her hands to her ears to block the sound of his words. 'Stop it!'

He pulled her hands away and carried on in the same angry, bitter tone, 'Did he make you scream when you came, Nikki? Did he make you so desperate for release you raked his back with your nails? *Did he?*'

'No!'

'You lie!' He threw the words at her. 'He held you on his arm like a trophy at every opportunity he could. I saw the photographs in the press. He was smiling like a cat who had stolen the cream. But it was *my* cream, wasn't it, Nikki? It still is, and you and I both know it. Last night proved it.'

'I am no man's possession,' she said, trying to get out of his hold. 'And certainly not yours.'

He refused to release her, his fingers biting into the flesh of her upper arms. 'I still want you and I intend to have you,' he said. 'It is only a matter of time.'

'I am *not* going to sleep with you.' Nikki hoped by saying it enough times it would somehow make it true.

'You will not be able to help yourself,' he said. 'I see the longing in your eyes every time you look at me.'

'You're imagining it. I feel nothing where you're con-cerned.'

He smiled tauntingly as he pulled her even closer so she could feel where his body burned and throbbed against her. 'You are feeling it now, aren't you, Nikki? The same burning desire we've felt for each other from the moment we met.'

Nikki could feel her body betraying her, every pore of her skin aching with the need to feel his touch. She couldn't think with the temptation of his mouth so close to hers, the jut of his hard body reminding her of the passion they had once shared. Her inner core tightened and melted simultaneously, like a secret pulse deep inside her body, where his had once moved with such strength and virile potency.

'I don't want you,' she said even as her mouth lifted to meet the descent of his. 'I don't want—'

His mouth cut off the rest of her pointless denial, his tongue delving into her moist warmth to meet hers in a sexy tango that sent shivers of reaction up and down her spine. Her limbs turned to liquid as he deepened the kiss even further, exploring every corner of her mouth with almost savage intent.

His evening shadow scored her soft skin as he tilted her head for better access, the sexy rasp inciting her to return his kiss with a wild abandon that made a mockery of everything she had said only seconds previously.

She wanted him.

Of course she wanted him.

She had never stopped wanting him, and loving him and missing him, aching for him and wishing things had been different.

But he was after revenge, not love, she reminded herself.

He wanted to right the wrongs of the past, but on his terms this time around. She could already guess how it was going to go. He would be the one to walk away when it was over, leaving her as devastated as he had been five years ago.

For a brief moment she considered telling him why she had done what she had done, but knew it wouldn't really change anything. He had hated Joseph Ferliani and all he represented. Telling him how his stepfather had helped her escape from her background would no doubt only incense him further. He would argue that Joseph had used money that wasn't his to gain her favour. And a small part of her had to admit he was right. She would never have married Joseph if he hadn't offered her money. Money had been her passport out of her past, and a way to give some measure of comfort to Jayden. And she had clutched at it with both hands, grateful that Joseph had never once asked why she had needed it.

However, Nikki knew that, even if by some miracle Massimo still felt something for her after all this time, learning about her background would surely kill it. He was a high-profile man, with investment clients from all over the world. Having a wife with a background such as hers would be the death knell of their relationship. If word got out in the press that the woman he was involved with was the daughter of one of Australia's most violent criminals, what would it do to his reputation?

With a superhuman effort she pulled back from his hold, pressing both of her hands against his chest to separate their bodies. 'No,' she said. 'This is all wrong.'

'What is wrong about fulfilling a need that we both share?' he asked.

'I can't do this, Massimo,' she said, so close to tears she

had to bite the inside of her mouth until she tasted the metallic sourness of blood.

'Because it is too soon?' he asked.

'Because it is *wrong*,' she said. 'Can't you see that? You hate me.'

He stepped away from her, his hand raking a jagged pathway through his hair as he turned his back on her. 'Perhaps you are right,' he said heavily. 'Hate and desire can be a lethal mix.'

'You have to let it go, Massimo. We had a past, but it's over. I admit I was wrong in leading you on to believe we had the chance of a future together, but I was young, and…and I had already made a promise to your stepfather.'

He turned to face her, his expression sharpened again by bitterness. 'You could have told him you had met someone else,' he said. 'Why didn't you?'

She swallowed against the lump of pain in her throat. 'I had already made a commitment to him. He had given me money, a lot of money, that I had already spent. I know it sounds horribly mercenary to you, but I was in trouble and needed his money to get out of it.'

'I could have given you money. Why didn't you ask me?'

'You told me you were still building your business,' she said. 'I could read between the lines enough to know you couldn't have given me the amount I needed.'

'What sort of trouble were you in?'

She shifted her gaze from the unwavering probe of his, glad she had already rehearsed her lie with Joseph. 'I was irresponsible over money,' she said. 'It happens to a lot of young people when they first get issued with credit cards. I suddenly owed more than I could handle.'

Massimo wanted to believe her. Everything in him wanted her to be the girl he had met five years ago, but something warned him about falling yet again for her doe-eyed innocence.

'Did you know who I was that week we were together?' he asked after a short, but tense silence.

Her eyes came back to his. 'No…no, I didn't, but I should have,' she said, snagging her bottom lip with her teeth for a moment. 'When I thought about it later there were so many connections I could have made, but for some reason I ignored them. I just wanted that week to be about us—two young people who had briefly fallen in love.'

'But you were not in love with me, though, were you?' he asked. 'For if you were you would not have married my stepfather.'

'You don't get it, do you?' she said, her tone bordering on despair. 'Sometimes in life, things go against your best-laid plans. I had responsibilities that I couldn't get out of, I had no choice. You have to accept that. I would do the same again.'

'Then you really are the coldhearted gold-digger I thought you were after all,' he said. 'You walked away without a backward glance, not even having the decency to tell me to my face that it was over.'

'I left you a note with your ring,' she said. 'I tried to explain as best I could why I couldn't see you again.'

'But I did not get the note or the ring, which makes me start to wonder if you had even left one,' he said. 'You sound so convincing—even those sparkling tears are worthy of an acting award—but I am not a fool, Nikki. I know what you are up to. You have had the financial rug you clung to so greedily ripped from under your feet. I can see the little plan you are hatching.'

'There's no plan. I just—'

'Of *course* there is a plan,' he interrupted her angrily. 'I can see it unfolding before my very eyes. What better way than to make me want you again until I am nearly mad with it? That is how it works, is it not? You want me to be so desperate for you I will agree to keep you in the manner to which you have been accustomed.'

'That's not true. I don't want anything from you.'

A five-second silence drummed in her ears until he broke it by saying, 'What if I said I would do it?' He paused, as if gauging her reaction. 'What if I said that instead of being a trophy mistress, I wanted you to be a real one?'

Nikki stood very still, her blue-grey gaze locked on his, her heart beginning to hammer so loudly she was sure he was able to hear it. She moistened her mouth, but it made no difference; her lips felt like ancient parchment as she moved them to speak in a cracked whisper of sound that didn't even come close to sounding like her voice. 'You don't mean that. You can't possibly mean that…'

He held her gaze for interminable seconds before lowering his mouth to hers in a brief, hard kiss. 'I will see you tonight.'

Nikki didn't even realise she had been holding her breath until the door closed on his exit. She pinched the bridge of her nose as tightly as she could to control the tears, but in silence they came, as if they had been waiting for this moment for years…

CHAPTER EIGHT

ONCE Nikki had spent most of the day unpacking her things in the bedroom she wandered out into the garden, her nostrils instantly flaring as the sharp, lemony fragrance of daphne drifted towards her. The garden was awash with colour, the crimson and pinks of azaleas and rhododendrons, as well as the delicate cream and white of camellias interspersed with the vivid electric-blue of cinerarias.

The verdant lawn was fringed by old beech and elm trees, their new spring-growth tipping their craggy limbs. The air was fresh and cool, the damp, earthy smell reminding her that, typical of Melbourne's weather, winter was not quite ready to move aside for the warmth of spring.

A small, black cat suddenly jumped down from the back fence and came over to her and began to weave its way around her legs, its deep, contented purr clearly audible.

Nikki bent down to stroke the silky black fur. 'Why, hello there, little puss. What's your name, I wonder?' She turned the tinkling identification tag over to find the name 'Pia' engraved there.

'Hello, Pia,' she said. 'I wonder who you belong to.'

The little cat meowed and bumped its head against her

hand. Nikki felt a smile tug at her mouth. 'I am pleased to meet you too, Pia,' she said. 'Do you live nearby?'

The cat trotted towards the back door of the house, stopping occasionally to check to see if Nikki was following.

'You want me to feed you?' Nikki asked. 'I'm not sure if Massimo will appreciate having a neighbour's cat come wandering into his house. But he's not home, and I won't tell if you don't.'

The little cat meowed again and darted indoors.

Nikki found a saucer and poured some milk into it, and watched indulgently as the little pink tongue lapped at it enthusiastically. She searched through the pantry and found a tin of tuna, and, taking out another saucer, forked some onto it and laid it beside the milk.

Once the cat was finished it sat and began to lick its paws, wiping each soft pad over its face before beginning all over again.

'What is it about girls and grooming?' Nikki asked with a wry smile.

The cat blinked at her for a moment before resuming her ablutions, and then after she was finished she jumped up on one of the kitchen chairs, curled into a ball and closed her eyes.

Nikki began to prepare dinner, somehow feeling better now that she had a companion. She even found herself talking to Pia as if she was a friend. 'I've never had a pet before, or at least not one I was ever allowed to keep for longer than a few weeks,' she said as she took out some vegetables from the refrigerator.

'My parents moved so many times when I was growing up, I would no sooner make friends with the local kids and we'd be off again. I was always lonely, the odd one out, the kid with the wrong clothes or shoes, or unkempt hair.'

The cat opened both eyes and blinked at her. Nikki gave her a twisted look and continued, 'Do you realise you're the first person I've ever told that to?'

The cat got down from the chair and came across and rubbed against her legs. 'I didn't even tell Joseph,' Nikki said on a little sigh.

'I told you I never want to hear that name mentioned again in my house,' Massimo said from the door.

Nikki spun around in shock, her heart leaping to her throat. 'I didn't hear you come in,' she said, her face feeling warm.

His eyes went to the cat still twining itself around Nikki's legs. 'So you've met our little neighbour Pia,' he observed.

'Yes…' Nikki said, wondering how much he had heard. She couldn't tell from his expression; if anything he seemed much more interested in the cat, who was now heading towards his long trouser-clad legs.

The cat began nudging his hand when he bent down to stroke her. 'You are a naughty little kitten,' he chided her affectionately. 'How many times have you been told to stay in your own garden, eh?'

Nikki watched in fascination as he picked up the cat and held it to his chest, his free hand stroking its head while its slanted green eyes closed in blissful contentment, the deep purring reverberating in the silence.

'I found her in the garden,' she explained. 'She seemed pretty keen to come inside. She was looking for food. I hope I did the right thing by feeding her.'

Massimo met her slightly anxious gaze. 'It is fine,' he said. 'She belongs to Mrs Lockwood over the back. Her husband has been in the hospital for several weeks, so she is away visiting him for most of the day. Little Pia here gets lonely.'

Yeah, well, I know all about that, Nikki thought, but then she became aware of his deepening scrutiny, and to cover her vulnerability she found herself saying in a resentful tone, 'You're home earlier than you said. I hope you don't expect dinner to be ready. I have barely started.'

His dark eyes glinted. 'You are sounding distinctly wasp-ish, Nikki. Has your day been a particularly unpleasant one?'

She pursed her mouth. 'No more than usual. I met with a sleazy lawyer first thing, then I read a pack of lies about myself in the paper, unpacked my things in the spare bedroom of a man who hates me, and talked to a black cat all afternoon,' she said. 'Pretty average, really.'

A smile began to lift the edges of his mouth at her dry tone. The cat jumped from his arms to the floor with a soft little thud that sounded loud in the silence.

'You are looking for more excitement, are you, *cara*?' he asked, stepping towards her.

Nikki stood her ground, determined to show she wasn't intimidated by him, but even so her legs felt weak all of a sudden. 'What do you think you are doing?' she asked as he put his hands to her waist.

'What do you think I am doing, Nikki?'

She fought back the urge to swallow. 'I don't know, but if it's got anything to do with revisiting our past relationship, you'd better stop right now.'

'You do not like the thought of having my body hot and hard inside yours, eh, Nikki?' he asked, brushing his body against her suggestively. 'Remember how hot and hard I was for you that night we were together? I am almost exploding now, just thinking about it.'

This time she did swallow, a great, big gulping swallow that she couldn't control in time. 'I don't like the idea of making this farcical arrangement between us any more complicated than it already is,' she said a little breathlessly.

He smiled as he looked down at her. 'You are already weakening,' he said. 'I can feel it in your body. You are fighting something bigger than both of us, *cara*. We met five years ago and the passion was uncontrollable.' One of his hands went to where her heart was kicking against her chest wall. 'It is still beating inside of you.'

'D-don't do this, Massimo.'

'Don't do what?' he asked, doing it. His lips brushed against hers, his hand against her heart moving to cup her breast.

Nikki couldn't control the urge to respond to the next soft brush against her mouth. Her lips clung to his, her body tilting towards him, her stiff arms loosening as they moved from her sides to wrap around his solid warmth. She closed her eyes as his mouth covered hers, the first stroke and glide of his tongue against hers making her whimper in rapturous delight.

She felt herself being swept away on a tide of longing that no solid sandbag of commonsense could ever hope to restrain. The kiss became frantic, almost savage, as if the last five years of separation had fuelled his desire for her to an unmanageable level. His teeth scraped against hers, his tongue dived and thrust, and his hands possessed the lush prize of her breasts with greedy intent.

'I have waited for this moment for so long,' he growled against her mouth as he ripped her blouse open, his warm, open palm covering her breast as he pushed her bra out of the way. 'I have never forgotten how you responded to me that night. In all these years no one has even come close.'

She began to paw at his clothes, her fingers as urgent as his as she accessed his chest, her mouth pressing against the base of his throat, her tongue tasting the salt of his skin. She heard him groan as her mouth went to the hard pebble of his right nipple, nestling in amongst the sprinkling of masculine hair that marked him as a man. She had often dreamed of kissing her way down his body. She had been too shy in the past, but the urge to do so now was almost uncontrollable. She wanted to taste him in the most intimate way possible, to feel his explosive release, to show him she had grown from a girl to a woman.

His body was taut as a trip wire beneath her fingertips, his every response to her touch leaving her in no doubt of his ongoing desire for her.

'We cannot do this here,' he said, pulling away from her to look down at her with passion-glazed eyes. 'I want to pleasure you, not against the kitchen bench, but in my bed where you belong.'

Nikki began to extricate herself from his hold, his words reminding her of the reason for her being here. For him this wasn't about a love that hadn't died, it was about revenge.

'No,' she said, pushing against his chest.

'You know you do not mean that, *cara*,' he said, holding her hands against him so she couldn't remove them. 'You want me, but you want me to beg, don't you?'

'I want you to let me go.'

'Ask nicely.'

She gritted her teeth, her eyes flashing with anger. 'Let me go, you arrogant beast.'

He shook his head at her in reproof. 'That is not the way a lover should speak to her partner, Nikki. I hope you did not speak to my stepfather in such a way.'

'Your stepfather was twice the man you are,' she threw back. 'At least he had a conscience.'

His eyes hardened into chips of black ice. 'Oh, really?' he said, dropping his hands from hers. 'Does that mean he confessed his sins on his death bed?'

'He told me he had some regrets over the way he took your father's money from him,' she said as she rebuttoned her top with shaking fingers. 'But your mother was just as much to blame. She encouraged him to take it, insisting it was half hers.'

His lip curled. 'What a pity he didn't apologise to my father at the time. Maybe then my father might still be alive.'

'He was devastated by your father's suicide,' she said. 'It was what, in the end, broke up his relationship with your mother. He felt so guilty.'

Massimo gave a harsh bark of mocking laughter. 'He really did a good job on you, didn't he? Guilty indeed. That low-life creep never suffered a moment's remorse for destroying my father.'

'You didn't know him, not the way I did,' Nikki argued. 'If you had taken the time to get to know him, you might have realised what made him the man he was.'

'I suppose he gave you some sob story about his tortured childhood, did he?' he asked. 'I have no time for people who use that as an excuse. He was no victim, he was a perpetrator.'

Nikki drew in an unsteady breath. 'You don't think a person's childhood has an impact on who they are as adults?'

'I think my stepfather pulled the wool over your eyes, that's what I think,' he said. 'But then maybe the amount he was paying to have you in his bed made you see him through rose-coloured glasses.'

She gave him a flinty look. 'I did not sleep with your step-father for money.' *I didn't sleep with him at all.*

His expression showed his scepticism in every sharp angle and line of his face. 'Maybe that is what you are hanging out for now,' he said, with an insolent slide of his gaze over her body. 'Am I not paying you enough, eh, Nikki?'

Nikki loathed violence, having grown up with it for most of her life, but she had to keep her hands pinned by her sides as the urge to slap him became almost uncontrollable. 'I am glad I rejected you when I did,' she said through tight lips. 'Joseph might not have been an angel, but he never once insulted me the way you have done.'

A flash of rage lit his eyes as they held hers. 'I think you are more than a little bit ahead of me in the insult stakes, *cara*. You will have to forgive me if I take every opportunity to level the score.'

'You never used to be so cold and calculating. How can you live with yourself?'

'Do not speak to me of being cold and calculating,' he growled. 'You are the one with the heart of ice. Even knowing you as I do, I was surprised when you agreed to move in with me so readily.'

'You gave me very little choice in the matter,' she reminded him. 'Waving huge debts over my head—debts, I might add, I knew nothing about until you told me.'

'And the one thing you do not like to be is short of money, is it, Nikki?' he said. 'You would do anything, including live with a man you rejected previously, for financial gain.'

Nikki knew there was no way to defend herself, for unless she told him of her reasons for marrying his stepfather, he would always believe her to be a gold-digger.

'I did what I thought was the right thing at the time,' she said. 'I'm sorry you got hurt. It wasn't my intention. I had no idea you were developing such strong feelings for me.'

'Do not play me for a fool!' he thundered. 'You knew exactly what you were doing. You led me on until you had me where you wanted me, and then you tossed me aside for the bigger prize.'

She turned away from him, her hands wrapping across her body, her emotions feeling as if they were unravelling. 'Please don't make me hate you any more than I already do, Massimo.'

'You are going to hate me even more,' he said. 'For I have uncovered even more of your late husband's debts for which I will want to be paid.'

Her knuckles whitened as she held herself even tighter. 'How much did he owe in total?' she asked.

'More than you would want to know,' he said. 'It seems my stepfather lost more than his flare for business in the months before he died. He lost his lucky streak as well.'

Nikki turned around to face him. 'He was very ill,' she said. 'I nursed him through each agonising second of it. I know he liked to gamble from time to time, but I saw no indication it was getting out of control.'

'Perhaps you should have kept a closer eye on the accounts,' he said. 'But then as I said this morning, I suppose you were far happier with the "he earns it you spend it" arrangement of a marriage such as yours.'

She glared at him resentfully. 'You know nothing of my marriage to your stepfather—nothing.'

'I know it cannot have been very fulfilling for you over the past few months.' His smouldering gaze ran over her suggestively. 'You have the look of a woman crying out for sensual release.'

Nikki clenched her teeth. 'Of course someone like you *would* think that,' she said. 'All you ever think about is satisfying your disgusting animal urges.'

He closed the small distance between them, his pelvis brushing against hers as his hand reached for a long strand of her hair. 'You have the very same urges, Nikki,' he said softly, bringing her hair up to his nose, his nostrils flaring as he breathed in the flowery fragrance clinging to the silky strands. 'I can see them, I can feel them, and I can smell them on your skin.'

Nikki held her breath as his dark eyes held hers, the tether of her hair keeping her so close to him she could see the widening of his pupils in desire.

'What do you say, *cara*?' He kissed the corner of her mouth before continuing, inching closer and closer to her already tingling lips. 'Why don't we get these disgusting animal urges out of the way, mmm?'

Nikki felt her heart going like a jackhammer in her chest. 'I don't like your reasons for wanting to renew our relationship.'

'By that I take it you mean revenge?'

Her tongue came out to moisten her lips. 'Yes,' she said. 'You hate me.'

'I do not love you as I did five years ago, but I do desire you.'

'Gee, thanks.'

He frowned at her dry comment. 'What did you expect me to say—that I have never stopped loving you?'

'No, of course not,' she said, biting her lip again.

'But you would prefer it if I had some sort of feeling for you other than lust?'

She frowned in distaste. 'Lust is such a horrible word.'

'I cannot wrap up in romantic wrapping what I feel for you now,' he said. 'But who knows? We might over time restore some of what we had that week five years ago.'

'You will never forgive me for marrying your stepfather, no matter what my motives were at the time,' she said.

'I do not wish to speak of him again.'

'He wasn't a bad person, Massimo.'

'I do not want him to be the third person in our relationship,' he stated implacably. 'I understand you loved him, but I would prefer it if you would refrain from reminding me of it at every opportunity.'

She pulled herself out of his hold, this time successfully. 'We do *not* have a relationship.'

'Not yet,' he said. 'But I have a feeling you will soon change your mind.'

She opened her mouth to deny it, but he pressed her lips together with the tip of his finger. 'Hush, *cara*,' he said with a mocking smile. 'I do not want you to have too many words to eat later, for there will be no room for our dinner, eh?'

She slapped his hand away from her mouth. 'There's not going to be any dinner—or at least none cooked by me,' she said.

Massimo watched her stalk out, her blonde hair swinging in fury, the door snipping shut behind her.

He blew out a breath and looked down at the little cat who was blinking up at him with green eyes full of reproach, as she waited for the door to be opened again so she too could leave.

'I suppose it is to be expected that you would stick up for her, Pia,' he said wryly. 'For you are both female and both not very good at following orders.'

Pia gave him one last look over her shoulder and stalked out, her long, black tail twitching in disapproval.

CHAPTER NINE

NIKKI had hoped to avoid another confrontation with Massimo, so deliberately delayed coming downstairs the next morning but he had clearly anticipated her actions, for she found him in the kitchen lingering over his coffee and reading the morning paper.

He looked up when she came in and informed her, 'I have made the travel arrangements for tomorrow. We leave at 6 a.m. in my private jet, landing in Palermo, where I have a villa.'

'How wonderful it must be to have so much money to throw around,' she said with a toss of her head as she reached for the orange juice. 'I don't see why we couldn't have taken a commercial flight just like everyone else. There is such a thing as business class, you know.'

'I have worked hard for what I have, and see no problem in making such long and arduous journeys as comfortable as I can,' he returned. 'However if your conscience is troubling you I can book you on a commercial carrier on a business-class fare—or perhaps you would prefer economy? I will of course continue with the arrangements I have made for myself.'

Her top lip turned up in disdain. 'Of course.'

He drew in a harsh breath and placed his half-finished coffee on the bench with a sharp crack. 'I am losing my patience with you, Nikki,' he said. 'I was thinking of your comfort as well as my own.'

'I just bet you were,' she tossed back.

'What is that supposed to mean?'

'I want my own room at your villa,' she said with a determined set to her chin. 'In fact, I want my own room wherever we stay.'

'I am afraid that will not be possible,' he said.

'Why?' She sent him a scornful glance. 'Is your billionaire villa too small or something?'

'No,' he said. 'There are numerous rooms, but each of them is serviced by my attentive housekeeper.'

Nikki felt a little alarm bell ringing inside her head. 'So?'

'So, *la mia piccola padrona*,' he drawled. 'We will have to share a room for the sake of appearances.'

Her eyes flared with anger. 'I will do no such thing!'

'You are travelling as my intimate companion, Nikki,' he said. 'My staff members are used to me having my latest lover share my room, and will expect you to do so, as well. Besides, my ex-lover will suspect something if things do not appear normal between us.'

Nikki drew her brows together. 'Your ex-mistress lives in Sicily?'

'Yes.'

'Then she must have incredibly long-range vision, for I thought the whole reason I was acting as your mistress here in Melbourne was for her benefit,' she said with a sharp edge to her voice.

'It is.'

'How does that work?' she asked, her eyes still narrowed in suspicion.

'Sabrina Gambari has family in Australia,' he said. 'I wanted them to hear of our relationship, so when we arrive in Palermo there will not be a problem.'

She folded her arms crossly. 'You hope.'

'I do not anticipate any trouble now that the news has gotten out about our involvement,' he said. 'Her family had hopes of a marriage between us, but hearing you and I are together will hopefully defuse such dreams.'

'You weren't interested in marrying her?'

'No,' he said. 'After what happened to my father I do not think it is wise to commit yourself to one woman, who can then turn the tables on you so heartlessly.'

'I suppose that is meant to be a dig at me, as well,' she said with a resentful frown.

He gave her a look which said 'if the shoe fits'. 'I will see you tonight,' he said. 'Do not bother to cook. We will dine out instead.'

'I don't want to go out,' she said. 'I need to pack.'

'You have the rest of today to pack, *cara*,' he said. 'You are a lady of leisure now, are you not?'

'For how long?' she asked with a glowering look.

'Until the debt you owe me is cleared.'

'How do I know you're not going to string this out indefinitely?' she asked. 'You keep finding debts to hang over my head.'

He came over to where she was standing and lifted her chin, making her eyes meet his. 'To hasten things up, you can make the first installment any time you like, Nikki.'

Her grey-blue eyes flashed at him. 'I'm not going to lower myself in such a way.'

His eyes turned black as they burned into hers. 'If I had

time I would make you eat every one of those foolish words. You are indeed very lucky I have a meeting to attend, otherwise you would be spreadeagled on that table by now, with me proving how much you want me.'

Nikki felt her stomach cave in at the sexy promise of his statement. Her heart fluttered and stopped, fluttered and got going again, but in an out-of-time rhythm. She stood transfixed as his head came down, his mouth swooping to capture hers in a bruising kiss that was brief, but no less devastating.

He stepped back from her, picked up his keys and briefcase, and, with a searing look that she felt at the very base of her spine, he left.

Nikki caught a cab to Rosedale House, spending the afternoon with her younger brother, pushing him around the gardens as she told him of her forthcoming trip.

'I won't be able to see you for a couple of weeks,' she said as she sat on one of the benches near a bed of colourful azaleas. 'I know it's very short notice, but I'll be back before you know it.'

Jayden blinked at her vacuously, and Nikki squeezed his hand as she fought back tears. 'I'm so sorry, Jayden,' she choked out. 'If I could turn back the clock you know I would do it. I should be sitting in that chair, not you. I can never forgive myself for moving out of the way. I saw him coming for me, and I didn't realise you would take the brunt of his violence instead…'

She clasped Jayden's hand in both of her hands, tears streaming down her face. 'I love you, Jayden,' she said. 'I know you can't really understand a word I say, but I love you with everything that is in me. I will fight for you with my last breath, I swear I will.'

Nikki spent the remainder of the afternoon with some of the other residents, reading to them and helping with the drinks and snacks that came around at tea time. The staff knew her as plain Nicola Burnside, and with her blonde hair scraped back in a ponytail, no make-up, and wearing her oldest jeans and sweater, no one had ever questioned her identity. Nikki was amazed she had been able to get away with it for so long, but it suited her to keep her public life totally separate. Joseph had never questioned her outings, assuming she was visiting friends or shopping, and she had never once enlightened him.

But occasionally, particularly in those last heart-wrenching weeks as he had slowly and agonisingly faded, she had felt tempted to reveal her private pain. She had wanted to thank him for what he had done in providing such wonderful care for her brother, but every time she'd tried to form the words she just hadn't been able do it.

Her past was in the past and talking about it wouldn't change Jayden's life one iota. His future had been stolen, and it was up to her to give him what comfort she could, no matter what the cost.

But as she left to make her way back to Massimo's house, Nikki had to concede that perhaps the price was going to be a whole lot higher than she had ever imagined.

Massimo found her sitting in the lounge with the cat on her lap when he came in from work. 'I called you several times today,' he said. 'Where were you?'

'I went shopping,' she said, almost but not quite meeting his eyes.

'What did you buy?'

'Nothing.'

He raised his brows. 'Nothing at all?'

The cat leapt off her lap as Nikki got to her feet. 'You did say I wasn't to be chained to the house, if you remember,' she said. 'Or would you prefer me to sign in and out?'

'I would prefer to know where you are,' he said.

'Why?' she asked. 'So you can monitor my movements like a prison guard?'

'Not at all,' he responded evenly. 'I am merely thinking of your safety.'

'I hardly think shopping is a life-threatening pastime,' she said.

'Perhaps not, but I would still prefer you to use Ricardo for transport rather than use public transport.'

'I can look after myself.'

His dark gaze wandered over her in an assessing manner. 'You are far too thin, Nikki. You look as if a breeze could knock you over. You would not stand a chance if someone was intent on snatching your purse or jewellery.'

'I'm a model, or at least I was until a couple of days ago,' she shot back. 'I'm supposed to be slim.'

'You are unhappy about me severing your contract?'

Nikki was, but not for the reasons he thought. 'I would have liked to discuss it first,' she said.

'We can discuss it over dinner. I also wish to discuss the design contract with you,' he said. 'Are you ready to leave?'

She gave him a heated glare without responding, and, snatching up her bag, accompanied him out to the car where Ricardo was waiting to take them to the restaurant.

The table they were led to a short time later was set well back from the others in a private corner, the lighting low and intimate.

Nikki buried her head in the menu rather than meet Massimo's gaze, her senses on high alert with him sitting so close. She knew she had only to stretch out her legs to come into contact with him, the sudden temptation to do so almost overwhelming.

'Relax, Nikki,' he said as she wriggled on her chair. 'I do not want people to think you would rather be anywhere but here.'

'I *would* rather be anywhere but here,' she said with a little scowl.

'So would I,' he returned with a slow, sexy smile. 'In bed, for instance, with your legs wrapped around mine.'

'I didn't mean that!' she said, and buried her head back in the menu again.

He chuckled softly. 'You are like an open book, Nikki. I can see you are doing your best to string out the period of time before we reconsummate our relationship, but it is getting harder and harder, is it not?'

'I'm doing no such thing.'

'Are you hoping by making me wait it will drive the price up even more?' he asked. 'If you are, it is working. I am hard just sitting here looking at you.'

She sent him a fulminating look, her cheeks flaring with heat. 'You really are contemptible. I hadn't realised until now how much so.'

'You want the whole deal, do you not?' he asked with an indolent expression. 'Being a mistress has never interested you. You want marriage, but I am equally determined not to offer it to you.'

She tossed her blonde hair back over her shoulders. 'I wouldn't accept it if you did.'

His dark eyes hardened. 'Do not play games with me, *cara*,' he warned. 'You will not win this time around. You and I have a past score to settle and we will settle it in my bed.'

Nikki glared at him. 'How many times do I have to tell you I don't want to sleep with you?'

'I would find it easier to believe you if your body was sending me the same message, but it is not,' he said. 'You *do* want to sleep with me, and sleep with me you will, as of tonight.'

She disguised her rush of panic with a voice dripping with disdain. 'You're going to have to try a whole lot harder if you want me to shove my memories of Joseph aside to make room for you.'

His anger crackled in the air separating them. Nikki knew she was being reckless, goading him, but she couldn't seem to stop it. It wasn't as if he could think any less of her than he already did.

'I swear to God, Nikki, that I will make you forget that man,' he ground out. 'I will have my name on your lips, not his. Do you hear me?'

She set her mouth, her eyes firing sparks of defiance at him. 'You think.'

He leaned forward, his voice a low, primal growl. 'Before this night is over I will have you sobbing my name like you did that night five years ago. Your body will throb and hum with the release I know you crave from me, and only me.'

Nikki opened her mouth to fling a retort his way when the waiter appeared to take their order. She schooled her features into a bland indifference and ordered the first thing she saw, knowing she wouldn't be able to get a single mouthful past the lump of pain tightening her throat.

She sat in a stony silence for the rest of the meal, refusing to engage in the attempts at conversation Massimo occasionally made for the sake of appearances. She could see the way his anger was rising with each of the chilly looks she sent his way; his lips turned white at one point, his eyes warning her there would be hell to pay for her very public insurgence.

She gave her head a toss and drank another glass of wine, her head swimming slightly from the unfamiliar amount of alcohol.

'You are going to regret that in the morning,' Massimo said as she put her glass back down.

'I don't care,' she said.

He tossed his napkin down and got to his feet. 'We are leaving,' he said implacably.

She gave him a belligerent look. 'I'm not ready to leave.'

His dark eyes warred with hers and won. She lowered her gaze and reached for her bag, following him out of the restaurant with a sinking feeling in the pit of her stomach.

He didn't speak for the entire journey, and Nikki knew she had pushed him too far. The swish of the tyres on the wet roads filled the brittle silence, the back and forth motion of the windscreen wipers making her eyes water as she tried to focus on them rather than the rigid figure beside her.

The car purred into the huge garage like a panther returning to its den, and Nikki felt her stomach tighten another excruciating notch as the engine gave a low growl before going silent.

She waited as Massimo came around to open her door, her eyes avoiding his as she exited the car.

The click-clack of her heels was almost unbearably loud in the cold, still night air. Even the key turning in the lock sounded like a gun shot, her tautly stretched nerves making her inwardly jump.

He put a hand in the small of her back and led her indoors, turning to face her once the door had closed behind them.

'I am not going to give you the satisfaction of acting like the unfeeling brute you think I am by responding to your very deliberate attempts to make me lose my temper,' he said. 'That is what that routine in the restaurant was all about, was it not?'

She couldn't hold his gaze. 'I'm sorry,' she whispered.

'Nikki, Nikki, Nikki,' he said, and drew her towards him with arms so gentle she felt tears well at the backs of her eyes. 'You make me so angry, I want to shake you, but lucky for you I am not a violent man.'

She burrowed closer, breathing in the male scent of him, her arms going around his waist almost of their own accord.

'What am I going to do with you, *cara*?' he asked.

She pressed back to look up at him, her bottom lip trembling ever so slightly. 'I don't want you to hate me, Massimo,' she said. 'I couldn't bear to make love with a man who hates me.'

He held her gaze for a lengthy moment. 'I cannot pretend feelings I no longer have,' he said. 'You surely understand that?'

Her gaze fell away from his. 'Yes, I do understand that.'

He lifted her chin. 'But it makes you sad, mmm?'

'A lot of things make me sad, Massimo,' she said softly. 'A lot of things.'

He brushed a loose strand of blonde hair back from her face, tucking it gently behind her ear. 'I am in two minds over you, *cara*,' he confessed wryly. 'One tells me to let you go, and the other tells me to have my fill of you. Which one should I listen to, I wonder?'

Nikki held her breath as his mouth came closer, the brush of his breath against her lips kick-starting her pulse. She swallowed as his tongue glided across the surface of her lips, the tantalising movement sending sparks of heat right to her toes and back.

She told herself to move out of his embrace before it was too late, but it was as if her body and brain were no longer connected. Passion had shorted the system until all she could do was move closer and closer, her mouth opening under the increasing pressure of his, her arms going from around his waist to his neck in blissful abandon, her fingers delving into the black silk of his hair.

He made a sound of pleasure deep in his throat as her tongue slid forward to meet his, the intimate, moist coupling one of fevered urgency as if all hope of control had finally slipped out of his grasp.

His hands were on her breasts, his palms moulding her, caressing her through her clothes, until she was desperate to feel his skin on hers.

When he lifted her in his arms she made a tiny token sound of protest, but his mouth came back to hers to smother it.

'No, *cara mia*,' he said as he carried her towards the sweeping staircase. 'There is no turning back now. It is our time again at last.'

Nikki shivered in pleasure as Massimo's hands dealt with her clothes, his mouth kissing every bare inch of flesh as he uncovered it. He removed her bra, his hands skating over her full breasts, his eyes feasting on her until she felt her belly quivering with anticipation. He bent his mouth to her right breast and suckled on it, drawing the aching nipple into his mouth, his tongue rolling over and over it until her back came off the bed. Her left breast was subjected to the same exquisite torture, the pull of his hot mouth triggering a moist response deep in her feminine core.

He slid the zip of her skirt down and peeled away her tights, leaving her with nothing but her tiny knickers. She felt the scorch of his gaze as he cupped her tender mound, his fingers so close to where she pulsed for him she was sure he would be able to feel the drumbeat of desire against his palm.

She sucked in a sharp breath as he tugged the black lace away. 'You're not undressed,' she said raggedly.

'I know,' he said, lowering his head to the tiny indentation of her belly button, his breath whispering over her abdomen. 'I have other things on my mind right now.'

Nikki clutched at the sheets with clawing fingers as his mouth moved lower, his tongue leaving a glistening trail of fire all the way down to the tiny landing-strip of closely cropped curls that shielded her femininity. She gasped as his tongue separated her, the first rasping stroke against her making every single fine hair on her body stand to attention.

'You still taste of salt and sugar,' he said, moving back up her body with deliberate slowness, each movement of his lips sending another current of fire through her system.

Nikki wanted to taste and feel him, too. She tugged at his shirt, pulling it out of his trousers and tossing it over the edge of the bed. She pressed hot, little moist kisses to the naked skin of his chest, her fingers lacing through the sprinkling of dark hair, delighting in the feel of his arrant masculinity.

She undid his belt and slid it out of his trousers, and sent it in the same direction as his shirt, her fingers going to the fastening at his waist before releasing his zip. His thickness tented his black underwear and she pulled it out of the way to access him.

He groaned as she bent her head to him. *'Eiaculò troppo velocemente.'*

She ran her tongue down the silky shaft before asking, 'What does that mean?'

He flinched as she did it again. 'I will come too quickly,' he said, groaning as she bent her head again.

She opened her mouth over him, tasting his musky saltiness, feeling the glide of his satin-covered steel.

'Il mio dio,' he groaned again, his fingers digging into her hair. 'Stop now.'

'I don't want to stop.'

He swore and rolled her off him, pinning her beneath him, his body surging forward, parting her in one rough thrust. Her slick moistness welcomed him, her tight muscles clenching him possessively, her hips rising and falling as she followed his frantic rhythm. Her breath came in fevered gasps as the pace increased, beads of perspiration peppering her skin where the heat of his rocked against her.

She was so close, but not quite there when he began to massage her intimately, his long fingers playing her like an instrument until she was suddenly soaring. She hit the highest note of pleasure, the taut strings of her senses reverberating with wave after wave of rapture.

She felt his body tense momentarily above hers, the precursor to his freefall into oblivion. She held him as he shuddered through it, spilling himself into the warm cocoon of her body, until he collapsed against her, his hurried breath feathering the side of her neck where his face was pressed.

She stroked her hands over his back with long, massaging movements, rediscovering his muscular contours, her body still tingling from the heat and driving force of his.

She felt the slow trickle of his essence between her legs, and suddenly stiffened. 'Oh, no…'

Massimo propped himself on his elbows and looked down at her, his expression shadowed with concern. 'I have hurt you?'

'No, it's just that I… I mean, we didn't use protection. I'm not on the pill.'

He got off the bed in one lithe movement, the anger coming off him in rippling waves even though his voice was deceptively calm. 'Do you not think it might have been appropriate to tell me that a few minutes ago?' he asked.

Stung by the tone of accusation in his voice, she shot back defensively, 'You didn't exactly give me much time.'

His mouth tightened to a thin white line. 'So you are blaming *me*?'

She met his glittering glare with an equanimity she was nowhere near feeling. 'If you were so concerned you should have protected yourself, or is it a habit of yours to have unsafe sex?'

'No, it is not,' he said, his eyes narrowing slightly as he added, 'But then perhaps you planned it this way.'

Nikki refused to respond; besides, she could almost guess where his mind was heading.

'It is indeed an old trick, but a good one,' he said. 'If you were to fall pregnant it would give you a much bigger bargaining tool, would it not?'

'I'd rather die than have any child of yours,' she said with a fiery glare.

His mouth tightened even further. 'I thought I told you I will not have you speak to me so insultingly.'

She pulled her shoulders back in defiance. 'I will speak to you any way I like,' she said. 'You paid me to be your pretend mistress, not your subservient slave.'

There was a thick, pulsating silence.

'Thank you for reminding me,' he said coolly and reached for his trousers on the floor.

Nikki's mouth went dry as she watched him take out his wallet from the back pocket, his fingers unfolding it to take out a wad of cash.

'That should just about cover it,' he said, and dropped the cash on the bed.

She opened and closed her mouth, caught between a fury so intense and despair so deep she couldn't get a single word out. She stood in a helpless silence as he stepped back into his trousers, socks and shoes before reaching for a fresh shirt from the walk-in wardrobe, tucking it in as he came back to where she was standing.

'I am going out,' he announced.

'Do you think I care?' she bit out.

'Probably not, but I thought I should tell you all the same,' he said. 'I wouldn't want you to wait up for me unnecessarily.'

'Isn't that what a good little obedient mistress is supposed to do?' she asked with a curl of her lip.

His eyes held hers in a battle of wills that saw her drop her gaze first. She turned away, holding her arms close to her body, pain filling her chest until she could scarcely breathe.

'It doesn't have to be this way between us, Nikki,' he said after another long silence.

She clamped her bottom lip between her teeth, determined not to respond. But in a matter of seconds she heard the rustle of his clothes as he moved across the room, and the soft click of the door as it shut behind him.

CHAPTER TEN

THE flight to Palermo was long and tiring, in spite of the luxury of travelling in a private jet with attentive staff seeing to their every need. More in an effort to avoid conversation with Massimo, Nikki pleaded tiredness and lay down in the sleeping compartment, and, although she barely slept for more than a few minutes at a stretch, she was relieved he didn't join her. What his flight crew made of it she was beyond caring. She was still nursing her hurt from the night before. If only he knew how deeply he had insulted her. It had been so tempting to defend herself but she knew he would never have believed her. After all, she had married his stepfather, and Joseph had obviously led Massimo to believe their marriage was a real one.

Yet another member of staff met them at the airport and drove them to the villa overlooking the chief seaport of Sicily. The salty tang of the sea was heavy in the air, the bright summer sunshine a stark contrast to the capricious winter of Melbourne. Nikki breathed it in, her skin feeling as if the top layers were swelling in response to the delicious warmth of the sun.

A housekeeper with the name of Carine showed her to the master suite once they had made their way indoors. 'Signore

Androletti has instructed me to unpack for you,' she said. 'Do you need anything pressed for dinner this evening?'

'No, thank you,' Nikki said with a small smile. 'I'm used to seeing to things myself.'

The young woman looked confused. 'But you are a model, no?'

'I haven't modelled for months. I'm not used to being waited on any more; I prefer to look after myself,' Nikki said. 'Please don't trouble yourself. I've brought easy-care clothes in any case.'

'You are very different from Signore Androletti's usual partners,' the young woman observed.

Nikki couldn't resist asking, 'In what way?'

Carine made a little moue with her mouth. 'That last one, she was nothing but trouble, always wanting things at all hours of the day and night. I had to run errands for her all the time until my legs hurt.'

'I promise not to do that to you,' Nikki said with another friendly smile. 'Believe me, I'm very low-maintenance.'

Carine tilted her head as she looked at her. 'You are very beautiful, much more beautiful than her, although she too is blonde and tall—although if you ask me her hair colour comes out of a bottle.'

So, he has a thing for tall blondes, Nikki thought with a sharp little pang of jealousy. 'I'll try not to be too much trouble for you,' she said.

'I do not think you could ever be anything but good for Signore Androletti,' Carine said with passionate emphasis. 'He used to be such an easygoing man, but over the last few years he has…how you say in English…a chip on his shoulder?'

'Um…yes,' Nikki said, her face feeling a little hot. 'That's right, a chip on his shoulder.'

'See? I am learning good English from you already!' Carine said excitedly. 'Signorina Gambari would not even speak to me in Italian, let alone English. But you are not like that, I can tell. You are a nice lady. You must have had good upbringing, yes?'

'Er, yes,' Nikki lied. 'Very good.'

'I knew it,' Carine said as she straightened the bed covering with a proud little stroke of her hand. 'A good background is *importante*, no?'

'Very,' Nikki agreed.

'If you want me to do anything for you just call me,' Carine said.

'I will. Thank you.'

Carine smiled. 'I hope he asks *you* to be his wife,' she said. 'It is what he needs, a wife and a couple of *bambinos* to make him settle down. He has been playing for too hard and for too long.'

'Carine, would you please leave us?' Massimo's voice spoke from the door.

'*Sì, signore.*' Carine bowed her head subserviently and scuttled away.

Nikki turned on him in anger. 'There was no need to dismiss her so coldly,' she said. 'She is fond of you, who knows why, but she is.'

'I do not like to be the subject of my staff's speculations,' he said. 'Carine has a habit of speaking out of turn.'

'She is very young,' Nikki said in the young woman's defence. 'She is eager to please and shouldn't be reprimanded for it.'

He raised a brow at her. 'You are very good at this, are you not?' he asked. 'Worming your way into everyone's affections.'

'Except yours, of course,' she said with an element of bitterness.

'I have made my feelings towards you very clear.'

She sent him a churlish look. 'Yes, that's true. More than clear.'

He came to where she was standing, his eyes holding hers. 'You are still angry with me, eh, Nikki?' he asked.

'Yes, I am,' she said, glaring at him. 'What you did was unforgiveable.'

'That was our agreement, was it not? That you would be my mistress for a price.'

'I didn't sleep with you for money, and you know it,' she said.

'Then why did you sleep with me?'

Good question, Nikki thought. She lowered her gaze from the intensity of his. 'I didn't really intend for things to go that far,' she said. 'I thought I'd be able to stop at any point...'

'But you could not?'

His tone brought her eyes back to his. 'No,' she said, releasing a small sigh. 'I could not.'

He touched her cheek with the end of one long finger in a brushlike motion. 'Nor could I, *cara*,' he confessed. 'You are like a fever in my blood. I can feel you running like a hot river underneath my skin every time I look at you. No one else has ever made me feel this way.'

'But you don't love me.'

His mouth twisted with a hint of cynicism. 'You sound so genuinely disappointed, Nikki. I am almost tempted to believe you are developing feelings for me.'

'Massimo, I…'

He pressed her mouth closed with the pad of his thumb. 'No, *cara*,' he said. 'I do not want to hear empty words and phrases from you. We have a relationship built on mutual need, let's keep it at that. We will have our affair and at the end of it you will be free from the debts your late husband left you with. That is a bargain, is it not?'

It is a sure path to heartbreak, Nikki thought as his mouth came down to cover hers. Her lips swelled under the intoxicating pressure of his kiss, the first touch of his tongue against hers sending sparks of desire up and down her legs and the length of her spine. Her whole body responded in a rush of heady feeling, her skin tightening all over at the thought of his hands touching her the way he had touched her before. She pushed herself closer, her breasts crushed against his chest as her mouth fed hungrily off his, her soft whimpers of need fuelling him to deepen the kiss to a mind-blowing assault on her senses.

His hands moved to cup the gentle weight of her breasts, his thumbs rolling over the already tight buds of her nipples, triggering another whimper of pleasure from her throat.

'You want me just as much as I want you,' he said, momentarily lifting his mouth from hers. 'I feel it in your body; the pressure of longing is uncontrollable.'

Nikki didn't bother denying it. She pulled his head back down to her mouth and pushed her tongue between his lips to find his, curling around it with seductive little movements that made him growl as he began to deal with the barrier of her clothes.

Her lightweight skirt and top were soon dispensed with, his clothes, under the frantic and fumbling movement of her hands, joining them on the floor at their feet.

She caressed him through the fabric of his underwear, teasing him with each stroke of her hand until he wrenched the fabric away with a muttered curse of frustration.

Her fingers encircled him boldly, the satin-covered steel of his body making her shiver in anticipation at its alluring control over her. She felt the thrumming pulse of her body between her legs until it became an intense ache for assuagement. She rubbed against him unashamedly, her lower body on fire for the heat and power of his.

He wrenched his mouth away from hers long enough to growl, 'You are making me crazy for you. I am not going to be able to hold back.'

Nikki didn't want him to hold back, she wanted him to be as desperate and needy as she was. She pushed herself closer, her fingers digging into the taut flesh of his buttocks to bring him to her needy core.

He pushed her away to remove her bra before his hands went to her tiny lacy briefs. She felt the delicate tickle of lace being pulled down over her thighs as he knelt before her, and then the hot breeze of his breath as he cradled her hips in his hands to explore her melting form. Each and every hair on her head rose at the first flicker of his tongue against her, and her back arched in delight as he tasted her. Her fingers dug into his scalp at that first, sexy rasp of his tongue against the swollen pearl of her need, the sensations building to fever pitch until she felt every nerve tightening to snapping point.

The first wave of release hit her, closely followed by a second and third, each more devastating than the previous one. Her whole body shook and shuddered with the aftershocks, her legs still trembling as he straightened.

Nikki found it hard to look into his eyes in case he saw the truth of her feelings shining back at him. She concentrated on the fine sheen of perspiration on his chest, pressing her mouth to each of his dark-brown nipples, running her tongue over each one in turn before trailing a pathway to his belly button. She felt his body jerk in response as she began to go lower, his hands burying into her hair, a deep groan issuing from his throat at the first brush of her lips against his turgid length.

She knew he was close to losing control, she could feel the hair-trigger tension in his body, his deeply in-drawn breath signalling he was moving beyond the point of no return. She opened her mouth over him and drew on him again and again, stronger and stronger, until she felt him explode with a hot burst of male power that made her stomach hollow out in reaction as she tasted him fully for the first time.

The raw intimacy of what she had just done surprised her no less than it surprised him.

'You have certainly learnt a few tricks from my stepfather,' he said with a flicker of something she didn't care for in his eyes. 'And here I was thinking perhaps he had been boasting about your sexual expertise.'

'He *was* boasting,' she said emphatically. 'I never slept with your stepfather.'

His mouth became white-tipped with anger. 'Do not insult my intelligence with such a pathetic lie.'

'It's the truth,' she said. 'He couldn't, for one thing, and I wouldn't have even if he had been able to perform.'

He scooped up her clothing from the floor and thrust it at her. 'Get dressed.' He clipped the words out savagely. 'I do not want to listen to any more of this nonsense.'

'It's not nonsense!' Nikki insisted as he turned away to retrieve his own clothes. 'I didn't have a sexual relationship with Joseph. He had prostate cancer. He didn't want anyone to know how he'd become impotent after the radical surgical procedure had been performed. It devastated him, as indeed it would any man.'

He turned around to face her, his expression communicating his disbelief. 'So you felt sorry for him and married him, did you, Nikki? For money, right? Lots and lots of money, if I recall.'

Nikki couldn't bear to see the contempt in his glittering gaze and lowered her eyes. 'I told you my reasons for marrying your stepfather,' she said.

'Yes, you did, and you are with me for the very same reason, are you not?' he asked. 'Money motivates you to do almost anything, right, Nikki?'

She forced her gaze back to his. 'I am not ashamed of marrying your stepfather. He helped me when I needed help and treated me with nothing but respect.'

His eyes hardened as they pierced hers. 'You are not ashamed because you are without shame,' he said. 'You use people to get what you want and suffer no remorse about it.'

'That is more accurately a description of you, not me,' she threw back. 'You have exploited me in the most despicable way, treating me like a whore, when in the last five years I have never slept with anyone but you.'

His bark of mocking laughter made Nikki feel sick with anguish. 'Nice try, Nikki,' he said. 'You almost had me there. It is certainly a cute story, but like all fairy tales totally outside the realm of reality.'

'There's no way I can make you believe me, I know that,' she said. 'You are too bitter and angry for the truth to get a foothold. But what if you're wrong about me, Massimo?'

His dark gaze stripped her. 'I know what you are, Nikki. You are a social climber. You have lied to me from the very beginning, just as you lie to everyone you meet—even my housekeeper Carine just a short time ago.'

Nikki felt a tiny tremor of alarm rumble through her at his tone.

'You see, Nikki,' he went on. 'I have made some interesting observations about you.'

She swallowed back her rising panic. She told herself there was no way he could know about her past. No one knew. She had changed her name when she'd moved from Perth. The police had assured her the witness-protection scheme was secure.

'Are you not going to ask me what I have observed about you?' he asked.

Nikki swept her tongue across her lips. 'No, but I'm sure you're going to tell me anyway.'

His eyes held hers in silence for several agonising seconds.

'I would not have thought anything of it, but I got to wondering why your family was not at my stepfather's funeral. Every time you spoke of them in the past you painted a picture of familial bliss. Where were they when you needed them most, Nikki?'

She lowered her gaze. 'We had a falling out a...a couple of years ago...'

'What was it about?'

'Um...' *Oh God!* Why couldn't she think of something convincing under the pressure of his dark, probing gaze?

'What are you trying to hide from me, Nikki?' he asked into the pulsing silence.

She forced herself to hold his penetrating look. 'I came

from an unhappy home,' she said, trying to control the wobble in her voice. 'I know it's not exactly unusual in this day and age, but I was always ashamed of where we lived. There wasn't a lot of money and we moved a lot.'

Massimo frowned. 'Why did you feel it necessary to hide that from me five years ago?'

'I hate talking about my family life,' she said, her bottom lip trembling ever so slightly he almost missed it.

She sighed and continued in the same deadened tone, 'I spent my childhood dreaming of a perfect home, with a mother and father who loved each other and their children. My brother and I were an inconvenience. My father made it quite clear we were to be seen and not heard. My mother spent most of her life trying to keep us quiet in case we upset him. That's pretty much it. I know it probably seems a bit lame to you, but I got tired of making excuses for my parents. They should never have had children.'

'Do you still see them?'

She shook her head. 'My mother is dead and I have since severed all contact with my father.'

'What about your brother?'

She hesitated, her eyes moving away from his again. 'My brother and I are not as close as we once were,' she said. 'We see each other occasionally, but we don't really communicate all that much.'

Massimo found it intriguing to hear of her past. Although he could not forgive her for how she had exploited him, it certainly explained a lot about her greed for money and security. She had married his stepfather for money and to launch her career as a model, a career which he could see now had been as far removed from her impoverished background as any could be. She had worn the best of clothes and jewellery, eaten at the finest restaurants, drunk the most expensive wine, attended red-carpet movie premieres and stage shows with other celebrities as if she had been born to it.

But finding out all this now didn't mean he was going to allow her another chance to get her hooks into him. He would have his affair with her and call an end to it when it suited him. For, he reasoned, if she had cared anything for him five years ago she would have trusted him with the truth of her past. He had told her of his pain over the death of his father, and yet she had not once let on that her life had been anything but perfect.

He wasn't sure what to make of her claim that she had not slept with Joseph Ferliani. The reasons she'd given were certainly feasible, but he had been a victim of her deceit before, and wasn't keen on repeating the mistake of trusting that wide-eyed innocence.

However, he would have had to be blind not to recognise it had been difficult for her to open up to him now. Her whole demeanour suggested her confession had been nothing short of emotional torture. Her eyes looked wounded, and her face pale and pinched.

'Thank you for telling me,' he said into the silence. 'I am sorry if it caused you unnecessary pain.'

'I am used to it, believe me,' she said. 'But I would prefer it if we didn't have to speak of it again.'

'If that is what you want then the subject will be closed as of now.'

She looked down at her clothes still clutched against her chest. 'I guess I should get dressed.'

'No,' he said, removing them from her grasp. 'Not yet.'

Nikki looked up into his dark brown eyes and felt herself melt with longing. His hands went to her waist, their warmth seeping into her skin as he brought her closer to his hardening body. She closed her eyes as his mouth joined hers, her whole body sighing in pleasure as his tongue flicked against hers.

Nikki felt the subtle change in his kiss and touch, as if the anger of how she had treated him had gradually faded to be replaced by a longing that had nothing to do with revenge.

Her heart bursting with long-held-back feelings, she kissed him back with fervent passion, her arms looping around his neck, her pelvis pressed against the burning heat of his.

He scooped her up and brought her down to the bed, his weight coming down over her, pinning her beneath him. She felt him reach across to retrieve a condom from the bedside table drawer, deftly applying it before moving between her legs to possess her with a tenderness she found totally enthralling.

He gradually increased his pace, pulling her along with him in an exhilarating climb to the highest pinnacle of human pleasure. She was tipped over the edge by the brush strokes of his fingers playing her like a delicately tuned instrument. He joined her moments later with a deep groan of release that reverberated throughout his body. She felt and heard his sigh, and, still intimately joined, she nestled closer, her eyelashes drifting down in contentment.

Massimo listened to the gentle sound of her breathing, his hands idly playing with her hair where it lay in a silken pool around her head and shoulders. Her beautiful face was relaxed, her mouth softly swollen from his kisses, the mauve shadows under her eyes reminding him of his own exhaustion after the long-haul flight.

He let out a long sigh that caught on something small and prickly in his chest, and, closing his eyes, he breathed in the scent of her body, promising himself he would not stay for too long…

CHAPTER ELEVEN

NIKKI woke late the next morning to find herself alone in the big bed. She ran her fingers over the indentation in the pillow beside her, a little quiver of delight rushing through her as she thought about the passion and tenderness of the night before. Massimo had turned to her again during the early hours of the morning, his love making taking her to new heights of ecstasy.

She showered and then dressed in a light cotton sundress, with her hair scooped up in a casual knot, and made her way down to the terrace overlooking the sea where Carine had set up fresh rolls, fruit, home-made preserves and freshly brewed coffee.

'Signore Androletti will be with you shortly,' Carine said after a cheerful greeting. 'He is taking a few business calls.'

'Thank you, Carine,' she said as the housekeeper poured coffee. 'Have you worked for Signore Androletti long?'

'For three years,' Carine answered. 'I took over from my aunt who worked for the family for many years.' She handed the rolls to Nikki and added with a little look of self-consciousness, 'I guess I must not seem very ambitious compared to someone like you, working as a housekeeper instead of going after bigger and better things.'

'I'm hardly what you would call ambitious,' Nikki confessed with a slight frown. 'I haven't worked in months, and don't intend to again if I can help it.'

Carine suddenly looked past Nikki's shoulder and blushed. 'Signore Androletti,' she said. 'Your breakfast is served.'

'*Grazie*, Carine,' Massimo said. 'Could you inform Salvatore that we will be ready for the car in approximately one hour?'

Carine bowed her head. '*Sì, signore.*'

Nikki waited with bated breath as the housekeeper disappeared inside the villa. She could feel the tension coming off Massimo like a charge of electricity pulsing through the air.

'So,' he said with a brittle look as he took the chair opposite. 'You have no intention of ever returning to work. Why is that, I wonder—because you intend to land yourself another rich husband?'

Nikki moistened her lips as his dark eyes burned into hers. 'You misunderstood what I said to Carine,' she said. 'What I meant was I didn't intend to return to modelling.'

Suspicion lurked in the shadows of his gaze. 'Because I cancelled your contract?'

'No, because I am tired of it,' she said, looking away. 'I never really liked it in the first place. It was always just a job.'

'There are many women who would give anything to have had the chance for fame and fortune you have been given,' he said. 'Your face is recognisable wherever Ferliani Fashions are sold.'

Her eyes came back to his. 'The constructed image of Nikki Ferliani, yes—but it's not really me,' she said. 'Look at me, Massimo. Do I really look like the woman on the billboards?'

Massimo studied her for a moment. Her face was devoid of make-up, her hair casually arranged, some of it already escaping its clip to cascade down the sides of her heart-shaped face. He had to admit she didn't exactly look streetwise and worldly. She had a hint of fragility about her. The slightly anxious pleat of her brow, and the soft lips that had a tendency to roll together in uncertainty when she thought no one was looking, made him wonder if what she said was true—that the woman on the billboards was indeed someone else.

'You are still a very beautiful woman, *cara*,' he said. 'Even without the accoutrements of the modelling trade.'

He watched as she crumbled the roll with her fingers, her nails without colour and short as if she had nibbled at them recently.

Her grey-blue eyes met his briefly. 'Thank you.'

'Have you thought any more about my offer of a design job within the business?' he asked as he poured himself a cup of the steaming coffee.

'I'm…I'm not sure I'm the person for the job,' she said after a slight hesitation. 'I have no qualifications, and I only helped your stepfather out because he was falling behind.'

'Is there something else you would like to do?' he asked. 'You worked as a personal assistant in the business before. Would you consider a return to that?'

'I don't think it would be wise for me to get too involved,' Nikki said with a wry twist to her mouth. 'After all, I'm a temporary diversion in your life. When our affair is over, I can't imagine you wanting me underfoot at Ferliani.'

'I am not intending to keep Ferliani Fashions for very long,' he informed her. 'I have sunk considerable funds into the business, and once it recovers from the slight downturn it has experienced recently I will sell it. I already have had several enquiries. I am just waiting for the price to be driven up.'

'Ever the hard-nosed businessman,' she commented darkly.

His brows moved together over his eyes. 'You surely do not expect me to keep it indefinitely?'

Her shoulders came down on the weight of a sigh. 'No, perhaps not. It's just that your stepfather worked so hard at making it what it is.'

'You are forgetting he defrauded my father to do it,' he said. 'He used my father's hard-earned savings to fund his own dream of a fashion label.'

'I understand your bitterness,' she said. 'But both Joseph and your father are now dead. You can't change the circumstances that existed between them.'

'No, but I want justice.'

'By that I suppose you mean paying me back for rejecting you?'

He held her flinty look for several pulsing seconds. 'As far as I see it, I am being extremely generous towards you in offering to wipe out all the debt your late husband left you with, in exchange for a brief period of time as my lover.'

'The agreement was I was to be your trophy mistress,' she said, capturing her bottom lip briefly.

He paused in the process of bringing his coffee cup to his mouth. 'So the circumstances have changed a bit. It is to our mutual benefit, however, if the last two nights have been any indication.'

Nikki felt her face heating under his scrutiny. She looked down at the little mountain of crumbs she'd made with her restless fingers, her heart contracting as she wondered how long he would want her for.

Would his desire for her burn out within days, weeks or months? They had only had a week together five years ago, and, as wonderful as it had been, it didn't necessarily mean an affair for any length of time would work out now. He could tire of her within a few short weeks, which would leave her devastated. She had found it hard enough to walk away from him before—how much worse would it be this time around?

The slight rattle of his cup as he put it back on the glass-topped table brought her head back up to meet his eyes.

'I thought we could take a drive to one of the villages where the designs are manufactured,' he said. 'After there, we can do a little sightseeing for the rest of the day before stopping for dinner somewhere.'

'Fine.'

He waited another moment before adding, 'You are meant to be enjoying yourself, Nikki. You are supposed to look like a woman who is being spoilt by her attentive lover. The least you could do is smile for the benefit of my staff.'

'There is no staff around at the moment,' Nikki pointed out.

'Perhaps not, but I would still like to see you smile,' he said. 'I do not think I have seen you do so in the whole time we have been together.'

'The circumstances by which we are together are hardly the sort to bring an involuntary smile to my lips,' she remarked.

The line of his jaw stiffened as his eyes skewered hers. 'You do not give an inch, do you, Nikki? You like to twist that little knife of yours any chance you can. What do you hope to achieve by it, mmm? An apology from me, or a proposal?'

Nikki was the first to shift her gaze. 'I am not expecting much from you at all,' she said. 'You seem incapable of being anything but bitter and twisted towards me.'

'As I've told you before, if I remain bitter towards you, you have only yourself to blame,' he said. 'I do not respect a woman who marries a man she does not love for money. I can think of no single circumstance where that would ever be acceptable.'

Nikki got to her feet and, brushing the crumbs off her dress, sent him a rapier look. 'Then perhaps you're not thinking hard enough, Massimo.'

Massimo watched as she turned for the villa, her gait jerky and stilted, as if she couldn't wait to be rid of his presence. He heard the door open and close with a snap, the sound of it echoing through the villa.

A small frown began to tug at his brow as he slowly rose to his feet, his chest rising and falling on a heavy sigh as he tossed his napkin to one side and followed her indoors.

Nikki hadn't expected to enjoy the day in Massimo's company, but after they had driven to a small village about an hour and a half from Palermo the frozen silence that had accompanied them gradually thawed. As the morning progressed she could tell he was making an effort to effect some sort of truce. He involved her in all of the discussions at the factory, introducing her to the various staff members, his manner solicitous and polite throughout.

Nikki fingered the beautiful fabrics she was handed with reverence, smiling from time to time when one of the seamstresses showed her a clever invisible zip, or the delicate stitching that was a signature of a Ferliani design.

She got a particular thrill out of seeing the first of her own designs being made, the soft fall of fabric as one of the girls held it up for her inspection bringing a tiny lump to her throat.

In a different life she would have loved to do a fine-arts degree. She had often thought about it over the last five years, but had felt too ashamed to admit to Joseph that she hadn't even completed senior school.

She moved past the garments to the office where Massimo was already speaking in rapid-fire Italian to one of the more senior staff.

She felt a sensation like a sharp pain in her chest when she saw the brilliant whiteness of his smile as he looked down at the woman he was speaking to. Why couldn't he smile at her like that, she wondered. Was there a chance he could resurrect the love he'd had for her five years ago?

He turned and found her looking at him. 'Everything all right, Nikki?'

She nodded. 'Fine, yes…everything's fine…'

'Good,' he said, taking her by the hand. 'Now it is time for lunch. Are you hungry?'

'A little,' she said, lowering her eyes.

He gave her hand an almost imperceptible squeeze. 'Come; you are looking pale and in need of refreshment,' he said, and led her out to the car.

Over a leisurely lunch in a café on a cliff overlooking the sea, Massimo told her some of the island's history, how Sicily was the largest island in the Mediterranean with a rich heritage of art and history.

'Sicily is considered to be the world's first multicultural

society,' he said. 'It has been ruled by Asians, Africans and Europeans, which makes for an eclectic history. You will see thirty centuries of history here, from Greek temples and Roman amphitheatres, Aragonese churches and Arab castles.'

Nikki lapped up the spectacular scenery as they drove back towards Palermo a short time later, the sheer height and drop of some of the cliffs that hugged the coastline breathtaking to say the least.

'We will go first to Cappella Palatina, or Palatine Chapel as it is also known,' Massimo said. 'It contains a wonderful blend of cultures—Byzantine, Norman, Arabic and Sicilian— and has some of the most beautiful mosaics in the world.'

Nikki took his proffered hand a short time later, and looked up in wonder at the wooden ceiling styled into Arab-style stalactites and alveoli dating back to 1143.

They moved on to the cathedral, built in 1184 by the Norman king William II, where Massimo informed her the many renovations over the centuries had resulted in the current neoclassical style. Nikki listened to the deep sound of his voice, the element of pride within it making her realise he was deeply passionate about many things besides business and making money.

He caught her looking at him intently at one point and gave her a rueful smile. 'I am boring you, yes?' he asked.

'No,' she said, a tiny smile pulling at her mouth.

He put a finger to where her lips had lifted slightly, his touch feather-light. 'You nearly smiled,' he said. 'Does that mean you forgive me for being a brute towards you this morning and the other night?'

'We are standing in a cathedral,' she said somewhat wryly. 'I can hardly say no, now, can I?'

His thumb brushed lightly over the surface of her bottom lip. 'I am getting tired of sightseeing. We should have dinner; are you hungry again yet?'

'Not really…' She brought her tongue out just as his thumb came back over her lips, the intimate contact sending sparks of sensation throughout her body.

Their eyes locked for a two-beat pause.

Nikki felt the magnetic pull of his body as hers began to sway towards his. Her heart began to flutter with excitement as his eyes dipped to her mouth, his head moving closer and closer…

The sound of approaching footsteps broke the moment, and with a barely audible sigh he took her hand and led her out to the brilliant sunshine.

Even before they were led to a table in a restaurant a little while later, Nikki could smell the aromas of Sicilian cooking in the air. The hint of wild fennel, mint, almonds, sardines and anchovies all made her mouth start to water.

Massimo ordered some local wine, and when it arrived raised his glass to hers. 'Let us toast to peace while in Italy,' he said. 'I do not want our time here spoilt by pointless bickering.'

She met his eyes across the top of her glass. 'I'm not the one doing the bickering.'

He frowned at her in disapproval. 'That is not helping, Nikki. Come; let us put the past aside for a few days and act like any other couple on holiday.'

She backed down with a sigh and touched her glass against his. 'All right,' she said. 'To peace between us.'

'Good girl,' he said with a smile. 'That did not hurt, did it?'

'Not so far.'

'You do not trust me to keep my promise?' he asked.

Nikki looked at the glass in her hand rather than at his face. 'It is hard for me to trust anyone,' she confessed. 'I guess it comes from my childhood.'

'Tell me about it, *cara*,' he said. 'Was it so very terrible? I know you said you did not want to discuss it, but perhaps it will help to talk of it.'

Her eyes flicked to his before moving away again. 'It doesn't help, Massimo. Talking doesn't change anything.'

Massimo felt his stomach clench as he looked at the shadow of deep sadness in her eyes. 'You were not…' he paused as he searched for the right word '…abused in some way, were you?'

The silence was broken only by the sound of crockery and cutlery being used on the nearby tables, the lively, convivial chatter a stark backdrop to the closed expression on her face.

'Nikki?' he prompted gently.

'Not in the way you mean,' she said at last. 'But there are other ways to make a child's life miserable.'

'Il mio povero tesoro,' he said, reaching for her hand.

She looked at him. 'What does that mean?'

He held her look for a long time before he spoke. 'It means I am getting soft where you are concerned, Nikki.'

She looked down at their joined hands and asked softly, 'Is that a good thing or a bad thing?'

He brought her hand up to his mouth and brushed her fingertips with his lips, his eyes locking on hers. 'I guess I will have to wait and see.'

CHAPTER TWELVE

NIKKI hadn't really trusted him to keep his word, but over the next few days he never once mentioned the past. She could feel herself gradually relaxing as each day passed, the hope in her chest gradually unfolding like the petals of a delicate flower each time he smiled at her.

The nights she spent in his arms, his passion for her seemingly increasing as each day passed. She gave herself up to the wild torrent of feelings that coursed through her at the first brush of his lips and the first touch of his tongue. His body surged into hers, his groans of pleasure like music to her ears. She loved the feeling of him losing himself; the total relaxation of his body in her arms made her feel as if she had touched him in a way no one had ever done before. She became increasingly bold with her worship of his body, relishing in the harsh grunts of response that came from deep within him when she pushed him to the brink time and time again.

The last night before they were to leave for Melbourne came all too soon. Nikki hoped the change in location wouldn't sever the atmosphere of friendliness that had grown along with their passion. So many times over the last couple of days she had wanted to tell him of her reasons for marrying Joseph. His gentled attitude towards her made her feel as if she might be able to trust him enough to reveal the dark pain of her past.

But each time she mentally rehearsed the words, her guilt over Jayden's condition would assail her all over again.

As unpredictable and violent as her father had been, she had never imagined that standing up to him that day would have such an outcome. The vision of that afternoon was etched on her brain for ever. The black bats of blame had haunted her ever since, circling her, flapping at her in accusation. 'Your fault, your fault, your fault,' they seemed to say with each beat of their wings inside her head.

She couldn't escape from the torture of it. The thought of talking about it in any detail would surely give her a return of the nightmares that had plagued her in those first harrowing years.

'You are looking very pensive this evening, *cara*,' Massimo commented as their main meal was cleared away. 'Are you not looking forward to returning home tomorrow?'

'Sorry,' she said with a tiny glimmer of a wistful smile. 'I'm not very good company tonight, am I?'

'What are you thinking about?' he asked. 'I have been watching you for the last few minutes. Is something troubling you?'

She toyed with her glass, the movements of her fingers nervous and edgy. Could she do it? Could she trust him with her pain? What if he was repulsed by the thought of having a permanent relationship with a violent criminal's daughter? For what man would want that tainted blood running around the veins of his future offspring?

'Massimo.' She brought her eyes up to meet his, the tip of her tongue snaking out to moisten her lips. 'There's something I have wanted to tell you…'

A flicker of disquiet came and went in his gaze. 'You are pregnant?' he said.

She blinked at him, momentarily knocked off course. 'No, of course not,' she said, blushing slightly.

'We made love without protection over a week ago,' he reminded her.

'So?'

'So one would assume, if you have conceived, then you will not have a period on time,' he said. 'When are you due?'

Oh, God, when *am* I due? Nikki thought in panic. She was hardly regular at the best of times, and with the strain of nursing Joseph over the last few months, and her lower than normal body weight as a result of stress and too many missed meals, she had no idea of the rhythm of her body.

'Nikki?'

'Um…next week,' she said. 'But with all the travelling I might go out of whack. I often do.'

'I think it would be best if you go on the pill when we return,' he said. 'I do not want any little accidents.'

Nikki felt her hopes come crashing down. If he cared anything for her, he would want to continue their relationship indefinitely. The conception of a child would not be seen as a burden but a blessing, an intimate bond like no other. How much worse would it have been if she had told him the truth?

She stripped her expression of emotion as she met his gaze. 'There won't be any little accidents,' she assured him. 'It is not necessary for a woman in this day and age to endure an unwanted pregnancy.'

He frowned at her statement. 'You would have a termination?'

Nikki suddenly realised she had backed herself into a tight corner. 'I have no issue with women having the freedom of choice, but for me personally I would try and find an alternative if I should be in that position.'

'You mean have the child adopted out?' he asked, still frowning.

'You make it sound worse than a termination,' she said with a twisted expression. 'My mother made the biggest mistake of her life by marrying my father because she was pregnant with me. By the time she thought about leaving him, she was pregnant again with my brother. Supporting two little kids when you've had very little in terms of secondary education is not easy, even with the government handouts available both then and now. She lost her confidence under my father's constant belittlement. She became complicit in her own subjugation. In her overburdened and tortured mind, Jayden and I became the enemy instead of our father.'

'So she took her frustration out on you and your brother?'

She gave a little shrug that should have communicated indifference, but in the end didn't. 'Occasionally.'

'But your father was the main perpetrator?'

Her eyes fell away from his, the movements of her hands becoming all the more agitated. 'I really don't like talking about this.'

'I know you do not, Nikki,' he said, reaching for one of her hands and squeezing it gently. 'But do you not see how important it is for me to understand what you have been through?'

'Why is it important?' she asked, her mouth turning down in bitterness. 'I'm nothing to you.'

'That is not true.'

She looked at him, hope inflating like a balloon in her chest. 'W-what are you saying?' she asked.

His dark eyes bored into hers. 'I want to understand you, Nikki. I want to know what secrets you are keeping from me. I feel it every time we are together. You always hold something of yourself back. The only time you do not do so is when we are intimate.'

She shifted her gaze, her mouth twisting ruefully again. 'Yes, well, I don't seem to have any control over that.'

He gave her hand another tiny squeeze. 'Neither do I, *cara mio*,' he said. 'I guess our bodies have a language of their own, mmm?'

Nikki moved her fingers against his hold, her stomach turning over at the realisation of literally being held in the palm of his hand.

'You do not like to be vulnerable, do you, Nikki?' he asked.

'Does anyone?'

'Perhaps not,' he conceded. 'But between lovers it is expected that a certain level of vulnerability and openness is a given.'

'We don't have that sort of relationship.'

'No, but we could have.'

Nikki felt her whole body stall at his words. 'What do you mean?'

He turned her hand over and began to stroke the soft skin of her exposed palm with his thumb. 'I am enjoying this truce we have agreed on,' he said. 'What do you say we continue it for a little bit longer?'

'How long are you talking about?'

'I have not thought about a time frame,' he said. 'We are both enjoying being together, are we not?'

It wasn't as if she could deny it, Nikki thought. She had given him plenty of proof of her satisfaction with their arrangement last night, her body rocking and shuddering beneath the surging weight of his. She could still feel him inside her, those tender muscles responding by contracting every time he looked at her with that dark, smouldering gaze.

'We should get a good night's sleep,' he said as the silence crept towards them. 'Although we do not leave until late in the day tomorrow, I do not want you to be too tired.'

Nikki got to her feet on unsteady legs. 'I'm not the least bit tired,' she said. 'I fell asleep this afternoon on the sun lounger.'

He brought her up close, his body brushing the entire length of hers. 'That is the best news I have heard all day,' he said, pressing a hard, brief kiss to her lips.

She slipped her hand into his as they went to their room, her excitement building with each step. She loved him in this mood; his playfulness made her forget about the reasons they were together. It made her forget about his need for revenge; he was just a man who was seriously attracted to her, wanting to be with her at every opportunity.

'Undress for me,' he commanded as he shut the door of the bedroom with a click.

Even a few nights ago Nikki would have baulked at his request, but with a week or so of sunshine and good food she felt her body had taken on a healthy glow it hadn't experienced in years. Her breasts felt fuller and more feminine, her hips less boyish and angular, and the kiss of the sun had made her pasty skin take on a golden hue that shimmered in the soft light of the bedside lamps.

'What do you want me to take off first?' she asked, with a sultry half smile.

'The top,' he said. 'I want to see your breasts.'

She undid her blouse, button by button, taking her time, sending him looks from beneath her lowered lashes as she gradually revealed herself to him.

'Now go lower,' he said. 'And touch yourself.'

That was harder, but she did it because he made her feel as if she was the most beautiful and desirable woman in the world. She watched as his eyes fed off her, the smooth glide of her hands over her breasts and her lower body making his pupils dilate and his throat move up and down convulsively.

'Come here,' he said roughly.

She stepped forward, her arms going up to loop around his neck, her breasts pushing against his chest. 'Like this?' she asked with another seductive half-smile.

He growled as his mouth connected with hers, his tongue driving through her softly parted lips in search of hers, tangling with it erotically. His hands shaped her breasts, his thumbs rolling over each nipple until he tore his mouth off hers to suckle each one, the pull of his mouth on her sensitive flesh making her shiver all over in reaction.

She felt the bed at the backs of her knees as he walked her backwards, his mouth returning to hers with increasing pressure. She opened her legs to accommodate him, the steely brace of his thighs sending her belly into another quiver of delight. There was barely time for preliminaries, although he managed to grab a condom before he drove into her silky warmth with a harsh groan of satisfaction.

Nikki dug her fingers into his back as he set a hurried pace, the urgency of each of his thrusts thrilling her. She felt tension build and build in every nerve of her body, until all she could think about was that final lift-off where all conscious thought was momentarily suspended.

His first intimate stroke of the tight pearl of her femininity sent her soaring, her whole body feeling as if it had splintered into a thousand tiny pieces.

She felt him come on the tail end of her release, the spasms of her body sending him over the edge. She held him as he rocked against her, her heart feeling so full of love for him she had to bite her tongue in case she said it out loud.

She knew he wouldn't believe it if she told him. He would think she was feigning love in an attempt to achieve financial security for herself.

Massimo lifted his head and looked into her eyes. 'What is that little frown for?' he asked.

Nikki tried to relax her brow. 'Am I frowning?'

He traced a finger over the space between her eyebrows. 'You will get wrinkles if you frown all the time.'

'Smiling is worse,' she said, lifting a finger to outline his top lip. 'You use more muscles to smile than to frown.'

He gave her a teasing smile. 'Did you just make that up?'

'No, I read it somewhere, in a magazine I think,' she said, moving her finger to brush over his bottom lip.

'Ah, but happy people live longer,' he said, capturing her wandering finger and pressing a tiny light-as-air kiss to the end of it. 'A positive outlook on life is a recipe for longevity.'

Her frown came back and her fingers dropped away from his mouth. 'But happiness is not always up to the individual,' she said. 'You can have the most positive outlook in the world, but some circumstances in your life can eventually drag you down.'

'Like your childhood?'

She turned her head away. 'You promised not to mention it again,' she said, her mouth turning down at the edges. 'It's taken me years to put it behind me. I don't want to have to bring it into every conversation we have.'

Massimo felt the aching loneliness of her soul, the sadness in her eyes making his chest feel tight. He couldn't help feeling a little guilty about the way he had forced her back into his life. He had been hell-bent on revenge, not really stopping to think if there was a reasonable explanation for what she had done. Even now he still couldn't think of a single set of circumstances that he would find acceptable for doing what she had, but, as she had said a few days ago, perhaps he hadn't thought deeply enough.

His childhood had been reasonably happy until his mother had deserted his father, but he knew of others who had suffered greatly at the hands of their parents. The newspapers were full of it almost daily—neglect, shaming, abuse both physical and sexual; the cruelty of some adults continually astounded him.

He thought about Nikki's young body being brutalised in some way, for what else had put those haunting shadows in her eyes? She tried to hide it, most particularly when arguing with him. Although she stood her ground with a defiant set to her mouth, he had noticed she never allowed herself to be backed into corners, as if she had already worked out the nearest and quickest escape-route if she ever needed to take it.

It surprised him how much he was affected by her every mood. He liked it when she smiled, and he liked it when she gave herself to him with increasing abandon. He liked the way she kissed him so passionately, her arms flung around his neck as she had done in the past. He hadn't expected his feelings for her to be reawakened in such a way.

Damn it! He didn't want them to be reawakened. He wanted to continue to hate her for betraying him, to make her pay for the heartache she had caused.

She had sold herself to his stepfather, and according to what the lawyer had said she had had numerous affairs during the five years she and Joseph Ferliani had been together.

He had to remember that.

She wasn't to be trusted.

A sneaking suspicion began to lurk at the edges of his mind, and although he hated allowing it purchase he reasoned he had to examine this from all possible angles. What if she was making the stuff about her childhood up? He had heard stories of such things before, a wayward child causing trouble by casting aspersions in order to destroy a parent. Whole families had been torn apart by such specious claims.

What if she had done the same in order to garner sympathy from his stepfather? If so it had certainly worked, as within a few short weeks of working for Joseph Ferliani she had married him.

And now she was doing it to him, reeling in his sympathy for her hard life, in the hope that he would relax his plan for revenge.

'Nikki,' he said turning her head around to face him. 'Where did you grow up?'

Her eyes flared with sudden anger, her hand pulling his away from her face. 'You're not listening to me, Massimo. I told you, I don't want to talk about it.'

He captured her hands and held them above her head as

she bucked and rolled beneath him. 'Stop it, Nikki. It is not such a difficult question, and if you do not tell me then I will have to engage the services of a private investigator to find out for myself. Which would you prefer?'

The fight went right out of her. She lay very still in his hold, her body now limp. 'I grew up in Mount Isa,' she said in a flat, toneless voice.

Massimo knew she was lying. He was starting to recognise the signs now that he had spent time with her. She couldn't hold his gaze, and her face took on a betraying hue of faint colour. 'I can always check that, you know,' he said.

She gave him a defiant look. 'Check it, see if I care. You won't find anything.'

'No, because you did not grow up there, did you?'

She clamped her mouth shut and turned her head away again.

Massimo let out a sigh and got off the bed. 'I am going to have a shower. Do you want to join me?'

She answered by pulling the sheets over her head.

The next morning he joined her at breakfast on the sun-drenched terrace with a frown on his forehead. 'It looks like you are going to get your business-class flight after all, *cara*,' he said as he pulled out the chair to sit down. 'I will not be able to accompany you back to Melbourne as planned. I have some unexpected business to see to. I will have to stay on for another week at the very least.'

Nikki tried not to show her disappointment, and concentrated on pouring him a cup of the delicious coffee Carine had set out just moments earlier. 'It's all right,' she said. 'I have plenty to keep me occupied in Australia.'

He took a quick sip of the coffee before placing it back

down on the table. 'Perhaps you can take a quick trip to Mount Isa to visit your father and brother, eh, Nikki?'

Her cup gave a small rattle against the saucer as she set it back down. 'I don't like the humidity at this time of year,' she said, meticulously avoiding his probing gaze.

'I will try to tie things up here quickly,' he said into the suddenly pulsing silence. 'But I should warn you not to try anything silly while I am away.'

She arched one brow at him. 'You mean such as act like an independent person for a few days?' she asked.

'I meant as in finding yourself another lover to fill in the time,' he said with a warning look. 'Ricardo is under instructions to keep a close eye on you.'

Nikki felt her anger rising like a hot lava-flow inside her. 'Don't judge me by your own despicably low standards,' she tossed back at him. 'I can just imagine what your business here involves.'

His expression darkened. 'I have tried to be patient with you, Nikki,' he said. 'We have had seven days of a truce, and yet you are throwing it away to score points off me.'

'I didn't break the truce—you did. You keep insisting we talk about things I don't want to talk about.'

'You have shared my bed and my body,' he threw back tightly. 'The very least you could do is honour me with the truth.'

'You speak to me of *honour*?' She glared at him. 'You don't even know the meaning of the word! For all I know you're probably bedding a dozen women behind my back as part of your plan for revenge. But I've got news for you—I don't care.'

'Good,' he said as he put his cup down with a sharp crack.

He got to his feet, his dark eyes glittering with barely suppressed anger. 'Enjoy your flight. I will see you in seven days.'

Nikki opened her mouth to fling a bitter retort his way, but stopped when she saw Carine coming out of the door leading to the terrace. The little housekeeper had to step sideways to avoid cannoning into Massimo, who glowered at her on his way past.

She came over to Nikki and set the rolls down, her expression grim. 'Signore Androletti is in a bad mood. I hope it is not because of the phone call he had this morning.'

Nikki picked up her cup with a shaky hand. 'What phone call?'

Carine blew out a breath. 'I should not really tell you, but I do not like that woman,' she said. 'She calls all the time and demands to speak to Signore Androletti.'

'You mean Sabrina Gambari?'

Carine nodded, her mouth pulled tight.

'What did she want?' Nikki asked, trying not to sound too interested.

'She wants to see him, of course,' Carine said. 'She will not take no for an answer.'

Nikki felt a mouthful of coffee come back up into her mouth from her stomach, the acid burn scalding her throat. 'Do you think that's the business he has to see to this morning?' she asked before she could stop herself.

Carine gave her a world-weary look. 'I was hoping it was over between them,' she said. 'When he brought you here I was so certain he would settle down with you, but now he cannot do so.'

Nikki moistened her lips. 'Why is that?' she asked, her throat feeling tight and scratchy.

The young housekeeper bit her lip, glancing back at the villa uncertainly. 'I am not sure I should tell you…'

'It's all right,' Nikki reassured her.

'But you are involved with Signore Androletti,' Carine said. 'I do not want to hurt you.'

Nikki decided to be honest with the young woman. 'Carine, listen to me,' she said. 'I am only a temporary interest of Signore Androletti. He is not in love with me. I have known that from the beginning.'

'But what about your feelings for him?' Carine asked with a concerned frown.

'My feelings are irrelevant,' Nikki said sadly. 'That's also something I've known right from the start.'

Carine took a breath and clutched at the back of the chair Massimo had not long vacated. 'Signorina Gambari is pregnant,' she said. 'I heard one of the villagers talking about it this morning when I was getting the rolls from the bakery.'

Nikki felt her chest tighten to the point of pain. She could scarcely breathe for the weight of it crushing against her chest.

His ex-mistress was having his child.

'That is why he cannot come back to Australia with you,' Carine continued. 'I am certain he is going to marry that woman. It will be expected. The Gambari family will insist on it.'

'But surely that is up to Massimo?' Nikki put in. 'He doesn't strike me as the type to be pushed around.'

'No, but a son and heir is what every Italian man craves,' Carine said. 'Signorina Gambari might not be his first choice for a wife, but she has taken the matter right out of his hands by producing a child for him. He will not allow a child of his to grow up illegitimate.'

'What if it isn't his child?' Nikki asked.

Carine began to clear the table, her expression still grim. 'I guess we will have to wait and see.'

CHAPTER THIRTEEN

NIKKI'S arrival in Melbourne was hampered by heavy fog, which meant the flight had to be redirected to Sydney and wait there for several hours until the airport was reopened.

Ricardo met her in the arrivals hall and transported her to Massimo's house, his glances from time to time as she surreptitiously brushed at her eyes making her wish she had better control over her emotions.

She had desperately hoped Massimo would come back to the villa in time to speak to her before she left, but the hours had dragged past without him returning. It made her realise how little he cared for her to send her back like a parcel, instead of a person with feelings, with hopes and dreams. Her mind filled with images of him with his mistress, perhaps celebrating the news of her pregnancy, planning their wedding and future together.

She clenched her sodden tissue in her hand and gulped back another sob, her tear-washed eyes staring sightlessly out of the window as the rain lashed down outside.

'Signore Androletti has instructed me to drive you wherever you need to go,' Ricardo said as he carried her luggage into the house forty minutes later.

'I know what he said, but I don't need a driver,' Nikki said. 'I prefer to use public transport.'

'You would be wise to do as he says,' Ricardo warned.

She gave him a scathing look as she moved towards the staircase. 'I don't take orders from Signore Androletti.'

'I do not want to lose my job.'

She turned around to look at him. 'If he fires you over me refusing to be chauffeured around then he's even more ruthless and dishonourable than I thought.'

'He is a good man,' Ricardo insisted. 'He will always do the most honourable thing.'

Nikki suppressed an inward sigh as she continued up the stairs. That was the whole reason her heart was breaking all over again. They had missed their chance five years ago, and in spite of all her hopes they were not going to get another one.

It was too late.

The phone was ringing as Nikki came out of the bathroom three days later. 'Hello?'

'Nikki,' Massimo's voice greeted her coolly. 'You took so long to pick up I was beginning to wonder if you had run away.'

'I can hardly do that with your little watchdog on my tail all the time,' she told him resentfully.

He gave a soft chuckle of laughter. 'Ricardo knows which side his bread is buttered,' he said. 'And hopefully so do you.'

'I want to move out,' she said. 'There's no point in continuing this arrangement now.'

There was a momentary pause.

'Are you forgetting the money you owe me?' he asked.

'Are you forgetting the woman you got pregnant?' she shot back.

This time the silence pulsated for endless seconds.

'As far as I know I have not impregnated any woman,' he said. 'Unless, of course, you have some news of your own to tell me.'

Nikki felt a flutter of panic deep in her belly. Her period hadn't arrived, and the tiredness she had assumed was jet-lag had continued regardless of the amount of sleep she'd had.

'Nikki?'

'No, of course not,' she said. 'But I thought—'

'I told you my ex-mistress was determined,' he said before she could finish her sentence. 'But I am not so foolish as to fall for that trick.'

'H-how did you find out it wasn't yours?' she asked.

'I insisted on a paternity test, but in the end it was not necessary, as Sabrina confessed she had been lying about being pregnant.'

'Oh…'

'So that is why I am returning to Melbourne the day after tomorrow,' he said. 'I will expect you to be waiting for me.'

'That's what I am being paid to do,' she said with a barb of bitterness in her tone.

'Yes,' he said. 'You are, and you had better not forget it.'

'You're an arrogant bastard,' she said. 'I should have known that the first time I met you.'

'You sound like you are missing me, *cara*,' he drawled. 'You are spoiling for another fight, mmm?'

Nikki ground her teeth. 'I can't wait to get away from you. I hate you.'

He laughed again. 'You are not going to get away from me until I say so, *cara*. That is the deal, remember?'

Nikki could feel her emotions spilling over again. With

Ricardo following her every move, she hadn't been able to visit Jayden since she'd returned from Sicily. She'd called and the carer on duty had told her he hadn't been well; his fits had increased alarmingly, and he'd had a bad chest infection which wasn't responding to treatment.

'I-I can't do this any more…' she choked. 'I just can't.'

'Nikki.' His tone softened a fraction. 'You are crying?'

'Of course I'm not crying,' she sobbed. 'I n-never cry.'

Massimo released a long-winded sigh. 'I am sorry, Nikki,' he said. 'You are feeling trapped, eh?'

'Y-yes,' she sniffed. 'Ricardo follows me like a shadow. I can't bear it any more. I hate being looked at all the time. I hated it when I was modelling. I can't be myself.'

'Stop crying, Nikki.'

'I-I'm not crying…'

'Yes, you are. I can hear you.'

'Why should you care?' she asked. 'You hate me, re-member?'

'I have not forgotten my feelings for you,' he said after another little pause.

Nikki gave another little sniff. 'I just want this to be over,' she said. 'How much do I owe you now?'

Massimo tightened his resolve. 'I will tell you when I get back,' he said.

'But I need to know now.'

'Why?'

'Because this is not working for us, Massimo,' she said. 'You know it's not. We can pretend to have a truce for a few days, but it doesn't last. There's too much bitterness.'

'You are my mistress now, Nikki. We have a commitment of sorts and I expect you to fulfil your side of it.'

'I don't want to be your—'

'Goodbye, Nikki,' he said. 'I am hanging up.'

'If you hang up I won't be here when you get back,' she threatened.

'If you are not there when I get back I will find you and sue you for the debts you owe,' he countered.

'So either way you win,' she said cuttingly.

'That is right, Nikki. And you had better remember it. You are mine for as long as I want you.'

There was no sign of Ricardo the next day so Nikki could only assume Massimo had called him off. It made her soften towards him, in spite of her anger at the way he was insisting she stay in his life according to the rules he had set down.

She wished she did hate him for it would have made things so much easier, she thought as she made her way to Rosedale House.

Jayden was sleeping when she arrived, his deathly pale face tearing at her heart strings as she sat by his bedside.

The doctor came past just after tea time and asked to speak to her in the office down the hall.

'I am afraid your brother's condition is worsening daily,' Julia Lynch said once Nikki had sat down. 'He's had several grand-mal fits, and in spite of an increased dose of medication it is not controlling them.'

Nikki swallowed back her dread. 'What are you saying?' she asked in a voice hardly above a cracked whisper.

Dr Lynch touched her on the arm, her caramel-brown eyes soft with compassion. 'I don't think he's going to hold on much longer, Nicola. I know we've discussed this earlier, but sometimes it takes a while for it to sink in.'

'I understand…'

'He's been going downhill for quite some time,' Julia continued. 'You did the right thing in getting him in here where the level of care has been consistent, but it's not going to cure him. Nothing was ever going to do that. You do understand that, don't you?'

Nikki nodded, her throat suddenly too tight to speak.

'We are offering him the best level of comfort we can,' Julia said. 'If there is any change we will call you.'

'Thank you.'

'I wish I could offer you more hope,' the doctor said as she got to her feet. 'We see a lot of sad cases in here, but Jayden's is one of the saddest.'

Nikki brushed at her eyes. 'He was such an active kid. He used to surf every morning, he was so good at it. He was bright too, he could have done anything he wanted… anything…'

The doctor gave her shoulder a gentle squeeze. 'Take care of yourself, Nicola.'

'I will…thank you.'

Pia was sitting on the doorstep when Nikki returned, which made her want to cry all over again. She scooped the little cat up in her arms and buried her head against the soft fur. 'How did you know I needed a friend right now?' she asked.

The cat gave her chin a nudge with its head which made a sad smile tug at Nikki's mouth. 'I missed you too, Pia.'

Ricardo appeared briefly to inform her he was going to pick up Massimo from the airport.

'But I thought he said he was coming back tomorrow,' she said with a confused frown.

'He changed his plans,' Ricardo said. 'He lands in just over an hour.'

Nikki couldn't sit still while she waited for Massimo to return. She paced and fidgeted so much Pia stalked out in disgust, and returned to her own home over the back fence.

Nikki heard the car come up the driveway and got to her feet, one of her hands tucking a loose strand of hair behind her ear as Massimo came into the lounge from the foyer.

'Nikki,' he said, his gaze sweeping over her. 'Come here.'

She stood very still, fighting with herself not to dash across the room and throw herself into his arms.

'I said come here.'

'I know what you said, but I'm not coming,' she said with a defiant hitch of her chin.

His mouth tilted in a sardonic smile. 'You are determined to fight me at every opportunity even when it hurts you to do so,' he said.

'What hurts me is being used by you.'

'I am not using you, Nikki. We are both benefiting from this arrangement.'

'How can I trust you to fulfil your side of the agreement?' she asked. 'You say I will be debt free once this is over, but I want proof.'

'All right,' he said after a little silence. 'I'll contact the lawyer in the morning and have something drawn up.'

'I don't want to see Peter Rozzoli. I don't trust him.'

'It seems to me you do not trust anyone,' he said.

'No, that's right, I don't.'

'Is that why you lied to me about growing up in Cairns?'

Nikki felt her throat move up and down but she couldn't get her voice to work.

'I see no reason why you should lie about where you grew up, unless you did something so bad that you have to keep your past a secret,' he said after another stretching silence. 'Is that what this is all about, Nikki? You did something you are ashamed of and want to keep it hidden?'

She drew in a shaky breath when he came closer, her heart thudding erratically when he lifted her chin with one long finger. 'Tell me your little secret, *cara*,' he said.

'T-there's no secret…'

His eyes glinted at her. 'Do I have to tease it out of you?' he asked.

She swallowed as his other hand went to her hip and brought her up against him, pelvis against pelvis, heat against heat, want against want.

He pressed a soft-as-air kiss to the edge of her mouth, making her lips begin to tingle to feel the crushing weight of his.

Her tongue darted out, trying to sweep the sensation away, but before she could close her mouth again his tongue snaked out to flick against hers.

Fire exploded in her belly.

Hot, liquid longing burst between her thighs as his mouth came down hard upon hers, his tongue driving through her already parted lips to mate with hers. She clung to him with desperate fingers curling into the front of his shirt, her mouth feeding hungrily off his, her breathing all over the place as his hands began to wrench wildly at her clothes.

The first touch of his warm palm on her bared breast had her gasping into his mouth as he deepened the kiss. Her body arched towards him, her nipples tight as he left her mouth to suckle each one in turn, his tongue both a torment and a salve as he subjected them to his attention.

She could feel her body singing with pleasure, every nerve end tightening in response to his fevered touch. She pressed herself closer, the hot, hard jut of his body thrilling her to realise he wanted her so badly.

He pushed her backwards towards the sofa, the solid weight of him as they landed in a tangle of arms and legs and half-removed clothes making her sigh with delight as his body nudged hers intimately.

'I want you now,' he groaned as he tugged her skirt upwards, his hands searching for the scrap of lace that barely covered her. 'Right now.'

She lifted her bottom to free her knickers as he gave one last tug on them, her gasp of need deflating her chest when without preamble he surged into her warmth.

She shuddered at the electric-like buzz of him moving inside her, each tender muscle stretching and contracting as the pressure mounted. Her breathing became shallow, her hands clawed at his back, her fingers digging in for purchase as he rode her with rough vigor.

'Look what you do to me,' he growled as he lifted his mouth off hers, his eyes burning into hers. 'You make me lose control.'

'I want you to lose control,' she panted as she lifted her hips to meet the downward thrust of his. 'I want you to want me like I want you.'

'I have always wanted you, Nikki,' he said. 'I do not think it will ever stop, no matter how many times I do this.'

She brought his head back down, her mouth hot and needy on his, her tongue searching for his as her hands held him tightly against her.

He kissed her back with passion that bordered on pain, his

body driving deeply into hers until there was nowhere else to go but paradise. He barely touched her with his fingers and she was there, her high cries of pleasure sounding almost primal to her own ears.

He followed closely, his body stiffening before the final plunge, the pumping thrusts as he spilled himself sending her backwards into the springiness of the sofa.

He lay against her, his breathing still ragged, his lips touching the soft skin of her neck, his words when he spoke tickling her. 'Do not move, Nikki. I want to feel you around me, holding me.'

Nikki let her fingers dance over the smooth skin of his back, her fingertips exploring each knob of his vertebrae, her stomach giving a little kick of lingering pleasure as she felt the moist heat of him between her thighs.

She gave a soft sigh as he brushed his mouth over hers in a soft kiss that was almost tender, and, opening her eyes, searched his face. 'Massimo?'

'What is it, Nikki?' he asked, brushing the hair off her face.

She traced a fingertip over the curve of his upper lip. 'Nothing. I just wanted to make sure I wasn't dreaming…'

He kissed her again, slowly, lingeringly, finally lifting his head to ask, 'Does it seem like a dream to you, *cara*? This thing we share?'

'A bit,' she said, her finger moving to his bottom lip. 'I keep thinking I am going to wake up and it will be over.'

'It is not over yet, Nikki,' he said, kissing her fingertip as it came past. 'Not by a long shot.'

Her eyes came back to his. 'But it will eventually, won't it?'

He frowned as he saw the glint of moisture in her eyes.

'Let's not talk about the future or the past,' he said as he brought his mouth back down to hers. 'Let's just concentrate on the here and now; it is all we have.'

Nikki sighed as his kiss carried her away on another tide of pleasure. He was right, she told herself. They had no future, and the past was too painful to contemplate revisiting.

They had here and now, and that was all.

CHAPTER FOURTEEN

NIKKI woke up to find Massimo lying propped up beside her, his dark gaze fixed on hers.

She began to sit upright, but a wave of nausea suddenly assailed her. She blinked back the white spots from in front of her eyes and flopped back down, her fingertips tingling as the blood drained out of her face.

'Nikki?' he asked, leaning closer. 'What is wrong? Your face is like chalk.'

She swallowed back the rising bile in her throat. 'I don't feel so good…'

'You don't eat enough,' he chided her as he got out of bed and reached for a towel to hitch around his waist. 'I'll bring you some tea and toast.'

'No.' She swallowed again. 'Please…I don't want any-thing…'

Massimo turned to see her lurch out of the bed and stumble towards the bathroom. 'Nikki?' He stepped on the bed rather than waste time going around it to get to her, but even so she had fallen to her knees in front of the toilet before he could get there.

He winced as she heaved and, kneeling down beside her,

pulled her hair back from her face as she finished. He rinsed a face cloth, gently wiped her face and neck and helped her to her feet. 'I think you should see a doctor,' he said, handing her a fresh towel.

Nikki buried her head in the soft, fragrant towel rather than look at him. 'Yes,' she said weakly. 'I think I will. I've been a bit run down for ages.'

Massimo felt guilt pierce him like a thin, serrated knife. How many times had she ministered to Joseph in the same way or even worse? Long periods of chemotherapy were notorious for making people desperately ill. How had she managed all on her own?

He tucked her hair behind her ear. 'Caring for my stepfather was very difficult, wasn't it, Nikki?'

She nodded, her face still hidden in the towel.

He let out a sigh and gently held her against him. 'He was lucky to have you.'

Nikki lifted her head to look at him. 'He was a good man, Massimo,' she said. 'I know you hated him, but he really tried to make amends for what he did.'

He put her from him, his expression losing its earlier softness. 'I have to go to the office,' he said. 'Will you be all right, or shall I call a doctor to come to the house?'

'I'll see my own doctor,' she said. 'But I'm sure it's nothing serious. I'm probably still a bit jet-lagged.'

He stood for a moment in the doorway, his eyes holding hers. 'Do you think there is a chance you could be pregnant?' he asked.

'No.'

'You seem rather definite about that,' he observed.

'I am,' she said, hoping he couldn't see the lie for what it was.

He held her gaze for another three beats before pushing himself away from the door. 'Do not bother to cook dinner tonight,' he said. 'We are dining out—that is, if you feel well enough to do so.'

'I'll be fine,' she said. 'Where are we going?'

'There is a dinner-dance being held to raise funds for one of the charities I support.'

She looked at him in surprise. 'You support a charity?'

He gave her an arched-brow look. 'You do not think I am a charitable person, *cara*?'

She nibbled at her bottom lip, her eyes falling away from his. 'I haven't really thought about it.'

'I have been very charitable towards you, have I not?' he asked. 'I could have taken legal action against you, but instead I gave you a chance to work off the debt.'

She brought her eyes back to his, an accusing glitter shining in their depths. 'Yes, by using me as a sex slave. That's hardly what I'd call charitable behaviour.'

'I am not using you in any such manner. Each time we have made love it has been your choice just as much as mine.'

'We do not make love,' she said. 'We have sex.'

'It amounts to the same thing, Nikki, no matter what term you use.'

She clenched her fists by her sides. 'It's not the same thing at all! You don't love me.'

'I do not *want* to love you,' he threw back angrily.

She blinked at him for a second or two. 'You mean…you mean you're *fighting* it?' she asked.

He raked a hand through his hair. 'I am going to work. Be ready by seven.'

She took a step towards him. 'Massimo?'

'Leave it, Nikki,' he dismissed her coldly. 'You killed my love for you five years ago. I cannot switch it back on again even if I wanted to.'

Nikki let out a ragged breath as the door snapped shut on his exit. She turned and looked at her reflection in the mirror, and grimaced. She had ten hours to get ready for this evening and she was going to need each and every one of them.

The doctor's surgery was crowded, which meant Nikki had to wait much longer than normal, which did nothing to settle her nerves. She flicked through the magazines on the table in the waiting room, every now and again finding a photograph of herself in one of the Ferliani advertisements. It was almost surreal, looking at that carefully constructed pose, the smoky made-up eyes, the lush painted curve of her lips, the sexy drape of fabric over her too-slim frame, the creamy perfection of her skin and the silky gloss of her long blonde hair so far away from what she was currently feeling. It was like looking at a stranger.

She looked up when her name was called and followed the doctor into the surgery, taking the chair opposite.

'It's been a while since you were in,' Dr Harris said, looking at her notes. 'What can I do for you, Nikki?'

Nikki decided to come straight to the point. 'I think I might be pregnant.'

Tracey Harris didn't bat an eyelid. 'Have you missed a period?'

'I'm not sure. I haven't been regular for months, but I have some of the symptoms.'

'I'll send off some blood to run a few tests, pregnancy included,' Tracey said. 'I can pull a few strings at the pathology lab. The results will be in by late this afternoon.'

'Thank you.'

Nikki spent the rest of the day with Jayden who, though awake this time, was listless and pale. She tried feeding him at lunch time but he seemed uninterested, and even when she wheeled him outside for some fresh air he screwed up his face, as if the watery sunlight was too bright for his eyes.

She left Rosedale House with a heavy heart, her grief and guilt consuming her all over again at what her brother had suffered on her behalf.

Her mobile rang just as she was coming up the driveway of Massimo's house and she took it out of her bag, her heart chugging unevenly when she saw Dr Harris's number flash up on the screen.

'Nikki, I have the results of your test,' Tracey Harris said.

Nikki held her breath. 'Yes?'

'It's positive,' the doctor said. 'You are pregnant.'

'Oh.'

'I'd like to see you again as soon as you can arrange an appointment,' Tracey went on. 'You are slightly anaemic, and there are some supplements we recommend you take during pregnancy—that is, if you wish to continue with it.'

'Of course I want to continue with it,' Nikki said.

'Sorry, I wasn't sure,' Tracey said. 'We didn't get around to discussing it this morning.'

'I'll call the receptionist in the morning and make an appointment,' Nikki said. 'Thank you for speeding up the results.'

'That's fine, Nikki. Have plenty of rest until I see you again.'

'I will…' she said, and ended the call.

* * *

Nikki dressed in a long, silvery Ferliani ball gown, the slight train on the back like a mermaid's tail, the silky fabric clinging lovingly to every slight curve of her body. She scooped her hair up high on her head, leaving trailing tendrils either side of her face. Dangling diamond earrings hung from her ears, and a sparkling matching pendant nestled in the shadow of her cleavage.

She put her hand on her flat tummy, and felt a quiver of nervousness rush through her at the thought of telling Massimo her news. She could wait for a few more weeks, hoping he might begin to feel something for her again, but she didn't like her chances. It would be better to get it over with, to deal with it head-on instead of drawing it out unnecessarily.

She waited for him in the lounge, her fingers gripping her evening purse until they ached, her stomach churning with anguish as each minute dragged by.

'I am sorry,' Ricardo said as he came into the room. 'Signore Androletti has instructed me to drive you to the function. He has been held up in a meeting. He will meet you there.'

Nikki got to her feet, her legs feeling like wet cotton-wool as the stores of adrenalin leached out of her. 'Thank you, Ricardo. I am ready to leave now.'

The hotel ball room was aglow with sparkling chandeliers and balloons, the banner of the underprivileged-children's charity hanging from one side of the stage to the other. Nikki stared at it for a long time, hardly aware of the buzz of people around her.

'Mrs Ferliani?' A photographer jostled closer.

Nikki was vaguely aware of smiling mechanically for the

camera, but the smile froze on her face when she saw a young woman enter the ball room on Massimo's arm. He was smiling down at her fondly, his eyes so soft with affection it tore at Nikki's heart like long, sharp claws. She felt nausea rise like acid in her throat, and her legs started to wobble beneath her.

'Mrs Ferliani.' A journalist pushed past a knot of people to get to her. 'Is it true you are no longer the face of Ferliani, that Abriana Cavello is taking your place?'

'It is true that I have terminated my contract with Ferliani Fashions—yes,' she answered stiffly.

'Have you met Miss Cavello?' the journalist asked.

'No, not as yet.'

'Are you aware of the rumours circulating about Massimo Androletti's relationship with Miss Cavello?' he asked.

Nikki gave him a cool smile. 'I make it a habit not to listen or even respond to rumours,' she said. 'In any case, they are rarely accurate.'

'How would you describe your current relationship with Mr Androletti?' he asked. 'Are you still living with him?'

'I have no further comment to make,' she said, and turned away to make her way to the powder room.

She locked herself into one of the cubicles and took some steadying breaths, her stomach still threatening to misbehave.

She heard the door of the powder room being pushed open, and the sound of female voices chatting over the basins as lipstick was reapplied.

'Looks like Massimo Androletti has traded in yet another lover,' one woman said. 'I thought he was seeing Nikki Ferliani.'

'He was, but I heard he's finishing with her,' the other woman answered. 'Off with the old and on with the new.'

'Nikki Ferliani is only twenty-four. That's hardly *old.*'

'I know, but you know what these rich playboys are like,' the first woman said. 'They can have anyone they like. Mind you, I think the Ferliani woman is a bit of a user herself. Fancy marrying a man old enough to be her father. Yuck. It makes my flesh crawl just thinking about it.'

'It's amazing what some people will do for money,' the other woman replied as the door opened and closed as they left.

Nikki got unsteadily to her feet and made her way back to the ball room, her face feeling tight as she searched the room for Massimo. She found him to the right of the ball room, chatting with a group of people, Abriana Cavello still hanging off his arm. His eyes collided with hers, and he bent his head to say something to the young woman before he came over to Nikki.

'Nikki, I have been waiting for you to arrive,' he said. 'There is someone I would like you to meet.'

She gave him a filthy look. 'I'm not interested in meeting your new mistress,' she bit out. 'I'm leaving.'

He took her by the arm and led her, out of earshot of the tables they were standing alongside, to the bar outside the ball room.

He waited until they were both seated away from the other guests before he announced, 'Abriana is not my mistress.'

She glared at him. 'You expect me to believe that?'

'I expect you to remember the agreement we made,' he returned.

'I'm not doing it any more,' she said, grey-blue sparks of defiance firing in her eyes. 'I don't care if you sue me.'

His eyes gleamed as they held hers. 'You are calling my bluff, mmm? Testing me to see if I will follow through on my threats.'

Nikki felt close to tears. 'If you sue me then you will be hurting your own flesh and blood,' she said.

He frowned as he looked at her. 'What do you mean?'

She moistened her lips with her tongue, her eyes flicking sideways to see if anyone was listening. 'I'm pregnant.'

It was a long time before he spoke.

'I suppose it would be impolitic of me to ask if it is mine?'

'It would be very cruel of you to do that,' she said, her eyes taking on a wounded look. 'But if you want a test done to establish paternity then I will agree to it.'

He let another silence pass for several moments.

'What have you decided to do?' he asked.

'I haven't had time to think about it,' she said, fidgeting with the clasp on her purse. 'I just thought you should know.'

'Thank you for telling me.'

Nikki searched his face, but his expression was almost impossible to read. 'I didn't mean for this to happen,' she said. 'You have to believe that, Massimo.'

'What is it you want from me, Nikki?'

'W-what do you mean?'

'That was your plan, wasn't it, Nikki?' he asked. 'You orchestrated it very well, I have to admit—playing cool and coy to begin with, ramping up my desire for you to such a degree I made love to you without protection. It was a clever tactic and timed to perfection.'

She opened and closed her mouth, trying to get her voice to work. 'I did no such thing!' she insisted.

'Do not play me for a fool,' he ground out. 'You forget, I have already been down this road recently. I am not going to believe you are carrying my child until I see evidence of it.'

She sent him a glittering glare. 'I have the test results at your house.'

He gave a little snort. 'That is not going to be good enough for me. I will want to see my DNA on the printout as well.'

'You are a heartless bastard,' she spat at him furiously. 'I wish I had never told you. I should have kept it a secret to punish you.'

'That is exactly the sort of thing a woman like you would do, isn't it, Nikki?' he asked in a snide tone. 'You love your little secrets. But, you forget, I have the means to uncover them. What will you do then, I wonder?'

Nikki stared at him as the fear chugged through her veins. She told herself it didn't matter any more. Jayden wasn't going to live much longer, so the issue of providing for him would be removed. Her own shame she could deal with. She didn't intend being in the public eye any more, so it wouldn't matter in the least. And, as for any future with Massimo, well, that was a dream turned to dust like most of her others.

'I am not going to offer you marriage,' he said into the tight silence. 'I will help you financially once it is established that the baby is actually mine.'

Nikki got to her feet in one rigid movement. 'Please don't bother. I can manage on my own. If I have to live on the streets I will do it rather than accept a single cent from you.' She swung away and stalked out of the bar, desperately trying not to cry until she was alone.

'Would you like a drink, sir?' a hovering waiter asked Massimo.

Massimo turned to look at the waiter and frowned. 'What?'

The waiter indicated the bar behind him and repeated his question.

'Yes,' Massimo said as he saw Nikki climb into a cab on the lower level. 'And you had better make it a double.'

Nikki stared at the passing streets with unseeing eyes, her heart feeling as if it had been crushed beneath a heavy weight. Pain filled her chest until she could hardly breathe, her throat burned and her eyes streamed.

She hadn't been expecting him to be happy about her news, but neither had she expected him to be so cold and clinical about it. During that wonderful week in Sicily she had felt such a change in him. She had hoped he was starting to care something for her again; she had even felt as if she was starting to trust him enough to tell him about Jayden. But then there had been the issue of his ex-mistress, which had ruined the atmosphere of peace between them.

Although, when she recalled his gorgeous and very young new lover standing beside him this evening, she had no choice but to assume he had only been using her as a temporary fill-in.

As revenges went, it was up there with the best. There was no better way to drive the nail home than have a quick fling with her and walk away, as he felt she had done to him five years ago.

Nikki opened her purse to get another tissue, and saw that there was a message icon on her mobile. She had turned it to silent when she had gone to meet Massimo at the dinner, but obviously someone had been trying to reach her. She looked down at the received-calls list and her stomach gave a sudden lurch. She dialled the message service, her heart thumping as she listened to someone who identified themselves as Jayden's doctor in Intensive Care, the short but urgent message sending another wave of panic and dread through her.

She put the phone away with shaking fingers and leaned forward to speak to the cab driver. 'I'm sorry, could I change my destination to the Western General Hospital? And please hurry; it's an emergency.'

'How long has he been like this?' Nikki asked Dr Cardle in Intensive Care.

'He was brought in a couple of hours ago,' the doctor said. 'Rosedale House tried to contact you earlier. He had a fit at tea time, but came out of it reasonably well. However, he had another one as they were putting him to bed. He fell and hit his head and has been in a coma ever since.'

Nikki bit the inside of her cheek as she looked at her broken brother hooked up to various machines, his tall, thin frame taking up so little space in the bed.

'I'm sorry to have to tell you this,' the doctor said gently. 'But there has been an intracranial bleed that has caused even more damage to his brain. There is no possible hope of recovery.'

Nikki brushed at her eyes and faced the doctor. 'Can he breathe on his own?'

David Cardle shook his head. 'The ventilator is keeping him alive. Dr Lynch thought you would want to be with him when it is turned off.'

Nikki swallowed. 'How long can I have with him?' she asked.

The doctor touched her on the shoulder. 'You can have as

long as you want,' he said. 'Is there anyone you would like to call to be with you? I noticed you are nominated as the next of kin, but is there anyone else who could support you right now?'

Nikki shook her head. 'No, there's no one I want with me right now,' she said, trying to control the tremble of her bottom lip.

'I will be in the office if you need anything,' he said.

'Thank you…'

Nikki sat by her brother's bed for seven hours. She stroked his hand, kissed each of his fingers, his nose, his forehead and each of his cheeks, telling him how much she loved him, how sorry she was, how she would give anything to change places with him.

At three minutes to two in the morning, before the ventilator was switched off, Jayden Bradley Jenkins passed away with his sister's hand in his.

Nikki walked out of the hospital a few hours later just as the sun was coming up on a new day. She walked to the tram stop in an invisible bubble of grief that even the chill wind couldn't penetrate.

The tram was crowded with the first wave of early-morning commuters, but as she jostled to find a position Nikki realised she had never felt more acutely alone in her life.

CHAPTER FIFTEEN

'I THINK you should see this,' Abriana Cavello said, pushing the morning paper towards her godfather a few days later.

Massimo put down his coffee and stared at the photographs, his brow furrowing as he read the article below. His throat went up and down, and his gut tightened the more he read.

'The funeral is today,' Abriana said into the silence. 'It's supposedly private, but I think you should go.'

He scraped a hand through his hair, still staring at the grainy police-photo of Nikki's father. He had heard of the brutal murder of Kaylene Jenkins in Perth several years ago. It had shocked the nation that a husband could be so chillingly sadistic. He had turned the axe he had used on his wife on his sixteen-year-old daughter Nicola, but she had managed to escape the first blow. The younger brother Jayden had tried to protect her and had suffered horrendous head injuries.

'Yes,' Massimo said, looking up at Abriana, swallowing convulsively again. 'Yes… I will go.'

'Do you want me to organise some flowers?' she asked.

'No,' he said, rubbing at his face for a moment. 'I will do that.'

'Would you like me to come with you, Uncle Mass?'

He gave her a grim look. 'No.'

'You didn't know about this, did you?' she asked.

He shook his head, his eyes taking on a bleak dullness.

Abriana looked back at the paper, still open on his desk. 'If I came from that sort of background I would want to keep it a secret too,' she said. 'But I wonder how the press found out.'

He got to his feet and walked to the window to look down at the city below. Guilt knifed through him. *He* had probably been responsible for the leak, given that he'd had a private investigator searching for information on her whereabouts. Tony Carpenter had finally located her, staying at a small hotel in the suburbs, but he hadn't gone to see her. Massimo had read a small interview in the paper, in which she'd been quoted as saying she had hooked up with someone else and was extremely happy. He had thrown the paper down in disgust, his anger towards her so intense he hadn't trusted himself to confront her personally.

'I don't know,' he said heavily. 'Maybe someone at the hospital recognised her or something.'

'Uncle Mass?'

'Mmm?' he answered absently, his mind filling with images of Nikki sitting alone by her brother's bedside, watching his last breaths of life leave his body.

'Finding out about her background hasn't changed the way you feel about her, has it?'

He slowly turned around to look at her. 'What do you mean?'

'I mean, you still love her, don't you?' she asked. 'It's not her fault she had an awful father. Lots of people have terrible parents, and even brothers and sisters. A friend of mine has a brother who is in jail for robbing a service station. She's only told me; not even her boyfriend knows about it. But you wouldn't hold something like that against Nikki, would you?'

He came over and, taking her head in his hands, kissed her on the forehead. 'Thank you, Abby.'

She wrinkled her nose at him. 'What did I do?'

'You made me realise what an absolute idiot I have been,' he said. 'No wonder she didn't tell me. I am a blind, stupid fool for not realising she had something like this to hide. She hinted at it a couple of times. God, I have probably ruined my chances of ever repairing the damage, but I am going to do my best to try.'

Nikki sat in the chapel waiting for the chaplain to arrive, her brother's coffin in front of her adorned with white flowers, the fragrance of lilies lingering in the air.

She had never been a particularly religious person, God had not seemed to be listening any of the times she had prayed for help. But somehow in the chapel she drew a small measure of comfort from the sweet cadences of the hymns playing softly in the background.

The chaplain appeared at the same time as someone entered the pew and sat down beside her. Nikki turned her head, her eyes widening as she encountered Massimo's dark-brown gaze.

'Nikki,' he said, reaching for her hand.

Her heart began to race as his fingers curled around hers, the tenderness in his eyes making hers glisten with tears, but she didn't have a chance to speak as just then the chaplain began the short but meaningful service.

Several journalists surged towards them as they left the crematorium a little while later but Massimo herded them off with a curt dismissal. Nikki felt the strong protection of his arms about her waist, and felt safe for the first time in more years than she could remember.

Massimo led her to his car, instructing Ricardo to drive them to his house before helping Nikki inside the vehicle, joining her on the seat and taking her hand in his again.

'I do not know where to begin,' he said, stroking the back of her hand with his thumb. 'When I saw that article in the paper…' He swallowed and continued hollowly, 'I cannot tell you how I felt. I have treated you unforgiveably. Can you find it in your heart to forgive me for my ignorance and arrogance and unspeakable cruelty?'

Nikki looked at him with eyes still red and swollen. 'I should have told you…I wanted to so many times…'

'I can imagine why you did not,' he said in harsh self-recrimination. 'I had not shown an ounce of compassion towards you. I talked of having my revenge, forcing you into a relationship no one of your nature would have been ready for. You had just buried your husband. My opinion of you was so misguided I did not think you capable of having any feelings for him or anyone. It was all about money, or so I thought.'

'It was all about money,' she said, staring down at their linked hands.

He brought her chin up. 'Yes, but not money for you—money for your brother.'

'Yes.'

'*L'oh il mio povero tesoro piccolo,*' he said. 'How you must have suffered.'

'It's over now,' she said on the tail-end of a ragged sigh.

'Jayden's at peace finally. I hated seeing him like that. He had been such an active and bright, intelligent kid. I will never forgive myself for what happened to him.'

'It was not your fault, *cara*.'

She looked at him with such aching sadness in her eyes, Massimo felt his chest tighten unbearably.

'It *was* my fault,' she said. 'I should have known something was wrong that day. I was usually so good at judging my father's moods. But he had killed my mother, Massimo.' She paused and when she spoke again her voice wavered. 'Killed her that afternoon, while Jayden and I were at school. I didn't know. He was so argumentative and belligerent, so I stood up to him, determined not to be reduced to the quivering wreck my mother had become. I didn't realise Jayden had heard us arguing. He was supposed to be at a friend's house that afternoon, but I later found out the friend had been sick so he had come home instead.'

Massimo pulled her into his arms, caressing the silky tresses of her hair as she told him the rest in fits and starts. He had tears in his eyes by the time she finished. She had been through hell and back, fighting for survival for most of her life.

Her courage astounded him. She had forged a career for herself, done everything in her power to protect the person she loved and believed she had let down.

He led her into the house a few minutes later and, pouring her a drink, joined her on the sofa, drawing her close. 'I can understand now why you were so derisive of my attitude towards my stepfather,' he said. 'My behaviour must have seemed so petty compared to your situation.'

'It wasn't petty—just a little pointless,' she said. 'Joseph had suffered enough. If you had seen him those last few weeks…'

He brought her hand up to his mouth and kissed it tenderly. 'You are the most compassionate person I have ever known. I thought so that first time we met. I was drawn to you as soon as you walked into the bar. It was like you were my other half, the missing half I had been searching for.'

'I'm so sorry I hurt you back then.'

He pushed her lips closed with his finger. 'No, I am the one who should be apologising. I am no doubt going to be doing it for the rest of our lives.'

She blinked at him. 'You want me to…?'

'Lo sposerete il mio tesoro?' he asked with a melting smile.

She smiled back, her eyes lighting up with joy. 'Are you asking me to marry you?'

'Yes, Nikki. I love you. I thought I no longer did, but my goddaughter Abriana made me realise I had never really stopped.'

Nikki gaped at him. *'Your goddaughter?'*

'Yes,' he said with a sheepish look. 'I promised her parents I would help her get into modelling. The press has made a bit of an issue out of us, but you know what they're like—never interested in the truth.'

'That night of the dinner when I saw you come in with her I was so hurt that you seemed to have moved on so quickly,' she said. 'When a journalist approached me the other day I told them I was seeing someone, but of course I wasn't. There has never been anyone but you.'

He hugged her close, his arms around tight to the point of crushing. 'I can never forgive myself for hurting you. I am ashamed of how I treated you when you told me about the baby.'

'I understand,' she said into his chest. 'It must have been hard for you, hearing it so soon after Sabrina's claims.'

He pulled back to look at her. 'I cannot forgive myself for uncovering your past the way I did.'

'What do you mean?'

He took a deep swallow. 'When I returned to the house the evening of the dinner I was sure you would be there waiting for me. I was convinced you would not leave without a large payout. But you were not there. You had not even taken a single article of clothing or your toiletries with you. I sent a private investigator in search of you. He phoned me the next day to say he had found you in a cheap hotel. But I cannot help thinking perhaps he leaked something to the press about you, although he said nothing to me of your background.'

'It wasn't anything you did,' she said. 'One of the nurses at the hospital recognised me from when I was living in Perth. I have spent the last eight years dreading someone recognising the girl I was back then—but, there you go, not even make-up and expensive clothes can hide who you really are.'

'I can understand why you wanted to keep that part of your life a secret, *cara*,' he said. 'But it makes no difference to me. You are still the sweetest, most adorable woman I have ever met.'

Tears shone in her eyes. 'You mean if I had told you all those years ago you wouldn't have run a mile?'

He brushed at her tears with his thumbs as he cupped her face in his hands. 'I would have done everything in my power to help you get your brother into the care he needed.'

She compressed her lips, her throat moving up and down

as she tried to control her emotions. 'I should have told you. Oh God…I should have told you…'

'Do not torture yourself,' he said. 'It is in the past, and besides you were a wonderful support to my stepfather. If he went to his deathbed a better man then surely it was worth the sacrifice of those five years.'

'I didn't sleep with him, Massimo. I need you to believe me.'

'I do believe you, Nikki,' he said. 'And I have also terminated all dealings with Peter Rozzoli. I had my financial people delve a little into his background. You were right about him. He has been siphoning off funds from Ferliani Fashions for the past year.'

'Poor Joseph.' Nikki said. 'I wonder if he knew…'

'To tell you the truth I was quite surprised when he called me in those months before he died,' Massimo said. 'I have been wondering lately if he did so in order to provide for you.'

She looked at him in puzzlement. 'But he knew you hated me for what I had done.'

'Yes, but he also knew I had not married anyone else,' he reminded her. 'He must have realised I still had feelings for you, otherwise he would not have offered me everything the way he did. But you still have not answered my question, *cara*. Are you going to give me a second chance?'

She touched the side of his face with the softness of her hand, her expression full of wonder that the heartache of the past had finally gone. 'Yes, I am,' she said. 'For remember I said five years ago if we were really meant to be together we would get another chance?'

He covered her hand with his and brought it to his heart. 'I remember, Nikki. This is our time now. We have had to both work for it in our separate ways, but it will be all the sweeter for the waiting.'

'You know something, Massimo?' she said, snuggling up to him. 'I think you are right.'

EPILOGUE

'WHICH do you like best?' Massimo asked as he leafed through their wedding photos with Nikki a few weeks later.

Nikki peered over his shoulder, pressing a soft kiss to the side of his neck. 'I don't know,' she said, nibbling on his ear. 'I kind of like the one where you're kissing me with the sunset in the background.'

He shivered as her tongue snaked into his ear. 'I like that too.'

'What about this?' she asked, raining hot little kisses all over his face. 'Do you like that too?'

He laughed and tugged her onto his lap, holding her against his hardness. 'You are a minx,' he said. 'I thought you were supposed to be resting each day. Isn't that what pregnant women are supposed to do?'

She pouted at him playfully. 'It's no fun resting on my own,' she said. 'Besides, you're the reason I can't fit into my jeans any more. I think it's only fair you should entertain me when I'm bored.'

He kissed her lingeringly, the sweet taste of her thrilling him all over again. He had not realised how deeply he could love until now. His child lay in her womb, its tiny limbs growing day by day just like his love for her. Each day brought him new awareness of her beauty and grace, her ready forgiveness for the way he had treated her totally humbling him.

The pain of her past was gradually fading. He had stood by her side on a lonely Victorian beach as she had cast her brother's ashes into the rolling waves, tears falling from her eyes as she'd told him how Jayden had been locked away for too long in a body that no longer worked, so it was only fair that he was free to swim and surf as he used to do.

He had felt a lump come to his throat as she'd lifted her face to the salty air, her eyes closing as the sun came out from between the clouds to shine on the water…

'So, how about it, darling?' she asked, pressing a soft kiss to each of his eyelids. 'Are you going to take me to bed and entertain me?'

There was a miaow from the doorway, and Massimo and Nikki both turned their heads in surprise and delight.

'Pia!' Nikki hopped off Massimo's lap and scooped up the wasted little body. 'Where on earth have you been? You're so thin! We thought you must have been run over or something. Mrs Lockwood told us you haven't been home for almost two weeks.'

Massimo gave the little black head a gentle stroke. 'Naughty little Pia, you had us so worried. Have you been getting up to mischief?'

The little cat blinked at him guilelessly before leaping from Nikki's arms to saunter to the door leading back out to the garden.

Massimo exchanged a quick glance with Nikki. 'Do you think she is trying to tell us something?' he asked.

Nikki took his hand and tugged him towards the door. 'Come on.'

A few minutes later they stood gazing down at four little squirming, silky black bodies, hidden away in a corner of the garden shed, their tiny eyes still glued shut.

'Do you think she's told the father yet?' Nikki whispered as she squeezed Massimo's hand.

He looked down at her, tears in his eyes as he drew her closer. 'I certainly hope so,' he said. 'For there can be no greater thing in life than having the woman you love bear your children.'

She smiled up at him, her heart swelling to twice its size as she saw his love for her shining in his eyes. 'Do you think we could keep one for our baby?' she asked.

'A boy or a girl?'

She rolled her lips together for a moment. 'I don't know, do you think it matters?'

'What about one of each?' he suggested.

Her eyes went wide. 'You want *two*?'

He pulled her into his arms and breathed in the sweet, fresh fragrance of her hair. 'I want it all, Nikki. Two kids, two kittens and you.'

'There's only one of me,' she said, her eyes dancing with happiness as she gazed up at him. 'Is that going to be enough for you?'

He lifted her in his arms and carried her back towards the house. 'More than enough,' he said, and kicked the door shut with his foot.

Valenti's One-Month Mistress

SABRINA PHILIPS

Sabrina Philips first discovered Mills & Boon one Saturday afternoon in her early teens at her first job in a charity shop. Sorting through a stack of pre-loved books, she came across a cover which featured a glamorous heroine and a tall, dark, handsome hero. She started reading under the counter that instant—and has never looked back!

A lover of both reading and writing since childhood, Sabrina went on to study English with Classics at Reading University. She adores all literature, but finds there's nothing else quite like the indulgent thrill of a Modern™ romance—preferably whilst lying in a hot bath with no distractions!

She grew up in Guildford, Surrey, where she now lives with her husband—who swept her off her feet when they were both just sixteen. When Sabrina isn't spending time with her family or writing, she works as a co-ordinator of civil marriages, which she describes as a fantastic source of romantic inspiration and a great deal of fun.

A decade after reading her very first Mills & Boon® novel, Sabrina is delighted to join as an author herself and have the opportunity to create infuriatingly sexy heroes of her own, which she defies both her heroines—and her readers—to resist! Visit Sabrina's website: www. sabrinaphilips.com

To Mum, for your unquestioning support, always.
And to Phil, for exceeding every
dream I ever had.

CHAPTER ONE

WOULD she look him in the eye and plead? he wondered. Or would she be reluctant to meet his gaze, knowing that the last time she'd held it she'd had her legs wrapped around him and had given herself to him so freely? Dante spread the report across his expansive mahogany desk and his mouth hardened. No, he doubted that. Reluctance was not a word to be associated with Faye Matteson.

Leaning back in the wide leather chair, he glanced at her name amongst the appointments in his electronic diary. When his PA had come to him last month, asking if he would agree to see her, he had immediately deduced what it was that she wanted. He knew only something like this would bring her back to Rome. But she needn't have bothered making the trip. *How* she stated her case would make no difference. He smiled wryly. It amused him that she actually believed he might be willing to help her. Like hell he would. But then why would she consider any outcome other than the one that *she* wanted? She never had before. He doubted six years had changed her. Yet it had changed him. The once angelic English waitress with the come-to-bed eyes no longer posed a danger. This time he knew she was a witch.

'Miss Matteson is here, Mr Valenti,' his receptionist purred over the intercom, interrupting his thoughts.

Dante stood up, preparing to savour the revenge.

'Send her in.'

Nothing had changed, then, Faye thought to herself as she took a deep breath and sank down tentatively on the pristine sofa indicated by the svelte redhead—the final obstacle between herself and his office. His empire might have grown, but the set-up was the same: employees still orbited around him and every woman gravitated in his direction like flowers towards the sun. No doubt he still plucked whoever took his fancy and then left them to wilt.

Faye shuddered and tried to relax her shoulders. The tension was only partly due to the after-effects of the cramped seating on last night's flight. Now was not the time to dwell on *back then*. She looked around the luxurious reception area. This world—his world—was unfamiliar to her now. Had she ever really been a part of it? She suspected that was just another delusion. There was no point even wondering. She had not *stayed* a part of it. After all these years she doubted he even recalled her name. But then it had dawned on her during the metro journey here that Dante Valenti did not allow his PA to make appointments for anyone he had not fully vetted first. So he must remember, and he had agreed for her to come anyway. Which meant… What did it mean? That the past was nothing to him, she supposed, and that business came first. *And business is all that matters now*, she berated herself silently. *It's about time you started thinking the same way*. The fact that he had agreed to see her surely meant there was a chance that he at least might be willing to help, didn't it? And there was no way she was going to blow Matteson's last hope by dwelling on a stupid, childish disappointment.

Faye checked her watch for the third time, catching sight of her freshly manicured nails, so alien to her, clutching the proposal. This had to work. It *had* to. She watched the immaculate redhead murmur into the intercom, feeling self-conscious, and swept a tendril of her own fair hair back into the clip which held it away from her face. Her budget had not stretched to a professional cut too. This would have to do.

'Mr Valenti will see you now.' The woman spoke as if bestowing upon her an undeserved honour, and ushered her towards the elaborately panelled door.

Faye smoothed down the skirt of her new grey suit unnecessarily, her heart racing, the pressure echoing at her temples. She had spent over six years believing she would never have to lay eyes on him again, and now she had brought it upon herself. But what choice did she have? Over the course of the last year she had appealed to every bank, every possible investor she could think of, but no one would lend her a penny. At first it had been disheartening, worrying. Now it was desperate. There *was* no other choice—because it was this or watch her family's restaurant go bankrupt before her eyes. And that wasn't an option. Not just because she felt instinctively that it was her daughterly duty to prevent that happening, but because *she* loved the business. So much so that she was sure even if she had been born into an entirely different family she would always have been drawn—like a bird to the south—to the simple yet deep pleasure which came from seeing other people sit together around *her* table, enjoying good food. The way people once had at every table in Matteson's. Which was why there was nothing left to do but to walk, as confidently as she could feign, into the enormous room.

He did not speak at first. Faye was silently grateful. For, though she had only dared flick a glance in his direction, the action had rendered *her* speechless. She had prepared herself for facing the old Dante, and that had been painful enough. What she had not taken into account was how time would have changed him. It was not the plush new office—he had always exuded wealth and class—nor the atmosphere of power that seemed to emanate from the ground where he stood. No, the years had somehow refined *him*. His luxurious dark hair seemed thicker, the irresistible slant of his jaw more chiselled, the curve of his full lower lip even more sensual. And those dark eyes, thrown into relief by that smooth olive skin, were the most changed of all: more piercing, more commanding—like ice. And, formidable though he looked, he was still the sexiest man she had ever met, and her treacherous eyes wanted to drink in every inch of him. Her memories had been distorted in so many respects, but she had never been wrong about that. No matter how much she wished that she had been.

'To what do I owe this unexpected pleasure, Ms Matteson?' His cut-glass enunciation of the English language with its seductive Italian undertone was as impressive to her now as it had been at eighteen, and sent long-dormant senses into overdrive. 'I can only *imagine*.'

She raised her head tentatively, not able to focus her eyes above his broad chest. He gestured brusquely for her to sit on one of the black leather chairs flanking the enormous desk whilst he remained standing, making him seem even taller than the city buildings outside the window. She perched on the edge of the chair. She wished he'd remained silent, for she had not predicted the arousing effect *that* voice would have on her in spite of the damning intention of his words. She felt the blood course faster around her veins, making her aware of pulse-points even her unrelenting nerves had not discovered.

'Hello, Dante.'

'No formalities, Faye? You need not have booked this appointment through my PA if this is, after all, a personal call.'

Faye had been more than relieved last month, when she had been able to arrange this meeting without actually speaking to Dante himself. Now she suspected this whole charade would have been easier over the phone. She had mistakenly presumed she could be more persuasive face to face, but she had she failed to anticipate the sway his physical presence seemed to have over her.

'Very well, Mr Valenti,' she said, mimicking his formal address though her throat was dry and constricted. 'I have come because I have a business proposition for you.'

'Really, Faye?' he counteracted. 'And what could you possibly have that would interest me?'

The colour rose in her cheeks and she felt utterly exposed—all the more so because of his hawk-like advantage over her. She could feel the intensity of his gaze burning through the fabric of her suit and she wanted to take off her jacket—but she didn't dare remove the layer of protection for fear that her cami would reveal the tingling buds of her breasts that thrust against the thin fabric against her will. *Straight on with the speech*, a voice inside her prompted. *Don't let him see he's getting to you.*

'My family and I are keen to find some additional investment for Matteson's, in return for a percentage of the profits. As someone who once showed an interest in our restaurant,

I thought you might be eager to see the proposal.' Her voice trailed off as she remembered his presence there back then: the delight that his approval had given her parents, the life he had breathed into it for her. She opened her folder on the desk and pushed it towards where he was standing at the other end. He ignored the papers.

'Eager?' She did not need to look at his face to catch his sardonic tone. 'You may have been fool enough to presume I had any interest whatsoever in *the restaurant* back then.' Dante dipped his eyes as he spoke, shaking his head. 'But you must be plain stupid if you think I don't know that Matteson's is on its last legs.'

Faye stiffened, wondering if there was anything he could have said that would have hurt more. So it had all been a facade. He had seen the opportunity to use *her*, nothing more. And if he believed Matteson's was irrecoverable, she might as well give up here and now. The thought spurred her onto the defensive. 'Much as it might please you to believe me to be *plain stupid*, Dante, for your information Matteson's is not on its last legs. I admit we need an injection of cash to continue updating some elements, but—'

'An injection of cash?' Dante cut in. 'You need a miracle. Who in their right mind is going to pump money into a business running at a loss?'

'We are *not* running at a loss.'

'But let me guess—you are not making a profit either?'

The shocking accuracy of Dante's judgement caused her cheeks to burn, and the air in the room was suddenly stifling. When her father had fallen ill, he had been unable to devote the time that Matteson's demanded, and yet he had been too proud to seek extra help, too stubborn to allow Faye to pull out of university and share the responsibility. Faye swallowed down a lump in her throat; she admired her father for that as much as she regretted his obstinacy. But since his death things had gone from bad to worse. No matter how hard Faye had tried to turn things around profits had continued to fall, and if they didn't increase soon she wouldn't even be able to afford to pay the staff their wages.

'Perhaps if you had gained a little more experience before taking on this venture, you might not have found yourself in this position, *sì*?'

The insinuation hurt. *He* was exactly the reason the broadening of her experience had been cut short. 'I have had experience. Just because it wasn't all under your guidance it doesn't mean it wasn't worthwhile. There *are* hotels and restaurants that aren't owned by you. Or hadn't you noticed?'

'I do not doubt you have had plenty of other experience since then,' Dante said slowly, deliberately running his eyes over her figure. 'But clearly none of it was quite good enough, since here you are standing before me. And we both know that means you must be desperate.'

Faye ignored the insult. He might be right about the last part, but he would mock her all the more if he knew how wrong he was about what else he was implying.

'Every business needs capital spent on it periodically. Circumstances dictate that Matteson's needs to look for an external investor now, for the first time in fifteen years. I don't consider that a failure.'

'Then open your eyes.' She recognised the harsh professional side of him she had once respected, but had never thought she would find directed at her. 'You didn't need cash back then because Matteson's was current, contemporary.

Now it's fallen so far behind it's dropped off the radar. People need change.'

Was that his personal motto? Faye wondered bitterly. And did he really suppose she was so dense that she didn't know that? She *had* tried her utmost to keep the place up to date, to turn things around after her father had passed away. But there was only so far she could get using a home printer to modernise the menus, or spending her own paltry savings on paint for the walls. She knew Matteson's needed a complete overhaul, and was desperate to give it one, but to do so she needed the means.

'It is our intention to use any funding to update the kitchens, the interior—'

'It's too late.' Dante's voice seemed to echo every rejection ever thrust her way. 'Matteson's is a failing brand.'

'Then we must agree to disagree.'

Faye raised her head, and her eyes met his for just a second before she looked back at Rome's skyline. He did not speak, but finally moved from the window towards her, making the room behind him seem larger, brighter, but the space around her feel minute. At last he rested on the desk next to her, one immaculate charcoal-suited leg casually resting over the other.

She could see the powerful thrust of his thighs and smell the earthy, masculine scent that was so distinctly his that she was transported back to another afternoon, so different from this, altogether too painful to contemplate. But forcing the images from her mind did not help to ease the old familiar pooling in her belly. She rose, unable to stand his close proximity. She wanted to scream for him to get away from her, though they must be at least a metre apart. There was no point remaining here in this room with him, enduring his vehement loathing and torturing herself when there was no hope left that this meeting would have the outcome she had wished for. No matter that when she had forced herself to consider this failure in her mind, she had thought the saving grace would be that when she walked away she would know that the way she had felt about him back then was all down to schoolgirl infatuation. She ought to be accustomed to finding that she was wrong where he was concerned.

'In that case I will approach alternative sources of funding,' she continued. His silence was unnerving. She leaned forward to retrieve the proposal, her voice laced with false optimism. 'Thank you for sparing me a moment of your precious time.'

He did not allow her to make even one complete step in the direction of the door. Before she knew what was happening he had blocked the entire movement of her body with the powerful grasp of one large, lean hand on her small wrist. Faye caught her breath.

'Leaving again so soon?' His voice was as mocking as before, only now it was cold and devoid of all humour. Faye was paralysed. 'Yet again you have done what *you* came for, but not waited to hear what I have to say. What a surprise.' The feel of his touch set her nerves skittering, enflaming her in places beyond the small area he touched.

'You have something else to say?' Her eyes were questioning, and suddenly she was the Faye of six years ago, her heart longing for some explanation to undo all the pain.

'The location *is* excellent.'

Dante released his grip on her wrist and moved back to lean against the desk. His words were like a fog and she searched within them for some hidden meaning, rooted to the spot despite the absence of his grasp.

'Wh…what?'

'You have not asked me outright whether I am interested in any aspect of your proposal—another business *faux pas*, you understand. As you rightly interpreted, I have no interest in funding Matteson's. There is, however, something that I do find extremely desirable.' Faye's head was reeling. 'The restaurant is in an exceptional location. It is in an outskirt of London I have been hoping to expand in for some time. I might consider buying the *site* for a very reasonable sum of money, if that is on offer.'

Swivelling round to face him, she felt things begin to fall into place in her mind. So *that* was why he had agreed to see her. She swallowed hard. It was his intention to finish her off completely, to usurp her family business with another Michelin-starred Valenti enterprise like the one in central London that she had taken pains to avoid for the last six years—not that she could afford to do anything but walk past. Hadn't he conquered enough already?

'Over my dead body. It is not for sale.'

'Not yet, perhaps.' He was smiling now, and it infuriated her. 'But I'll wait.'

'What do you mean by that?'

'Ahh—of course. How could I forget that waiting is a virtue that so eludes you, Faye? What I mean is I'm guessing it won't be long before it *is* for sale.'

Faye felt the colour rise hotly in her cheeks, as much at the accusation of loose morals he had just made as at the realisation of just how much he knew. For Dante was not the kind of man who *guessed* anything. He hadn't become a billionaire by burying his head in the sand. He clearly knew more about the financial state of Matteson's than she had originally thought, and it wasn't because of any distant interest he might have had in the restaurant, or in her. It was because he had seen an opportunity for himself. The thought was like a waterfall of ice down her spine. So now, if their profits failed to increase, Matteson's wouldn't just slowly fade away. He would be there to launch his brutal takeover attack.

'Well, it looks like I'll have to try my powers of persuasion elsewhere, doesn't it?' she retorted, raising her eyebrows and flashing him a smile right back. She would not let him have the satisfaction of thinking this was a *fait accompli*. So what if he had been her last possible resort? There was no harm in calling his bluff. Faye saw the wave of anger that momentarily crossed his face disappear as quickly as it had come. She suspected it was a rare thing for a woman to refuse him whatever it was he had set out to get.

'Perhaps we can come to some arrangement,' he ground out.

'Meaning what, exactly?'

'A compromise, of sorts.'

Faye doubted he knew the meaning of the word.

Suddenly the intercom in the middle of the room burst into life. 'I am sorry to interrupt you, Mr Valenti, but Mr Castillo from the Madrid office is on the line, and he says it's urgent.'

Dante swooped down to the device on the desk. 'Thank you, Julietta. Please ask him if he would be so kind as to hold for just a few minutes. I am almost finished here.'

'Of course.' The woman's voice was silky, reverent. As hers must have once been, Faye thought wretchedly. She could not help shuddering at the seductive way in which he had spoken the woman's name in return, the compassionate response that suggested he was actually something other than a cold, calculating bastard. Something like jealousy coursed through her veins, and she hated herself for it.

'Where are you staying?'

'Sorry?' His question caught her unawares.

'In Rome—where are you staying?'

'At a guesthouse near the airport. Not that it's any concern of yours.'

'No, you're not. I will have someone collect your bags, and my driver will take you to Il Maia.'

Il Maia? What was he talking about? She had never wanted to see Rome again, let alone his hotel. Now he had made it clear he had no intention of helping her, she planned to catch the next flight home. 'Even if I could afford to stay at Il Maia, it won't be necessary. I fly home tonight.'

His voice was dangerously low. 'No, you won't, Faye. Unless you want to sit back and watch the remains of your family's business crumble around you. I am willing to reconsider your proposal—on *my* terms. I will be in the hotel bar at eight, and we will discuss this over dinner.' He spoke matter-of-factly, as if the prospect could not be more unappealing. 'Since I recall that you never fulfilled the duration of your previous stay, I will kindly overlook the cost.' He motioned towards the door. 'I have more pressing business now. Julietta will show you out.'

'I am not agreeing to this when all you've told me so far is that you wouldn't touch my proposal with a bargepole!' she exclaimed, incensed by both the idea of returning to Il Maia and the prospect of spending an entire evening in his company. For one thing, she hated the thought that she might feel indebted to him, and for another, the emotions he had evoked in her during this short meeting alone quite frankly terrified her. But he was already on the intercom, telling Julietta to arrange a driver, and to put through the call from Madrid.

'Give me one good reason why I should consent to your

ridiculous proposition!' she fired out helplessly, her eyes burning with defiance.

Dante took a deep breath and turned to face her, shaking his head patronisingly. 'Because your consent is not a requirement, Miss Matteson. You will do what I tell you because I am going to make you an offer that you can't refuse, and because if you don't I'll ruin you.'

And with that he switched into perfect Spanish, and continued with his call.

Dante replaced the phone in its receiver, having rectified Castillo's supplier crisis without issue. Faye had stormed from the room the instant he'd turned his attention away from her, exactly as he'd anticipated. It was not the first time a woman had left his office sulking when things had not gone her way, and he doubted it would be the last. And yet, as he glanced at the chair where she had been sitting, he had to admit that he had been wrong about one thing. She had practically refrained from looking him in the eye for the entire meeting. The only time she had met his gaze had been when she was being bloody defiant about the dire financial state of her restaurant, and then she had looked away again just as quickly. It frustrated the hell out of him. Did she think she could fool him all over again with that feigned look of modesty?

But she had been innocent last time, hadn't she? a voice piped up in the back of his mind. It was accompanied by something else that felt disturbingly like guilt but which he refused to give any such name to. For her apparently artless innocence—which had to have been the trigger for the uncontrollable attraction she had once awakened in him—had lasted all of about five minutes! Yes, she had soon proved just how keen she was to rid herself of the *burden* of her virginity before moving on to her next victim. How long had it been? Two weeks after she had gone before she was swapping sexual favours on the other side of the Atlantic?

But God, she was just as tempting now—if not even more so. Once was not enough. Despite her coming to him begging for his money in clothes he knew she could not afford—no wonder Matteson's had reached rock bottom!—with her fingers artificially manicured when everything about her had used to be so natural, he still wanted her. It surprised him. He had felt it as soon as she had entered his office. Just like the moment he had looked up from the menu at Matteson's all those years ago to find a girl unlike any other looking back. A shy and talented young English waitress with hair like honey and legs to die for he had forbidden himself to touch. Her innocence had proved to be as false as those nails, but she still turned him on.

Saying no, telling her that the closest she was going to get to what she wanted would be watching him buy the land from under her, was not going to be enough. He needed *her* under him again. He would make her gaze into his eyes and cry out his name in pleasure, powerless to look away. Even if it did mean changing his plans a little. The end result would be the same: she would be forced to sell everything to him, to realise that if only she had been capable of a little restraint she might have been a success. He had once thought her to be unique, deserving of his respect, and he had given her the opportunity to learn from him. But she had proved that she was the same as every other woman who had tried to sink her claws into him. And now she wanted his help? Well, she had made her bed, and he was going to make damn sure she lay in it, whenever and however he chose.

CHAPTER TWO

FAYE slammed the door as soon as the hotel porter was out of sight, and flung her suitcase onto the bed. She could not remember another time in her life when she had felt her independence so utterly undermined. Yet what choice did she have but to acquiesce? She couldn't go home knowing that Dante might have considered a compromise that would stop the family business from going bankrupt and her own dreams from being torn to shreds—that rather than sacrifice her pride and go along with his egotistical demands she had decided to fly home instead of hearing him out. How could she?

It was just dinner, she supposed. When it came down to it, she had nothing to lose. If he offered her some ridiculously small sum of money for Matteson's she would simply refuse again, then get a taxi back here and head straight to the airport, knowing she had done everything she could.

Therefore, forty minutes earlier, Faye had begrudgingly followed his assistant to a car, exactly as he had instructed. Thankfully she had managed to persuade the driver to stop at the guesthouse so she could at least gather her own things on the way, rather than have someone else collect her luggage as Dante had suggested. And now here she was, back at Il Maia.

It was a very different arrival from that scorching hot July day when she had first set foot here, just over six years ago. That day her life had never felt so full of promise. Six weeks before she had been working at her parents' restaurant, waiting tables, when the most alarmingly attractive man she had ever laid her eyes upon had strolled in with such self-possession she had felt as if she was part of a film set and the star of the movie had just walked in.

'Catch of the day,' one of the other waitresses had said, and winked at her, following her line of sight.

Faye had blushed and turned away, but despite being far from alone in her awareness of him she had suddenly found herself to be the only waitress not attending to a customer. Clasping the pen and pad to her chest like a schoolgirl hugging her books, she had tentatively approached him.

'What can I get you, sir?'

He paused for a long moment, his head down.

'Whoever is responsible for this,' he said, tapping the menu with what looked to be utter disgust.

Faye froze, convinced that he was about to launch into a heated complaint. She cursed her chances for being the one to bear the brunt of it.

'Our chef is responsible for the choice of dishes on offer, sir. If there is something in particular you'd like…' Faye smiled as placidly as she could and took a step back towards the kitchen, in a gesture she hoped suggested it would be no trouble to ask.

'Not the food,' he ground out. 'The person who is responsible for this design.'

Faye felt the liquid pink that had slowly begun to drain from her cheeks rising with a vengeance.

'Actually, I am,' she said, hoping she didn't look as small as she felt.

'You?' His tone was disbelieving as he raised his head to study her face, but for one long, earth-shattering moment his eyes seemed to look deep into her soul with a burning intensity unlike anything she had ever experienced before. He shook his head and continued, 'You have this incredible talent, yet you are *waiting tables*?'

Faye was too taken aback to notice the censure in his voice, for it was then that he invited her to sit and Faye explained everything. That this was her father's restaurant and she was working there temporarily, whilst awaiting her A-level results, and that she had a passion for the whole business of hosting which came second only to her love of designing things. And that was why, whilst she was debating going to university or trying to get a job in marketing, this summer her father had finally let her loose on his menus.

When he had finished asking her every question imaginable, she realised she was beaming all over her face. It felt as if she had been invisible her whole life and that he had just bathed her in sunshine and seen her for who she really was.

'My staff, who have had years of training,' he said, lost for a moment in his admiration for her enthusiasm and talent, 'are incapable of producing something even half this original.'

And that was the moment her life had changed for ever. For in response to her wide-eyed amazement, he had announced that he was the owner of the most successful new restaurant and hotel in Rome, and that there was no way he was leaving this restaurant until she agreed to become part of his team.

It had felt as if she had just won first prize in a competition she'd never even known she had entered. Out of nowhere had come this man, as far from boys her own age as wine was from water, well-dressed, exotically Italian, with a charisma that held her in its thrall, who had created the best there was in the industry she loved. And he'd wanted *her* to work for him.

Faye remembered the feeling of pure excitement, the sensation of having arrived in every sense of the word when she had waved goodbye to her proud parents and then arrived at Rome International Airport, to find him waiting for her in his bright red sports car to personally oversee her safe arrival. But she had fallen under his spell even before that. For he could have arrived on a moped and revealed that he was actually a pizza delivery boy and she would have been just as captivated. But he *had* been everything he had said he was—and more besides. Just as the hotel had been beyond her wildest imagination—Il Maia: goddess of growth, indeed. Here, she had not only been introduced to the glamorous world of five-star hospitality, she had also lost her innocence and her heart.

Yes, this arrival at Il Maia was a very different one. Rather than being filled with a sense of freedom and anticipation, now she felt trapped here, because it was the only hope she had. But if being forced to relive the desolation of six years ago meant there was even a small chance of saving Matteson's, she was just going to have to face it.

Filled with a grim determination, Faye opened her suitcase and began hanging what few outfits she had brought with her in the enormous wardrobes along one side of the room. She sighed. She had not packed with *any* kind of dining in mind, let alone dining at one of Dante's exclusive restaurants. Eating out was, ironically, a rare thing for her these days. Though she occasionally went out for a drink with some of the girls from the restaurant when she could, it had been a long time since she had been out on this scale—and longer since she had agreed to a date. Not that this was a date, she reflected, pushing something like regret to the back of her mind.

She held up the only dress she had brought with her. It was a high-street fern-green wrap-over number that was rather too short, but she had brought it knowing the temperature here in September could still be stifling during the day. It was her only option. So what if he wouldn't consider it appropriate? He could hardly have expected her to have planned for tonight. She had spent the last of her savings on her suit for the meeting, stupidly thinking she could fool him into believing that the restaurant just needed a little extra cash to expand its already adequate profits. But now she knew he was only too aware of their dire financial situation there was no point pretending.

Faye looked in the mirror and unclipped her hair, fanning its honey-coloured length over her shoulders. In two and a half hours' time he would be downstairs, waiting for her. A frisson of anticipation shot through her. *Stupid girl*, her reflection seemed to mock. So her body still wanted him? So much was different. So much of what she had believed to be real back then was not. But she had never been wrong about the level of desire he evoked within her. She had thought it was the rose-tinted glasses of nostalgia that made her remember how her body had gone into meltdown the moment he touched her, how she had longed for his hands upon her whenever he was near, but today proved that nostalgia had nothing to do with it. Even when his touch had been simply to restrain her, rather than designed to ignite her sexually, she had not wanted it to end. Or maybe that had been precisely its purpose? she speculated as she collected fresh underwear and headed for the luxurious bathroom. She'd only had to see the way Julietta eyed him so coyly to know that he had the same effect on all women. And Dante was not the sort of man who was unaware of his own appeal. It would be exactly his style to torment her with the way he made her feel for his own ends. But it was just sexual attraction, she reasoned. Though her body might be weak, she most definitely was not. Once she had naively fallen for his charms, gladly surrendered her virginity and then slipped out of his life compliantly. But she wasn't eighteen anymore. She was older, and wiser, and had absolutely no intention of surrendering anything.

Eight-twenty. He saw her the moment she entered the room. So he would not have to go up to the suite and drag her down here. Pity. To his annoyance, several other men at the bar turned on their stools and gave her the once, then twice over. No wonder, in a dress that damned short; she always had had the most fantastic pair of legs he had ever seen. He fought the urge to walk straight up to her, wrap his hands in that golden mane of hair hanging loose over her shoulders and claim her as his own with all the force of his kiss. All in good time, he thought.

He finished the remainder of his wine and stood up before she reached him. 'I trust you had no trouble finding your way here?' he mocked, eyeing the watch at her wrist and looking upwards, as if through to the floors above.

Faye did not answer him. She had had no intention of arriving on time, even if she had been ready since seven forty-five.

'Our table is ready—do not let us refrain from the pleasure any longer.' Dante motioned for Faye to walk ahead of him.

'I agree. Let's get this over with.' She felt him place one hand lightly at the small of her back and begin to guide her through the bar into the restaurant. His touch was electric. The heat of his hand spread throughout her body. She swallowed, wanting to yell at him to back off, but she was aware that eyes were upon them. No doubt wondering what the hell the head of Valenti Enterprises was doing in one of his restaurants with *her*, and not one of the usual supermodels he did more than dine with, if the tabloids were anything to go by.

Like the rest of the hotel, the Tuscan restaurant had been simply and elegantly updated, Faye acknowledged as he led her to their table, and she didn't need to be in the restaurant business to know it remained one of Italy's most celebrated.

'Please, sit.' He held out her chair for her. 'Welcome back to Perfezione.'

Faye raised her eyebrows. Perfection; she had forgotten. Along with the rest of the staff she had known the restaurant affectionately as Fez during her month here. How had the egoism of the name never struck her back then, even if he did have a point?

'I have explained to the staff that we have important matters of business to discuss this evening. They have assured me that their disturbance will be minimal.'

Faye was not sure that was necessarily a good thing. They were seated in a fairly isolated corner. The tables cleverly concealed by vines that were the restaurant's trademark. If it was possible Dante looked even more forbidding than earlier, in a dark lounge suit and a maroon shirt open at the neck that revealed a potently masculine sprinkle of dark hair.

'I trust your room is satisfactory?' His politeness was utterly unnerving.

'*Perfezione, naturalmente.*' Two could play at the butter-wouldn't-melt game.

'I should hope so. You approve of the changes?'

'It is beautiful,' she answered genuinely, thinking how con-
tradictory it was that in her desperation to see Matteson's
tables filled with people enjoying themselves once more she
had forgotten to allow herself the pleasure of eating out for
what must have been months—too many to count.

Dante nodded and turned his attention to the menu. Faye
watched him, unable to focus on her own. She wondered if
he had any involvement in deciding what was served these
days. She was not sure he would have time for the kind of attention to detail that had once so impressed her now he was
based in a separate office, with restaurants all over Europe.
He seemed to be looking critically, his thick, black eyelashes,
outrageously long for a man, shrouding his eyes. She remembered how they had felt against her cheek, and subconsciously
raised her hand to touch her face.

'I recommend the seafood.' He looked up at her, mistak-
ing her gesture for puzzlement. 'I took the liberty of ordering
an accompanying wine at the bar, but if you would prefer
something else I will order another.'

'The seafood will be fine, thank you.' Faye shut her menu.
'But I will pass on the wine.'

'A mistake, you realize?'

'Perhaps.' Faye did not trust herself to keep her head on
anything more than mineral water.

'And the seafood will be better than fine.'

'I don't doubt it.' Faye forgot herself for a moment, her
nerves making her garrulous. 'My father used to say, "To eat
well, look to the plate of your host."' The memory conjured up
a childhood image of her father serving up his favourite glazed
chicken and rosemary dish as the whole family waited expec-

tantly. She remembered announcing loudly at the very same moment that she wanted to do her Brownie hostess badge.

'A wise man,' Dante agreed, his voice unusually soft. 'I was sorry to hear that he is no longer with us.'

Faye was taken aback. She had not expected Dante even to know of her father's death, let alone offer his sympathy. She could bear anything but that. Much, much easier to remember that the reason he knew was because he was waiting for Matteson's to fail in the aftermath. She nodded swiftly.

'So tell me,' she said, changing the subject, 'what offer is it that you are going to make that you think I can't refuse?'

'Patience, Faye. My grandfather used to say to me, "Do not chew over an idea until you have digested your food."'

Great, thought Faye, as Dante swiftly made their order with the waiter. *He intends to keep me dangling*.

'So, tell me, what you have been up to since…we last saw each other?' he asked, his hands together in front of him, his eyes upon her, their intensity stifling.

Trying to forget you, Faye thought, forcing down the parting image of his naked body pressed to hers.

'I travelled for a year.' Her tone was polite, stilted; she did not notice the nerve working at his jaw, her head too flooded by truths she would rather not acknowledge.

I left the country indefinitely because I couldn't bear looking up at the door in the restaurant every time it opened, jumping at the phone every time it rang, hoping it was you, finding it wasn't. Funny, how her travelling always sounded like the single most important thing she had done with her life when it had been nothing but an escape. At least going to the States to do research with Chris, who couldn't have been any more different from Dante if he'd tried, had vaguely taken her mind off him. It had beaten sitting at home wondering if she would ever hear from him again. Learning not to hope had become second nature as the months had passed. A pity forgetting him altogether had not.

'And I studied marketing,' she continued without elaboration. 'I graduated just before my father passed away. After that I naturally returned to the restaurant.'

'And that is where you wish to stay?'

At the time she had never stopped to consider whether or not it was what she wanted. That hadn't come into it. All that had mattered was that her father had devoted his life to Matteson's and there was no way she would let everything he had worked for fade to black just because he was gone. But when she thought about it, despite their dire financial situation, deep within her she knew that the restaurant business was so close to her heart that it *was* where she belonged.

Faye nodded. 'In particular my passion still lies in the design side of the business, when I get the chance.' Though that was rarely, now she was practically managing the place as well as doing shifts waiting tables.

'Really?' He raised his eyebrows. 'I was rather convinced your *passion* lay elsewhere.'

Faye's face dropped immediately. She felt as if she had been foolish to let her guard down even for a second.

'*Buon appetito.* Enjoy.'

The waiter had placed the seafood in front of them, the meals an artwork in themselves. Was the service always this immediate, or did they have every dish on standby when he was in the house?

Dante lifted his fork and looked down at his plate, his face breaking into an unadulterated smile. Faye wondered if this was another deliberate attempt to turn her on, because it sure as hell was working. She forced herself to look away, emotions warring within her. *This is the man who made love to you and then walked away.*

'You're not hungry?'

She shook her head. He looked insulted as he watched her move the food around her plate. But that only frustrated her more, for she knew damned well it was as important to him as it was to her that guests enjoyed their meal—it was just one of the things about him that had once appealed so much to her. But she didn't care; she couldn't force her appetite right now if her life depended on it. Even the very act of sitting opposite him made every muscle in her body contract.

'Contrary to popular belief, a man who takes a woman out to dinner does not find it alluring to see her eat a single lettuce leaf.'

If the misogynist in him had not been apparent earlier, it had just been biding its time. 'I am not here for your pleasure.'

'Aren't you?' He put down his knife and fork and challenged her with his full attention.

It sent a shiver down her spine, and she felt suddenly conscious of the thin layer of fabric between her breasts and the cool air of the restaurant.

'No. I am not.' She concentrated on sipping her mineral water. 'I am here because, before you so rudely cut short our business meeting this afternoon, you suggested you had something worth saying.'

'Ahh.' His pause was arrogant, his eyelids low. 'So *you* prefer to digest an idea *before* your food? But patience has its rewards.'

Did it? she wondered. What good had the months of hoping he would call done for her?

Dante signalled for the waiter and spoke to him briefly in Italian.

'Very well. You came here to join my marketing team six years ago, and you made it perfectly clear that your interest in doing so was—how shall we say?—*to gain experience of a different kind*. Once you had achieved that goal, you vanished.' He trailed his finger pensively across his jaw, as if she was a rather irritating conundrum that had just fallen out of a Christmas cracker. 'And yet you presume you have the knowledge to run a successful business? Perhaps if you had stayed longer and paid a little more attention your family's restaurant would not be where it is now.'

She had heard it all now. Was he actually arrogant enough to suggest that if she had hung around it would have prevented this whole crisis? Had he actually *expected* her to stay and face the humiliation of his rejection when he had practically packed her bags for her? She shook her head in disbelief.

'But still, despite your failing in this, Matteson's is in an excellent location,' he continued.

Here we go again, she thought. *He's just trying to convince me that I'm such a failure I might as well sell now.*

'Therefore I am willing to take a chance and transfer a small advance to your business account now, with the rest of the sum you desire to follow in a month.'

'You are?' Faye was so shocked that she almost knocked over her glass. But he had refused point-blank earlier. This made no sense. He hadn't even looked at her proposal.

'On one condition,' he continued, his eyes glittering in challenge. 'For the next month, you will take up where you left off six years ago, and you will learn everything you need to make Matteson's a success. Then, and only then, will I loan you the full sum you request. When you return home you will have one further month to double your profits.'

Faye looked at him, wanting to see something in his expression that would suggest he was joking. It wasn't there.

'And if I fail?'

'The restaurant is mine.'

CHAPTER THREE

TAKE up where she'd left off? Her chest constricted at the thought. As Faye reeled from his ultimatum and all it spelled for Matteson's, that was the only thing her brain seemed capable of processing. Surely he didn't mean—? She shook herself. He was talking about her *work* experience. Yet even the thought of living back here at Il Maia, where she had spent the best and worst four weeks of her life, filled her with alarm. Where would that leave *her* at the end of the month? How could she see this man every day when she was torn between wanting to scratch that triumphant smile from his lips and wanting to taste them?

It seemed a foregone conclusion that she was ruined whether she accepted his ridiculous proposal or not. Doubling the turnover within such a short space of time was near impossible. Yet refusing his offer was out of the question. For if she did she'd be willing to bet he'd make sure Matteson's folded in double-quick time, just so he could pick up the pieces, work his multimillion-dollar magic and then flaunt his success in her face.

'I suppose the fact that what you expect me to achieve within a month is impossible is part of the joke?'

She watched his lean fingers with their neatly shaped nails stroking the stem of his wine glass ominously. His eyes rested threateningly upon her, as if she were his prey and the slow kill was his preference.

'I never joke about business. You asked for my help. These are my conditions.' His arrogance was almost tangible. He sat completely still. It only seemed to emphasise that, to him, this whole affair was barely worth his energy.

'This is a game to you, isn't it?'

'Life is a game.'

'People's livelihoods are at stake.'

'Then win.'

Faye leaned back in her chair, feeling the pulse throb at her temples. 'Could I not have the full sum now? Have the renovations well underway by the time I return?' She subconsciously shook her head as her mind tried to fathom some way of achieving the unachievable.

'Ahh, what a surprise. Miss Matteson is both loath to wait and unable to see that the *priceless* offer of working with me is worth more than any payout.'

'You always did have the most monumental ego.'

'And yet you have come back for more?'

Faye glowered at him.

'Silence, Faye? Just when I was growing so fond of your new spirit.'

Anger bubbled within her veins like volcanic lava, and her eyes dropped to her glass of water. She was racked with a sudden desire to see it splashed all over his smouldering features. Only the buzz of other diners made her hesitate. He second-guessed her.

'Go right ahead,' he challenged, as her eyes darted around

the room. 'You think it will hurt *my* reputation? You're the one who will be working here. I, on the other hand, am used to the childish behaviour of clients unable to control themselves when they do not get their own way.'

'And what about when *you* don't get your own way, Dante? You blackmail your *clients* until they do?' Faye rose, placing her serviette on the table.

'Blackmail?' He made it sound as if she'd just accused him of murder. 'I think you'll find I've offered you a lifeline.'

She'd hate to see him offer the opposite.

'Sit, Faye.' Could he be any more patronising? 'If you walk away, my offer is withdrawn, and the day you go under I will be there—waiting. I will offer you even less than the site is worth, and you will be forced to accept. Now, sit down.'

His tone was low and silky, and the effect it had upon the muscles in her legs would have made the decision for her even if the cold truth of his words had not. Slowly she resumed her seat, her face stony. She could not bring herself to look up at the expression of self-satisfied triumph he undoubtedly wore.

'Dessert.' She was grateful for the interruption as the waiter positioned large plates in front of them.

'Torta di Ricotta,' Dante announced.

Faye did not answer him. She could be eating ambrosia, the food of the gods, and it would still taste bitter to her.

'You imagine that Matteson's will be able to cope without me?'

'Presumably someone has been running it the last couple of days.'

Technically, Faye's mother was in charge of the restaurant in her absence, but whilst Josie Matteson was desperate to see Matteson's restored to its former glory, she had always played a supportive role. In reality the workload would be spread between the head waitress and the chef. She trusted them both, but it was far from ideal.

'Do not tell me that you, who are so critical of my ego, consider yourself indispensable, Faye? I can assure you, you are not.'

No, she doubted any woman was indispensable to Dante Valenti. How long had it been after he had walked away from her bed before he had taken another lover. Hours? Days?

'Impetuous change may be part and parcel of your hectic lifestyle, Dante, but I can assure you it is a rare thing for us lesser mortals.'

'Ah, but when there is opportunity you are only too eager?'

'Not on this occasion.'

'And how coincidental that your reluctance comes when it means not getting your cash at the click of your fingers.'

'I can assure you that my reluctance has nothing to do with your money and everything to do with you.'

'And yet you used to be so keen for both?' His voice was husky now, and Faye almost dropped the first spoonful of dessert that she had taken. 'Or has it slipped your mind that you once begged me to make love to you?'

So he was not going to let her forget it. Though she had been trying to prevent herself reliving that fateful afternoon since the moment she had arrived, he had every intention of using it against her. She sank back in her chair, feeling defeated.

It had been the first of August. Saturday. She would never forget the date. The evening before they had worked cease-lessly to meet a deadline, with Faye sketching idea after idea for the new hotel brochure. Production meetings had run late into the night. Not that Faye had noticed the unsociable working hours. She had been too exhilarated that she was a part of all this.

In fact, even during her time off she'd caught herself wishing she were back at the office, with that feeling of awareness zipping around her veins at a double-quick pace just at knowing he was close by, which quadrupled when he looked at her. And there had been many times in the course of the last four weeks, unbelievable though it was, when she had caught him doing just that. And not in the way that an employer usually looked at his employee. More in the way an art lover might examine the ceiling of the Sistine Chapel. But he would always look away the moment she noticed, his brows furrowed, as if he had really been contemplating some complex business problem and had just alighted upon the answer. Which had left Faye caught between believing she was too young and too awkward for him to see her as anything other than the teenage girl she was, and sensing something else within him that he seemed reluctant to acknowledge.

'Faye?' He had spoken her name as if coaxing a child from sleep. She'd finished off the section of the cover design she was working on and attempted to steady the pounding of her heart before looking up to see him standing before her desk.

'I'm almost done.'

'It's late.' He looked at his watch and raised his eyebrows. 'It's the weekend, and I've been working you like a Trojan. Go and get some rest.'

Faye's eyelids did indeed feel heavy. 'OK. I'll pop back tomorrow morning—get this finished before Monday.'

'No, you won't,' he said, his voice insistent. 'You deserve a break. Go out—soak up Rome at the weekend.'

Faye nodded hesitantly. She had taken herself out on a sightseeing bus tour the weekend after she had arrived, but magnificent though the sights were, seeing them by herself, without anyone to share her amazement, had somehow diminished their appeal.

'Perhaps.'

It was then that Dante looked around the room thoughtfully, at the rest of his team slowly packing up and making their ways home.

'I suppose there isn't really anyone else here your age.' His expression was guilty. 'I'm sorry.'

Faye knew it was true, although it was not something that had bothered her. Until he had pointed out how young she was again. She didn't *feel* young.

And then he said it.

'I could always show you the sights tomorrow, if you like.'

And those words changed everything.

For the Dante who was waiting for her in the lobby the next morning—a Dante without the immaculately pressed suits he wore to work—was everything she had hoped for and more besides. It felt as if somehow they were equal, like any other couple getting lost amongst the crowds. For not only did he make the sights come alive—from the wonder of Vatican City to the Baroque fountains hidden amongst the lesser-known ancient sights—he also had insisted she experience the intimate *trattorie*, the sensational boutiques in Piazza di Spagna.

She marvelled at their windows, not daring to go in. Until he called her over to one particularly exclusive display and she saw the most exquisite red evening gown she could ever have imagined. The kind most women never got to wear, let alone own.

'Go in,' he commanded, sensing her appreciation. 'Try it on.'

'Oh, Dante—don't be ridiculous. Why would I try on a dress like that? The assistants will only have to take one look at me to know that I don't have the money to even buy the hanger, let alone an occasion to wear the dress.'

'Nonsense,' he said, as if she had just suggested the earth was flat.

And the sudden understanding of just how powerful and how rich Dante really was began to seep in as she was ushered to a fitting room that was so large it could have given the entire upstairs in her parents' house a run for its money.

The dress fit like a glove, but it was with some trepidation that she stepped out, feeling like a peasant masquerading as a princess. Slowly he turned around, and then did a double-take, as if to check it was really her. She hadn't anticipated that it would be the way he looked at her rather than the dress itself that would make her feel as if her whole body was glowing. But she knew she wanted to bottle the feeling and keep it for ever.

'Faye…*bella*,' he said guardedly, his voice a purr. 'You look …' He shook his head like a man torn and turned to the shop assistant. 'We'll take it.' The woman smiled from ear to ear and waltzed off to the till.

'Dante, what are you doing?' Faye protested under her breath, trying not to move for fear she might damage the priceless gown. 'I can't afford this!'

'Think of it as a thank you for all your hard work,' he said abruptly, avoiding looking directly at her. 'Now, go and get changed.'

And, despite her protestations, Dante paid for the dress before she even emerged from the changing room.

Feeble though it was in comparison, she insisted she buy him a *gelato* in return. Puzzled by her insistence, he reluctantly agreed—on the condition that he take her to the best place to sample delicious ice cream. But just as they were approaching the winding street he had in mind, the heavens opened.

By the time they had run back to Il Maia, her hand reaching for his to stop them losing one another in the crowds of shoppers, her light summer dress was soaked through and stuck to her body, and his pale shirt was clinging to his broad chest, his jeans moulded to his lean hips. Finally they reached her room, and, breathless and laughing, she unlocked the door and flew in.

Dante hesitated in the doorway.

'My apartment's only a few blocks away. Let me head back and get changed. I'll meet you downstairs.'

'Dante, it's raining even more heavily now—here, have a towel.' Faye slipped off her shoes and flitted through to the bathroom. He stood there, poised like a man who had been asked to do a bungee jump without a rope.

'No, Faye, I shouldn't—'

'Come on, you'll get cold.' Faye pulled him into the room, laughing, and put the towel around his shoulders, shutting the door behind him.

And the moment the catch clicked shut, something snapped. The air in the room changed, and her naturally quick movements seemed to slow as she became conscious of every move her body made. The smell of rain mixed with her faint floral perfume and his musky cologne. Their damp clothes seemed to long to be removed. She was thrilled at being caught out by nature, as if it was urging them to come together.

She stood before him, the intensity of the look he gave her

making her nipples peak beneath the wet cotton of her dress. His silence was unbearable.

'Let's get out of these clothes,' she said, reaching her arm behind her back, turning around. 'Help me with this zip.'

He did not answer, but she felt him move behind her and his hands begin to release her dress, agonisingly avoiding contact with her skin. Faye heard her breathing fall in time with his. It was as if those lingering glances had reached fever pitch and there could be no more looking away. Faye...*bella*. The words echoed around her mind, refusing to be forgotten, and her body was crying out for him as the rivulets of water ran over her body, mingling with its own heat.

'Touch me, Dante.'

She did not know where the words came from. She whispered them in a voice she did not recognise as her own—knew only that she needed him in a way she had never understood needing anything before. His warm breath stirred the hairs on the back of her neck, but still he did not move.

'Please.' She turned round to face him and looked up at him, her eyes wide, imploring. 'Please, touch me,' she urged.

Dante drew in a ragged breath, his eyes boring into her with unfathomable intensity. She saw his hands move up as if to encircle her waist, and then drop to his sides again.

'I want...' Her voice was bolder now, seeing his temptation. 'I want you to make love to me.'

'Damn you, you little temptress,' he bit out, his voice thick as he shook his head slowly. 'Don't you know what you do to me?'

She nodded slowly, her lips parted. And then he raised his head and looked deep into her eyes for one final moment, before he brought his mouth crushing upon her own.

And it was then that Faye truly learned what it was to be touched. To feel the exquisite pleasure of being claimed by the man you loved in the most intimate way there was. And the sudden searing of pain was replaced by a mounting pleasure which exploded with all the unexpected welcome of a late-afternoon storm. A sensation which, to Faye, was only surpassed by the feeling of lying beneath a cool white sheet, with Dante just inches away afterwards, and the sound of the easing rain outside the window. The sound of his breathing was steady and deep.

'Couldn't you just stay here for ever?' she whispered.

It was the eye of the storm she had never seen coming.

'I thought you had got everything you wanted.'

Faye's face crumpled. She didn't know what he was supposed to say *afterwards*, but she knew that wasn't it. Seconds before he had been crying her name in ecstasy—and now? Now the harshness of his tone made it sound as if he almost *despised* her.

Faye rolled away from him, whipping the sheet around her. 'What are you talking about?' She suddenly felt as if she was playing a complicated game and no one had told her the rules.

'I'm talking about little girls who cast all dignity aside the minute they get a taste of the high life.' He glanced towards the designer bag containing the dress and curled his lip in distaste. 'Those who are so hot for a man they do not see the value of their virtue amidst their haste to lose it.'

He swung his legs over the bed, shameless in his nakedness, and reached for his damp jeans.

'You came here to learn, *bella*? Then today you learn this is not the kind of behaviour which makes a man *stay* anywhere. Why would he, when he has taken all that is worth taking?'

And with that he scooped up the rest of his clothes and headed towards the door. Suddenly it didn't feel like a game at all.

'What are you talking about?' she repeated helplessly, searching his face, willing him to take the words back.

'Your true colours, *sì*?' he said with finality before closing the door calmly behind him.

As Faye stared helplessly at the door, nausea rising in her belly, she felt her heart break in two. Felt all the humiliation of loving so blindly, of discovering just why it all felt so unreal. Because it was. Every moment, from the instant they had met until now, turned sour in her mind, as if someone had poured acid into her brain. And something changed irrecoverably within her. Not because she had just made love to a man for the first time in her life. But because all her foolish childhood dreams had just crashed out through the door with him. She had wanted to give herself to him, and he detested her for it. How could she have got it so wrong?

Faye choked back the sobs as realisation seeped in, and suddenly she was caught by a need to get dressed—as if angry at her own body, determined to cover its nakedness. The open wardrobe caught her eye, with its skirts and blouses neatly ordered for her weeks of work ahead. Yes, she thought, there *was* something worse than this: staying around to face the humiliation day after day, having him look at her thinking he had *taken all that was worth taking*, having him look at her at all.

And so she packed her bags. Understanding that her leaving would have about as much impact on his world as a pebble skimming the surface of the ocean, but knowing it was preferable to being swallowed up by the ocean completely.

* * *

Faye raised her head to look at him, sitting opposite her, her heart numb with the steady ache she had not allowed herself to feel for so long. She felt ashamed—that she had had no choice but to swallow her pride and return, that she had allowed him to get to her once more—and she felt terrified that she was capable of letting him do it all over again.

'As you said yourself, Dante, we all make mistakes.'

He seemed oblivious to the pain in her eyes. 'You mean you realised that you could have got more for your virginity than a few weeks working here?'

What was he talking about? She had wanted nothing from him but for it to have been real. Yet *he* was angry with *her*? She looked at his cruel, arrogant, despicably handsome face. He seemed to tire of waiting for her to answer. She was glad.

'It was fortunate that you were offered *opportunities* elsewhere, in spite of having come straight from me.'

'Not everyone is such as Neanderthal as you, Dante. Some men do not consider a woman's virginity the only thing she has to offer,' she bit out, furious at his assumptions, and even more furious that she had never brought herself to take up any such *opportunities*, as he put it, on the occasions when they had come her way. But what would have been the point? She hadn't even once got close to feeling anything like she had felt that afternoon with anyone. Until she had walked into his office again today, she thought wretchedly.

'Faye, do not misinterpret me. I meant opportunities in the business world. Not many people walk out on a contract with Valenti Enterprises and are still offered work elsewhere.'

Bastard, she thought. Like hell you meant that. And as for business opportunities—those that had come her way since, she had had to turn down for the sake of Matteson's. Faye felt all the tension in her shoulders return as she put down her spoon.

'Champagne to finish, I think. A toast to my new…right-hand woman for a month.'

Faye gritted her teeth. There was no reason to refuse. She had sold her soul to the devil. If she was worried about losing her head, it was too late.

As he chinked his glass against her own, the blood in her veins slowed to a more languorous pace, no less insistent. She wished she had brought her *faux* pashmina to cover herself from that penetrating gaze which lingered upon her as she took a sip. Did he want her? He hated her, wanted to ruin her—she knew that. But she also knew that was not an issue he'd have difficulty putting aside if he did. The bubbles fizzed on her tongue. She took a deep breath as the alcohol reached her bloodstream, making her more conscious of her surroundings. Two days ago she had woken up to face a day like any other at the restaurant: vacant tables, piles of bills, tired décor, tired people. And now here she was, sitting in Perfezione, the antithesis of her life back home. Surrounded by so much luxury, so much life, in a restaurant where it took months just to secure a booking. Unless you happened to be accompanying the man who had haunted her dreams to this day. For a moment she wondered if she had conjured up this whole scene in her imagination.

'I will have a contract drawn up, which you can sign tomorrow.'

No, not a dream. She nodded reluctantly. He *was* the devil in disguise. So she had no choice but to stay, but she did not have to stay *here*. She would return to the guesthouse. Even if it meant having to put it on a credit card and negotiate the busy metro every morning, she needed her escape.

'Excuse me.' Faye caught the attention of a passing waiter, ignoring Dante as he stiffened. 'Please could you order me a taxi to Piazza Indipendenza? *Grazie.*'

'That won't be necessary, Michele. I will drive Miss Matteson. Thank you,' Dante interjected, almost before she had even finished. The waiter was dismissed instantly and was so professional that not a hint of perplexity crossed his face.

'You've been drinking. You're not driving me anywhere!' Faye made no effort to tone down the volume of her anger now. She had had enough of this rollercoaster of emotions. One minute he was masquerading as a reasonable human being, and the next he was verging on the tyrannical.

'I'm glad you agree. I will not be driving you anywhere, because we have established that you will stay here—have we not?'

'I have agreed to *work* for you. Where I stay has no bearing upon that. I will make sure I am on time, if that is your concern.'

'That is not my concern, and it shall not be yours either. Living here is as much part of your experience as your work here during the day. It is not up for debate.'

No, nothing *he* decided was up for debate, was it? And no wonder, when his world was full of people pandering to his every need, treating his every word like the Holy Grail. But whilst he might get her diffident agreement, he would not have this ridiculous facade of civility any longer. She would get on with what she was here to do, and spend as little time in his company as possible.

'I wish to go to bed. I had a late flight.'

'Bed? Why, you should have said earlier.' He rose, his hand moving to her elbow and his mouth lifting into a lazy lopsided grin that was at odds with the brooding intensity she had seen on his face for most of the day.

How was he allowed to look so good when he was so damned unscrupulous? She tried not to notice. She had allowed him to trample over her youthful emotions wearing that sexy smile once before, and she was not going to let him do it again.

'I can make my own way up three flights, Dante.'

'I insist on seeing you back to your room, *bella*.' He whispered the word in her ear as they walked away from the table. *Bella*. She wondered how her legs kept moving with such tantalising remembrance flooding back.

Faye led the way up the stairs, not prepared to face the intimate space of the lift with him. She could feel him close behind her, the sounds of the foyer and the restaurant dying away as they ascended. She would never be able to escape him; she never could. Even nine hundred miles away, he had always been there in her head, making every other man appear as a mere shadow.

They came to a stop outside her room, and she fixed her eyes firmly on the thick wooden door, determined to put it between them. This close he was dynamite. She wanted—no, needed to defuse it.

'Goodnigh—'

'Look at me,' he ground out, one hand suddenly tilting her chin so that she had no choice in the matter, his other hand against the wall behind her head, trapping her. His face was so close to hers she could see the angry flaring of his nostrils and the first sign of stubble on his chiselled jaw. She fought the urge to touch it. 'You can't hide any longer.'

'I'm not trying to hide.'

'Liar.'

She looked into his eyes. Their black depths glittered with hunger, and they were her undoing. She wanted to tell him not to look at her that way. And at the same time she never wanted him to stop. She let out a sigh she was not even sure was hers, all the fight from her gone. His gaze dropped to her lips. He did want her. She could see it in the way he almost clenched his teeth in resistance as his thumb came up to touch her bottom lip invitingly.

'Dante!'

She closed her eyes, almost out of fear that if she kept them open she would awake from this moment. She did not. Half of her was convinced he would back away, whilst the other half expected him to claim her mouth in one fierce, demanding stroke. Neither. Her lips parted as if he had coaxed them subliminally at the exact moment he brought his own down to meet them, and for a second he held them there, as if they were some timeless statue, caught for ever in the most sublime moment of anticipation. And then slowly, painfully slowly, he brushed his lips against her own, gently exploring her, teasing her into deepening the kiss, beginning to taste her. His tongue found hers and slid across it, sending feelings of anticipation throughout her entire body, the movement loaded with sensual promise. Hunger enveloped her. His hand at her chin reached to tangle itself in her hair, cradling her head at the perfect angle for him to kiss her more and more deeply.

What had he done to her all those years ago that made him the only man on earth who could melt her with a single gaze? He had imprinted himself upon her very soul. But as yearning flooded her body like a drug she gave up wondering and surrendered to the urgent sensation that threatened to take her over, sliding her arms behind his broad back, crushing her breasts against his powerful chest, her whole body throbbing with need.

But in that moment she felt his lips break away from her, creating a new and unwelcome void that demanded to be filled by him alone. Yes, she thought, amidst the blur of desire in her mind. Not here. Inside. She lifted her eyelids drowsily, ready to lead him into her room. And the piercing black stare that met her own lust-filled gaze chilled her to the bone.

'You think, perhaps, that a speedy capitulation might encourage me to part with the entire sum early?' His tone was merciless. He shook his head and tutted. The arms that she had wrapped around his body fell to her sides. 'I know you are gagging for me, *cara*, but patience is one of the first rules of business. Never offer your best assets first. You have made this mistake in the past, yes? See—you learn the first lesson already. We have all month to sample dessert.'

Faye's teeth bit down on her kiss-swollen lips, hot colour staining her cheekbones, the desire that had coursed through every inch of her replaced with a humiliation equally difficult to quell. She turned away from him, wanting to knock the satisfaction from his face, but feeling a moistness in her eyes that she would rather die than have him observe.

'Forgive me,' she muttered, her voice like poison as she unlocked the door of her room, 'for assuming that conceding to your barbaric behaviour was a requirement of this deal. I obviously misunderstood. Now I know I am excused in that department, I assure you nothing will give me greater pleasure than to stay as far away from you as possible.'

Dante laughed—a loud, shameless laugh that shook her to the very core. 'I will teach you about pleasure too, *cara*, but all in good time.' Before he had even finished his sentence she had flown into the dark room and closed the door hurriedly behind her, her hands still shaking. She stood with her back to the wall, a shiver rushing over her as the cool evening breeze blew the curtain at the balcony in an ebbing and flowing motion that reminded her of an old horror film. She had never felt so utterly rejected. She held her breath, unwilling to exhale until she was sure he was gone. Finally she let out a long, deep sigh. The moment she did, his voice penetrated the thick door.

'You begin work tomorrow morning at seven-thirty, in the kitchen. Do not be late.'

CHAPTER FOUR

FAYE caught the white apron that was thrust into her hands and grudgingly tied it around her waist. Attempting to blink herself awake, she followed the petite kitchen hand who had introduced herself as Lucia to an enormous sack beside a space at one of the work surfaces. She wanted to ask precisely how peeling sweet potatoes at this time in the morning was going to help her rescue her family's business, but she held her tongue. Though she knew this was contributing to nothing more than Dante's already inflated ego, there was no reason to take it out on Lucia, who was simply another member of the army of staff that gladly catered to his every whim.

As Lucia left her to it, Faye looked around the enormous kitchen and sighed. Yet oddly, as she took in the sea of whites, stainless steel and concentrated expressions, she somehow felt impelled to prove to him that, regardless of what he thought, she was not afraid of hard work. As she knuckled down to her task the minutes soon ticked by, and she began to find the repetitive action strangely therapeutic.

She had had a restless night, caught between sleep and waking, fighting the feeling of utter rejection and the overwhelming desire to open the door just to check whether Dante was still hovering there like some elusive phantom, even though she knew he was long gone. At least the fastidiousness of the Perfezione kitchen kept her mind from wondering whether she was simply here to amuse him, even if this whole exercise was actually an extension of that.

She had almost expected him to be here this morning, if only to check that she had not gone AWOL during the night. But when she discovered that Lucia was to be responsible for her *experience*, today at least, Faye realised that in complying with his scheme she had no doubt relinquished any special treatment. Now he as good as had a free employee for the month, and when she failed in her task Matteson's would be his. Even if for some unthinkable reason she succeeded, he would get his money back and she would be gone from his life for good. From his point of view it was a win-win situation. She, on the other hand, had everything to lose, she thought as her mind wandered over the brief telephone conversation she had had with her mother that morning.

'Oh, Faye, that's wonderful news!'

Faye had tried not to inject her voice with too much optimism as she'd told her mother that she had secured enough funds to contract the first renovations, but after endless months of bills and 'application refused' letters dropping through the letterbox at the restaurant, it was no surprise that Josie Matteson had been delighted.

'It's not a simple loan, though, Mum. There are…conditions.' Faye pushed the disturbing image of Dante's *conditions* to the back of her mind. 'I'm going to have to stay here for the next month.'

Aside from telling her mother that she was going to Italy in one final bid to secure a loan, Faye had been vague about her exact plans. But she *had* said that she would only be gone a couple of days at most. If only.

'I'm sure we can cope,' her mother replied, fretful for a second. 'Yes—of course we can.'

Though Josie Matteson was as desperate as Faye to see the restaurant restored to its former glory, she had always been happier keeping the place spic and span than getting involved in the managerial side of things.

'Was last night busier?' Faye asked hopefully. If only some miracle had occurred whilst she had been away. Then she could tell Dante what to do with his contract and get back to where she was needed. But she knew she had about as much chance of having drummed up enough business with that last frantic leaflet-drop as she had of being married with a baby by the time she was twenty-five.

'It was quiet again, I'm afraid, darling. Even that anniversary booking was cancelled. Apparently they hadn't been to us for years, and when one of them popped in to see the place they changed their minds.'

Faye felt her heart sink as she envisaged another empty table. But at the same time it seemed to fill her with a renewed sense of resolve to see this whole excruciating but necessary charade through to the end. It was the only thing that offered her a chance to change all that.

'But let's not dwell on that now, when we've just had good news about this kind soul offering us a loan,' Josie continued.

Faye was grateful that her mother couldn't hear the alternative opinion of Dante running through her head, for the thought of explaining just why he was anything but a *kind soul* was too loathsome to contemplate. Nevertheless, whilst her mother wasn't one to probe, this was about Matteson's, and she at least deserved to know where the money was coming from.

'I…um…approached Valenti Enterprises,' Faye said, as if avoiding his Christian name would stop Josie making a connection with the past—though she doubted her mother had forgotten. After all, though it had been many years ago, it wasn't every day that she found her daughter over the moon at being offered the opportunity of a lifetime, only to have her return out of the blue, suddenly desperate to take up Chris's long-standing offer, with a list of excuses for leaving Italy as long her arm. That the job hadn't been what she was expecting. That the language barrier had been too difficult. That there had been no one her own age. In hindsight, Faye realised she had protested so much that it had had nothing to do with *him* that she had given herself away.

Her mother's momentary silence seemed to confirm it.

'That can't have been easy, Faye. Mr Valenti is a formidable man. But he was once impressed with what he found here. He must remember.'

Oh, he remembers, all right, thought Faye as she steered the conversation back to the practicalities of her absence. That's precisely the problem.

Several hours later, when she had finished the potatoes, Faye was surprised that Dante had arranged for her to be shown how some of the dishes on the day's lunch menu were prepared. She was delighted to find that the chef in charge was Bernardo, who had started as a junior the season that Faye had first arrived at Il Maia.

'Faye! Come. I show you risotto!'

It's lucky, she thought, that his English isn't good enough to ask me what the hell I'm doing back here.

It was amazingly inspiring, watching the staff work so harmoniously together in this high-tech set-up, and she couldn't help but admit that the experience did give her a fresh outlook. It reminded her of her own enthusiasm for serving good food, that in recent months had become buried under the stress of poor profits. For, whilst Dante's attitude to her might leave plenty to be desired, she couldn't deny his skills as a restaurateur.

Faye was laughing raucously at Bernardo's gestures as he tried to demonstrate how the mushrooms for the risotto were harvested, when she felt the air change. The doors to the kitchen had been opening and closing all morning, but somehow she knew that the person who had just entered the room was not simply any other member of staff. She stopped laughing immediately as she sensed footsteps behind her. *Dante*. For some reason she felt utterly guilty, like a small child caught with her hand in the sweet tin. Even Bernardo looked as if he wished he were not there, despite the fact he had been carrying out his boss's wishes. She turned round, knowing without looking exactly where he stood. He was wearing a jet-black suit that only enhanced the darkness of his hair, contrasting lucidly with the gleaming bright white of the kitchen. His mouth was fixed in a hard line. For a man so well-known for his control, he looked as if it might evade him for a moment.

'Good afternoon.' Faye smiled brightly, determined to counteract her unwarranted guilt. 'What can we do for you? Lunch, perhaps?' She thought she saw a nerve move at his jaw, and turned to Bernardo, grinning. 'I can recommend the mushroom risotto.' Bernardo shifted on his feet a little uneasily, and turned back to his preparations.

Dante did not seem willing to dignify her question with an

answer. Did he have to be such a brute? She supposed he would have preferred to find her elbow-deep in potato peelings, lamenting her fate.

'I see Bernardo has had plenty of time to share his expertise. If you speak to Lucia, she will see that you are organised to serve lunch for the rest of the afternoon.' He delivered his speech as if he was diagnosing a disease, and turned on his immaculate heels to head for the door without waiting for a response.

'Believe it or not,' she called after him, 'I have waited tables before. Just as I'm quite capable of preparing vegetables *and* following a recipe. Could you explain to me how this is supposed to help me increase my profits?'

The kitchen went silent, save for sound of billowing steam from a large saucepan. The other workers continued diligently, ears undoubtedly pricked. Dante swung round and closed the gap between them, so that his face was level with hers and disturbingly close. His eyes were full of challenge, as if she had dared him.

'I am going to make you fall in love,' he announced, his voice smooth and low.

Faye stood on her tiptoes, as if the extra inch was some small semblance of defence against him, and drew in a breath. She parted her lips, half in shock and half because she felt she should say or do something, without knowing what. She knew what had flashed into her brain, but there was certainly no question of doing *that*.

'With this business,' he finished nonchalantly, as if his sentence had never suggested anything else. 'With the sights, the smells, the tastes of Perfezione. I am going to make you want to give *your* customers the pleasure you will see on people's faces here, and you are going to learn how to instil that same want in your staff.' His voice assumed an acidic timbre. 'But I see you have already learned something of the wants of my staff this morning.'

Faye fell back on her heels, not following Dante's glance in the direction of Bernardo, who was now furiously working away at the stove. She was momentarily stunned, and when she raised her head to look at him again he was eyeing her as if he wished she would disappear. As the words sank in, it infuriated her that his intention had worked—for she had always loved this business, and yet she had felt more inspired this morning than she had done for years.

'You need to change,' he said casually, as he looked her up and down, before walking towards the door. It took until he was long gone for Faye to realise literally what he meant.

Dante sat down at a table by the window, tossed his jacket aside, and loosened his tie. The manipulative temptress! She had been here less than twenty-four hours and she had already found a way to pout those kissable lips and flash those bewitching green eyes to her advantage in the most assiduous kitchen in Italy. *His* kitchen. How had he ever been stupid enough not to see through her?

Unwillingly, he thought back to the day he had by chance set foot in Matteson's. He'd been in London checking out potential sites for expansion and any likely competition. He hadn't expected to find the fresh new look he wanted for his branding staring up at him from his lunch menu. But then he knew that the best things in life were never be to found where you most expected them. Recognising that had been the secret of his success. But how much easier it would have been on that occasion if the innovative design before him had been the work of some hugely expensive marketing company in some far-flung corner of the world. He could have simply bought it up and claimed it without complication.

Instead he had discovered it was the work of a waitress, a girl who was barely out of high school. A girl he had not only found irresistibly attractive, but who had evoked in him another feeling he couldn't quite lay his finger upon—and that had surprised him. Had it been because she was English? No, he had had English lovers. Because she was beautiful? Yes, she had a fresh-faced beauty women would kill for and men would die for, but it wasn't the kind that would be wholly captured by a photograph. Because a photo wouldn't have been able to capture her unaffected *joie de vivre*, or her innate enthusiasm for the business that he'd been surprised to find reminded him of his own, but without any of the cynicism that had come from his being too often surrounded by people who lacked it. He never usually looked twice at women that young or that innocent. But when had been the last time—no, when had he *ever* come into contact with a woman whose innocence he truly believed so wholeheartedly? The truth was, he had both admired and *respected* her. Which was why—the minute he'd offered her an opportunity to work with his marketing team—he had made a pact with himself never to touch her.

But, *Dio*, how she had seen an opportunity for something else entirely! So quick to rid herself of the purity that he had held in such regard that he had suppressed his own longings— which was something Dante Valenti simply didn't do. And how little she had deserved it! He remembered that fateful day, when he had seen what he should have recognised the first time she blinked those enormous earnest eyes at him. Eyes which had spoken even louder than her cries for him to take her. What man could have fought against it any longer? Dante swallowed defensively, pushing down the feeling of something like shame as he removed his tie completely and attempted to control the insistent press of his erection against his inner thigh, as strong now as it had been then.

Why had he presumed that her age and innocence made her different from every other woman he had ever known? For they had only proved to be even deadlier wiles than the practised artifice of the coquettes he was used to, prompting him to spend time with her because she had made him think she was lonely. Making him believe her small cries of protest when he bought her that damn dress were genuine, and not the reverse psychology of a mistress-in-the-making.

His mind jumped to the moment two weeks later, when one of his maids had nervously approached him, telling him Miss Matteson had left a red dress behind. For one rare moment he had *actually* hoped he was wrong. Because leaving the dress was not the only thing that had surprised him about her reaction afterwards. If she *was* just like other women, why had she not hung around and pleaded with him to change his mind? Or at the very least milked him for another gift or two? Such questions had left him on the verge of admitting to himself that the true object of disgust was himself, for taking her virginity and pushing her away rather than facing his own guilt.

Until he had buried his pride and rung England—and discovered she was already on a plane to God knew where with her next lover! The evidence had been unequivocal—worse, even, than discovering she had wanted him for what he could buy her. She had made a sexual conquest of him! He understood then what that feeling was that he hadn't been able to lay his finger upon. No, she wasn't like any other woman he had ever met. She was a hundred times worse. And now here she was again, six years down the line, returning for no other reason than to get her claws on his cash. And hadn't she proved last night just what she was willing to do to get it?

Dante shifted his legs and tried to focus on perusing the lunch menu. Despite his belief in the importance of stopping to eat, he realised it was a long time since he had even sat down at this time of day. But then today was not panning out as his day usually did. His morning had been strangely unproductive, and he had found himself wondering if there was something he really ought to be going to Il Maia to do every time he'd looked at his schedule. One thing in particular had kept popping into his mind, and, hell, he probably should have done *that* last night. He could not have had a more enthusiastic invitation. That hot, responsive mouth, the small moan of pleasure as he had taken her in his arms that had seemed to break from her subconsciously. So the little witch still acted as if it was the first time that a man had ever touched her that way.

That was why she still got to him. Because she had fooled him, made him believe her little performance until he lost control completely. But never again. This time he was going to make her sorry for everything she had thrown back at him the day she had surrendered her virtue and tossed away the opportunity he had given her. She would live to regret making a conquest of *him*. He was going to have her on his terms—when she knew full well that doing so wouldn't gain her a penny, when she could admit she wanted him for no other reason than that if he didn't have her desire would drive her mad. And then he would get her out of his system once and for all.

* * *

Faye felt as if it was herself on the plate as she was handed stuffed tomatoes and instructed to take them to him. Apparently Signor Valenti was in no mood for mushroom risotto. The restaurant was as busy as, if not busier than, the night before, with executive men and women discussing business at every table. But despite the multitude of suits her eyes were drawn instantly to the brooding figure he cut against the window. It was like walking a gauntlet; his mesmerising eyes were fixed upon her, his potent masculinity coiled in that easy pose, belying his danger. He had planned this, of course. The irony of the moment. Yes, he still made her feel that everyone else but the two of them were invisible, but he had not one iota of respect for her now. Now it was as if he was the emperor and she some offering, his to sample or disregard. But she felt oddly removed from the Faye of all those years ago, as if for Matteson's she had grown another skin of responsibility and purpose that kept her from breaking down at this perverse distortion of her memories. Except her skin was not so thick that she was impervious to the physical effect he had upon her. It took all her effort to place one foot in front of the other, willing herself not to look down to check that her legs were obeying her scrambled brain as she approached him. She wondered whether she had remembered to breathe.

'I am getting a little *déjà vu*, Faye. Do you feel this also?' The lightness in his tone had returned, as easily as if he was remarking upon the weather.

'Well, it was only last night that we were here, Dante. I expect that's it.' She had no intention of letting on that the first time they had met still stuck in her mind. 'As for me, like I mentioned earlier, waiting tables is a forte I have already mastered. So it is not so much *déjà vu* as a common experience.'

He looked perturbed. 'You consider working at Perfezione

a common experience for the second time in your life, Faye? I pity the man who seeks to give you the uncommon.'

Was that what it had all been about? The Italian billionaire bestowing a special experience on plain little Faye, whose life was a *tabula rasa*, just longing to be scrawled upon? Heaven forbid she should have felt anything as human as desire.

'I do not rely on men to fill the meaningless void that you consider my life to be, Dante.'

'Really? You just rely on them for money—is that it?'

Faye was still holding his plate a few inches away from the table. Although she stood taller than him he still somehow dominated her. His six-foot-five frame was at ease, like some predatory animal ready to pounce on the elfin prey in front of him. What was the point in arguing with him? Telling him that the idea of using men for money disgusted her, that this was the first time in her life she had ever asked any man for help? After her actions yesterday he was hardly going to believe her. Better he think that than know the truth. Her weakness would give him too much satisfaction.

'*Buon appetito*, Signor Valenti. Enjoy your meal.' Faye placed the plate in front of him, flashed him a counterfeit smile, and made to walk away.

'Have you eaten?' he asked, as though the thought that she was human had only just crossed his mind.

'You mean I am allowed a lunch break? I had no idea your terms were so civil.' She turned back to face him.

'Sit down, Faye. Eat with me.'

'Why?' It was ludicrous to feel so threatened, but she did. The question took him aback.

'Because we are both hungry, *cara*.'

He flashed her a look that was loaded with sensual promise, sending her senses into overdrive.

'Thank you, but I will have something with Lucia,' she replied calmly. 'Get to know life below stairs. Isn't that why I'm here?'

'Then just have a coffee,' he suggested casually, as she watched him take a sip from his own cup, which looked minuscule in his large hand. Her eyes were drawn to the sprinkle of dark hair at his wrist against the white cuff of his shirt, and then to his lips. She remembered how they had tasted her own, how it would feel to taste them again. She shook herself.

'I have just had an espresso that Bernardo made for me, thank you.' She saw him flex his other hand momentarily. 'I'd better be getting back. I am sure it does not project the right image, having a waitress loiter around for too long as it is.'

'I think you can leave it up to me to decide what image is Perfezione,' he murmured, so that she only just caught his words as his eyes undressed her with a single look.

'I would hate your tomatoes to get cold. Please excuse me.'

The rest of the afternoon passed in a blur of speed. Faye had gone back to the kitchen feeling as if she had just completed an endurance test, and then taken a quick break before promptly returning to work. By the time she was back on the restaurant floor Dante had already gone, the absence of his proud, dark head oddly conspicuous. Lunch at the restaurant had lasted several hours, and had been closely followed by a new flux of people arriving for coffee. At five o'clock, when the evening staff arrived, Faye felt dead on her feet, and after the restless night and the events of the day she was delighted to be able to slip away.

Tempting thought it was to go straight up to her room, her

unexpected need to remain in Rome longer than she had anticipated left her needing some supplies, so she went straight to the *supermercato* to pick up some basics. On the way there she passed the hotel's outdoor pool, and looked longingly at its shimmering depths. Faye had not swum competitively since her teens, but it was something she loved to do regularly. It gave her time to think, and not to think. The latter of which she suspected would be essential over the coming month. So when she spotted a fuchsia-pink bikini in one of the less expensive boutiques on the way back to the hotel—although never usually prone to impetuous spending—Faye treated herself. Believing she was only going to be here for a day or two at most, she had barely brought more than a few changes of clothes, let alone a swimsuit. Think of it as necessary for your sanity, she told herself. But much as she longed to change into her bikini at once, to go and release the frustrations of the day, she supposed she ought to check that Dante didn't mind her using the pool first.

As she whipped up a quick chicken salad and sat back to admire the view of St Peter's Dome from the balcony, she could not help wondering where he was this evening. Having dinner? Probably, and she doubted he was alone. Lucia had discreetly mentioned that he rarely dined at Perfezione, and that twice in as many days was unprecedented, so perhaps he took his other women elsewhere, somewhere more private. Not that she cared. The peace was a relief. She was just wondering because she didn't know what he had planned for her next, and she wasn't used to living like that.

The trill of a phone ringing broke her thoughts and almost made her leave her seat. Was it coming from the room next door? She hadn't even noticed a phone in here, though she

supposed there must be one somewhere. She followed the
sound, which led her to a table in the bedroom that she had
not really noticed, and picked up an ultra-modern device.

'Hello?' There were only two options. No one but Dante
knew she was here. So either it was a wrong number, or—

'Where were you?'

Or him. His voice was a low growl and it licked through
her body. She leaned against the wall. Where was she? What
kind of a question was that?

'Working, Dante. You employed me, remember?'

'After that.'

'What do you mean, after that? I didn't finish until gone
five.'

'And now it's seven-thirty. I've been trying to call you.'

'I went shopping. Was I supposed to inform you if I left
the building?'

'Don't be ridiculous.'

Look who's talking, she thought. 'I have to eat, Dante, or
had you forgotten again?'

'And you mean to tell me you weren't tempted by any of
the boutiques along the way?'

Faye was furious that technically speaking he was right,
but not in the way that he thought. She was glad he was not
there to see her cheeks burning.

'Anyway, that's precisely why I was trying to call. I'm
having dinner sent up to you. I'm on my way to Lazio and
won't be back until tomorrow night.'

'Thanks, but I've already eaten.'

The silence suggested it was a rare thing for his plans to
be thwarted, even if it was something so minor. Either that or
it had never crossed his mind before that women were capable

of fending for themselves. She suspected his next question would be whether she'd eaten her five portions of fruit and veg, but if it was he didn't voice it aloud.

'Tomorrow Lucia will talk you through the importance of seasonal produce to our menu, amongst other things. In the evening we have an event to attend.'

'What sort of event?' she asked, hearing nothing but *we*.

'The Harvest Ball.'

Did all ridiculously gorgeous billionaires attend a school where they were taught to drop bombshells like that into everyday conversation? The Harvest Ball: an internationally renowned event that was like the Oscars of the hotel and restaurant industry. The one Chris was always talking about, and which he could only bear to miss if he was soaking up the sunshine on the opposite side of the world.

'How is that beneficial to my training, Dante? Surely it is nothing more than a glorified party.'

'If that is what you think, that is precisely why you need to attend. In reality it's a marketplace—work under the veneer of pleasure. It will be exceptionally beneficial to you.'

Work under the veneer of pleasure? A good description, Faye thought.

'Will I not hinder your negotiations?'

'Every man there knows a beautiful woman at his side is an exceptionally useful tool—almost a prerequisite, so to speak.'

The flutter of pleasure that had risen treacherously in her chest sank like a hot air balloon that was out of gas. How stupid of her to think even for a second that perhaps he *wanted* her there. Why did she keep forgetting it?

'I will be back in time to collect you at eight.'

'I have nothing to wear.'

'And didn't I know you'd be only too quick to point that out, *bella*? You will have, I promise. Remember what we learnt last night? You must be patient.'

And with that he rang off.

CHAPTER FIVE

THERE was something different about the room. Faye sensed it the moment she opened the door and slipped off her shoes, grateful for the feel of soft carpet beneath her feet after her second busy day in the Perfezione kitchen. But she was not able put her finger on exactly *what* was different until she entered the bedroom. And then she saw it: a large, cream rectangular box that under normal circumstances would have been completely conspicuous. But what was normal about anything that had happened in the last forty-eight hours? So, Faye thought, the answer to who he expects me to be at the ball tonight lies within that box. She looked around the room, wondering if he had been there. No, she reminded herself. Aside from being away on business, Dante would not concern himself with delivering an outfit for her himself, when she was nothing but a mere *accessory* for the evening.

She remembered his mocking comment about her impatience, and made a point of getting herself a glass of water and tidying a little before allowing the box any of her attention. Whatever was in it wasn't important. He would no doubt have asked whichever stylist was currently at his beck and call to send something over, the way he probably did for any woman he took out, so as to be sure she didn't show him up. He probably wished he had done so the night they had eaten in Perfezione. Perhaps that was the reason why he had had them seated at the most secluded table there was.

Sitting down on the bed, she inspected the box, running her finger across the luxurious embossed surface with a sense of foreboding. Funny how he could even make a gift feel like shackles. But she was unable to quell her curiosity. Removing the lid revealed swathes of soft tissue paper, and slowly, slowly, she peeled the layers back. What she saw underneath made her recoil in horror as the years fell away. Faye jumped up from the bed as if the dark red fabric she had revealed was poisoned. It might as well have been. Her dress. The dress he had bought her that afternoon in Piazza di Spagna—the dress she had been wearing when he had looked at her as if she was the most beautiful woman on earth. The dress she had left behind the day her heart had been torn in two.

The thought of putting it on again made her shudder, and she crossed her arms close to her chest, suddenly cold. So he had kept it. Why? It made no sense. Dante was hardly a man who needed reminding of his conquests with such tokens. And she was sure it was not because he might have qualms about the money he had spent on it. No, it was as if he had kept it knowing that she would return one day, determined to make her wear it as a badge of her depravity. She could not let him see that he had got to her, she thought, as she leaned over the box and tentatively picked up the garment by the shoulders. She held it up and let out a sigh. The galling part of it was that it was still the most beautiful dress she had ever seen. The colour was deep maroon, but not a single shade at any one time; it changed in the light, rich and lucent, like her favourite garnet earrings. She recalled the way it had made her feel when Dante had insisted she try it on; utterly feminine, alive, sexy. As if she was dressing up as someone else, because *she* would never have any occasion to wear it. Until now.

Two hours later, having showered and piled her hair in loose curls upon her head, Faye stood in front of the mirror wearing the gown. She had forgotten how much the shade suited her, having rarely brought herself to wear it since. And if she had worried about not fitting into the same size she had worn at eighteen, she needn't have. The places she had grown shapelier only served to improve her silhouette. The neckline scooped elegantly over her high, full breasts, and the tailored cut enhanced her small neat waist and curved softly over her hips, until it fell in luxurious flutes over her strappy shoes. Despite her initial reservations, she could not help smiling at the result as she put on her favourite earrings and finished applying her mascara. It had been a long time since she had dedicated so much time to her appearance, and she would never normally make herself up so—well, provocatively. But if Dante thought for one second he could unsettle her with this allusion to the past, then she was going to make sure it was he who was going to find himself out of his depth.

'Miss Matteson? Mr Valenti instructed me to inform you that the car is waiting directly outside.'

The man she had come to recognise as the reception manager greeted her as she stepped from the lift and led the way to the door, holding it open for her. She knew it was futile—knew there was no point imagining that this evening was anything other than business—but she could not deny the thrill of anticipation that shot up her spine as the driver held open the door of a long, black car. The sky was a beautiful mix of darkness tinged with apricot and orange hues. It was a balmy evening, and she could smell all the warmth of the September day that hung in the air. The inside of the car, with its black leather interior, was awash with shadows, and as she carefully sat down she did not immediately notice the still, unwavering presence on the other side of the seat until he spoke.

'Have you not got a wrap of some sort?' His question came out of the darkness, his tone accusing.

'I don't believe one was provided. But it is a mild evening, is it not?'

'Yes, it is. In fact I would go so far as to say it is *too* warm in here. But that is not what I meant.'

She saw Dante try to stretch his long legs out in front of him, as if he was uncomfortable. The streetlight was throwing his formidable features into relief, and his eyes were examining her with the intimacy of a touch.

'I had not recalled that dress being so...'

'So what?'

'So revealing.'

Faye could not help breaking into a smile that began at the corner of her mouth and lifted slowly to her eyes. She turned her head to the window as the car drew away.

He was evidently displeased. 'Does something amuse you?'

Faye looked back at him. His mouth was a thin, hard line, his features the picture of disdain. 'Not at all. I was just thinking that if this dress *were* revealing, which is hardly the case, it would provide exactly the distraction that you seem so eager to create.'

Faye thought she heard Dante mutter something in Italian under his breath, but she could not be entirely sure as they

zipped along the main roads to the converted theatre where
the Harvest Ball was held. He did not speak to her for the rest
of the journey; the result was an atmosphere even closer than
the night air. But Faye tried to ignore it as she switched her
attention to the landmarks of the city as they flew past the
window, conjuring up half-forgotten memories.

When they finally reached a standstill outside the impressive stonework building—so impressive that if she had not
been consumed by nerves she would have felt the urge to whip
out a sketchbook—she felt her optimism devoured by apprehension as she caught sight of the huge crowd of the elite.
Could she be any more out of her depth? She was expected
to rub shoulders with people who attended events like this
every night of the week all over the world, when on any other
night of the week she would be one of the dozen waitresses
circling with canapés. But if Dante thought she would stick
out like a sore thumb he didn't show it as he got out of the car
and came to open the door beside her, offering her his hand.
It was idiotic to feel weak at the gesture. His perfect manners
were as inherent within him as his Italian roots. And yet Faye
could not help feeling a surge of pleasure as she placed her
hand in his. He curled his fingers gently and protectively
around her own, and for a small moment the gap between
them, as wide as the Mediterranean, felt a little bit smaller.

Standing beside him, bathed in the orange glow of the
sunset, she felt the full force of Dante in his pristine black
dinner suit and bright white dress shirt hit her. He was magnificent; his broad, hard shoulders and narrow, lean hips had
her lips parting subconsciously, and the expensive fabric of
his trousers with their thin vertical line seemed only to high-
light rather than cover his taut, muscular thighs. He looked

regal, and yet possessed a natural ruggedness that suggested he wouldn't have a second thought about crumpling every inch of his suit given the opportunity.

In the car he had been folded into the seat like a caged panther, unwillingly restrained in the shadows, unused to being out of the driving seat in every sense of the word. Now he stood tall, each one of his six feet five inches exuding a magnetism that had the women in the crowd looking longingly out of the corners of their eyes and the men subconsciously straightening their posture in a worthless attempt to assert themselves beside him. Faye reluctantly remembered how wonderful it had once felt to be by his side because he wanted her there, however temporarily. It had not been the envious glances of other women she had enjoyed that day in Rome. It had been knowing that this man, whom she admired so much, had chosen to spend time with her. She drew in a deep breath; now was not the time to get sentimental.

Dante led her swiftly through the grand doors, the heat of his hand creating havoc on her skin, domineering and yet oddly reassuring as they entered the throng of the party. The ornate walls and ceiling were bedecked in gold, and the heady scent of expensive perfume mingled with the sound of air-kisses set her head spinning. She watched him beside her, the consummate professional, as he weaved through the crowd, making brief and polite greetings, stopping at those people who clearly meant something to Valenti Enterprises in whatever capacity—to make introductions.

And Faye held her own in spite of her nerves, making polite conversation as she sipped the rosé wine he had handed her, grateful to discover that small talk was still small talk, even in the company of some of the world's wealthiest people.

Only Dante didn't seem pleased. Even when she swallowed her natural instinct to stand her ground, and took a step back to allow one woman after another to approach him and whisper something indiscernible in his ear before sashaying away with all the subtlety of a bird of a paradise. But finally she saw the hard lines of his face break into a soft smile as a woman with long, dark hair and a dress of midnight-blue approached them.

'Elena,' he said. 'I am so glad you could make it.' The woman's broad smile mimicked Dante's, her eyes alighting on Faye. Dante turned to her. 'Faye, meet my sister Elena. Elena, this is Faye.'

Elena nodded warmly, as if in recognition. 'A pleasure to meet you Faye,' she said in perfect English, offering her hand.

'Likewise,' Faye replied as she did the same, feeling immediately comfortable with the beautiful Italian woman who had the same sophistication as her brother, but coupled with a homely air that Dante lacked.

'I am not quite sure what possessed Dante to bring you along to an evening of what boils down to overdressed business negotiations, but I am glad to have a comrade.'

Faye laughed. 'Me too,' she admitted.

Dante seemed to spot someone in the distance as the two women exchanged pleasantries. 'Excuse me for just a moment,' he said, nodding towards a large group of black suits on the other side of the room. 'I won't be long.' His hand brushed Faye's arm before he moved off, sending a rush of heat through her body.

'My husband, Luca, is somewhere over there too,' Elena said, looking in the direction Dante was headed, out across the grand room. 'I told him I'd be happy to stay at home and look after Max to save on the babysitter, but he insisted on bringing me along.'

And Faye bet it wasn't because he considered her a useful tool, she thought, observing the look of adoration in Elena's eyes. She was surprised how natural it felt, standing here talking with her as they watched the men, as if she and Dante really were a couple. She felt as if she needed to explain that their situations were far from comparable, but Elena did not give her the chance.

'Dante tells me you're doing some work for him?' she asked with interest. 'I understand marketing is your speciality, so you probably feel much more at ease here than I do.'

Whatever Dante had told his sister about her, it obviously hadn't been strictly accurate. 'I'm just here for a month,' she said, as Elena smiled at her, 'and I'm afraid my marketing experience is on a much smaller scale than this.'

'I'm sure it is still fifty times greater than mine!' Elena laughed. 'I haven't a clue, and to be honest Luca's equally out of his depth, but since we bought the farm in Tuscany he's expected to be here.'

Faye could just imagine Elena in a farmhouse, surrounded by crops and animals and children. She did not know why the image filled her with a dull pang of wistfulness, why the incongruous image of Dante in a similar house seemed to pop into her head.

'Faye?'

She heard her name being called from somewhere on the other side of the room, interrupting her thoughts. The voice was familiar, but it took until she swung round to face him for her to place it.

'Chris!'

Dressed as fashionably as ever, and sporting his trademark Californian tan, Chris leaned back. He looked her up and down, then nodded his head approvingly before kissing her dramatically on both cheeks.

Faye embraced him affectionately before introducing him to Elena, who smiled genuinely, seeming to sense his instant likeability which was as striking as his boyish good looks.

'I thought you were still in the States?' Faye exclaimed, her mind still playing catch-up. The last time she had spoken to Chris had been six months ago, when she had called him about Matteson's. She knew he had no money of his own to invest after blowing his inheritance on his ventures abroad, but his father had been a friend of her parents for generations, and for all his impetuous spending she had always valued his refreshing eccentricity and loyal friendship.

Chris rolled his eyes and let out an enormous sigh. 'No such luck! I spend years researching American cuisine to take it back to the British public and what do I discover? It's conventional old Europe which sells! So here I am—for the next few months, at least—soaking up the restaurant scene in Roma.'

Faye laughed at the way he made it sound as if the results of his research were a surprise, and as if being here was such a chore. He had never looked more at home than amongst the world's fashionistas, and had waxed lyrical about Rome's Harvest Ball being *the* event of the year for as long as she could remember.

'But never mind about me. Tell me what on earth *you* are doing here, and who is responsible for this *fabulous* transformation! You look positively *glowing*.'

Faye stifled a blush, aware of Elena looking on, and ignored Chris's implicit but harmless criticism of her usually subdued wardrobe.

'It's not what you think,' Faye said, shooting him the kind of look only an old friend would understand. 'I'm just here in connection with a possible investment in Matteson's.'

'And who could refuse you in an outfit like that?' He winked.

'Quite.'

Dante's voice sliced through the air behind her. She had no idea how long he had been standing there, but when she spun round his face was as dark as deadly nightshade.

'Dante!' Faye did not know why she should feel as if all the breath had been whipped from her lungs, but she didn't like it. She fought to fix a smile on her face. 'You remember I told you I went travelling to the States?' she said, as casually as her voice would allow. 'This is Chris. He's now doing some research here. Chris, this is Dante. Dante—Chris.'

Faye watched the two men shake hands as the orchestra began to strike up, thinking that the two of them meeting was like a double bass meeting a tambourine and clashing on sight.

But Chris seemed oblivious, looking at Dante in awe, as if he had just announced that Elvis had entered the building. 'Dante *Valenti*? I'm such a fan of your restaurants—*so* inspiring.'

'Even for conventional old Europe?' Dante said sardonically, proving he had probably heard the entirety of their exchange. 'Elena, I believe your husband is looking for you,' he shot out abruptly, before he jerked his head round to face Faye. 'Care to dance?'

His tone left Faye in no doubt that it was an order, not a request. Chris seemed to willingly recognise his cue to leave, and directed a shrewd look at Faye accompanied by a friendly nod which said, 'Don't worry. I understand.' *If only he did understand,* thought Faye, as the haunting melody of a tango began to strike up. *If only I did.*

Dante did not wait for her assent, but led her to the floor. A few other glamorous couples were moving the same way. She did not kid herself that this was anything but an exercise to ensure he was in control of exactly where she was and who she was talking to, but nevertheless to think of Dante dancing for any purpose seemed at odds with everything she knew of him. It seemed too expressive, too meditative, to be something he would find time for in his fast-paced, work-obsessed life.

'Do you always dance at these occasions?' she asked as he snaked one hand around her waist and placed her own hand upon his shoulder. Awareness shot through her the minute his body came into contact with her own.

'Never,' he drawled, his mouth disturbingly close to her ear as he took the lead, making her feel so light it was if he had changed the force of gravity.

She had danced with men before, of course, at university. So why did it suddenly feel as if she was experiencing the pleasure for the first time? As if all of a sudden she understood why people described it as sensuous, erotic? Because you're dancing with *him*, a voice said in the back of her mind. Because this isn't a minute of ungainly swaying with some guy who seems to hear *yes, please* instead of *no, thanks*. This is dancing with Dante Valenti, who is as proficient at this as at everything else he touches. Like Midas, she thought as they moved in time to the sultry rhythm, feeling as if she was turning to molten gold beneath his fingers.

'You *never* dance at these occasions?' she whispered breathlessly. 'Then how did you get so good?'

She felt him tense slightly. 'Some things come to us instinctively, wouldn't you say?'

So he was reluctant even to discuss something as innocuous as where he had learned. Because small talk with *him* wasn't part of this deal?

'You are talking about sex, I suppose?' Faye shot out, fired by a need to bring down the barrier he had put up in front of his emotions, and only realising once the words were out of her mouth just how risky it was to articulate the image she didn't seem to be able to budge from her mind.

'Ahh, Faye, you speak of it so matter-of-factly for a woman.'

'For a woman?' she asked incredulously. 'Is it not a fact of life when two people want one another?' She was all too aware that she had steered the topic of conversation into dangerous territory, and that she was speaking on a subject upon which she could hardly be any less of an authority, but his misogynistic comment irked her.

'And you have always been so clear about your wants, *bella*.' His voice was loaded with suggestion, his thumb moving provocatively in small circles on her back as he moved them deftly around the floor. So he still thought every woman who wasn't a nun was as good as a harlot, she thought, cursing him.

'And what of *your* wants, Dante? Oh, but of course—you are a man. So you are not only permitted to have such indiscretions, you celebrate them. Heaven forbid a woman should do the same!' Faye did not know quite whose corner she was arguing, but his double standards made her blood boil.

'So you wish to celebrate your sexual triumphs, do you, Faye?'

Why had he supposed that bringing her here would be any

different from when he had let her loose in his kitchen? He thought. To her this was just a bigger playground!

His voice was acidic as he continued to manoeuvre her across the floor, his languid movements replaced with a precision and sharpness that suddenly made her aware of her own inadequacy.

'Does it thrill you to think there are two men in this room tonight you have given yourself to? Or perhaps there are more?'

His arms opened in disgust as he spoke the words, releasing her from his punishing embrace, and although he moved towards her once again she took a step backwards, too insulted to continue.

'Perhaps there are, Dante. Who knows?'

And with that Faye turned on her heel, losing herself in the crowd as the orchestra beat out the song's climactic ending.

'I apologise for my brother.'

Elena found Faye queuing at the bar—for the want of something to do to prevent herself from looking round to see where Dante had gone as much as for needing refreshment after the heady experience of that dance.

'Sorry?' Faye said, suddenly terrified that even half of what they had been discussing had somehow carried across the dance floor.

'The way he felt the need to "rescue" you from your friend. Dante is a very possessive man where the women he cares for are concerned.'

Faye nodded, thinking that it didn't matter whether he *cared* or not. Possessiveness seemed the order of the day.

'You can imagine what he was like when I had my first boyfriend.' Elena laughed. 'Luca was the only one he deemed even remotely suitable after months of scrutiny. Which was convenient since I'd already agreed to marry him long before I told Dante.'

They had just made it to the front of the queue when Luca found them both, and Elena made the necessary introductions.

'It's a pleasure to meet you, Faye. Any woman who can get Dante on the dance floor has clearly made an impression on him.'

Faye was not surprised to find that Luca shared the same look of adoration for his wife as she did for him. But when Luca curved his arm protectively around Elena, Faye was unprepared for the pang of jealousy which hit her. Funny how no matter how used she got to being alone something so small had the power to remind her of what she didn't have.

It soon transpired that Luca had finished the networking he admitted was a necessity of the evening and had come over in the hope that Elena was ready to go home. Elena protested that they could not leave Faye alone, or go without finding Dante, but Faye convinced them that he had no doubt just stepped outside, and that she would find him immediately and pass on their farewells rather than them having to negotiate the now-busy dance floor to reach the French doors which led out onto the terrace. Reluctantly they agreed.

In truth Faye had no such intention; she had told herself she would find Chris, catch up on old times and leave Dante to his own black mood. But as she stood alone, watching the couples twirl hypnotically across the floor, something more powerful determined her path.

The back of the theatre was surrounded by a large oval veranda with wrought-iron railings that reminded her a little of the foyer at Il Maia, and somehow she knew immediately that her instincts about where he had gone were right. As she stepped out of the enormous doors she felt surprised there were not more people taking a break from the evening's festivities, but as she moved farther away from the warmth of the party cool night air nipped at her skin.

He must have heard her footsteps approaching, but he did not turn around. She could see from his pose that he did not want company, and felt instinctively that to go to him now would be to dice with danger. Yet as he stood there, like some devastating gothic hero, a picture of strength and solitude in the dark shadow of the evening, she was drawn to him. Slowly she walked towards him, the cool wind playing with the honey coloured tendrils of her hair that had worked their way loose.

'Go back inside. You'll catch a chill.'

'The change of scene is refreshing.'

'And yet you seemed to be in your element.' He remained focussed on the dark hills in the distance.

Her eyes flicked over the profile of his face, the high bridge of his nose, the hard jut of his jaw, fortified with a tension that refused to dissipate. She realised she had never seen him look *so* Italian.

Faye did not answer him. She had done exactly what had been asked of her—mingled with his associates, his sister and brother-in-law—yet somehow she had still ended up riling him.

'Elena and Luca asked me to pass on their goodbyes.'

He nodded, as if it went without saying.

'I liked them very much.'

The comment seemed to surprise him, and he snapped out of his dazed look, as if the idea of her having any affable feeling was impossible. How little they really knew of each other, she thought, a shiver rushing over her.

In an instant his jacket was off and he was behind her, draping the heavy fabric around her shoulders. His heady, musky scent surrounded her. It felt so intimate, and yet everything tonight seemed just the opposite. Faye tried to ignore the distracting sensation of having him behind her, turning her eyes back towards the people indoors.

'You never told me where you learned to dance like that, Dante.'

There was silence for a moment, and then he said, 'My mother.' His tone was curt, and he turned back to face the darkness of the night sky.

Faye immediately sensed that it had not been a pleasurable experience and did not push him. But slowly he continued.

'Let's just say she was something of an expert on the *advantages* of frequenting every ball in every hotel in Europe. She made me practise with her.'

Faye knew little of Dante's childhood, and what she did know was only from what the papers said about this self-made billionaire. According to them, his mother had died before he was in his teens, and he never spoke of his father. After her own secure and loving childhood, she could only imagine the horrors of the experience his brief but telling words hinted at. What would that do to a young man? Faye wondered. No wonder he had been so protective of his sister.

'I'm sorry,' she whispered.

'Sorry for me, or for my mother?' he asked, turning on her.

Faye frowned softly. The revelation which seemed to have dulled her own anger had plainly had the opposite effect on him. 'For you, Dante.'

'Why? When tonight you have proved just what an expert you are in exactly the same field? How does it feel, Faye, to pout your lips and know every man is wanting you? To walk across the floor ticking off each conquest in your mind, planning the next?'

She almost wanted to laugh at just how wrong he was, how unfounded was his sexual jealousy. Yet the realisation that *that* was what all this was about made her anger return. *He* didn't want her, but still he was so chauvinistic that he didn't want anyone else to have her either. It cut her to the quick.

'You think working with men is synonymous with sleeping with them?'

His face was the picture of distaste. 'No, *bella*. I *know* it is where you're concerned. How else do you explain why you begged me to make love to you and only a fortnight later you were *working* halfway around the world with a man who still can't keep his eyes off you?'

Faye stared at him, knowing she should retaliate but too dumbstruck by the fact that he was saying things he couldn't possibly know.

'How did you know that?' Her voice was low, urgent. 'I never told you when I went travelling.'

There was silence for a moment.

'Let's just say I made a call to be sure I was right about you. One of your colleagues kindly informed me exactly where you were. Did he offer a higher price for sharing his bed, Faye?'

She shook her head in disbelief, her eyes focussed on the hard stone beneath her feet. The furious shade of molten gold that burned in his eyes was too dangerous for her to look at. He had called and she had never known. The revelation was like an ice-cold shower down her spine. And yet did it really make any difference? He had made up his mind about her long before that. What good would it do to tell him now that she had gone to escape her feelings for him? What good, when the only way to escape the pain was to keep those exact feelings locked away?

'A shake of that pretty little head of yours means nothing, princess. But let me guess. You can't look me in the eye? Now, why might that be? Because you're a damned liar, perhaps?'

'Why can't I look into your eyes?' she questioned desperately, her voice racked with emotion, her breathing rapid. 'You want to know why?'

She lifted her head to meet his gaze and her body began to tremble.

'Because I'm afraid that if I start I won't be able to stop.'

CHAPTER SIX

SHE was right. As her wide, fearful eyes met the onyx-dark depths of his Faye was lost. But if she had thought that he would accept her words as proof of her innocence, the unforgiving set of his features told her that he did not. He might be the expert on change, but he was no more capable of opening his mind to the truth than she was capable of looking away. It struck her that if anyone had come out onto the terrace they would have thought the two of them were lovers, locked in an embrace of requited love and contentment, and she wasn't sure whether that made her want to laugh or cry.

There was no question of what was coming. No wondering if he would or he wouldn't. But it would hold not one inch of affection. The suggestion of tenderness—his jacket around her shoulders, the soft curve of his lower lip, the languorous spreading of heat throughout her limbs—were all part of fate's joke at her expense. Yet she could not deny that she longed for it to come, as if it was the air she needed to breathe to stop herself from fading away.

She did not know how long they stood there, with the cool breeze of the evening beginning to whip around them, each defying the other, unmoving. But the moment their defences shattered was sudden and mutual. Hungry and reckless, his lips crashed down upon her own and she pressed her body wantonly against him: the culmination of anger and of hurt. Was it possible all those years ago he had regretted his words? Had tried to reach her and found her gone? No—and even pondering that question would be a terrible mistake. Worse even than entwining her tongue with his now, as it slipped in and out of her mouth, promising intimacies of a much deeper kind.

His kiss was condemning and furious, as if it sought to erase everything but the wanting between them. Until suddenly he dragged his mouth away. For one hideous moment she feared he was going to take his revenge by rejecting her again. But if that had been his intention his self-control had failed.

'Home. Now,' he bit out, his voice throaty, his need obvious.

He did not wait for her agreement; he read it on her face. Words were unnecessary as he led her artfully to the front of the building, via a side passage that avoided the crowded dance floor, and took them straight to a waiting taxi as if he had willed it into existence.

They sat deliberately on opposite sides of the back seat, both knowing they didn't dare go near each other—yet. *Not long now*, his eyes seemed to say to her, looking, if it was possible, even more predatory than they had when he had arrived. She ought not to continue to feel like some startled gazelle, yet somehow she felt even more apprehensive than she had at eighteen, when she'd had all the daring of youth and been blissfully unaware of the fallout that would follow. Ever since desire and recklessness had been words that had virtually slipped out of her vocabulary. Until now. Now they were written in bright red ink across her mind, obliterating the fears scribbled beneath. And never had she so longed to give in to those words as she eyed him hungrily, imagining his tanned hands against her pale skin, on her breasts, *lower*.

Home indeed, she thought, with desire unfurling deep within her. But as she turned to look at the moon, low in the sky, she realised that they were not headed in the direction of Il Maia, and that there was only one other home he could have meant. *His* home.

Her heart thrilled at the thought of the intimacy of arriving at his domain, though she knew really that he was simply bringing her there because it was the most discreet and sensible option. Yet she was not sure sensible applied in any way to her state of mind as he paid the taxi driver and whisked her up the steps to the luxurious apartment block that was tucked away in a quiet and exclusive street just outside the city centre. His was the top two floors, naturally, but the detail of the layout eluded her as he led her through the expansive rooms, his hand upon the base of her spine playing havoc with her grasp on anything except the feel of his body in contact with her own.

He did not turn on the lights, and Faye felt the butterflies in the pit of her stomach multiply. Moonlight was streaming through the enormous glass windows, projecting the shadows of their bodies onto the wall. How many women had he brought here? And how much more skilled in giving him pleasure must they have been than her? Was it even possible that he wanted her—she who had displeased him so much before? For nothing had really changed. Because, whatever he presumed, after her moment of naive boldness had proved to be such as disaster, sexually she had retreated back into her shell. A shell that no one had been able to prise open since. So why did it seem to *fall* open for him?

'You hesitate, Miss Matteson?' His eyebrows were raised in mock rebuke as she wavered at the foot of the stairs, running the tip of her tongue over her lower lip nervously in a movement that drew his black gaze. 'Surely not?'

It was the moment to stop—the moment to walk away and end this ridiculous charade right now. But she couldn't have even if she had wanted to. As she stood in the dress he had bought her, the jacket he had cocooned around her, with the delicious taste of him on her swollen lips, she did not even feel the decision was her own. It was as if her fate, however cruel, had been decided long ago.

She shook her head.

'Then touch me,' he commanded.

And she understood what he asked—knew that this was about *him* possessing *her*, on his terms. But for once in her life she didn't give a damn about whether that was right or wrong. Because she could ponder that as long as she lived, but not acting now would be to deny herself the only thing that made her feel truly alive.

She reached up her arms in willing surrender, entwining them around his neck, running her fingers greedily through his thick dark hair, glorying in the feel of it as she pulled his head down for a long and lingering kiss that was hot and wet. His lips found her neck, below her ear, and his warm breath sent her senses haywire as he trailed feather-light kisses lower. Emotions rushed over her like a wave; she was unprepared for such tenderness amidst their mutual urgency. Deftly, he threw his jacket from her shoulders and ran his hands over her as they sank down together on the stairs. Slowly, he discarded one flimsy strap of her dress, peeling back the dark red fabric from her naked flesh to reveal a thrusting nipple which peaked expectantly under his gaze. Faye let out a sigh of need that was matched by his exhalation of breath as he took it in his mouth and ran his tongue slickly over it, causing her to grip on to the stairs for dear life.

'Not fair,' she cried out breathlessly, her hands tugging at his tie, which she removed with ease, pulling it impatiently from under his collar and letting it fall to the floor. She relished the feel of unbuttoning his shirt. But before she could finish he caught her hands in his own and held them behind her head. A bubble of excitement broke from her throat.

'Not fair?' he questioned silkily, raising his eyebrow in challenge. 'I completely agree.'

Faye expected him to remove his shirt for her, but he did nothing so self-centred. He revealed her other breast in lightning-quick time and treated it to the same sensual exploration, his left hand stroking the other. She had never been so turned on in her entire life as she lay there, her evening dress exposing her to the waist, her body crying out for more and more of the man who held her captive with the sheer force of the yearning he stirred within her. But more than that, it felt as if dreams she had never believed herself capable of dreaming again were being handed back to her, piece by piece. Delighting in the realisation, she arched her back to allow him to take more of her soft peak into his mouth, one of her hands still tangled in his hair, encouraging him.

'Dante!' She guided one of his hands lower down her body.

'Patience, Miss Matteson,' he said, lifting his head, a mischievous glint in his eye as he replaced his hand on her shoulder.

The allusion to exactly why she was there and at his bidding ought to have set an alarm bell ringing through her, but the idea of him bestowing more pleasure upon her silenced it before it even rang.

'Stand for me,' he ordered, allowing her the space to do as he requested, lying back on the stairs lazily to watch her, propping himself up on his elbow.

She did exactly as he asked, only realising as she did so the consequences of her actions. The dress that had gathered at her waist slipped effortlessly to the floor, leaving her standing there in nothing but her flimsy lace panties and her despicably high-heeled shoes.

Dante muttered something indiscernible in Italian and was at her side in a flash, sweeping his warm hands under her bottom and lifting her up into his arms.

'If I don't get you to the bedroom right now,' he ground out, 'you are going to have some nasty carpet burns on this delectable body of yours.'

In no time at all they had reached the top of the stairs, and he carried her towards the master bedroom, where an enormous bed made up with pure white cotton sheets was just visible through the darkness. He laid her down with the utmost care, his gaze lingering upon her body. She liked the way he looked at her, as if he almost—no, as if his need for her was the one thing he couldn't control. It might not be the way a man gazed at the woman he loved, the way she gazed back at him, but she knew that at this moment he wanted her, and it was enough. Because he was Dante, whose hard, rugged body had filled her dreams for so long. She kneeled up on the bed provocatively.

'Now, let me finish what I started, Mr Valenti.' She cocked her head as he stood looking down at her, and moved to unbutton the rest of his shirt.

'My thoughts exactly, *bella.*' Though her hands stalled for a moment, as she realised she had insinuated more than she had meant to, she had no intention of stopping to reflect. She stripped his chest bare and sat back on her knees, looking him up and down with sultry eyes.

'You have no idea how much it turns me on when you look at me that way,' he murmured as her tongue subconsciously went to the roof of her mouth.

Her lips parted as she eyed every inch of bronzed flesh and rigid muscle, sprinkled with whorls of dark hair. She moved towards the edge of the bed as he lay down beside her, the throbbing heat of his desire pressing against her stomach through his dark trousers.

'Please,' she cried raggedly, pressing herself into him so her nipples grazed his chest as she moved her hands clumsily to discard the remainder of his clothes. He took over the task for her, deftly removing both his trousers and his shorts, his proud, hard length springing free. Her breath caught in her throat at the sight. She was sure she was not supposed to find it so beautiful, but the undeniable evidence of his masculinity, so smooth and hard, did things to her insides. More things than she dared admit even to herself. She reached out to touch it, but he moved away.

'Ladies first.' He smiled wickedly, the moonlight throwing his striking face into relief.

Ever the gentleman, she thought, as his finger trailed over her flat stomach and hesitated for a moment on her inner thigh before casting aside the small scrap of lace. She let out a small cry as he dipped one finger inside her and then began to circle rhythmically, sending tremors through her body that slowly sent her higher and higher. She saw the satisfaction in his eyes as he watched her clasping herself to him, but she wanted him to share the pleasure—to feel as helplessly bound to her as she felt to him. She reached out, wrapping her hand around his hard shaft, and heard him groan.

'Do you have any idea what you do to me, *cara*?' His accent was stronger than ever as she stroked his length, matching the rhythm of his hand at her feminine core. And though his tone held a note of all too familiar condemnation, it made her realise that for all his demands she held the ace. He wanted her, whether he wanted to or not.

'I have an idea what I am *going* to do to you,' she said seductively, placing one leg on either side of his taut body, her boldness returning as if it couldn't help itself when faced with *him*.

His eyes suddenly shot open as he realised what she was about to do, and for one terrible moment she thought he was going to stop. 'Wait,' he said, one arm reaching across to the bedside table, and in one swift movement he protected himself.

Ever the professional, she thought. But then all thought was swept away as he ran his hands over her hips and encouraged her downwards, entering her in one hard thrust. Faye's body opened for him invitingly, welcoming him home as if created for him alone, and she wondered deliriously at how, despite her being on top of him, he had still managed to take control.

Determined to regain some power, she moved above him, slowly dipping up and down on his length, and the pleasure in his eyes was palpable as she built a slow and steady rhythm that he matched with his own hips. Gradually she picked up the pace, sending them both to a place without language, with only feeling and sensation. The realisation that she was making love to Dante all over again, was connected to him in the most inseparable way there was, filled her with as much heat as the physical pleasure of having him inside her. She did not know how she held off her climax as the intensity grew stronger and stronger, but as she watched his face, knotted with passion, she was determined to make him lose his grip on reality first. As she heard a low groan beginning to break forth in his throat, and felt his movements reach even deeper, rubbing against the sensitive folds of the innermost part of her, she could not hold on any longer. Her own cry of ecstasy was matched by his as he made his release, sending them both over the edge, shattering into a thousand pieces like a firework lighting up the night sky.

And for the most perfect moment he held her there, in a gesture which seemed the most tender she had ever known, his arms wrapped around her as their breathing slowly grew more steady, like two people attached to parachutes who were floating back to earth. Flooded with so much emotion, Faye felt inexplicable tears prick at her eyes—the spontaneous kind that no one ever warned you to expect.

But with her eyes still closed she realised that for the second time in her life she had landed in the all too familiar territory of limbo-land, where she didn't know what she was supposed to do or say *afterwards*. Only this time there was no future to misconstrue. For though *she* felt as if she couldn't have acted any more impulsively, she realised with a jolt that all she had really done was live up to everything he had expected of her from the minute she had walked into his office three days ago. The realisation made her open her eyes suddenly, and the tangle of their bodies, with her limbs on top, only served to remind her exactly how *thoroughly* she had proved him right.

'There is no need to feign surprise on my account,' he murmured, his eyes barely open. 'We both knew it was on the menu.'

Faye didn't answer, but freed herself from his embrace. Once he had made her feel embarrassingly brazen. Now she just felt embarrassingly predictable. *But alive*, a voice inside her head whispered in her defence; *you made your bed, now lie in it*. So she did, perfectly still; not a single part of her touching a single part of him. And as he made his way to the bathroom she realised that remaining detached was the only possible hope she had of seeing this contract through.

Dante was not gone for long, but when he returned she was dead to the world. The role reversal made him uneasy. Most women usually swanned off to the bathroom to reapply their make-up afterwards, leaving *him* to fall asleep. Not Faye Matteson.

But then she was all about contradiction, wasn't she? He stood a metre or so away from her. Her sweet fresh scent was like an aphrodisiac lingering upon his skin, and one honey-coloured strand of hair stroked her cheek lightly as she breathed slowly in and out. She looked almost *vulnerable*. And knowing what a lie that was didn't banish the unfathomable discord in his chest.

It was not disappointment. Heavens, no—that had to be some of the best sex he had ever had: the responsiveness of her hungry lips upon his own, the way she had whispered his name like a siren song and wrapped those extraordinary legs around him. This was what he had planned, after all.

Yet it hadn't happened *how* he had planned. Yes, that was why it hadn't put an end to that old feeling he couldn't put his finger on in the way he had expected it to. For he hadn't counted on dredging up his past. Nor had he expected her to frustrate him to such a degree that he had been almost unable to prevent himself taking her there and then, at the most sophisticated ball in Rome. How many men had she ensnared with that enticing body of hers? he wondered. Using that facade of virtue to ensnare her victims like a spider weaving a web of deceit. Why had she even bothered to argue against what he knew to be true? And *why* had he felt that wretched swelling of guilt all over again when she had shaken that angelic little head of hers? *Dio!* He knew it was all an act to turn him on, and she had damn well succeeded!

He drank in one last look at her before turning back to the door, furious that his moment of pleasure was tinged with such frustration, furious that what he wanted most was to rouse her from her sleep and take her again and again. But that would mean relinquishing control, and Dante never relinquished control to anyone or anything. Least of all to a woman who was only after his money and had just slept with him to get it.

Sweet autumn sunshine poured through the wide glass windows, gently rousing Faye from her languid slumber. She stretched out her arms as wide as they would go, as if she was some synchronised swimmer, keeping her eyes closed. She froze as she reached the pinnacle of her tautness, realising just how far her limbs had stretched without meeting the edge of the bed. This was not *her* bed. Which meant only one thing. She kept her eyes shut, willing either the faint tenderness between her thighs to dissipate, or the hand that was frantically searching the empty space next to her to rest on him. But neither. She opened her eyes to find herself alone, and realised that she had no way of knowing whether Dante had even come back to bed last night at all. She had fallen straight to sleep as he had headed for the bathroom, and she hadn't stirred until now. For all she knew he could have retired to one of the other bedrooms.

She stared at the empty space beside her, trying to discern whether it was body-shaped. Could this whole scene be any more clichéd? she thought. The room spelled bachelor pad. The whitewashed walls, the dark angular furniture, not a family photo in sight. What had made her think for one moment that waking up next to the enigmatic Dante Valenti was any more likely now than it had been six years ago? She closed her eyes again and drew in a deep breath, sitting up and leaning back on the obscenely comfortable pillow. Yes, this was all too familiar—and there was no way she was going to stick around and endure a conversation like *that* one again.

But just as she was about to alight upon a plan for slipping away from him unnoticed, the bedroom door slowly opened. As she scrambled for the duvet to avoid exposing herself, she wanted to yell that he should have knocked—until she remembered that was this was his apartment, and had he not snuck away he would be lying there naked with her.

But he wasn't; he was already dressed for work, looking despicably handsome in a pale grey suit and a white shirt with dark pinstripes. He was missing only his tie, and even the slight shadow at his jaw that she had felt against her skin last night was shaved cleanly away. The only anomaly was the steaming mug of freshly ground coffee he carried in one hand.

'Thank you,' she said tentatively, accepting it from him.

'There are fresh croissants downstairs.' The timbre of his voice was as unfathomable as the look on his face.

Was this one of the perks of a one-night stand with Dante Valenti, then? Mind-blowing sex with an emotion-free continental breakfast included?

She composed herself. 'I can be ready for work in half an hour.'

'You surprise me.' He cocked his eyebrow sardonically.

'Like you said, *that* isn't going to get me my money any quicker.' She gave a brittle laugh. At least the cutting remarks were something she was accustomed to dealing with.

His face turned to thunder as he paced over to the window. So he was furious even though she had acknowledged that last night didn't change their deal? There was no pleasing the man.

'Then you should be able to catch the eleven forty-five flight to Tuscany,' he said, still focussed on the city view.

'Tuscany?' Faye could not hide the surprise in her voice.

'I have arranged for you to meet some of my suppliers there. I had planned for you to go next week, but I see now that today is just as convenient. It is a unique opportunity.'

'You are going there on business?'

'No.' The sunlight seemed to have faded, the room no longer so warm. 'I have meetings here.'

He would be here. She would be gone. Suddenly breakfast felt like the booby prize.

'They speak English?' Faye questioned, wondering if the practicalities had eluded him in his sudden desire to banish her from his sight, and determined to alight upon some get-out clause.

'Some. But my sister will accompany you anyway.'

'Elena?'

'Yes. She lives near to my villa. You may use the facilities whilst you are there.'

He made it sound as if the concession could not be more repellent to him. She supposed now he had taken what he wanted he had no other way of disposing of her between now and the end of their contract. Faye stared at him, not sure why she wanted to ask him how long it would be before she saw him again, and cursing her treacherous heart for feeling only that she would miss him, rather than hating him for toying with her all over again.

'Elena will meet you at the airport and take over things from there.' He tossed her some keys. 'I will leave the flight details on the table downstairs. Lock the door as you leave.'

And would you like me to carve an extra notch on your bedpost for you? she wanted to fire back at him, but he was already out of the door.

CHAPTER SEVEN

IT WAS her second day here in Tuscany, yet Faye could still scarcely believe that the man who owned the stark, clinical apartment she had been left to dispatch herself from just thirty-six hours before also owned *this* room. She adored it all: the warm cream walls, the natural fabric of the terracotta suite, the understated olivewood furniture. It was spacious, of course, but not excessively so. In fact the one word she would use to describe the place was homely. And as she looked out at the groves of citrus fruits and cypress trees visible from the wide living-room window, the image of Dante at a family home in the country that had popped into her head at the Harvest Ball no longer seemed so illogical. But it was delusional, she reminded herself, because he'd made it perfectly clear that, regardless of how he kept his house, he ran his life like a business: supply and demand. And the minute she had willingly given in to his demand and supplied him with her body he had made it plain she was surplus to requirements.

Thankfully this was the first opportunity she had really had to dwell on that since she had arrived. When she had got here, late yesterday afternoon, Elena had collected her from the airport, bursting with enthusiasm to show her the countryside, and their scenic journey back to the village where Dante's villa was located had lasted until it grew dark. Beset with the sheer exhaustion of travel and the events of the night before, Faye had fallen into a deep sleep until Elena had called early this morning for her to begin their tour of the producers. From that moment on her day had been too full of this bittersweet utopia for her to completely succumb to the visions of Dante still dancing through her mind.

But whilst the part of her that faced the world felt truly in awe of the things she had seen—ripe figs being plucked from the trees, fresh cheeses being pressed—underneath she had never felt so utterly raw. And now she was alone she was forced to confront the rejection that she had once promised herself she would protect her heart from feeling ever again. Yet even though she reminded herself that she had gone into this knowing what the outcome would be, no amount of reasoning made it any easier. Nor did being apart from him, though on the plane journey here she had told herself it would be preferable to staying in Rome. Quite why, she wasn't sure, when even going to America before hadn't made a blind bit of difference. But she hadn't expected to find it *harder*—to feel his presence everywhere.

Elena spoke to Faye as if she was practically Dante's wife-to-be, rather than some redundant mistress. And each place they went it took only one mention of his name and the same look of reverent adoration crossed people's faces, as if he was not just part of the community, but some kind of local deity. The very notion was completely alien to Faye. This was the man who was as changeable as the wind, who got through women like cups of coffee, but the connections he had here were plainly loyal and longstanding. Perhaps he paid these people extortionate prices for their goods? But that still did not explain their steadfast pride when talking of their involvement with Signor Valenti.

'It must be a great contrast for Dante when he comes here from the city,' Faye had suggested to Elena casually, desperate to grill her on the two personas her brother seemed to have without seeming discourteous. But Elena had only shrugged, nodding as if it was no big deal.

This evening Elena was otherwise engaged, and Faye had been looking forward to having some time to herself, to explore the villa and its grounds. The darkness when she had first arrived, along with her early start this morning, had offered her little opportunity. Only now was she beginning to wish that she didn't have such a long night ahead of her to sit and think, surrounded by evidence which suggested that somewhere in that hard but delectable chest of his he had a heart. How much easier it would be to sit in his dispassionate apartment in Rome, believing the space beyond his ribcage was empty.

She twisted in the armchair, thinking how little compassion he had shown *her*. Or had he? He had made it clear from the moment he had taken her to dinner that he fully intended to have her and then let her go. Inwardly, she castigated herself. She had stupidly believed that their conversation at the ball had changed things, that just for a second he had let her in. But here she was, banished from his sight all over again. She drew in a deep breath. How long did he intend to leave her out here? The entire month? Was it devised to be the ultimate torture—being left to imagine what it would have been like to be one of the women he usually accompanied here, forced instead into exile with only her memories for company? She cast her mind over the events of the last few days, trying to convince herself that all was not lost, that this was actually what she had wished for: to sit out the month quietly, until she could get the money Matteson's so desperately needed. But as she touched her fingers to her lips she could only think of needing him, of the taste of perspiration on his skin, of how it would feel to take him in her mouth...

Good God, what had he done to her? She who prided herself on qualities like restraint and self-control. Qualities? Or were they barriers to hide behind? she wondered ruefully. All the time too scared of getting her fingers burned? But if they were the only scars that being around Dante Valenti left her with then she could cope. The trouble was he set her whole damn body aflame, and she needed to cool off.

Faye had spotted the inviting waters of the Olympic-sized pool from her bedroom that morning. Yes, she thought, convincing herself that aside from needing to douse urges she had never known she possessed, it would be a practical way to fill her time, release some of the tensions of the past week and to be sure she was physically tired enough to be guaranteed the release of sleep. She was thankful now that she had had the foresight to buy that bikini, however guilty he had made her feel about it at the time.

It was 5:00 p.m. and the air was beginning to cool as Faye made her way out onto the terrace and tentatively approached the edge of the water, testing it with her toes. To her delight the temperature was glorious, the heat of the sun having warmed it perfectly during the day. She plunged in gracefully, entering the water like some sleek mermaid, barely causing a splash.

The silence was utterly calming and tranquil as she began to swim from end to end, losing herself in the rhythm of the strokes. There was none of the crowds or noisy echoes she was used to contending with at her local pool, only herself, the water, and the beautiful backdrop of acres of green. She swam as she had done as a child, without inhibition, as if only the motion of her body mattered, not caring how many lengths she pounded out, knowing only that she would stop when she was ready and it wouldn't be any time soon.

That was until she felt the air change halfway through one length in the direction of the villa. Though she told herself there could be no distraction, she felt compelled to open her eyes.

'Making the most of the facilities, I see.'

The deep, sardonic voice broke across the water at the exact moment Faye laid her eyes upon the imposing masculine body at the edge of the opposite end of the pool, shocking her out of her meditative state with a start. The previously still water flew in all directions as she struggled to regain her composure and began treading water. Though droplets laced her eyes she did not for a second need to speculate as to who it was. Apparently her body didn't either. Her stomach felt as if she had just taken her first mouthful of food after days without eating. She hadn't realised until now just *how* hungry for the sight of him she had been.

'What are you doing here?' The words broke from her huskily.

'I live here, or had you forgotten?'

Forgotten? She thought. *I can barely think about anything else.*

'I thought you had business in Rome.'

'It's the weekend. Surely that hadn't escaped your notice?'

'I was working today,' she answered automatically, as if he wouldn't have known.

'I am well aware of that. For you it is essential. I, on the other hand, am not the one who needs to learn.'

Maybe you need to learn *you* can't treat people like this, she wanted to retort, as she clasped her hands around her body, suddenly aware of just how intently he was looking at her. It was just beginning to grow dark, and the faint lights around the pool gave the air a smoky quality. It drew her attention to the irresistible tanned skin of his muscular arms beneath his black T-shirt, and highlighted the taut contours of his patrician face. She noticed his hand move as she pushed her mane of water-logged hair from her face and wiped her eyes. Hell, he was taking the T-shirt *off.*

'What are you doing?'

'What does it look like? I'm joining you for a swim.'

A million thoughts flashed through Faye's mind—*He knew I was here. Maybe once was no more enough for him than it was for me? But this is his home, and me being here is inconsequential, isn't it? What good would more than once do anyway? It would only make things harder.* But her reasoning came to a standstill as she watched him fling the T-shirt to one side. Harder indeed.

Faye wanted to escape, and swim closer to him all at the same time. As she dragged her gaze over his magnificent chest and down to his lean hips she longed to run her hand over his taut stomach, to feel her body pressed close to his all over again. He removed his dark jeans in one swift movement and she felt something she erroneously branded as relief when she saw he was wearing swimming shorts, however brief, beneath them.

He dived proficiently into the pool, and Faye's senses were heightened as the ripples reached her. Her body thrilled just at the knowledge that he had entered the same expanse of water. She felt her nipples harden involuntarily beneath the surface, despite the warm temperature. His head came up a few metres away from her.

'When I heard you splashing about in here I thought perhaps I might have caught you skinny-dipping,' he said, his voice low, his face close to the water. 'But it seems that sadly I was right about your shopping extravaganza in Rome.'

'And what makes you think I didn't bring a swimsuit with me?' She angled her head defiantly whilst avoiding his gaze.

'Because I know you, Faye,' he said, sending a chill through her with a look that seeped deep into her soul. 'And, much as I like the idea, I don't think stripping down to your bikini in my office was plan B in getting me to show an interest in your offer.'

'High praise indeed. I thought that was precisely what you thought of me.' Was he actually beginning to believe otherwise? She felt herself weaken.

'Well, if you care to prove me wrong,' he whispered, moving slowly towards her, 'please feel free.'

'I wouldn't dream of it,' Faye answered, mock demurely. 'Even when I thought I was completely alone I was being a good girl, doing lengths in my perfectly modest two-piece.'

'Is that what you call it?' he asked, raising his eyebrows skeptically. His face was now so close to hers that she could see the rivulets from his damp hair running slowly over his broad shoulders, as if wavering in order to allow her lips the chance to kiss them away.

'Precisely,' she said standing up so her bikini-clad breasts met the water level. 'And since I was unprepared for an intrusion, I think perhaps I will retire to my room.' She began to move towards the steps.

'I don't think so.'

He offered her no chance to escape, stretching out a single arm and encircling her waist, holding her fast. She gasped, the sudden close contact startling. As he twisted her round to face him one of the triangles of her bikini top slipped sideways. It was only when Dante's gaze dropped to her exposed breast that she noticed, flailing her arms to re-cover her proud, exposed nipple.

'And this is what you call modest, is it?' His voice was grim, and Faye flushed as she straightened the offending fabric—though she could not help noticing the way his tongue met his bottom lip unconsciously as she did so.

'I cannot be responsible for its effectiveness when I am being manhandled, but as a piece of swimwear I consider it is perfectly reserved.'

'I'd sign Il Maia over to you this instant if you could find me one man on this earth who would agree with you on that. But then you do have the ability to make a sheet look like lingerie. No reason why a bikini should be any different.'

Dante's arm still held her, and as he spoke her eyes fell to his mouth. There was no denying the hunger she read there, and no denying to herself how much she wanted him—in every way it was possible for a woman to want a man. His hands toyed deftly with the strings that held the offending clothing in place, and she arched her back as the top fell readily into the water, freeing her to the cool night air. Even the moment it took for his warm hands to come forth and cup her eager breasts seemed too long, but as his thumbs began to circle the tender buds in the water she knew she would wait for ever if he asked her.

'Dante,' she whispered. The hypnotic motion coupled with the lapping water was sending shock waves to her inner core, willing greater intimacy. She was grateful for the buoyancy of the water, for without it she was sure she could not have remained standing. The thrill of his hands on her body, his presence after missing him more than she dared admit, overwhelmed her. And the eroticism of having him strip off her bikini right here, in the water, drove her to distraction.

She felt the heat of his arousal and reached her hand into the water, holding him through the thin fabric of his shorts.

'You see now how I know it is improper?' he ground out, indicating the thin scrap of pink that was now the only barrier between her and her nakedness.

'I can't miss it,' she replied huskily, a smile spreading across her face as she gloried in the feel of him touching her, in the knowledge that, whatever else was true, he had come because he wanted her as much as she wanted him.

He whisked away the tiny bikini bottoms in one swift motion and brought her legs around his waist. His hand made a small but thrilling journey from her inner thigh to her honeyed warmth, open for him, and he began to concentrate his slow, steady movements. Faye had never felt such intimate sensation, never known such wild abandon. His mouth went to her nipple, revelling, kissing and teasing as he continued his expert exploration below the water. Somewhere in the recesses of a mind swamped with pleasure she realised that he must want to satisfy her, that he could take her right here in the water but was choosing to bring her to her own point of ecstasy rather than satiate his own obvious need. Her shock and elation at such consideration reminded her of her own inexperience, but was instantly replaced with a sudden and foolish wonder at what pleasure it would be to come home here to this, every day for the rest of her life. But her body was too receptive to his touch to allow any thought, futile or otherwise, to remain in her mind for long. And as his slow movements brought her to her peak, every nerve-ending and emotion rose to the surface. She clamped her mouth down upon his shoulder in sheer ecstasy, the aftershocks convulsing through her body.

'That was…' she whispered as the water stilled around them, almost too overwhelmed with emotion and disbelief to find the word '…remarkable.'

'You sound surprised,' he ground out, as if his prowess usually went without saying.

'I've never done that before,' she said quietly. 'Just me, I mean.' She was sure as hell it would inflate his ego, but right now she was past caring. She was too infused with satisfaction.

'You mean your other lovers have been selfish?' Dante said, his words stunted. 'Then they are fools.'

He did not give her a chance to correct him, thought she hardly saw what difference it would make if she tried. He had already made up his mind about her six years ago.

Dante launched himself out of the pool, his pressing erection still evident as he passed her a towel. 'I'm hungry,' he said, and Faye wanted to smile at the irony, but his expression was severe. 'Get changed. I will make us some dinner.'

When Faye emerged from the shower twenty minutes later, she was mystified by the myriad of delicious scents wafting from the kitchen. Old-fashioned, homely smells—that word again. They had to eat, of course, and his knowledge of excellent food went without saying, but the thought of him actually cooking surprised her. And what was more he had decided to get creative in the kitchen *now*, after they had just been intimate. Could it be any more different from the last two occasions when they had made love? When what had followed was him ensuring she was as far away from him as possible? Faye tried to quell the ludicrous excitement that zipped through her. For, as experience had taught her, dinner was likely to be just another step up from the morning-after breakfast, and he was about to dispose of her all over again.

'There's some clean clothes in the wardrobe, *cara*.' His voice rang through from the kitchen as she was towel drying her hair, contemplating the inscrutability of it all.

Faye wandered over to the large mirrored wardrobe, his words not really sinking in. As she opened the doors she fully expected to see nothing but the grey suit and the couple of other casual numbers she had been surviving on. But the rail was full of outfit after outfit of beautiful clothes. For one naive moment she wondered if Elena had sent some over for her to borrow, but as she picked out a white linen skirt and a raspberry-coloured top she saw the tags: they were all brand-new, and designer to boot.

Faye exhaled through her teeth. So that was what this was about. When Dante had demanded that she become *his* for the month he had meant it. His to control, to make helpless at his touch whenever it suited him, to dress in whatever he wished. *That* was why he was here now.

'Put them on.' His voice echoed through to her, as if he had sensed her hesitation through the wall.

She shivered as she held up the outfit in her hands and compared it to her tired clothes squashed together at one end of the rail. Yes, it was easy to *reason* that the whole set-up went against everything she believed in, but why did it have to *feel* so damn good?

'Is this really necessary?' Faye strode into the room, trying to ignore the delightful swish of the new skirt against her legs as he swung round to face her, saucepan in hand. She was momentarily taken aback by the way steam rose from the hob, causing one strand of his dark hair to flop distractingly across his brow.

'*Bell-a*,' he said, pronouncing it so deliberately it sounded like a caress.

The look on her face pleased him. It had frustrated him that she hadn't made a single protest about being brought out here when all the while he had been in Rome, at war with his libido over how many days to keep her dangling. Finally her perplexed little pout felt like a victory.

'The fortune that little lot cost would no doubt have gone a long way towards the refurbishment needed at Matteson's,' she said, attempting reprimand but suspecting she was failing miserably as her heart softened at those two haunting syllables.

'Ahh, Faye,' he said softly. 'Still you underestimate the severity of your financial problems.'

'No, I'm just saying I could have managed on the things I had.'

'Surely you are not suggesting that clothes are not a requirement of this month, *cara mia*? Because if you are I might have to make you prove it.' He broke out into an irresistible smile and Faye knew she had lost. 'It wouldn't be fair to expect you to survive on the things you brought for only a short trip,' he said, turning back to the hob, 'and I promised I would provide everything you needed whilst you are here.'

Whilst I am here, thought Faye, realising how easy it was to forget that before long she would be back in England and, aside from the money and that ridiculous profit target to meet, it would be as if she had never been here at all. To him, at least. So why didn't she start being the woman whose point of view she had argued at the ball? Just because she was female it didn't mean she couldn't enjoy a purely physical relationship with him until it was time to go their separate ways, did it? She watched him deftly tossing vegetables in the pan. Yes, that was the only way to deal with this. Live for now, she thought. Dare to change your stupid obsession with the consequences, take a leaf out of his book and treat this as though it's perfectly normal.

'Do you cook often?' she said, a little too unsteadily to pass for *normal*, as she fetched cutlery from the sideboard and began to lay the table, already bedecked with a beautiful burnt-orange cloth and candles burning at either end.

'When I'm here, always.'

'The rural way of life inspires you?' Faye queried, trying hard to connect the quintessential city-slicker with the image before her.

'My grandparents' way of life.'

Faye stopped arranging the place settings for a moment and looked up at him, unable to disguise her curiosity. 'They lived in Tuscany?'

'Yes, in this house. I grew up here.'

'I didn't realise.' Faye was taken aback. It seemed to explain so much, and yet at the same time to raise even more questions. From what she had gathered he had spent the early part of his life trailing after his mother from one city to the next.

'Elena and I moved here after my mother died. I was eleven—'

It was telling that he defined from that moment onwards as his *growing up*.

'That can't have been easy.'

'Easier than you would think.' His voice was flat. 'Everyone who knew my mother thought she was destined to die young. She was—how is it you say?—like a moth to a flame, drawn away from the country to the bright city lights in search of rich men.' His lip curled in distaste. 'Children were no more desirable to her than growing old would have been.'

Faye frowned, unable to comprehend how any woman could lack basic maternal instincts. 'And your father?'

'Who knows?' He shrugged in a gesture that was exaggeratedly Italian, though his muscles were a little too taut for it to pass as customary indifference. 'Perhaps not even him.'

Faye sensed her cue to change the subject. 'So this is where you began?' she asked, spinning around on her feet, taking in the kitchen, imagining him here as a young man.

'Before I lived here, sitting around a table to eat was something I had only seen other people do through restaurant windows. As for preparing food itself, I knew even less.'

'Your grandparents taught you to cook?'

He nodded, as if the cooking part went without saying. 'They taught me how much it mattered. I made sure I never forgot.' He shrugged again. He made it sound easy, but she knew better than most how hard this business was, how tirelessly he must have worked to create an empire based on nothing more than that belief. She realised she had never admired him more.

'You must miss your grandparents,' she said, wishing she could do her father even half as proud.

'What they taught me about the meaning of sitting down and eating good food remains.'

Faye was not sure she had ever felt so close or so distant

from him all at the same time. In one sentence he had summarised exactly how *she* felt about Matteson's, and explained the roots of his own motivation which she had never fully understood. But suddenly she also saw how his need for change and his grounding in the things he was passionate about could co-exist. The Dante of Rome and the Dante of the Tuscan hills. Yet what was *this* whole set-up all about, when she seemed so clearly to fit into the *destined for change* category?

'And what about eating with me? What does that mean?' Faye's voice was quiet, as if she hadn't really meant to speak her thoughts aloud.

Dante looked up, any emotion that he had unwittingly allowed to creep onto his face replaced with a wry expression. Her words sounded suspiciously familiar to him, like those used by women who mistakenly supposed that when he released some detail about his life it put their relationship on a deeper level than sex. But this was Faye Matteson. The chances were *that* was exactly where she wished to steer this conversation.

'It means we are two adults, with the same taste in life's mutual pleasures.'

'You once led me to believe we had tasted all that was worth savouring.' Faye lowered her head.

'You want to hear me say that I still burn for you, *bella*. Is that it?' His voice was loaded. 'You are tired of hearing of my past, and instead you wish to know that around you I find my appetite is insatiable?'

Faye shook her head, trying to ignore the dart of pleasure that shot through her. She motioned to her clothes, the dinner. 'No. I just wonder where the word "mutual" fits in to all of this.'

'You are trying to pretend you are not crazy with longing

too, *bella*?' He mocked. 'After earlier tonight? You needn't bother. Even with your vast experience you must admit the sexual chemistry that exists between our bodies is rare.'

'That's not what I meant. I mean—me having no say in any of this.'

'But isn't that exactly what turns you on, Faye?' He looked at her mercilessly as she blushed. 'As well as precisely what you signed up for? For, despite all your protestations of female supremacy, doesn't knowing I might take you right now drive you wild?'

Faye tried to look away, but he reached his hand across the table and tilted her chin so that she was looking straight into his ebony-dark gaze.

'And when I do you will beg for me to do it again,' he murmured. 'Are you foolish enough to argue that I am wrong?'

Faye could make no answer. Her body had reached its own conclusion.

'Then I suggest you put down that knife and fork.'

CHAPTER EIGHT

IT FELT like a sexual awakening. Yes, they had made love before he joined her in Tuscany, but that night something changed. It was as if they had both surrendered to what Dante had described as the 'rare chemistry' between their bodies. To Faye, his analysis sounded painfully like the narrative in a science textbook, but, paradoxically, it somehow rationalised things in her mind. As if the only way to deal with the desire that existed between them was to live for the moment and savour it in exactly the way he described.

And savour it they did. For not only had Dante's words broken through her defences, but he seemed determined to prove just how *mutual* their needs were. And for the next few days, as if she was on some delicious sensual voyage, she learned for the first time in her twenty-four years what it was to exist in a world where there was only you and your lover. The kind of experience she supposed her friends had been having with boyfriends for years. Where you didn't ask questions like, *When is this going to end?* or *Shouldn't we be at work?* The kind of relationship that his rejection six years ago had ensured she'd never got close to. They were shut away from the rest of the world, learning each other's bodies, discovering a whole new scale of sensations. She could barely recall what else they did with their time but make love, wherever and whenever their desire struck them, with breakfast becoming brunch, only stepping outside to cool off in the pool or pop to the local shop for fresh bread and milk.

Watching the palpable enjoyment on his face, feeling him reach for her again and again, she found it astonishingly easy not to think about the consequences. It was only times like now, late in the night, as she listened to him sleeping, that questions began to grate on her. Like when would he be returning to Rome? Because today was Wednesday, and though he'd said he was only down for the weekend he was still here. She was desperate to ask, and yet it felt vital to her survival to pretend she didn't care.

'We will resume your tour tomorrow.'

His voice cut through the darkness. So he was not asleep. Faye felt her senses return to high alert, as if he had flicked a switch.

'Oh?' she mumbled, feigning drowsiness and wondering, not for the first time, if he possessed the ability to read her mind as well as the cravings of her body. Or had the undiscussed boundaries of the situation got to them both?

'You have much still to see, and I wish to visit some of my suppliers whilst I am here.'

'You no longer have pressing business in Rome?' Now it had arisen, she couldn't pass up the opportunity to discover if he had always planned to replace Elena as her guide, or whether it was the last few days that had persuaded him to alter his plans.

He moved towards her. 'I discover I have more pressing business here *at the moment*.'

It felt like a cleverly dropped reminder of her place in his 'temporary' file, and yet as he came closer her hormones went into overdrive, and all she could think was, *He's staying. I have changed his mind.*

'One of the perks of being head of Valenti Enterprises?' she asked lightly, telling herself to take his admission with a pinch of salt. 'A bank balance guaranteed to rise without anyone dictating where you must be and when?'

Dante stilled. For one long moment he looked at her through the dim night light as if she had said something in another language, and he was slowly translating and discovering the meaning was repugnant.

'Precisely.'

The moment he spoke the word it seemed to change the temperature in the room to an icy chill. He rolled away from her. The sudden sense of emptiness left her feeling utterly bewildered, and sleep was even further from her grasp.

Eventually, in the early hours, the pleasures of the day before finally outweighed the disquiet of their exchange and Faye fell into a deep sleep. He was standing over her when her eyes flicked open.

'Finally she wakes,' he drawled.

'Sorry.' She reacted instantly, rubbing her eyes and sitting up, peering at her watch on the bedside table. Nine a.m. He was fully clothed, his arms crossed in front of him. It was a far cry from being woken up by those self-same arms snaking around her waist yesterday. Yes, *he* might be staying, but had *business Dante* returned?

'You should have woken me earlier.'

'Believe me, I was tempted. We leave in half an hour.'

Faye nodded and scrambled out of bed, momentarily forgetting her nakedness.

He threw a towelling robe in her direction. 'We won't be going anywhere if you continue with that,' he growled, determined to reassert some control. If she was going to make snide little comments that intimated that him telling her where to be and when was such a chore, she could damn well do some work. 'I'll meet you outside.'

Faye nodded obediently as he left the room. It was gratifying to know she turned him on—she couldn't pretend it wasn't, or that the feeling wasn't mutual. But far harder to deal with were all the other things she had discovered about him, just by living alongside him for this short time. Like the way he constantly surprised her.

When she slung her bag over her shoulder and headed out through the door twenty-five minutes later, determined that she would not provoke his mood any more than she'd had already unknowingly done, the last thing she expected was to find him with his legs slung either side of a gleaming black motorbike. So, she thought with bemusement, even his mode of transport outside of the city was simple, carefree, fun.

But if he noticed the look of pleasure on her face he ignored it. He was silent as she walked towards him, the sight of his body on the powerful machine, clad in dark jeans, a white T-shirt and a black leather jacket, causing somersaults in her belly.

'Put your arms around my waist,' he commanded, seeming to sense her ineptness. Though her not having been on a motorbike before wasn't exactly the reason why she was so frantically gnawing her lower lip.

She did as he told her and they set off immediately. Beautiful countryside zipped past, the wind whipped through her hair, and the press of her body against his

powerful back as the machine roared beneath them almost
pushed his black mood from her thoughts. For wasn't his
unpredictability the very reason that being with him was so
exhilarating?

And when they arrived at a vineyard she was reminded that
she was far from alone in her admiration. For, though she was
well accustomed to seeing women fawn over him and men
pandering to his success, she had not expected the owners to
greet him almost as if he was family, not in the least intimidated that the man responsible for their livelihoods had
dropped in unannounced.

'Did your grandparents introduce you to suppliers in this
area?' Faye asked, her curiosity too great to remain silent as they
followed the old man down into the cellar. It occurred to her
that she was as captivated by Dante at work as she was by Dante
in bed. 'They treat you as if they have known you all their lives.'

He hadn't fully anticipated how bringing her here would
only serve to reawaken her enthusiasm for every element of
the business, and to remind him just why he had admired her
so much when he had first met her in Matteson's all those
years ago. It didn't sit well with him; much easier to believe
her passion lay in one place alone.

'Some of them, yes. Others, like Grumio and his wife,
here, I sought out because I tasted something so good that I
wanted to serve it to others.'

Faye dropped back as Dante spoke rapidly to Grumio in
Italian, discussing what looked to be a new red he had
produced. And as his words sank in Faye realised with a start
that it was exactly what he had done with her back then:
spotted her talent and decided he wanted it for himself. But
it made her feel as if *she* was wine being swilled in a glass,

for what ought to have been the most positive, defining moment of her life had ended up as the complete opposite.

'Faye?' Dante beckoned her over to taste the deep purple liquid, and Faye was forced to snap out of her contemplation. 'What do you think, will this suit Perfezione as the new house red?'

Faye smelt the fruity aroma of the rich dark drink and took a mouthful, closing her eyes the way she always did, as her father had once shown her. She was grateful; it wiped out the enticing sight of Dante's fingers upon the stem of his glass and allowed her to form something like a coherent response.

'It's good.' Faye nodded as she opened her eyes. 'Not too heavy.'

Dante held his glass up to the light and nodded in agreement.

'But is it more expensive than your current choice?' she asked, looking down at the bottle on the table.

Dante turned his head sharply to face her. 'That is what Grumio and I were discussing. I will not make the switch unless it is like for like. Has your Italian improved?'

'Sadly not.' Faye shrugged. 'I recently decided to update Matteson's wine list. Unfortunately our merchant presumed we had made up our minds to make changes regardless of price, so I went elsewhere.'

Dante put down his glass, taken aback. He had supposed that she was keeping her pretty head out of it, hovering at a distance because the negotiations were out of her depth. He hadn't anticipated that the opposite was true, or being reminded that her talents in this business still existed.

'Very wise.'

He sounded surprised. She looked in the direction of the winemaker, taking the steps down to the lower cellar to replace an unopened bottle in the rack. That was it, wasn't it? If, like Grumio, she had been a *man* whose skills had impressed him back then, he wouldn't have doubted her abilities now. It suddenly dawned on her that a woman capable of business *and* sex appeal simply couldn't exist in his mind; the minute she had shared his bed, in his eyes she had become incapable of any other achievement. The reality of their differing ideologies slammed into her. She felt as if all this time she had been running blindly, assuming there was a finish line in sight, however distant, and now she had just looked down and discovered she had been on a treadmill all along. No matter what she did she would never change his cast-iron prejudice.

'Just because I am a woman it doesn't mean my father didn't teach me anything but how to wait tables.'

'I wasn't basing my assumptions on your gender,' he breathed. 'But on your track record.'

'Matteson's, or mine?' Faye shot back.

'Both.'

'You once wanted me to work for you, Dante.'

'And what was it *you* wanted? Let me think—'

'So because I made love with you it automatically transpires that I did not want to do anything else with my life from then on?' Faye interrupted.

'No, Faye. *That* transpired the minute you disappeared and—how would you like me to phrase it?—found an alternative *employer* within the space of two weeks.'

Grumio hovered awkwardly at the top of the stairs. Their expressions were no doubt as clear as if they had been speaking in his native tongue. It was tempting to yell back at Dante regardless, to blast his outdated views and to ask how *he* would have reacted if he had had to face the humiliation he had put her through, but it seemed pointless. He only ever dished it out. He didn't feel it.

Faye turned her back on him, knowing she was as likely to alter his viewpoint as she was to find a pot of gold at the end of a rainbow. What did it matter what he thought? She had faith in her own capabilities, and once she had the money she needed she would prove them. Instead she spoke to Grumio, as much from a determination to demonstrate her professionalism as to dispel the tension. *'Grazie, è squisito.'* Thank you, it's delicious.

Grumio bowed and spoke rapidly, obviously presuming her Italian was better than it really was. She only caught a couple of words. *'Bella...vostra foto.'*

Faye furrowed her brow, unable to fully comprehend and all the more frustrated for having no choice but to turn back to Dante.

His tone was clipped. 'He says it is his pleasure, for you are just as beautiful as your photo.'

Faye turned back to Grumio, still perplexed. *'Foto?'*

'In the newspaper.' Dante translated his response without waiting to be asked, shrugging his shoulders nonchalantly. 'It seems you are splashed all over the tabloids *cara.* Congratulations.'

'Me?' Suddenly it felt as if the bubble they had been existing in for the past few days had well and truly burst.

Dante ignored her look of horror. 'Did the myriad of flashes escape your notice when we arrived at the Harvest Ball, Faye? Surely not? The world's press are no doubt swarming over each other, trying to discover who you are.'

In the emotional rollercoaster that came with being around Dante she had forgotten that he was practically royalty when it came to the papers. It was stupid to have done so when she had seen so many photos of him with supermodels and A-list stars over the years. It was part of her daily routine to avoid the news stands on her way to Matteson's. She had just supposed that because this was nothing, because she was a nobody, they wouldn't be interested. And now it seemed that not only Dante but the world saw her as his mistress.

'I want to see them.' Her tone was demanding, edgy. It might be a day-to-day occurrence in *his* life, but it wasn't part of hers. God knew what the headlines said—what people back at Matteson's would think if they saw them.

'Just when you were doing such a good job of convincing us that business was your only priority.' Dante's mouth slanted sardonically, ignoring her request. 'We're finished here. Let's get something to eat at the villa before we head east to the olive groves this afternoon.'

He moved forward to bid a puzzled-looking Grumio a charming goodbye, leaving Faye no choice but to quickly utter *arrivederci* herself.

Why was it that the minute she consoled herself with faith in her own abilities something else transpired which seemed only to back up his derogatory opinion of her? And why had she played right into his hands?

As Dante led the way out, Faye lagged behind like a sulking child.

'I'm not hungry.'

'But let me guess—you would be suddenly ravenous if I suggested we go the café opposite the newsagents?'

'Is it a crime to want to know what lies they've printed?'

'Why? So you can sell *your* story in exchange for more cash and extend your fifteen minutes of fame?' he said, turning on her like a viper disturbed.

'Do you really suppose I would do something so de-grading?'

'Do *you* suppose I am fool enough to believe that you are some moral high-grounder?'

'What's that supposed to mean?'

'It means that if you really were so *proper* you would have no reason to worry *what* they printed.'

FLAVOUR OF THE MONTH! DANTE VALENTI HAS MYSTERY MISTRESS EATING OUT OF HIS HAND AT ANNUAL HARVEST BALL.

Faye stared at the headline on his computer screen. The minute his phone had rung as they were finishing lunch she had seen her chance to slip away. He had given her permission to use his personal office to stay in touch with Matteson's earlier in the week; there was no reason why she shouldn't check the internet now. But with his accusations circling in her mind like a hungry shark she couldn't help feeling as if she was doing something forbidden.

Yet, more than that, as she saw herself through the eyes of the world she was forced to confront exactly what she had become. For whilst being around Dante made it hard to retain faith in herself and in Matteson's, or to believe that she was capable of the emotionless sex this bizarre situation demanded, seeing the words in black and white made it damn near impossible.

Dante's latest arm candy is thought to be an unknown Brit by the name of Faye Matteson, daughter of little-known late restaurateur Charles Matteson, whose once

*passable eatery has fallen on hard times. Whilst the
appeal of Italy's richest and most eligible bachelor to
Miss Matteson goes without saying, critics have been
stunned by the über-hunk's departure from haute cuisine
to what can only be described as pot snack.*

The article was accompanied by two pictures. The first was
of Dante, looking devastating but blasé as he ushered her into
the theatre. Her expression was so startled and meek even she
felt like giving herself a good kick. The second was a hazy
photo of the two of them dancing, which was all the more
erotic for its lack of clarity. The two of them together looked
like some comic strip in which a poor little match girl looked
up at an Italian billionaire with dollar signs in her eyes and
decided to get raunchy. It made her stomach turn.

Not that she should have been surprised, of course. What
had she expected? She *was* nothing more than his mistress,
and though she might have told herself that she accepted that,
she'd been wrong. Her one job had been to keep her feelings
at bay, to live only in the present, and she had failed. Because
she had found delight in much *more* than their lovemaking;
she had adored hearing stories of his childhood here in the
Tuscan hills, and meeting Elena and Luca, had relished
sharing meals and ideas with him as much as she had savoured
sharing his bed.

'Is seeing your name in print the thrill you were hoping for?'

Faye jumped up from her seat, the unexpectedness of his
presence behind her causing a flush to her cheeks. She turned
and shook her head, feeling as if she had been caught planting
a ticking bomb. 'I have seen what I needed to see. Shall we go?'

'No.' For a moment his eyes licked over her in such blatant

sensual appraisal that she wondered if it had always been his intention to come home for more than lunch. But he continued. 'That was Elena on the phone. I've asked her over this afternoon to thank her for showing you around last week—and to see Max.'

Faye swallowed. He expected her to meet Max—another member of his family who in a few weeks would exist as nothing more than a memory of something she would never be a part of again.

'What about visiting the olive groves?'

'Like you said, one of the perks of my job is not having anyone dictate where I need to be and when,' he replied flippantly.

Faye knew in that instant she couldn't do it. Couldn't go through an afternoon of playing happy families. She was his *mistress*, and he would never see her as anything more, so why put herself through this added heartache?

'I thanked Elena myself, actually,' Faye said, taking a deep breath and rising from the office chair to face him full on. 'So if we are taking the afternoon off I think I will go shopping instead.'

'Do you indeed?' His voice was razor-sharp.

'Yes. Seeing these photos reminds me I have nowhere near enough clothes for the duration of my stay.'

His eyes narrowed. 'And what about the wardrobe full of clothes I provided?'

'Wardrobe *full*? Men never seem to realise the real extent of that concept.'

Faye did not turn to face him, but she could sense anger billowing from him like steam. 'You *will* be here when they arrive.'

'Why? Do you wish me to give the impression of being a permanent fixture in your life? Surely that demands a higher fee?'

'What are you playing at, you little witch?' Dante took one step towards her.

'Being your mistress, I thought.'

'And doesn't it come so naturally?' His eyes glittered as he flicked them first over her, then down to the headline on the screen.

'You should know, Dante.' Faye shrugged, picking up a pen and pretending to write a shopping list that came out as a garbled mess of misspelled designer boutiques she was grateful that he couldn't see.

'Why don't we put it to the test?' he said, his voice husky. 'Since you are so desperate to be treated like one.'

Faye froze. The pen was suspended between her finger and thumb like a pendulum.

'Take off your dress.'

Faye turned on one foot, like a netball player who had just been passed the ball but dared not move for fear of losing the game. 'What did you say?'

'You heard.'

Faye hesitated, her eyes darting to the clock, then back to him. But he was leaning rakishly against the wall, as if he had all the time in the world and would wait as long as it took.

'Concerned you'll lose precious shopping time, Faye?'

He was daring her to say yes. But though the word was on the tip of her tongue she was immediately consumed by something stronger than speech. The slow pulse at the base of her throat. The all-consuming need to have him look that way at all of her, to know he needed her as much as she needed him.

Though her mind fought against her body, Faye slowly raised her hands and began to undo the zip at the base of her neck. An exultant click issued from deep in his throat.

'And when you're done with that, lose your underwear.'

Dante pulled the chair away from her and sat down to watch. It was like being some exotic dancer. So exposed. And yet as she stripped down to her panties and bra she felt only exhilaration. Not just because she didn't know exactly what was coming next, but because now, when it felt as if they were worlds apart, the promised intimacy of their bodies was like finding a bridge.

Edging down one strap of the bra, she heard him release a low growl of anguish. If she had not been prey to her need to be close to him she would have teased him longer. She tugged the delicate French knickers over her hips and bottom, feeling his eyes follow the movement down over the length of legs that had grown bronzed in the days of Tuscan sunshine, and growing warm once more beneath his gaze.

'Come here,' he commanded.

She walked slowly towards him, reaching out to encourage the T-shirt from his jeans, running the flat of her hands over the naked skin beneath, watching his emotionless yet widening dark pupils. Yes, to him this was having sex—but to her it was making love. It always had been and always would be, she thought, wondering why it felt like a goodbye.

He stood up, kicked off the jeans and sheathed himself swiftly. His hands cupped the soft globes of her bottom and exulted in the feel of them. The gesture felt more tender to Faye than she was sure he intended, but as he turned her around to face in the opposite direction he reached forward to stroke her breasts with equally tantalising softness.

'Dante—please!'

He did not hesitate, and entered her from behind. She felt her body, tight but eager, as his strong thighs brushed against her smooth skin, wicked and yet so—so *intimate*. For didn't he realise that she would never even have the desire to act this way unless she loved him with so much of her heart that none was left to protest? He moved within her slowly to begin with, building pace, and with every thrust he claimed a little more of her soul—filling and completing her in a way she had never known she was missing until now.

Faye had lost herself every single time she and Dante had made love, but this time she was not sure she possessed even one shard of control. She was in a world other than the one inhabited by the Faye Matteson of reality, a world where dreams no longer stopped short of eluding her grasp, and she never wanted to return. She sensed him reaching the edge, but she could not hold off her own orgasm any longer as he touched her, whispering something indiscernible but fierce in Italian. And as she cried out his name she felt something else—a warmth, an opening. His own spectacular climax followed, gripping her in his rapture. But as he met his release she realised exactly what that feeling was: the splitting of his carefully applied contraception.

She heard his intake of breath, which confirmed his own recognition. As his seed spilled forth into her body she breathed deeply, not willing even to articulate the foolish dreams that were running through her mind. Dreams that belonged in the cloud-nine moment of orgasm but not a second after. For as he withdrew from her she felt swamped by the realisation that if a new life had just begun inside her, it was the last thing a man like him would want of any woman—least of all her.

The deep sigh he released seemed to say it all. It was not the satisfied exhalation that marked the beginning of their bodies returning to their usual steady breathing after making love. It was the kind of sigh that usually came just before you offered someone your condolences—like *I'm sorry to hear he passed away*. A sigh that marked the end of something. She stood up, reaching for her clothes and putting them back on in an orderly fashion, one item at a time, as if it might work as some antidote to the chaos in her mind.

'I believe there is a pill you can take, if you're concerned.'

Faye continued to straighten her dress, focusing on some inanimate object on the other side of the room, like a ballerina determined to pirouette without losing her balance, whilst his dismissive words rampaged through her heart like a tornado.

'Of course,' she replied evasively, with what she hoped was equal detachment. 'These things happen.'

He had never seemed so cold to her—never so devoid of emotion. *If you're concerned*. But in Dante's world sex had no upshot but pleasure, did it? Was this another one of those unwritten rules that his mistresses were expected to know? That if the contraception he deemed adequate happened to fail then it became their responsibility to rectify the problem? Faye felt sick at the thought.

'Ahh, I was forgetting that you are a woman of the world,' he said, as if he had just won against himself in a game of solitaire.

No, Faye thought, I'm not. And I can't pretend I am anymore.

CHAPTER NINE

'HIS stamina never ceases to amaze me!'

Faye smiled politely, and attempted to sip the steaming cup of espresso in a manner which suggested that her heart was not breaking in two whilst she and Elena watched the spectacle of Dante and Max. She only prayed Elena shared her brother's lack of emotional intuition. Though inwardly she doubted it were possible that anyone else on the planet could have a heart quite so impenetrable.

'Faster, faster!' Max ordered Dante as he charged at full speed around the conservatory with his three-year-old nephew on his back, their dark heads pressed together, laughing like naughty schoolboys. The irony was not lost on Faye as she watched them.

'He's been up since six.' Elena laughed, watching her son with a look of motherly adoration. 'And still such energy. Mind you, I'm not sure which one of them's encouraging the other most!'

Faye helplessly followed her gaze. This was exactly what she had been dreading, only worse. Ten times worse. Being embraced like a sister again by Elena, whom she had come to care for in her own right, and now being introduced to Max too. She had known it would be difficult, meeting another member of Dante's family as if they were in a real relationship with some kind of future, but she hadn't anticipated that he would be as sensational with children as he was with everything else he touched. Or that she would feel as if she was looking through some nightmarish kaleidoscope, where one minute he was instructing her how to be sure she was not pregnant and the next playing the family man.

'Max does seem very confident.' She turned to Elena and, remembering the way her mother had somehow gained the ability to put on a brave face at her father's funeral, forced herself to replicate it. 'I would have expected him to be more timid with an uncle he must not see very often.'

'He is very sure of himself even with strangers.' Elena nodded. 'But Dante is around more than you'd imagine. I think he's even more enamoured with his nephew than his nephew is with him.'

'I can see that.' How much easier it would have been to hear that his visits here were fleeting, to think only of the Dante who lived in that stark apartment in Rome.

'You'd like children of your own one day?' Elena's eyes followed Faye's. Dante and Max were now engaging in a particularly athletic wheelbarrow race, their faces red and full of exhilaration.

'One day, perhaps. Under the right circumstances.' Faye nodded and moved her gaze to the trees beyond the window, whose leaves were just beginning to turn brown.

'Are you not close to the right circumstances now?' Elena coaxed.

'I couldn't be further from them,' Faye replied, a little too loudly as she turned back to face her.

It was the first time Dante had looked at her since she had emerged in the living room, not long after he had answered the doorbell that had put an end to their agonising exchange. He had not batted an eyelid at her tousled hair, hastily tied back into a ponytail, nor the flush still present in her cheeks when she had excused herself for her slightly delayed entrance. No, his handling of the whole situation had been far too practised for that. But now, as Elena handed Max his juice, the look of utter disdain he aimed at her the minute his sister's attention was diverted was undeniable.

'Would you like a biscuit, Max?' Faye asked, holding out the plate, determined to distract herself.

Max gratefully accepted the proffered snack and flew from his mother's arms to place his chubby hands around Faye's neck, planting an enormous kiss on her cheek.

'Well, thank you,' Faye said playfully.

'Something tells me he's going to be a hit with the ladies,' Dante drawled.

'Just like his uncle,' Elena said instantly, but then bit her lip, as if she wished she could take the words back.

Yet Faye was numb to Elena's pained expression. Nothing she said could hurt her any more than *he* already had. Even if she had just confirmed that Faye was nothing more than one in a long line of women second only in length to the line still queuing. She knew it all already.

The room was still save for the sound of Max quietly draining his cup of juice. Elena seemed desperate to break the silence.

'So, has Dante convinced you to stay in Italy longer than just a few weeks yet, Faye? It is so easy to fall in love with it here.'

Out of the corner of her eye Faye saw Dante raise his eyebrows quizzically. What could she say? *I would stay here for the rest of my life if your brother wanted me even half as much as I want him. But I can't go on, knowing I'll never have all this, pretending it's not tearing me apart.*

'It is beautiful. But far from convincing me to stay, Dante has made me realise the necessity of keeping things varied in life.' Faye looked at him, foolishly willing him to contradict her. She'd expected him to visibly breathe a sigh of relief, but saw only condemnation in his face.

'As you can see, the fleeting nature of our arrangement suits Faye down to the ground.' He turned to Elena. 'Now, let me drive you home. It is beginning to get dark, and Max is looking tired.'

Elena stood up and wiped the blackcurrant moustache from Max's mouth, her questioning look gone in an instant, as if everything she had just heard was the most natural exchange in the world. Faye felt paralysed.

'Goodbye, Faye—and in case I don't see you before you return home, have a safe journey.' She met Faye's eyes in a look that seemed to hold a meaning Faye could not quite fathom. 'I feel sure we will meet again.'

You're wrong, Faye wanted to say. Elena's words had somehow clarified exactly what she must do to prevent any further pain. *You're wrong because I have to stop the heartache now, and I am never, never putting myself through it again.*

'Thank you for everything, Elena,' Faye said finally, kissing her on both cheeks with affection. 'And goodbye, Max. It was a pleasure to meet you.' Faye bent down to shake his tiny hot hand and lifted the corners of her mouth in what she hoped looked like a smile. But his perplexed expression as he followed his mother and uncle to the door told her she had failed.

The minute Faye heard the front door click behind them she sank to the floor like a puppet whose strings had been cut, bewildered by the events of last twenty-four hours. But what had suddenly changed? She had known all along that she was nothing more than a brief affair to him—hell, hadn't the contract set it out clearly enough? She could hardly accuse him of not being honest. No, she was the one who had changed—because she had allowed herself to *feel*, and that was precisely what she had forbidden herself to do. She had told herself she was capable of being like him, but she was as wrong now as she had been at eighteen. Only this time she couldn't pretend that she hadn't seen it coming.

And she had done it again for what? The conditional offer of money with a demand that was—when she considered it without the rose-tinted glasses she had chosen to view it through—utterly impossible to meet? She was fighting a losing battle in every corner. What would sticking around and tormenting herself for another few weeks achieve? The longer she was here, the more deeply she'd fall in love with him.

Love. She hated to admit it. It was the stupid teenager's word she had gamely attributed to her feelings for him before she'd known how foolish it was to give her heart so readily. The word she could excuse herself for thinking during sex, but which in the cold light of day simply made her feel pathetic. Yet, try as she might to use grown-up definitions like lust or chemistry, there really was no other description for the feeling in her chest when he whispered her name, when he held her in his sleep, when she watched him playing with Max. He might be incapable of anything but a temporary affair, but love didn't ask questions like *Is he suitable?* or *Will he love you back?* did it?

Which was precisely why she had to leave. For if she stayed there would only be more waking up in his arms, more admiring the way he went about his life and his work, whilst knowing just how little respect he had for her. What would he do next? Arrange a taxi to take her to the local chemist for a morning-after pill the moment he returned? Then resume their arrangement until the hour of reckoning came, when he would shake her hand to close the deal and thank her for her services? No, she couldn't bear it. She had to go.

Much as she couldn't endure the thought of returning to the restaurant she loved and watching it fall around her, nor bear to see the crushed look on her mother's face the moment she told her there was no hope, she knew if she stayed here it would destroy her. And then he would destroy Matteson's anyway. Maybe she could appeal to the banks again? There had to be something she hadn't tried, didn't there?

Although she knew in her heart the answer was no, there suddenly seemed only one way to proceed. Leave now, or break down completely. Hauling herself to her feet, she made her way to the bedroom she had not slept in since the first night she arrived and pulled her suitcase from under the bed.

Faye was packing up her toiletries in the bathroom when she heard the click of the front door again. She felt her heart sink. Not that she could have possibly hoped to vacate the villa before he returned; Elena only lived five minutes away, and the taxi Faye had ordered in her broken Italian was bound to take its time. She just had to pray that he would not attempt to halt her progress simply because her departure flouted their contract. Pray he would make this easy, agree that whatever *this* was, it had run its course.

'Going somewhere?' His tone was loaded with wry surprise as he appeared at the bathroom door, his dark figure suddenly making the room seem tiny.

'Yes. Home.'

'Really? How foolish of me to think you had signed a contract to the contrary.' His eyes bored into her. 'If this is a tantrum because I refused you your shopping trip, then save it. I'll order a car to take you wherever it is you desire.'

'That won't be necessary. I've ordered a taxi to the airport myself, thank you.' She almost felt him wince that she had dared to undermine his control. She was glad.

'Is this an attempt to get my money early, Faye? Because if so you'll be sorely disappointed. I'm afraid I *never* alter the terms of a contract.'

'I don't doubt it. And, no, believe it or not it's because I wish to go home.'

'And why might that be?' He was close behind her now, as she looked down at the cream marble floor, unable to bring herself to meet the reflection of his gaze in the mirror. 'Do not tell me it is because you have not been enjoying yourself, because I know that is not true.'

She could feel the warmth of his breath on her neck playing havoc with her insides. 'I can't do this any longer.'

'This?' His tone had the unique quality of being both deceptively soft and wholly merciless. 'Has living in luxury with every pleasure you could wish for at your fingertips in exchange for exactly what you asked me for *and* more become too much of a strain, Miss Matteson?' He stepped back, raising his eyebrows in mockery.

'I came to you about business, Dante. You were the one who insisted on treating me as your mistress.'

'How ironic, when I once brought you here for business and you insisted upon *acting* like my mistress.'

Faye wished the room would expand, or that his damn reflection didn't dominate everywhere she tried to focus.

'I was a teenager. I'd never—'

He would not let her finish. 'And what is your excuse for falling into the role so easily now?' he spat, refusing to revisit the guilt he had once felt, knowing she deserved none of it. 'Is it because you are so experienced at playing the part that it comes naturally? Maybe that is why you're walking away? Because you have found you can get your precious money in half the time by selling yourself elsewhere?'

She closed her eyes and took a step towards the door, determined to harden her heart to him for the last time. 'Like you said, this was never going to be a permanent arrangement. I'll return your initial advance. Best to leave before one of us grows tired of the other, wouldn't you say?'

If he had made just one move to stop her she would have been powerless against him, Faye thought vainly as she lugged her suitcase up the stairs to the front door of her flat in the pitch dark. The hallway light was out again. But nothing. She had expected him to call her a liar, to demand she make good on their contract—hell, even seduce her into taking it back. For heaven knows she would have succumbed. But he had stood resolutely still whilst she had walked past his hard, heartless body for the last time.

But then he'd had no reason to stop her, Faye thought wretchedly as she fumbled to find the keyhole before dragging her small suitcase in behind her. For wasn't she as easy to replace as a blown bulb? There were countless women who would no doubt be glad to share his bed, happy not to question their position in his life when it came with so many material benefits.

She turned on the light and glanced around her tiny flat, at the practical brown armchair, the putrid digits of her alarm clock flashing 12:45, and tried not to think about just how much it contrasted with where she had gone to sleep last night. The place had never looked so dreary and devoid of life. Even her answering machine winked no green light. She wondered where on earth *she* was in the boxy intersecting rooms—she who loved to contemplate design. It looked as if their occupant was someone who had spent her life living by the rules, and suddenly she hated it.

But look what happened when you followed emotions and acted impulsively, she thought. She was returning to Matteson's more in debt than when she'd left, her heart no longer whole but shattered into pieces that she couldn't put together. She stood up and moved to methodically begin her unpacking. Except she couldn't do it. For once in her life even the thought made her feel sick, as if he had rearranged the internal organs in her body and no amount of organisation could restore her to the person she had been before. Faye sat down, and for the first time in years she allowed herself to cry.

It was nausea of a very different kind which overcame her the following month as she held the white stick in her hand and closed her eyes, trying to think inconsequential thoughts the way she would if she was waiting for a bus.

And there was plenty to think about, for thinking was the one thing she had forbidden herself to do since the moment she had gone back to Matteson's the day after she had re-turned. Because although she had walked through the door preparing to admit defeat, the first thing she had laid her eyes upon was the initial renovation Dante's advance had set in motion: the new shop front, the first steps towards a new, improved kitchen. And though it ought to have plunged her into an even deeper pit of despair, knowing that she now owed even more money and that they could not afford to *proceed* with the plans, somehow it had had the opposite effect. For the change had made Faye instantly refocus and remember her deep-rooted passion for the business that had resurfaced in the Perfezione kitchen, and she'd suddenly felt sure that the good work that was already underway would help her cause in finding investment.

And, to her open-mouthed astonishment, she had been right. Thanks to photos of the first few renovations, and her happening to mention her recent experience abroad, the bank had actually showed real interest in her plans for the first time, rather than treating them as the naive pipedreams of an inexperienced graduate. And upon examining how, in spite of difficulties, she had now completed a year of successful mortgage repayments, *finally* the stern face of the middle-aged bank manager had softened, and he had spoken the words that were music to her ears.

'Very well, Miss Matteson, we will grant you a loan in order to cover the main improvements you propose.'

It was the break Faye needed—that Matteson's needed—and she had immersed herself in what needed to be done im-mediately, determined this was one opportunity that she would not let slip through her fingers. She'd taken on the young interior designer she had approached previously, keen to showcase her talents, because she was at last able to pay for the materials. She'd sent pre-designed marketing material to proper print houses, adverts to newspapers, had interviewed and appointed the restaurant manager that they hadn't previously been able to afford to replace.

The days had passed in a blur of speed as each change was completed and, thanks to her widespread publicity generating interest about their new look, the customers slowly began to trickle back. Of course it was early days, but on the face of it life *looked* more promising than it had done in years. Even if behind closed doors, when she came home to her flat at night, she forced herself to watch trashy television rather than dwell on the fact that she was eating alone. Where once she had relished her independence, now the best she could hope for was reaching for the banana she ate for dessert without wondering where *he* was eating, and with whom. With the redhead who had so closely guarded his office against female intruders, perhaps? Or skipping food altogether and lounging in the back of some taxi, making eyes as he had once made eyes at her?

And although she had promised herself she would not think about him again until after the official grand reopening next weekend, there was only so long that she could go on ignoring the more physical reminders of her time in Italy. Reminders that since returning to England it had been convenient not to consider. Like the fact that her period was late, or that she had been sick every morning for almost a week and there wasn't a bug going around.

Which brought her back to the present with a start.

When Faye opened her eyes, it felt as if she had got someone else's holiday snaps accidentally mixed up with her own. But when she shut her eyes and opened them again it was still there.

The thin blue line.

It was as if the bus she had imagined waiting for had arrived and mowed her down.

So, she thought, he *was* so damn virile that once was enough for his seed to take root in her womb and create a tiny life inside of her. *Pregnant.* She rolled the word over in her mind, as yet too strange to say aloud. She had known it was a possibility, of course, but the difference between the idea floating around in her head like a dream and the reality of the evidence before her were worlds apart. Rather like imagining she was capable of a no-strings-affair, she thought wretchedly. But as she stroked her hand over her abdomen, the thought that she was carrying *his* child felt as natural and inevitable as waking up to find it was morning. For one insane moment her eyes darted to the telephone and she envisaged dialling his number. And then she remembered how plainly he had instructed her to take a pill—how she knew within the very depths of her soul that there was nothing he would want less than this. She imagined trying to explain it to him. Surely he would want nothing to do with his child? Six years ago she would have put money on it, but now she had seen him with Max, and given what she now knew of his own childhood, she couldn't help thinking that he would be only too determined not to let history repeat itself. But wasn't it also a given that he would assume she was trying to trap him for money? The thought made her heart sink. Making that call *would* inevitably force him to re-enter her life against his wishes, because his damn traditional Italian views would make him feel duty-bound to do so. She couldn't think of anything worse.

It would be selfish not to tell him. She knew that. She owed it to their unborn child to do it. But at this moment in time, when she needed to get used to the idea herself, she couldn't. She walked across the landing to the spare bedroom, currently awash with the art materials she had used to inspire her new ideas for the restaurant, and tried to visualise it as a nursery. She could work and bring up their child here, couldn't she?

Faye drew a slow, ragged breath. It wasn't ideal, it wasn't the way she had always dreamed she would bring up a child, but she would manage. And she *would* tell him—once next weekend was out of the way, once Matteson's required less of her energy. But until then she would refrain from wondering *how* for just a few days longer.

CHAPTER TEN

HER leaving early had saved him a small fortune. Saved, too, the inevitable and troublesome exchange that came when an affair lost its spark. So why wasn't he still in Tuscany thanking his lucky stars? Or back in Rome knocking on the door of that striking French actress who had taken such pains to whisper to him exactly which room she was staying in when she had introduced herself at Il Maia last week?

His eyes rested upon the tormenting sight of Faye's bottom sashaying to and fro through the narrow sliver of glass in the kitchen door, and the blood rushing around his body filled him with anger as rapidly as it rushed to another place entirely. At first he had assumed his annoyance would pass. The way it always did on the rare occasions when a deal didn't go his way and he later discovered a better one. But as the weeks had gone by he'd been irritated to find that, on the contrary, it only grew. In fact, his frustration at the memory of that ice-maiden face of hers as she had walked away—not a *glimmer* of emotion— was surpassed only by the hot, fervid dreams that filled his nights, spilled over into his days and refused to subside.

Was it because the instant he had made up his mind that the best course of action was to return to the social scene in

Rome he had run straight into the notorious Chris and been forced to concede that he *had* been wrong on that account? Or was it just because *she* had had the audacity to end their affair before he did? Probably. After all, he couldn't remember another occasion when a woman had walked out on *him*, let alone a time when anyone had turned their back on a contract with Valenti Enterprises. Twice. Had she really supposed there would be no consequence?

Dante shifted slightly, in order to watch as a waitress whispered in her ear, and he saw her face drop instantly. Yes, he thought, allowing himself a small, throaty murmur of triumph as she slowly turned her head and he saw her eyes widen in shock, it seemed she had.

It was the worst thing she could have imagined, and the last thing she had expected—tonight. Tonight, when what she needed most was to focus on Matteson's. Faye looked reluctantly, as if she had been asked to identify a body at some horrific crime scene as the hubbub of activity in the kitchen continued around her, unprepared for the instant pang of need that ricocheted through her gut as her eyes met his. But it was not just the carnal desire that seemed to be his God-given gift to evoke in women everywhere, but a new need that was unique to her. The need to go to the father of the baby growing inside her, to have him envelop her in the protectiveness of his arms. And that was the most dangerous need she had ever known.

Her self-preservation instinct was to turn and run, never to know why the hell he was here, rather than face him. But her gut feeling was for once outweighed by something stronger. For the moment she saw him it was as if he turned the key in the ignition of her unassailable guilt, and it was gaining speed.

It was a sensation which moved her limbs before she gave them permission to walk the all too familiar gauntlet. She was pushing open the door, ignoring the dryness in her mouth, the sound of her heartbeat so loud in her ears that it drowned out the sounds of the other diners. She should have told him—had to tell him. Whatever she thought she had been doing she had simply been putting it off. She only wished she had thought about *how*.

Her stomach tied itself in knots as she reached his table. 'Dante.' Her voice was strained as she stood there, taking him in as if unable to believe he was real, not having a clue what else to say. 'What are you doing here?'

Though she had promised herself not to think of him since the night she had returned home, she realised she had pictured him so often that she knew his face off by heart. He had lost weight, fractionally. How typical that it only made his olive skin cling more closely to his chiselled jaw beneath the permanent five o'clock shadow, making him appear even more startlingly male if that was possible.

'What everyone else is doing here, I imagine. Having dinner.' The place looked good. She looked good. Too good. The way she moved around the restaurant exuded talent and an enthusiasm for the place that lingered in her wake, reminding him precisely why she had gained his respect and admiration once before, and threatened to do so all over again. But her prim black dress and her hair all pinned back from her face seemed only to reinforce that expression which said *I'm untouchable. Dio!* How tempting it was to rip the dark fabric in two right now and toss those hairpins all over the newly polished floor until she purred that she would go mad *unless* he touched her.

'I heard there had been some changes—new menu, innovative décor. It sounded—how do you say?—my cup of tea.'

Part of her wanted to blurt it out, to wipe the sardonic smile off that outrageously sensual mouth and silence his merciless repartee once and for all. The other part thanked God that she wasn't any further along, that her body at least was giving nothing away.

'And you just happened to be in England?' Her voice was hushed but insistent. Had he come to see whether she had failed as thoroughly as he had been convinced she would—in the hope that the whole evening would be a total disaster and he would be able to swipe the restaurant from under her nose?

'I never just *happen* to be anywhere, Faye. Surely you know that by now?' he chided her, clicking his tongue and making no attempt to lower his own voice. 'I have business in London.'

Faye frowned. He had no business *here*. Which was what made it all the more unnerving. Could he know? No, she hadn't told a soul. It might feel as if he was capable of reading her mind on occasions, but he wasn't psychic.

Her puzzled look irked him. 'Let me refresh your memory. Did you not sign a contract which stated that a month after you returned here I would require a cut of double your profits if you succeeded or a cut of the business if you failed?

Faye stared at him blankly, wondering if she had heard him correctly, whilst at the same time a tiny tremor of fear began to judder at the base of her spine.

'The contract is null and void, Dante. I transferred every penny you gave me right back to your account.'

'And in your eyes that constitutes the contract being null and void, does it, Miss Matteson? Clearly we didn't spend long enough studying the legal side of running a successful business.' Patronisingly, he shook his head and tutted. 'Oh, wait—that was due to be covered at the *end* of the month. I seem to recall you took the decision not to see your side of the contract through and stay until that point. Regrettable, you might say.'

Faye's face fell, but she stood her ground. She had worked too hard.

'I owe you nothing. The cash has been repaid.'

Though she had dared to believe that Matteson's takings were slowly beginning to improve, any profit was being ploughed back into the business, into repaying the bank. Even if she did owe him a penny—which she didn't—she had none to give.

'But what about repayment for the *skills* you acquired under my tuition? You are making a profit, yes? Do not stand before me and pretend *experience* means so little to you.'

The sensual drawl of his voice seemed to reach into Faye and tweak every nerve-ending in her body. She began to shiver, but tensed her shoulders to counteract it, determined not to let him see.

'If you had taken the time to read my proposal you would know that every change I have made here was based on plans I created before I even arrived in Rome.' It was true. Yes, she might have rediscovered her passion for the business in Italy, but the ideas for here were hers alone.

'So what was it that persuaded the bank to loan you the money, *cara*, given that nothing had changed? Could it have been perhaps that they saw from your account that *I* had been willing to invest? Did you inform them you had undergone a period of learning alongside me?'

Colour shot hotly through her cheeks. She was furious that

she was even wondering whether his words held any element of truth. The bank had finally agreed because she had kept up her repayments, because they saw potential—hadn't they?

She looked at the way he was lounged back in his chair, with the river outside the window behind him, as if he was king of the whole bloody world—whilst she stood there like some minion who had been summoned for his amusement once more. Wasn't it about time he learned that the world turned of its own accord, without him twirling it? Yes, it might always be in the shade when he wasn't there, but that was beside the point.

'The thought of a woman making her own way in this world really gets to you, doesn't it, Dante?'

'Still such fire, Faye. You know, if you are unable to come up with the cash there may be another way to see the contract through to a mutually satisfying conclusion.' His eyes licked over her, sensual promise written all over his face. 'How about I take you for a drink when you're finished here. Toast your success?'

It was more than she could bear. He had played with her as a tomcat tormented a mouse, and now he was back for the kill. And for no other reason than that the sport amused him. It was time.

'I'm afraid that won't be possible, Dante.'

'And why might that be, when every inch of your body is craving my touch, right here, right now, even in this public restaurant?'

'Because I'm pregnant.'

Faye would have laughed and made a mental note to write that one down as the all-time greatest conversation-stopper if it hadn't been true—if the look on his face hadn't been everything she had feared. It hardly mattered that she hadn't allowed herself to think about how to say it or when, because even if she *had* thought about nothing else she would have known it was always going to be this hideous, regardless of whether she built up to it slowly or blurted it out so spectacularly.

For once in his life Dante was still, his face creased in such disbelief that she might as well have just revealed that she was extra-terrestrial.

'How is this possible?'

She wanted to patronisingly deliver a concise biology lesson, to point out that nature had invented sex with a greater goal than his pleasure, but his voice had lost its cut-glass quality, his Italian accent was stronger than ever, and instinctively she knew it would be the wrong thing to do.

'This pill—it did not work?'

Faye drew in a deep breath. 'I couldn't—no.'

He raised his head then, the look of bewilderment that had been aimed nowhere in particular suddenly directed unequivocally at her.

'Couldn't?'

'It was not something I wished to do.'

'In the same way as *telling me* was not something you wished to do?' His sardonic tone was back, the stillness it had been so rare to witness in him replaced by movement as he threw one leg over the other. 'How long have you known?'

'Only a week—for certain.' She wished it did not sound so predictable, so *pathetic*. 'I was going to tell you.'

'When?' he questioned accusingly, drumming two long fingers on the table. 'When it suited you to milk the benefits of my paternity at some later date? Save yourself for one lump sum?'

'I want nothing from you, Dante. I can raise this child alone.'

He stood up immediately, his full height beside her slender frame never so striking.

'Alone? You are suggesting that you would raise this child without him even being aware of his father, his Italian heritage?' he boomed, so that several diners turned around, before politely looking back at their meals and pretending they had seen nothing out of the ordinary. 'If you even *try*, I will fight you every step of the way.'

The trembling that had begun at the base of her spine spread through her limbs as the full weight of his threat seeped into her. The most dangerous implication of telling him hadn't occurred to her before. Now it was blindingly obvious. He had the power to extradite her from their child's life completely.

'But this is hardly the place to discuss the legalities,' he continued brusquely, as a sheepish-looking waitress hesitated at Faye's side before placing Dante's meal before him. 'I will wait for you to finish here.'

Faye barely registered the words that followed his threat, only hearing her cue to escape this intoxicating battleground she had walked into unarmed. For as she reluctantly nodded in response to his request—no, his demand to continue the conversation that she never had wanted to have, she felt as if up until that point she had been standing on a rug that had been slipping from under her so slowly she had barely noticed. Now he had torn it away in one single stroke.

He wanted their child and he would show her no mercy.

'You look like you've seen a ghost.'

Her mother was on the other side of the kitchen door, the

delight that had lit her face at the start of tonight's grand re-opening now replaced with concern.

Faye breathed weakly as Josie Matteson looked past her and out across the tables. She didn't doubt news of the striking Italian seated at the best table in the house had already done the rounds.

'Signor Valenti is here because he regrets not continuing his involvement, perhaps?' Josie questioned softly.

Faye shook her head dejectedly. 'The multimillion-dollar profits from his own restaurants ensure regret is not an emotion he need trouble himself with, Mum.'

Josie took hold of her arm, sensing her fragility, and moved them both out of the thoroughfare of the waitresses before turning to face her.

'I wasn't talking about the restaurant.'

Faye raised her head, blinking first in astonishment and then to stop the tears which threatened to fall. Her mother swept the strand of hair that had fallen across Faye's eyes to one side.

'It makes no difference.' Faye shrugged. Matteson's, her, the baby. Dante built his success out of having no regrets, working every situation to his advantage.

'And yet he is here, looking at you like I have only ever seen one other man look at a woman—'

'No,' Faye protested helplessly.

'The way your father used to look at me,' Josie continued.

'He's nothing like Dad.' The speed of her rejoinder was more revealing than she knew.

Josie sighed. 'Your father would have been very proud of you tonight, Faye. *I'm* proud.'

'I only did what needed to be done.'

'It is no small achievement,' Josie said calmly, in the voice of a mother who understood that at times her daughter was her own worst enemy. 'But what about what you need to do for yourself, Faye?'

Faye frowned, fearing she had made it sound as if this had only been about doing her daughterly duty. 'I didn't mean—'

'I know you didn't, and I know you love this business, but Matteson's itself was your father's dream. That was why he never wanted you to give up your studies. He wanted you to find something that made you as happy as you were the day you got offered the job in Rome.' She smiled slowly and kissed Faye's cheek. 'It's time to live your own dreams.'

If only it was that simple, Faye thought. If only she could have breezed through the unmitigated success of this evening believing that Dante was waiting in the wings to realise her dreams for her. But whatever Josie thought she had read in his eyes, the meaning of his words the minute he had discovered her pregnancy had been unequivocal. *I'll fight you every step of the way.*

That was all that lay ahead—the only vision in her mind as she plastered on an aching smile that belied the anguish of her heart, clinging to the futile hope that if she stayed here late enough he might grow tired of waiting for her to leave, and she might not have to face the words she dreaded tonight.

She shook her head at the other staff as they entreated her to go home. Found a million jobs to occupy her time. But as she locked up and wound her chunky knitted scarf around her neck against the cold bite of the late-October night, unable to stretch out the evening any longer, she saw it immediately. The sleek, low-slung vehicle on the opposite side of the street. Affluent though this neighbourhood was, there could be no pretending, even through the hazy streetlights, that it was the kind of model your average wealthy businessman would drive. It was in a class of its own.

'Do not tell me that your usual method of transport at this hour is on foot?' His incredulous voice cut through the half-open tinted window, penetrating the darkness.

Faye froze on the pavement. 'I only live a few streets away.'

'That doesn't make it any more acceptable. You're a woman. You should not walk alone in the middle of the night.'

'Yes, well, we're not all billionaires.'

'And we're not all pregnant either.' He said the word as if it was new, unfamiliar. 'Now, get in.'

Faye walked over to the car, irked to find herself grateful that she did not have to walk. The exhaustion of the day's events and the tiredness of being pregnant were beginning to catch up with her.

'I'm having a baby. I'm not terminally ill,' she ground out as he held open the door for her. She sank into the luxurious heated leather seat, the weariness in her limbs seeping away, though she couldn't help feeling this mode of transport couldn't be any more different from the carefree motorbike he had driven in another place, in what felt like a different lifetime.

'Which is why you *should* be taking the utmost care of yourself.' His voice was laced with both anger and concern. For *his* child? she wondered. A pity he had been devoid of such humanity when he had told her to take a pill, or demanded she become his mistress for a month and then repay him over the odds for the experience.

'I have profits to double—remember?'

But he ignored her, as if in his mind she had slipped into

a new female role because of her *condition*. From fallen woman to vessel carrying his child, she thought.

Dante crunched the gears, his frustration evident as he swung the car lithely around the end of the street in response to her directions. How crazy it was that there were so many day-to-day details about each other's lives that they didn't know—like something as simple as where she lived. No doubt that was precisely why affairs suited him: all the benefits of a relationship but none of the banalities a man who was head of an international empire wouldn't have the time or the inclination to learn.

'Doubling your profits, or should I say *attempting* to double your profits, will no longer be necessary.' His words were delayed, his voice reluctant, like a football manager forced to retract a boast after losing at home.

'Necessary for whom?' she asked, maddened by his pronouncement. 'Believe it or not seeing Matteson's do well again has always been *my* priority—even if it doesn't matter to you.'

'You cannot seriously be suggesting that you would carry on working these hours with a child?'

'Why not? It *is* possible for a woman to juggle the responsibilities of a career and a family, you know.' In an ideal world she would like nothing more than to raise their child without the pressures of work, to give their child the idyllic upbringing she had been lucky enough to experience. But life didn't always turn out the way you wanted it to.

'Juggle?' He spat out the word in distaste, raking his hand through his hair. 'Pass my child from pillar to post whilst you focus on your *career*, as if my child is some raggy doll?'

'Rag doll,' Faye corrected, and would have smiled in any other situation at how endearing it was on the rare occasions when English phrases eluded him. Would have if they had not been fighting over the one thing that ought to bond a man and woman inseparably together, but which only seemed to be driving them further and further apart.

'You will not need to juggle anything. I will see to that.'

So now he would *gladly* throw money at her? 'And what if I *wish* to continue working?'

'No child of mine will come second to the wishes of his mother.'

His, Faye noted, and not for the first time. Of course he would presume it was a boy. But then she looked into his eyes and saw something of the little boy he had once been, the little boy who had come second to *his* mother's wishes, and for one insane moment she wanted to reach across and obliterate that look on his face with a kiss.

But as Dante drew up outside her block of flats and killed the engine, she felt only a chill where there had once been fire. No, whatever passion there had once been on his part seemed to have died the moment she had confessed—to what she supposed in his eyes was a mistress's ultimate transgression.

'Thank you for the lift,' she said meekly, raising her hand to the handle on the car door, hoping that somehow this would be the end of it. Praying that whatever demand he had hinted at earlier would keep for another day, when she was stronger, when maybe *she* might have built up some immunity to him.

But he was ignoring her. 'This—' he stared grimly out of the car window '—is where you propose to raise my child?'

Faye followed his gaze, seeing it in the way he must see it instead of as the adequate, functional place she had chosen to rent after uni, when she had first come back to Matteson's. It was true that the antiquated block looked a little as if it could model for a cover shot of Dickens' *Bleak House*, but it was the middle of the night, on a cold autumnal evening in the suburbs. And it was starting to rain. What did he expect? To drive round the corner and find a spacious family home akin to his villa in Tuscany, miraculously bathed in the golden glow of sunshine? No, of course he didn't, and that was precisely his point.

'It's better than it looks,' she threw out defensively, her hand still resting on the door handle. 'And anyway, I don't consider it matters *where* a child is brought up, so long as it is loved.'

'No? You suppose that being an illegitimate child, brought up by a mother working full-time to pay the bills, is an ideal start in life?'

Faye noticed the way he visibly blanched at the word *illegitimate*. Yes, she had always imagined that if she were ever blessed with children she would be married, but considering *he* was supposed to thrive on adapting to change his views were immovable!

'Not ideal, no. But better than being torn between two parents caught in some hideous legal battle.'

'My thoughts exactly, *cara*,' he said slowly, his eyes glittering.

Faye looked at him in the light of the dim streetlamp, perplexed as much by the look on his face as by the words he had spoken.

'Then what do you propose, Dante?'

'That you become my wife.'

CHAPTER ELEVEN

No, FAYE thought, that's not a proposal at all. You're informing me that this is how it's going to be. As if I'm some newly discovered supplier for your business whose goods you want to buy, so you're blinding me with an offer beyond my wildest dreams without even considering what that might do to me.

She stared at him, searching his face without knowing what she expected to find there, as the rain beat down harder upon the windscreen. There *was* nothing to find there. She was pregnant with his child so he felt duty-bound to wed her, to ensure that the heir to Valenti Enterprises was legitimate, to make sure the mother of his child did nothing so crassly inappropriate as work for a living. Nothing else.

Against her will, an image of the villa in Tuscany entered her mind unbidden, of herself standing at the door waiting with their child as Dante came home to them. It caused something deep within her to blossom. No, she told herself, it would be nothing like that. Because *that* picture of marriage was filled with love, and his *proposal* was about anything but that. And suddenly the daydream changed into a nightmare. Their child tucked up in bed whilst she waited for him, not knowing where he was or who he was with, only knowing that she was expected to turn a blind eye. And how could she live alongside him, loving without reciprocation, when even just one week in Italy had almost broken her?

'You consider it a necessity for a mother and father who do not love one another to suffer living together for the sake of their child?' Faye asked.

His mouth hardened. For one tiny moment Faye felt a tiny surge of triumph amidst all the pain. She could just imagine the way Dante would have envisaged a woman replying to the offer of becoming Mrs Valenti, and it would be nothing like the response she had just uttered.

'I doubt the odds of our being able to bear living with one another are any worse than any other couple's,' he shot out, his vexation tangible. He raised one eyebrow sardonically. 'At least we already know we are compatible in the bedroom.'

Faye looked at him dismally. For where would she be left when he grew bored with her, as he inevitably would? 'There is more to a marriage than sex, Dante.'

He felt a surge of frustration. She dismissed her desire for him as if it was nothing more than a memory she had taped up in a box and left in baggage reclaim! How satisfying it would be to run his hands over that soft and supple body beneath that oh-so-functional coat and feel her infused with so much heat that she would be unable to think of anything but making love to him. Yet for once in his life there was something else he wanted more.

'Yes, there is more to a marriage than having sex,' he ground out, determined to dampen his own insistent desire. 'Like having children.'

What about love? Faye's heart screamed. Doesn't that enter this impossible equation?

'Plenty of people have children *without* being married. What if I wish to stay here?' The rain was lashing down so hard now that her block of flats was barely visible. Why was it she always seemed to end up arguing for that which was furthest from what she actually wanted when it came to Dante? How was she even pretending that *here* was a better alternative? Because she had her own pride, she thought brokenly, her own dreams.

'Why? Because you would have your freedom?' His voice was clipped as he turned away from her, disgust written all over his face.

'Because I'm needed at Matteson's.' Funny how arguments like *this is my home*, or *maybe I hope to one day find a man who'll love me back* didn't even enter her head. Because there had only been once in her life when she had felt as if she had really belonged somewhere, or truly loved someone, and it hadn't been here.

'I was impressed tonight,' he said frankly. It caused a swelling of pride deep within her. 'Money need no longer be a concern. I see no reason not to release you from your commitment to the bank and invest myself.'

It ought to have been her moment of sheer triumph, of proving him wrong, but it had come too late. He had believed she deserved nothing, and now he was throwing money at her for no other reason than to get to his baby. And yet she couldn't deny that he was making accepting his marriage demand seem feasible, doable.

'You can continue with the design side of the business from abroad, if necessary.'

'You wouldn't *rather* I stay here? Have your lawyers fight me for full custody?' She was daring to play devil's advocate with a scenario that made her stomach feel as if she had done ten rounds in a boxing ring, but she needed to understand.

'I believe a child needs his mother.'

His decision made sense. Deep down she believed a child needed its father in equal measure. But he couldn't have spelled out more clearly that her role would effectively be that of biological nanny. The thought made her chest ache.

He grew impatient at her silence. 'But if this is to be your answer then you leave me little choice but to take legal action.'

Faye felt the blood drain from her face. She was silent for a long moment, knowing this was the hour of reckoning, that she had a split second to make her choice. Except there wasn't really a choice to make, was there? How could there be?

'No, Dante, that is not my answer. Yes, I'll marry you.'

She had never imagined that she would say those words and in her heart feel anything other than the promise of sunshine. But as he saw her to the door under an enormous umbrella she wondered why he was bothering to shelter her from the rain when she felt as if it was destined to be forever winter in her heart. For he had made his offer as coolly as if it were a business takeover, and she knew the only way to survive was to match his coldness in equal measure.

'You have seen a doctor?' Suddenly it felt as if the door had been closed on any exchange other than practical details for evermore.

Faye shook her head.

'No?'

'I took a home test. I haven't had time.'

'Then we will go first thing tomorrow morning.'

Of course, Faye thought. He wants conclusive proof before he parts with any cash or even gets close to making this legal.

Never mind that I've got every physical symptom in the book. She doubted he would be convinced by something as flighty as the rhythms of her body; he had made it perfectly clear what he thought of women succumbing to those before.

'I'll book an appointment, though I doubt I'll get one straight away,' Faye said, searching for her keys. 'I'm due at the restaurant from late morning onwards as it is.'

'Matteson's will cope without you, Faye. I'll see to it.'

Two months ago she would have done anything to know that Matteson's was finally safe. Now it just felt as if she had handed him another piece of her soul.

'And as for a doctor—I'll inform the London practice of the private clinic I use that we will be arriving just after nine.'

Of course. His was a world in which people waited for *him*.

'We'll head to a jeweller afterwards. The press will no doubt expect you to be sporting a ring of epic proportions when I make the announcement.' He looked at her scathingly, as if waiting for some reaction, but her face was stony.

She had forgotten the media circus that would be bound to surround them, but suddenly it paled into insignificance as the true reality of her decision slammed into her. She remembered how, returning to her flat a month ago, she had hated just how little she seemed to have stamped her own personality on her living space. And now look at the future ahead of her: her life from now on was to be guided by where he wanted her to be and when, living up to what people expected of the wife of Dante Valenti and of the mother of his child. Never mind living space. There would be no space for *her* to have a personality whatsoever. No, but she would have her baby—would wake every day no longer eaten up inside because she missed him so much that it felt as if one day the pain would stop her waking up at all.

'Very well,' she said, the realisation suddenly making compliance easy. 'See you at nine.'

But life, Faye was about to discover, was never so easy that the moment you resigned yourself to the path ahead you could just get on with walking it. Because the minute she opened her eyes the following morning she knew something wasn't right. No, something was very *wrong*. Instinctively she sat up in bed. The objects in the room came into focus though she did not really *see* any of them. It was not nausea. She found the carpet with one bare foot. It was not the unpleasant but reassuring sickness to which she had been growing accustomed. It was something else.

She stumbled to the bathroom through the half light, willing her sense of foreboding to be nothing more than the remains of last night's exchange with Dante. But the moment she stood up she felt it: the slightly damp sensation that ought to have been impossible.

Because she was pregnant, a voice screamed inside her head as she screwed up her eyes tightly and felt the coldness of the white tiles beneath her feet as she reached the bathroom. Because her last period had been weeks ago. Because her body had been telling her for days and the test had confirmed it. Which meant if—

Faye crumpled like an inflatable doll which had been pricked with a pin the minute she saw it. The dark red stain. And suddenly it felt as if she was falling from a very high building as everything she held dear was left at the top. Then everything went black.

* * *

Dante gave up pressing the bell, doubting its operation, and let himself through the inadequate security door that led into the block of twelve flats. The place did look marginally more tolerable this morning, but maybe that was because he no longer had to imagine Faye attempting to remain here and bring up their child.

Except last night could not have felt less of a victory. He had wanted her to acquiesce, of course, to admit that it made perfect sense. And he had not supposed for a minute that she wouldn't put up a fight—she was too goddamned independent not to. But did her submission have to be so cold? He had always thought he would admire detachment in a woman, so why did it make him feel as if he was doing her a wrong, trapping her when he had just promised her everything? Hell, she had played the martyr so well it had even made him think better of proving her wrong about the importance of sex when that had been his whole reason for coming here in the first place—hadn't it?

Dante took the stairs two at a time. No doubt she would come round when they swapped Harley Street for Bond Street later. Even if she had barely seemed to bat an eyelid at the prospect last night.

He had knocked three times without an answer when he began to suspect that something was wrong. She might be defiant, but this morning was about the baby, and the minute she had dropped the bombshell of her pregnancy he had witnessed within her a motherly instinct he never would have anticipated. He didn't doubt her promise that she would be here for a second.

'Faye?' he bellowed through the thin wooden door, assessing its weight with his fingertips. There was no answer. It had one catch. If needed, he could force it easily. 'Faye?'

And then he heard it. A low moan that sounded like an animal in pain.

He was inside the flat in an instant, the full force of his shoulder more than enough to break the bolt. He took in the layout of the sitting room quickly. Empty. One doorway led to what he could see was the kitchen, another to what he presumed must be the bedroom and bathroom.

'Faye!'

Faye drifted in and out of delirium as if she was watching the scene from above, observing the pitiful collection of shivering limbs and pyjamas piled on the floor as if that was all that remained of her. Somewhere in a world she was unable to identify as the one in which she was existing she heard a vague knocking, and then the calling of her name.

'*Dio*! What's the matter—the baby?'

His voice was urgent, his dark presence in the cool white room unfathomable as he got to his knees beside her, the uncharacteristic gesture only adding to her bewilderment.

Faye made another noise that seemed to come from deep within, her agony so palpable it was like smoke pervading the air.

'We're going to the hospital. Now.'

The minute he said the words, suddenly, like a blinding light, Dante felt all the fear of powerlessness coursing through his veins. And with it came the startling realisation that he had broken the rule of detachment by which he lived his life. But if it caused him to forget to take breath for a second, in the next instant his hands were scooping her up, raising her limp body into his arms.

The sensation of his warm hands against her own clammy, pallid skin shocked her into consciousness. 'No.' She shook her head from side to side, as if the action took every remaining atom of energy within her. 'The baby is…gone.'

The minute the word was out she felt the tears she had been too stunned to release begin to roll in great beads down her face.

'There's no need,' she said helplessly. 'Go—you're free now.'

'I'm not going anywhere.'

Dante felt something twist in his gut, as if he had just looked down and realised he had been crushing a small bird in the palm of his hand, and that he needed to set it free as much as it longed to fly. Throwing his grey cashmere coat round her trembling body, he kicked open every door on the way to his car, laying her gently down upon the back seat before flying behind the wheel and starting the engine.

It was the local hospital she knew: the one where she had been born, had had her tonsils removed as a girl. She supposed it ought to have been comforting. No Harley Street clinic now, for what a leveller the failure of the human body really proved to be, she thought absently, as Dante insisted she sit in a wheelchair whilst he pushed her to the relevant department. All around them were husbands pushing wives, wives pushing husbands, children pushing parents and vice versa. Everyone was being pushed by someone who cared about them.

Except they would all go on caring after they had exited through those same doors. But Dante? Could she bear to have the doctor confirm what she already knew? Have him take her home and with a pitying look break off their engagement now that the one thing that had given him reason to be here had failed to exist? It felt as if in the space of twenty-four hours fate had served up every dream she had ever had, like delicious fruits, and then left her alone to discover that every one was poisoned.

'Dante, I can't,' Faye sobbed. 'Please, let me go home.'

'No, Faye.' His voice was firm, but filled with a tenderness she barely recognised. 'I can't do that.'

For once in her life she understood that there was a time to let someone else take the reins, and that time was now.

It was the longest thirty minutes of her life. She did not know what the medics were doing, only that Dante had demanded they were seen immediately and of course he had been obeyed. Now they were checking her from head to toe, as she lay back with her eyes closed, praying that it would all soon be over. Dante never left her side—against the doctor's recommendation that he wait outside. And, regrettably, it was now that she appreciated more strongly than ever before that Dante was the man she truly loved.

Not because when he spoke she never wanted to stop listening, or because when they made love she never wanted it to end, but because he was the man she wanted with her when she was in need. She'd thought she had built her life up so independently that she didn't *need* anyone, but she needed him. And not just because he had carried her here, or had demanded that she be seen immediately. But because somehow, in this terrifying moment when she thought she was losing everything, his very presence gave her more strength than she could possibly possess alone. Yet, paradoxically, it was as if she had never been joined to him by anything more substantial than a length of cotton, and now it had grown as fine as a spider's web that any second would break. And with it the baby she had dreamed of and the man she loved would be gone, like a change in the wind, as if to all the world but her the web had never existed at all.

'Well, Faye.'

She opened her eyes and raised her hand to wipe away the tears, shaken from her semi-conscious state by the first words to have been aimed at her for what felt like an age. She shuffled up on the bed slightly, to take in the benign face of the doctor as she tried to paste on the mask of someone who could cope.

'I apologise for all the examinations, but I'm afraid it is something you are going to have to get used to.'

Faye frowned and instinctively looked to Dante. The lines she now realised had been furrowing his brow were somehow more apparent for their absence.

The doctor continued. 'A bleed in the first trimester of pregnancy is, unfortunately for the stress levels of a new mother and father, quite common. But if you look at the screen before you you will see the beginnings of your perfectly healthy baby.'

Faye suddenly registered the small monitor at the end of the bed and stared at it open-mouthed, the doctor's words still lying on the surface of her mind like precious droplets she didn't dare allow her brain to absorb.

And then she saw it. Amidst the black-and-white grains a small, perfectly formed dark shape, and the tiny beat of a heart she could just make out. To anyone else it would have looked like nothing. To Faye it was like the greatest gift she had ever been given—an artistic masterpiece that evoked within her an emotion that transcended everything else she had ever known. Her heart seemed to swell in her chest.

'Everything is OK?' Faye said, as if testing the words, still unable to believe the sight before her wasn't some mirage her mind had conjured up to protect her heart. Unconsciously she reached out her hand to Dante, resting it upon his as he stared at the screen, equally humbled and lost in his own thoughts.

The doctor smiled. 'Everything is fine. You are free to go. I recommend you refrain from work for a few days, but we won't need to see you again until your next scan at around twelve weeks.'

'Thank you.' Faye smiled at him and Dante silently shook his hand before the doctor disappeared back into the busy ward, leaving them alone.

It was then that the relief truly hit her. Relief, and a joy so impossible to contain that she forgot her pact with herself and allowed the dam that was keeping her emotions at bay to burst its banks. Their baby was OK. This was normal. She had seen it with her own eyes. As she would see it again at twelve weeks—seven weeks from now. Would she be on Italian soil? Married even?

She looked at Dante, unusually still. He might be a man whose heart was as impenetrable as a fortress, but there was no denying that he had been moved by the tiny dot on the screen before them. Faye worked her way off the bed, with his help, and hugged his jacket around her.

'Well, it looks like the ring will have to wait, I suppose,' she said lightly as they made their way towards the door, attempting to disperse some of the intensity of the moment that had caught them both unawares.

There was a time when her comment would have struck him as being the words of a true gold-digger, but that moment was past. Now it seemed only to reinforce every wrong move he had made since the minute he had returned—how irreconcilable their two worlds really were, despite the fact that they had collided to create that tiny shape on screen that had made his heart turn over like nothing else ever had.

'That won't be necessary.'

For one second Faye stupidly wondered if he was about to whip out some symbolic gem from his pocket and place it on her finger, the way they did in the movies. But she had made the mistake of believing him to be a romantic hero long ago. She shouldn't have needed to see the grim set of his side profile to know that this was no fairy tale.

'Today has made me think about what you said.'

It was the kind of sentence Dante never uttered—one in which he admitted to seeing her point of view—and yet she had never heard him sound more resolute.

'And I agree. Two parents marrying for the sake of their child is not necessarily the best option.'

Faye stopped in her tracks as they reached the corridor, to check she had heard correctly. And when she couldn't rearrange the sounds in her mind to make a sentence any more palatable she shut her eyes, praying life had an 'undo' button—like when you made a mistake on a computer and you could take away the last thing that had happened as if it had never been. But as she looked into his face she was forced to confront that it didn't. She had never seen his angular features look so *closed*; the knowledge that this was truly the end had never felt more real. As real as the baby inside her. And yet it was over anyway. The spider's web had snapped, and never in her twenty-four years had she felt so debilitated that there weren't even words.

'What about what *you* believe,' she whispered helplessly. 'About a child needing both parents?'

'I changed my mind.'

CHAPTER TWELVE

HE HAD changed his mind: of course he had. The way he changed everything. What did it matter whether the consequence was a new colour scheme at Il Maia, or her future torn apart by what might have been?

Faye sat curled on the sofa in her flat, going over the events of two days ago for what must have been the hundredth time. What *could* she have said in return? She had been the one trying to persuade him to alter his dated views on child-rearing only hours before, desperate for some alternative to spending her life living alongside a man who would never love her. She couldn't exactly turn around and beg him to marry her now, when the minute he had been forced to confront the reality of what being her husband might entail he had blatantly wanted to run a mile. Telling him would have only made him want to run farther.

Yet it wasn't as if he had done the age-old male bunk when faced with the evidence of her pregnancy. No, after casually announcing that there would be no marriage he had helped her to the car, escorted her home, insisted she rest—in fact he had acted like the perfect gentleman. He had even called yesterday morning to check she was OK. But she couldn't help wishing that he hadn't been a perfect gentleman at all. At least when she had been his mistress she had felt wanted, if only physically. Now it felt like any concern for her well-being was simply because his child was growing inside her—rather like checking that his oven was on at the right temperature.

If she hadn't been so dazed after the frightening events of that morning she might have immediately assumed that he was sweetening her up prior to commencing his custody battle after the birth. But he had even been keen to clarify that *that* was not his intention.

'We will discuss the future at another time,' he had said as he left. 'But I am sure we can come to some mutually convenient arrangement between us.'

And, though she knew he was ruthless, she also knew that dishonesty simply wasn't his style.

Which meant what, exactly? That she would be stuck in the limbo of *afterwards* for evermore? That her involvement with Dante from now on would be nothing more than stilted conversations and endless details, starting with the dates of scans until her calendar became marked with when she was to hand her child over to him, and then he back to her. She would go on loving him helplessly whilst he got on with his life, and she who had once tried so hard to bury her memories would have no hope of ever doing so. Because every time she looked at their baby she would see him. Somehow, it felt as if it would almost have been easier to fight him. It seemed preferable to facing a lifetime of his indifference.

Faye put down her pencils and looked at the sketchpad resting on her lap, all energy drained from her. She wasn't used to the rest the doctor had recommended, and which Dante had been adamant she adhere to, and she had intended to pass the time by planning a design for the spare bedroom that would become a nursery, working out where she would fit all the bits and pieces a baby would need. Except as her mind wandered she had ended up sketching an idea for a fresco—all orangey sunshine and ripe fruit trees and farm animals. The perfect scene for the wall in a bedroom in a farm-house in Tuscany. Too big and too vivid for the greying space she had here.

She closed her eyes, feeling her throat tighten. What a blessing it had been, she thought, when she had first left Italy and had been able to throw herself into work—too busy to have moments like these, when she realised that dreams she'd never meant even to have had ingrained themselves so deeply in her soul. Now she didn't even have the luxury of losing herself in Matteson's. Because even if Dante allowed her to go back she knew that over time it would require her presence less and less; the newly appointed restaurant manager looked as promising as their takings, and she could pretty much do the marketing from home.

She supposed she ought to have felt as if a great weight had been lifted from her shoulders, but she didn't. She was truly glad, of course, to see the tables full of smiling diners once more, to see employees full of new enthusiasm and no longer fearing for their jobs. To know her family's business was restored. But the events of the last few days had forced her to confront the fact that there was something even more impor-tant to her.

Because from the second she had thought she might be losing her baby she had experienced a sense of both terror and clarity unlike anything she had never known. Most immedi-ate—like being forced under water—had been the fear that this child growing inside her, for which she already felt so much love, would never have its own chance at life, or become a part of hers. Secondly, like the crest of a wave crashing down upon her, had come the fear that in losing this baby she would also lose the person she cared for the most in this world. *And* it was out of her control. She had suddenly realised that twice before *she* had brought about her separation from Dante, by walking away rather than daring to take a chance and tell him how she felt. Yes, maybe it was what he had wanted, but she had never said aloud that she couldn't continue as his mistress because he meant too much to her, or that she'd given him her virginity not because she was the harlot he supposed but because she had fallen in love with him and in her naivety had thought he might be capable of falling in love with her. The thought had made her realise that maybe she ought to have done things differently—maybe she shouldn't have tried so hard to protect her own heart. For hadn't she failed anyway?

Except what had followed was the discovery that her moment of lucidity had coincided with his—at the opposite end of the spectrum. Had it been finding her on the floor like that which had made him realise he couldn't spend his life caring for a woman he didn't love? Or seeing his baby's heart beating that had made him aware of his haste, aware that putting his fiercely traditional views into practice was going to involve a lot more than he had thought? Whatever it was, she had never known so indisputably that he did not want her to be a part of his life. And suddenly it seemed nothing good would ever come of telling him that for her the opposite was true.

She couldn't blame him, of course. He had taken the steps to ensure she never got pregnant, and he had never been anything but honest about what she was to him: first his employee, then his mistress. She had failed on both counts. She couldn't even be angry anymore. He was the man he was. The man she loved as much in spite of his frankness as because of it.

Faye was grateful that at that instant the doorbell rang, interrupting her wretched thoughts. Why did no one warn you that the aftermath of a storm could leave the heart even more desolate than when it was being beaten by the wind and the rain? Wearily, she placed her slippered feet on the floor and moved towards the door, hoping that it was someone from Matteson's, come to tell her they couldn't manage without her after all.

'Oh! It's you.'

It was ridiculous to be so surprised at the sight of him. He had said they would have to discuss details, and he had made it clear that he intended to check up on her. But as she looked at him standing there, the pale shirt open at the neck beneath his dark suit telling her this was nothing but a brief visit in between business meetings, she felt shaken nevertheless. Would she still get this preposterous whoosh of excitement ten years from now, when she sat beside him at a parents' evening listening to how their child was doing, whilst all the time she was thinking about what *she* longed to be doing with him, wondering who he was currently doing it with? Faye shook herself.

'May I come in?'

It was tempting to say no—her flat was free of him. If he came in again, then every time she looked around she would imagine the incongruous image of his dark, powerful frame dominating the small room. But hell, it was swimming before her eyes most of the time anyway.

She nodded and stepped backwards to allow him to pass her, suddenly cringing at her tasteless slippers—a gift from Chris years before, emblazoned with the word *Tart* and depicting a large cherry-topped confection. She placed one foot on top of the other.

'Coffee?' she asked, closing the door behind him and swivelling round to face him, desperate to busy her hands.

'I'll make it. Sit down,' he commanded, frowning, as if she shouldn't even be standing up—as if she should have used nothing less than telekinesis to open the door.

'No, Dante. I'll make it.'

She walked through to the kitchen, wishing she could resist snatching a glance at herself in the mirror on the way, but failing. Once out of sight, she kicked her slippers under the radiator and loosened her hair. There was little she could do about the oversized grey jumper and faded jeans. Were his women usually pampered and preened on the off-chance he might drop in? Probably, she thought. Which is precisely why *one of his women* isn't a definition that will ever apply to you again.

'I've only got instant, I'm afraid,' she called, wishing that kettles whistled as they'd used to, in order to fill the void.

'Sorry?'

She stuck her head round the door to the living room. 'Instant decaffeinated coffee, Dante, as opposed to hand-blended latte. Will that do?'

'That will be fine, thank you.'

Would she have to explain to him what a state school was, too? Or a packed lunch? No, she thought. I doubt he'll give me the chance.

He was standing by her second-hand sofa, examining the sketchpad that she had left open on the coffee table. She paused at the door, mugs in hand, wishing she had had the foresight to put it away.

'Are you feeling better?'

No, Faye thought, I'm not. *Because you're here when I know you'd rather be anywhere else.*

'A little, thank you.' She motioned to the sofa. 'Please, sit.' How had she got to this point? Where she was incapable of anything but small talk with the man she loved, the man whose child was growing in her belly, as if he was nothing more than a guest she had just met at a ball.

'Still good,' he said, nodding to her designs and stretching his legs out in front of him as if sitting was an alien experience. 'What's it for?'

She placed the mugs down on the table, not even thinking to find the coasters she usually insisted upon, and closed the sketchbook.

'I was just passing the time.' She sat down on the chair opposite and crossed one leg over the other.

Dante opened his mouth as if to continue, but as he did so his mobile phone rang. 'I'm sorry—I have to get this.'

He stood then, and turned to look out of her window, speaking rapidly in Italian. As he did so he ran his hand absent-mindedly over the swimming trophy on her windowsill—the one she had dug out on her return from Tuscany, when she had been determined to put a little of herself back in this room. But at this moment in time she felt as if she was barely there at all, for Dante seemed to fill every inch of it.

Faye was still watching the movement of his finger when with his other hand he replaced the slimline mobile in his inside jacket pocket, revealing a flash of deep red lining, and turned to face her. 'I apologise.'

'Don't worry about it,' she said frankly. Business would always come first with him. It was who he was. And if she had remembered that he only respected people who shared his view they wouldn't be here now.

'You needn't feel obliged to come round and check up on me, Dante. You have a business to run; I know you're needed elsewhere.'

'That was actually why I came.'

To discuss business? Faye nodded slowly. 'The interest I owe on your initial advance can be paid direct to your account in Italy at the end of the month, if that is what you mean.' It might mean she missed her first loan repayment to the bank, but that was preferable to being indebted to him.

He looked directly at her then, the hard lines of his face taut with incredulity. 'No, Faye, that is not what I meant. I told you I will gladly invest.'

Why? Because it suited him for her to feel as if she owed him something?

He sat back down on the sofa and continued. 'That call was my office in Rome. These last two days I have been looking for suitable premises for my new head office. In London. The sale is going through as we speak.'

Now it was her turn to stare in disbelief. He was moving? To *London*? Faye felt as if all her worries had just been placed under the microscope and magnified by one hundred. So when he had said they would come to some arrangement he hadn't intended that he would only see their child at high times and holidays. He had genuinely meant they would share. Which meant she would never escape him—that whatever he did, whoever he did it with, would be right under her nose.

'But why?' she asked, truly amazed. Of course it made

logical sense—but when had Dante ever paid attention to that? Would he really change his whole life, leave his beloved Italy and alter the direction of the company he had spent his life building, to take on this role he had never asked for?

He frowned, as if the reason was as obvious as a simple times table. 'I wish my child to be brought up equally, by two parents. That is not feasible if we live in different countries. You wish to live here. I can work anywhere.'

There he was again, turning the situation to suit what he wanted. Faye felt defeated.

'Two parents in the same place, but who are not married,' she whispered, almost to herself, as if to stop her mind imagining otherwise. This conversation seemed so similar to the one they had only nights ago, yet so different.

'It was a mistake to ask you to marry me.'

An expression clouded his eyes that she had never seen before. It was something like remorse, and it didn't sit well on him. But the pity in his voice sat even worse on her. Did he have to spell it out?

'You considered you were doing what was right for this child.' Faye looked down, folding the hem of her jumper into a concertina, her voice such a monotone it was like a phone line gone dead.

'Yes,' he said, and the word had never sounded so laborious as he was forced to admit to himself that in spite of his desperate attempts not to repeat the mistakes his mother had made he had failed anyway. For he had been just as incapable of seeing any point of view other than his own, and in doing so had tried to trap Faye into a marriage that could never have worked.

He stood up suddenly, as if he was eating a date he hadn't

realised contained a stone that needed spitting out. 'But that wasn't the only reason I asked.'

Faye looked up from her mug of coffee, knitting her brows tightly together. Was he attempting to make her feel better? Because whatever game he was playing it just felt as if he was twisting the knife even deeper, and it made her livid.

'What then, Dante? You waltzed into Matteson's fully intending to get down on bended knee before you even knew I was carrying your child, but you just thought you'd set the scene first by demanding more money?' she bit out sarcastically.

'I didn't come because of the damn money.' His charming mouth twisted, as if he had bitten down on that stone by mistake. 'I came because I missed you.'

Faye hardnened her heart against his empty words.

'You missed our affair, you mean?' she asked, expecting his expression to intensify the minute she referred to it so recklessly, and surprised to find it did not. '*That* is why you came? Because you doubted I could repay you any interest on the sum you had lent me, and therefore you intended that I repay you in sexual favours?' Faye forced down the erotic image that popped into her head unbidden. 'I'm sure you can find yourself another willing mistress. If the papers are anything to go by, they're just queuing up to replace me!' Faye drained her coffee cup and banged it down on the table.

'I thought so too, at first,' he admitted, his expression grim. 'But I discovered I didn't want anyone else.'

'Because I am the only woman to have ever ended an affair before you did, perhaps? After all, you had no desire to come after me the *first* time you left my bed.'

He shook his head. She did not know if it was in denial or regret. 'I did you much wrong Faye, I know that. You were an employee in my care, and when I robbed you of your virginity the only way I could justify it to myself was by blaming you— by thinking you were a temptress to whom I had fallen prey.'

'I'm sorry I fell short of your standards.'

'It was my standards that were the problem. It was easier to push you away, to blame you, than it was to admit my own guilt. When I discovered you hadn't taken the dress I knew I had been wrong to judge you by every other woman I had ever known, and I decided to call you. But then I found that you were already abroad with someone else, and I was too jealous to entertain even the idea that it might have been innocent.' He paced uneasily. 'When you returned, begging for money, I had all the evidence I needed and none of the guilt to stop me taking you as my mistress.'

It explained things, of course—made them crystal-clear, in fact. But knowing his motivation, even understanding where it had come from, wasn't easing her pain. It didn't change anything. Their two worlds were still as irreconcilable as they had ever been.

'And what now? You choose to believe the truth because I am carrying your child?'

'A few weeks after you left Tuscany I was at a function in Rome when I ran into Chris.' He looked at her shamefacedly, as if that one sentence was enough. 'He was with his partner.'

'Rick?' Faye asked coolly. 'What about him?' So he had finally worked out that Chris was gay. What did he want? A medal?

'I realised that I might have got things wrong. But then to come to Matteson's and discover you were pregnant and hadn't even told me!'

Faye felt her own anger soften. 'I should have told you.'

She raised hooded eyes to look at him as the severity of her own mistake seeped through her. But Dante was lost in his own thoughts.

'When I thought about why you hadn't told me—though you could have come to me for money, or ensured you were never pregnant at all—I realised it was because you fully intended to raise this child alone. Worse still, I knew you were perfectly capable of making a damn good job of it.'

'You were angry because you thought I'd be a good mother?' Faye asked, bewildered.

'No. I was angry because after you had given yourself to me all those years ago I should have kept you for myself.'

Faye remembered something Elena had said about how possessive he was over the women he cared about, but her head was still spinning.

'I was even angrier at myself two days ago.' The admission was quiet, almost under his breath. 'When you—' His voice had started loudly but now softened, his Italian lilt suddenly prominent. 'When you thought you had lost our baby.' The anguish on his face was like watching something being crushed. 'I knew it was breaking your heart, but you were glad to be free of me. I realised that although I had thought we could make a marriage work, you had only agreed because I gave you no alternative if you wished to see your child. And I hated myself. That is not a pleasant feeling.'

Faye let out a deep sigh. She bet that feeling was an improvement on loving someone blindly for your entire adult life. How much they had both got wrong.

'Do you suppose I only agreed to become your wife because you blackmailed me?'

Dante frowned—the way he always did, she now realised

with affection, when he was forced to confront any perspective other than his own.

'If that is the case, how do you explain why I gave myself to you at eighteen? Or why I barely put up a fight against becoming your mistress?'

Dante began pacing again. 'I may not like to admit it, Faye, but I do know a woman has the same—needs—as a man. Which is precisely why…' he pursed his lips '…it would be wrong of me to marry you and take away your freedom.'

'You think if I do not marry you I will find some other man?'

'I may be a consummate lover, Faye, but I have no doubt that you will find someone else, no.'

She remembered her moment of clarity, which had hit her like the swell of the ocean. Would it be laying her heart too bare to tell him? No, it would be denying she had a heart not to.

'Then for once in your life you underestimate yourself, Dante. You have been my only lover.'

There had not been many moments in Dante's fast-paced life when it had felt as if the world froze for a moment on its axis, but this was one of them. In fact, when he thought about it, he could only recall one other occasion when time had seemed to stop: it had been many years ago, when he had looked up from his menu in a particular restaurant at a particular waitress.

'How is this possible?'

They were the same words he had uttered when he had discovered she was pregnant, Faye noticed. Funny how he was so intelligent in every way she knew except when it came to the things which ought to be blindingly obvious.

'After a rejection like that I wasn't exactly inspired to go looking. Not that anyone ever crossed my path who made me want to,' she said uneasily.

They looked at each other for a long moment before he spoke again, breaking their gaze. 'But like you said, for a marriage to work it requires more than sex.'

She got to her feet then, and reached out to take hold of his fingers gently in her own, making him face her. 'You're right. It does. So why do you suppose I *still* tried to resist becoming your wife—even though Tuscany is where I would most want to bring up our child—even though you told me if I accepted I had no need to worry about Matteson's and that I could continue my designing if I wanted to?'

It was the biggest risk she had ever taken, but suddenly she knew it was time.

'Because I love you, Dante. Because the thought of hiding that every day, as I had to when I was your mistress, tore me apart.'

He raised his eyes to meet hers, and for the first time ever she saw the look of cynicism vanish and the hard lines of his face soften.

'You love me.' He repeated. It was not a question. He was testing the words on his lips, exploring them, revelling in them. It was many years since he had heard them spoken—a lifetime since he had heard them and known that nothing was being asked from him in return. And Faye realised that maybe what had changed most fundamentally of all was Dante himself.

'This means you will reconsider becoming my wife?' His voice was soft, tentative.

'That depends why you are asking me, Mr Valenti,' Faye

teased. A smile was beginning to spread across her lips, and then, as if it was infectious, to Dante's face too.

'You know why, Miss Matteson. Because I think I've loved you since the minute I laid eyes on you,' he said, reaching for her other hand with his. 'And more than anything I want you to be my wife, to have a family with you.'

He had always dreamed of a family sitting down around a dining table. Suddenly, the family had faces: theirs.

'Well…' Faye said, pausing for a painfully long moment, her finger raised to her lips in seductive consideration. 'I think I can agree to your contract.'

'Then you are even more foolish than I thought,' Dante replied, only able to keep his sensuous lower lip from curving into a wicked, self-satisfied grin for a second.

'How so?' Faye tilted her chin at him provocatively.

'Because, *bella*, your lips are not yet upon mine.'

And with that he took her possessively in his arms and kissed her, until they forgot who and where they were—forgot everything except that they belonged to each other.

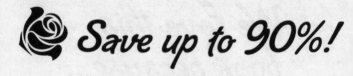